ROBINSON CRUSOE

DANIEL DEFOE (1660–1731) was born in London, the third child of James Foe, a tallow chandler, and his wife Alice. He attended Charles Morton's dissenting academy in Newington Green before establishing himself as a hosier and general merchant in Cornhill, and married Mary Tuffley in 1684. A year later he joined the Duke of Monmouth's disastrous rebellion against James II, and was lucky to escape the 'Bloody Assizes' following Monmouth's defeat at Sedgemoor. Persistent overinvestment precipitated his bankruptcy in 1692, after which he turned to writing.

Defoe's first great success came with his satirical poem *The True-Born Englishman* (1701). *The Shortest Way with the Dissenters* (1702), an audacious parody of High Anglican extremism, brought him a charge of seditious libel and he was briefly imprisoned. Defoe was employed by successive ministries as a polemicist until about 1717, and continued to write prolifically thereafter in a range of fields including politics, economics, and religion.

Between 1719 and 1724, Defoe produced the pioneering fictional narratives on which his reputation has come to rest. The first part of *Robinson Crusoe* was published on 25 April 1719, with a sequel in August. A third part, *Serious Reflections*, followed in 1720, in which year *Memoirs of a Cavalier* and *Captain Singleton* were also published. *Moll Flanders*, *Colonel Jack*, and *A Journal of the Plague Year* appeared in 1722 and *Roxana* in 1724, to be followed by further major works of non-fiction, including *A Tour thro' the Whole Island of Great Britain* (1724–6) and *The Complete English Tradesman* (1725–7). Defoe died following a stroke on 24 April 1731 while in hiding from a persistent creditor. He is buried in Bunhill Fields.

THOMAS KEYMER is Chancellor Jackman Professor of English at the University of Toronto and a Supernumerary Fellow of St Anne's College, Oxford. His books include *Richardson's Clarissa and the Eighteenth-Century Reader* (Cambridge, 1992), *Sterne, the Moderns, and the Novel* (Oxford, 2002), and *The Cambridge Companion to English Literature from 1740 to 1830*, co-edited with Jon Mee (Cambridge, 2004).

JAMES KELLY has published widely on Defoe, voyage narrative, and related topics, and serves as a council member of the Hakluyt Society. He is Senior Research Fellow and Lecturer in English at Worcester College, Oxford.

OXFORD WORLD'S CLASSICS

*For over 100 years Oxford World's Classics have brought
readers closer to the world's great literature. Now with over 700
titles—from the 4,000-year-old myths of Mesopotamia to the
twentieth century's greatest novels—the series makes available
lesser-known as well as celebrated writing.*

*The pocket-sized hardbacks of the early years contained
introductions by Virginia Woolf, T. S. Eliot, Graham Greene,
and other literary figures which enriched the experience of reading.
Today the series is recognized for its fine scholarship and
reliability in texts that span world literature, drama and poetry,
religion, philosophy and politics. Each edition includes perceptive
commentary and essential background information to meet the
changing needs of readers.*

OXFORD WORLD'S CLASSICS

======

DANIEL DEFOE

Robinson Crusoe

======

Edited with an Introduction by
THOMAS KEYMER

and Notes by
THOMAS KEYMER *and* JAMES KELLY

OXFORD
UNIVERSITY PRESS

OXFORD
UNIVERSITY PRESS

Great Clarendon Street, Oxford OX2 6DP

Oxford University Press is a department of the University of Oxford.
It furthers the University's objective of excellence in research, scholarship,
and education by publishing worldwide in

Oxford New York

Auckland Cape Town Dar es Salaam Hong Kong Karachi
Kuala Lumpur Madrid Melbourne Mexico City Nairobi
New Delhi Shanghai Taipei Toronto

With offices in

Argentina Austria Brazil Chile Czech Republic France Greece
Guatemala Hungary Italy Japan Poland Portugal Singapore
South Korea Switzerland Thailand Turkey Ukraine Vietnam

Oxford is a registered trade mark of Oxford University Press
in the UK and in certain other countries

Published in the United States
by Oxford University Press Inc., New York

British Library Cataloguing in Publication Data

Data available

Library of Congress Cataloging-in-Publication Data
Defoe, Daniel, 1661?–1731.
Robinson Crusoe / Daniel Defoe ; edited with an introduction by Thomas Keymer
and notes by Thomas Keymer and James Kelly.—New ed.
p. cm—(Oxford world's classics)
Includes bibliographical references.
ISBN–13: 978–0–19–283342–6 (alk. paper)
ISBN–10: 0–19–283342–1 (alk. paper)
1. Crusoe, Robinson (Fictitious character)—Fiction. 2. Survival after airplane accidents,
shipwrecks, etc—Fiction. 3. Castaways—Fiction. 4. Islands—Fiction. I. Keymer, Tom.
II. Kelly, James William. III. Title.
PR3403.A2K49 2007
823'.5—dc22

2006026022

Typeset in Ehrhardt
by RefineCatch Limited, Bungay, Suffolk
Printed in Great Britain
on acid-free paper by
Clays Ltd, St Ives plc

ISBN 0–19–283342–1 978–0–19–283342–6

1

CONTENTS

ACKNOWLEDGEMENTS

The present edition of *Robinson Crusoe* is based on the text established by J. Donald Crowley and his research assistant Nancy Splinter Zguta for the Oxford English Novels edition of 1972, and we gratefully acknowledge their textual work. Our debts to some of the leading scholars of Defoe and his age, especially Max Novak, Claude Rawson, and John Richetti, are personal as well as intellectual. Financial support was generously provided during preparation of this edition by the Leverhulme Trust, Major Research Fellowship Programme (Thomas Keymer), and the Provost and Fellows of Worcester College, Oxford (James Kelly). We are grateful to Nuala Koetter for providing images of the title page and frontispiece to *Serious Reflections During the Life and Surprising Adventures of Robinson Crusoe*, which are reproduced by permission of the Rare Book & Manuscript Library of the University of Illinois, Urbana-Champaign.

INTRODUCTION

FEW literary works have as strong a claim as *Robinson Crusoe*—or, to use its original title of 1719, *The Life and Strange Surprizing Adventures of Robinson Crusoe*—to classic status. With over 700 editions (a fraction of the total) listed in the British Library catalogue, and an enduring global reach in countless translations, Defoe's first and most celebrated novel easily passes the test of Samuel Johnson, for whom 'length of duration and continuance of esteem' were the indicators to watch.[1] In the rich interpretative possibilities offered by the text to successive generations of readers, *Robinson Crusoe* also chimes with modern definitions of a literary classic, which stress the hospitality of complex works to multiple, divergent readings. The novel rewards analysis as many things—an exotic adventure story; a study of solitary consciousness; a parable of sin, atonement, and redemption; a myth of economic individualism; a displaced or encoded autobiography; an allegory of political defeat; a prophecy of imperial expansion—yet none of these explanations exhausts it. In the political purposes to which it has been put, and the cultural needs it has been made to serve, Defoe's masterpiece even answers sceptical accounts of canon formation as a process owing as much to ideology as to disinterested aesthetic evaluation.

The canonization of *Robinson Crusoe* has its origins in the second half of the eighteenth century, propelled by prominent arbiters of taste in Britain and beyond. In a conversation dating probably from the 1770s and published after his death, Johnson took care to exempt the novel (with *Don Quixote* and *The Pilgrim's Progress*) when asking rhetorically if there was 'ever yet any thing written by mere man that was wished longer by its readers'.[2] Other commendations by Johnson are recorded elsewhere, and they herald a recognition of Defoe's importance that grew in strength during the Romantic period, notably in a major essay by Walter Scott and in Coleridge's brilliant

---

[1] *Johnson on Shakespeare*, ed. Arthur Sherbo, introd. Bertrand H. Bronson, 2 vols., The Yale Edition of the Works of Samuel Johnson vii–viii (New Haven: Yale University Press, 1964), vii. 60.

[2] Hester Lynch Piozzi, *Anecdotes of the Late Samuel Johnson* (1786), 281, quoted in Pat Rogers (ed.), *Daniel Defoe: The Critical Heritage* (London: Routledge, 1972), 59.

marginal commentaries on style and psychology in *Robinson Crusoe*. The most influential early champion of the novel was Jean-Jacques Rousseau, who hailed it in *Emile* (1762) as 'a complete treatise on natural education', a fable of development that could teach to perfection the place of humanity in nature.[3] Yet Rousseau also dismissed as redundant almost a quarter of the text (the episodes before and after the island story), and the novel has owed its success ever since to the power of its castaway myth. It was above all as a celebration of pioneer self-sufficiency that *Robinson Crusoe* ran into more than a hundred American editions between 1774 and 1830, and reprints gathered pace in Britain and Europe over the same period.[4] Later, the widespread use of Defoe's protagonist to illustrate theories of supply, demand, labour, and value in nineteenth-century economics gave new resonance to the work, Karl Marx being one among many thinkers to ground his arguments about *homo economicus* in the Crusoe figure. In the same period, the rise of mainstream evangelism enabled Defoe's religious themes (like those of Bunyan in *The Pilgrim's Progress*) to shed the provocative air of Dissenting radicalism that surrounded them on first publication, and the novel was widely valued for its pious content. Wilkie Collins satirizes the dual foundation of the Victorian vogue for *Robinson Crusoe*, at once utilitarian and evangelical, in Gabriel Betteredge, the ponderous lead narrator of *The Moonstone* (1868), who regulates 'all the necessities of this mortal life' by using the work as a manual of spiritual solace and practical advice.[5]

For the pioneers of modernism in the twentieth century, the spare style and vivid specifications of *Robinson Crusoe* made it the founding text of fictional realism, a status later fleshed out in Ian Watt's influential study, *The Rise of the Novel* (1957), which identifies the particularizing solidity of Defoe's technique as the crucial formal breakthrough for the early novel. For Virginia Woolf, *Robinson Crusoe* displayed a 'genius for fact' that could achieve effects 'beyond any but the great masters of descriptive prose', using just the plainest

[3] Jean-Jacques Rousseau, *Emilius and Sophia; or, A New System of Education*, 2 vols. (1762), ii. 59; a modern translation is in Rogers (ed.), *Daniel Defoe*, 52–3.

[4] Clarence E. Brigham, 'Bibliography of the American Editions of *Robinson Crusoe* to 1830', *Proceedings of the American Antiquarian Society*, 67 (1958), 137–83.

[5] 'When my spirits are bad—*Robinson Crusoe*. When I want advice—*Robinson Crusoe* . . . I have worn out six stout *Robinson Crusoes* with hard work in my service' (Wilkie Collins, *The Moonstone*, ed. John Sutherland (Oxford: Oxford World's Classics, 1999), 9).

snatches of nouns and verbs. Likewise, Defoe was for James Joyce 'the great precursor of the realist movement'.[6] But Joyce's interest in the novel was also political, and he found in Crusoe a national spirit of enterprise and conquest that was a harbinger of global empire. Joyce's reading highlights the ways in which, as an energizing fable of exploration and colonial encounter, *Robinson Crusoe* could be enlisted throughout the nineteenth and early twentieth centuries to promote the claims and values of empire across Britain and her dominions overseas. A ubiquitous book in Victorian schools, it was also the most popular book among boys, according to a survey of the 1880s. For one witness at the height of imperial expansion, it 'exerted over the minds of Englishmen an influence certainly greater than any other of modern times', and it was to this influence that England owed 'many of her astonishing discoveries, and no inconsiderable part of her naval glory'.[7] Yet on closer inspection Defoe's novel also suggests some of the most salient anxieties and scruples of the imperial project, and could equally become an enabling resource for colonial and postcolonial writers. Not only Columbus but also Proteus, the Crusoe figure was 'part of the mythology of every West Indian child', as the poet Derek Walcott recalled of his schoolboy reading in wartime St Lucia. With his rich symbolic potential and flexible rough-hewn prose, Defoe's hero offered Caribbean writers a voice that was 'various, contradictory and as changeable as the Old Man of the Sea'.[8]

Crusoe in the marketplace

In Defoe's own lifetime (he died in 1731, almost twelve years to the day after publishing the novel) the reputation of *Robinson Crusoe* was far less exalted. A brazenly commercial production, defiant of traditional literary decorum and accessible to all readers, Defoe's novel

---

[6] Virginia Woolf, '*Robinson Crusoe*' (1919), in *The Common Reader: Second Series* (London: Hogarth Press, 1932), 57; James Joyce, 'Daniel Defoe' (1911), ed. and trans. Joseph Prescott, *Buffalo Studies*, 1.1 (1964), 12.

[7] George Borrow, *Lavengro* (1851), ch. 3, quoted in Rogers (ed.), *Daniel Defoe*, 124. For the survey, conducted in 1884 and reported by Edward Salmon in 1888, see Richard Phillips, *Mapping Men and Empire: A Geography of Adventure* (London: Routledge, 1997), 51, 174.

[8] Derek Walcott, 'The Figure of Crusoe' (1965), in Robert D. Hamner (ed.), *Critical Perspectives on Derek Walcott* (Boulder, Colo.: Lynne Rienner Publishers, 1997), 37, 35.

was one of the most conspicuous successes of the early eighteenth-century market for print, yet also one of the most suspect. No doubt it found an audience of some kind within the educated elite, and the leading poet of the era, Alexander Pope, privately confessed to admiring the work. But the earliest recorded responses to *Robinson Crusoe* fix above all on the scandal of its lowbrow appeal, as though the outpour of print released by the novel crystallized the anxieties about cultural democratization and decay that pervade so much of the period's satire, from Swift's *A Tale of a Tub* to Pope's own *Dunciad*. Published on 25 April 1719, *Robinson Crusoe* reappeared in five further authorized editions within four months, and it is a mark of the work's brisk sale that three different printers had to be enlisted in order to keep up with demand. As the surviving ledger of one of these printers indicates, the typical print-run for each edition was about 1,000 copies.[9] The absolute figures may not be huge, but early sales of *Robinson Crusoe* were enough to make a mid-century biographer of Defoe marvel at 'the many editions it has sold, and the sums of money which have been gained by it'.[10] They were unprecedented in the case of prose fiction. As in the jaundiced vision of Pope or Swift, where the relentless effect of popular print is to propagate more (and worse), *Robinson Crusoe* then multiplied itself in a series of second-order texts. The continuation tentatively floated in Defoe's closing lines—'All these things . . . I may perhaps give a farther Account of hereafter' (p. 258)—materialized in August 1719, offering readers not only a crowd-pleasing return to Crusoe's island but also exotic travels through China and Muscovy. After a fourth stand-alone edition of 1722, *The Farther Adventures of Robinson Crusoe* was then frequently republished in tandem with the original text, only dropping away from view after the mid-nineteenth century.

Defoe followed up again in August 1720 with an enigmatic book of meditations, *Serious Reflections During the Life and Surprising Adventures of Robinson Crusoe: With His Vision of the Angelick World*. Some items in this rather pragmatic compilation have little bearing

[9] K. I. D. Maslen, 'Edition Quantities for *Robinson Crusoe*, 1719', *The Library*, 24 (1969), 145–50. Two entirely separate printings were published as the 'third' edition, and two more as the 'fourth'.

[10] Robert Shiels, *The Lives of the Poets* (1753), iv. 322, quoted in Rogers (ed.), *Daniel Defoe*, 50.

on the novel, but others have rich and intriguing implications, including a discourse 'Of Isolation' and a preface (reprinted in the present edition as Appendix 1) that strategically confuses Crusoe's voice and identity with Defoe's own. This display of religious enthusiasm did little to head off criticism, however, and may even have intensified it. 'There is not an old Woman that can go to the Price of it, but buys thy Life and Adventures, and leaves it as a Legacy, with the *Pilgrims Progress*, the *Practice of Piety*, and *God's Revenge against Murther*,' sneered Charles Gildon, a fading hack who railed against (while profiting from) the novel's vogue in *The Life and Strange Surprizing Adventures of Mr. D—— De F—* (1719), a scurrilous attack that was soon in its third edition.[11] Where Gildon damned the novel by association with popular piety and Dissent, others saw it as a cynical exercise in the kind of far-fetched travelogue that Swift was shortly to mock in the deadpan implausibilities of *Gulliver's Travels* (1726). Naive adults marvel at 'common Books of Travels and *Voyages* . . . stuff'd with . . . monstrous and incredible Narrations', one contemporary scoffed, while their offspring 'are little less delighted with such Books as the *Lives and Adventures of Robinson Crusoe*'.[12] With its offer of low pleasures to low readers, from vulgar religiosity to sensational adventure, the novel was a commercial triumph to be envied, but in almost no recorded case a literary achievement to be praised.

Several explanations can be given for this downbeat reception. For Defoe and his publisher, the widespread denigration of *Robinson Crusoe* was a simple case of sour grapes, and spoiling copy, on the part of professional rivals. As the 'Publisher's Introduction' to *Serious Reflections* protests, the work had elicited 'a thousand hard Words from the Men of Trade; the Effect of that Regret which they entertain'd, at their having no Share in it'. But Defoe's controversial personal reputation must also have been a factor. A prolific writer on trade, religion, and politics for decades before *Robinson Crusoe*, he was known above all as a journalist and agitator with ideological roots in the revolutionary Puritanism of the civil war era. Educated at a prominent academy for Dissenters (Protestants who refused to conform to Anglican doctrine as laid down after the Restoration

---

[11] Charles Gildon, *The Life and Strange Surprizing Adventures of Mr. D—— De F—, of London, Hosier* (1719), pp. ix–x.

[12] Anthony Hilliar, *A Brief and Merry History of Great-Britain* (Dublin, 1730), 23–4.

of 1660), Defoe was a lifelong campaigner against the claims of divine-right absolutism in church and state, though also something of a loose cannon at a time when categories of party allegiance were beginning to harden. As a young man he took arms against James II in the Duke of Monmouth's disastrous west-country rebellion of 1685, and was lucky to escape the 'Bloody Assizes' that autumn, when several of his former schoolfellows—'your *Western* Martyrs that, had they lived, would have been extraordinary Men', as Defoe remembered them[13]—were hanged or transported. When James was successfully deposed at the 'Glorious Revolution' of 1688–9, Defoe became a zealous propagandist for the incoming monarch, William III, who claimed to have inaugurated a newly benign and consensual mode of government based on contractual relations between ruler and ruled. William was nothing less than 'the restorer of English liberty', as Defoe put it in *The Original Power of the Collective Body of the People of England, Examined and Asserted* (1701).[14]

Defoe came to the peak of his notoriety as the Tory and High Anglican interest moved back into the ascendancy under Queen Anne. He was arrested for or otherwise implicated in the production of seditious libel on several occasions, the first time following his authorship of *The Shortest Way with the Dissenters* (1702). This pamphlet was a brilliantly provocative work of ventriloquism that aimed to discredit Anglican extremists by tipping their rabble-rousing rhetoric into outright calls for violent, even genocidal, suppression of the nonconformist minority. Although *The Shortest Way* is identifiable on second reading as laced with ironies that undercut the surface argument, its immediate function was as a hoax designed to ensnare or flush out his unwary political opponents. As Defoe later explained, 'The case the Book pointed at, was to speak in the first Person of the *Party*, and then, thereby, not only speak their Language, but make them acknowledge it to be theirs, which they did so openly, that confounded all their Attempts afterwards to deny it, and to call it a *Scandal* thrown upon them by another' (*Present State of the Parties*, 24). A quarter of a century later, one of the cleverest lines in Pope's *Dunciad*—'Earless on high, stood unabash'd Defoe'— plays on Defoe's adroit stage-management of the punishment that

---

[13] Daniel Defoe, *The Present State of the Parties in Great Britain* (1712), 319.

[14] Daniel Defoe, *The True-Born Englishman and Other Writings*, ed. P. N. Furbank and W. R. Owens (London: Penguin, 1997), 109.

ensued. Sentenced to stand in the pillory as (in the words of his indictment) 'a Seditious man and of a disordered mind, and a person of bad name, reputation and Conversation', Defoe was protected by a ring of heavies, and pelted with flowers, while supporters distributed copies of his defiant new poem, *A Hymn to the Pillory* (1703). With finely judged absurdity, Pope also keeps in play the contaminating link with radical Puritanism of the civil war years, as embodied in William Prynne, the Presbyterian activist whose ears were cropped for seditious libel in the 1630s, and the thwarted revolutionary hero of Milton's *Samson Agonistes*, 'eyeless in Gaza', 'patient and undaunted'.[15]

Even in Whig and Dissenting circles, Defoe inspired little trust. No side escapes incrimination in his political satires and tracts, least of all Dissenters prepared to compromise (through the practice of 'occasional conformity' at Anglican communion) with the political and religious establishment. After the questionable service done to nonconformist interests in *The Shortest Way*, Defoe then worked for years as the hired pen of the moderate Tory minister Robert Harley, in whose service he also set up an espionage network and became a key player in negotiations leading to the union of England and Scotland in 1707. Thereafter he grew in notoriety for his apparent readiness to write on opposing sides of any controversy: 'a hireling Scribler'; 'a mercenary Fellow that writ for and against all parties'; 'a thorough-pac'd, true-bred *Hypocrite*, an *High-Church Man* one Day, and a *Rank Whig* the next'.[16] By the time of *Robinson Crusoe*, he was a leading contributor to the most rabid Tory periodical of the day, *Mist's Weekly Journal*, albeit probably in a spirit of damage limitation.

Defoe's notoriety as a seditious libeller and literary mercenary was not alleviated by sporadic allegations of other crimes and misdemeanours, from smuggling, fraud, and horse-stealing to the

---

[15] Alexander Pope, *The Dunciad Variorum* (1729), ii. 147 (see also i. 101 n., which explicitly connects Defoe and Prynne); John Milton, *Samson Agonistes* (1671), lines 41, 1623. The Old Bailey indictment of 1703 is quoted by Paula R. Backscheider, *Daniel Defoe: His Life* (Baltimore: Johns Hopkins University Press, 1989), 104.

[16] William Pittis, *The True-Born Englishman: A Satyr, Answer'd*, 2nd edn. (1701), 77; contemporary manuscript note in a copy of Defoe's *The True-Born Englishman* (1701), University of London Library, quoted by Backscheider, *Daniel Defoe*, 349; *Judas Discuver'd . . . Being a Full and True Account of the Apprehending and Taking of Mr. Daniel De Foe, on Saturday Last, for High-Treason* (1713), 3.

cuckoldry of a personal friend. Nor was it helped by the roller-coaster swings of his business career. A spectacular bankrupt in early life (he broke in 1692 with debts of £17,000, more than a million in modern money), and a fugitive from creditors at the time of his death, Defoe was wealthy enough in other periods to ape a gentry lifestyle, with his handsome retreat at Newington Green and his trumped-up coat of arms ('three griffins passant counterchanged'). His early experience of debtors' gaol was followed by another bankruptcy in 1706 and further arrests for debt in 1713, but did not deter him from keeping up an exotic series of projects and ventures alongside his literary career. He dealt or speculated at different phases of his life in almost every commodity imaginable, from hosiery, bricks, and timber to civet cats, anchovies, and even a diving-bell for salvaging treasure. Then there was the flamboyant figure he affected in taverns and coffeehouses, the lavish tasselled wig and outsize diamond pinky ring he famously sported expressing the same upstart energies and ambitions that characterize his fictional heroes. Not only a fanatic and an incendiary (two of the insults that dogged Defoe most closely in his lifetime), the author of *Robinson Crusoe* was also an egregious spiv, and a slave to bling.

Personal factors apart, denigration of the kind suffered by Defoe's novel was standard treatment at a time when prose fiction had yet to position itself as a serious or legitimate mode of writing—a process of generic elevation that only took hold with Richardson and Fielding a generation later. Yet the sheer vigour of the attacks on *Robinson Crusoe* also indicates a sense that something new and important was poised to emerge on the literary scene, with disruptive long-term consequences for the established hierarchy of genres. In the years that followed, Defoe did little or nothing to minimize the scope for censure. Between 1720 and 1724 he produced a spate of further novels about lives of transgression, beginning with the exuberant *Captain Singleton* (1720) and closing in grimmer tones with *Roxana* (1724), a work originally entitled *The Fortunate Mistress* (probably in wry response to Eliza Haywood's *Idalia; or, The Unfortunate Mistress* (1723), a scandal narrative by Defoe's only significant competitor as a writer of fiction at the time).[17] For all his sins, Crusoe looks a

---

[17] *Captain Singleton* was preceded by a borderline candidate for designation as a novel, *Memoirs of a Cavalier* (1720); *Roxana* was followed by another, *A New Voyage round the World* (1724).

model of respectability alongside the lawless protagonists of these follow-up works: Singleton is a pirate, Roxana a courtesan and borderline murderess; the heroine of *Moll Flanders* (1722) is a street robber, the hero of *Colonel Jack* (1722) a pickpocket and mercenary. In each case, Defoe's choice of material was compounded by the insidious tendency of his first-person style to foster vicarious involvement in, even sympathetic identification with, the cause of each narrating subject. As Roxana disarmingly puts it, her design as a narrator is to 'move the Pity, even of those that abhor the Crime',[18] and this morally destabilizing effect was only partly mitigated by the expressions of repentance, some notably perfunctory and fragile, that typically frame the novels.

Further tarnishing the reputation of *Robinson Crusoe* was its rapid penetration into the murkiest depths of the book trade, beyond the control of Defoe and his publisher William Taylor, who even went to law in a forlorn attempt to protect his copyright. Taylor may have authorized the first popular serialization of the work, which ran for a year from October 1719 in a halfpenny newspaper, the *Original London Post; or, Heathcot's Intelligence* (where instalments had the interesting side-effect of dramatizing for readers the incremental pace of Crusoe's journal). But numerous other publishers cashed in without permission or payment. Alongside the usual unauthorized Dublin editions came several piracies and abridgements (including an error-strewn collector's item, *The Life, and Strange Surprizing Adventures of Robeson Cruso*), while cheap, simplified chapbook digests were produced for the literate poor. Then came the imitations, beginning with a novel entitled *The Adventures and Surprizing Deliverances of James Dubourdieu and His Wife: Who Were Taken by Pyrates, and Carried to the Uninhabited Part of the Isle of Paradise*, written by Ambrose Evans and cheekily marketed as 'very proper to be bound up with *Robinson Crusoe*'.[19] This work came out in October 1719 as a double bill with another castaway fiction (*The Adventures of Alexander Vendchurch, Whose Ship's Crew Rebelled against Him, and Set Him on Shore on an Island in the South-Sea*), thus inaugurating

---

[18] Daniel Defoe, *Roxana*, ed. John Mullan (Oxford: Oxford World's Classics, 1996), 39.

[19] *Daily Post*, 9 Oct. 1719, quoted by Backscheider, *Daniel Defoe*, 599; on *Heathcot's Intelligence*, see H. C. Hutchins, *Robinson Crusoe and Its Printing, 1719–1731: A Bibliographical Study* (New York: Columbia University Press, 1925), 157–66.

the long-lived subgenre of the 'Robinsonade'. Other early works in this vein, marked not only by the island theme but also by titular claims to strangeness or surprise that were almost the Crusoe trademark, include *Ashton's Memorial; or, An Authentick Account of the Strange Adventures and Signal Deliverances of Mr. Philip Ashton; Who . . . Liv'd Alone on a Desolate Island for about 16 Months* (1726), and *The English Hermit, or the Unparalell'd and Surprizing Adventures of One Philip Quarll, Who Was lately Found in an Uninhabited Island in the South Sea* (1727).[20] All these novels adapt Defoe's prototype in different ways, but all converge on the same basic plot of isolation, survival, and providential care, often with other borrowed motifs such as capture by pirates or Moors.

Voyager, castaway, improver

As the many imitations of *Robinson Crusoe* make clear, the appeal of the work for many readers was simply as an adventure story, and here Defoe was tapping into a vogue for voyage literature that was rife as he wrote. The expanding range of exploratory and privateering activity undertaken by mariners of the period made voyage narrative a genre in healthy supply, and demand was ensured by the armchair fantasies it offered of perilous quest, heroic trial, and often spectacular reward. As the Earl of Shaftesbury loftily complained in 1710, voyages 'are in our present Days, what *Books of Chivalry* were, in those of our Forefathers'.[21] Prominent examples include William Dampier's *A New Voyage round the World* (1697) and his associate Woodes Rogers's *A Cruising Voyage round the World* (1712), both of

---

[20] For a survey of the 'Robinsonade' subgenre, see Martin Green, *The Robinson Crusoe Story* (University Park: Pennsylvania State University Press, 1990). *Ashton's Memorial* is a fictionalized memoir, ghostwritten by John Barnard; *The English Hermit* is a novel by Peter Longueville, frequently republished in the eighteenth century, once as *The New Robinson Crusoe* (1797). Among the best-known Robinsonades are three German novels that recast Defoe's original with significant twists: Johann Gottfried Schnabel's *Insel Felsenburg* (*Felsenburg Island*, 1731–43), a utopian satire that coined the term *Robinsonaden*; Joachim Heinrich Campe's *Robinson der Jüngere* (*Robinson the Younger*, 1779–80), which makes the crucial move of stranding its hero without tools, thereby providing the real prototype for 'Crusoe economics'; Johann David Weiss's *Der Schweizerische Robinson* (*Swiss Family Robinson*, 1812), a myth of patriarchal community that makes the island a symbolic refuge from the chaos of revolutionary Europe.

[21] Anthony Ashley Cooper, Third Earl of Shaftesbury, *Soliloquy; or, Advice to an Author* (1710), 178, quoted by Philip Edwards, *The Story of the Voyage: Sea-Narratives in Eighteenth-Century England* (Cambridge: Cambridge University Press, 1994), 3.

which went into new editions—the sixth in Dampier's case—shortly before *Robinson Crusoe*. Like other mariner-authors of the period, Dampier and Rogers may have sought professional assistance when reworking their journals, but both take characteristic pride in their own simplicity of utterance and corresponding authenticity of report. In their respective prefaces, Dampier rejects the idea that in matters of style 'a Seaman should affect Politeness', while Rogers announces it as his deliberate choice 'to keep to the Language of the Sea'. Much of the vigour of both accounts flows from this demotic plainness, and a particular success of Dampier's text is his immediacy in representing not only nautical and buccaneering exploits but also something of his own inward state in the face of uncertainty and peril. Other voyage narratives made more of the religious element that remains a background feature of Dampier's account, weaving episodes of deliverance from storm and shipwreck into narratives of individual reprobacy and salvation.

These are all aspects of the genre that Defoe would exploit, and his appeal to the market for voyages is evident in the elaborate title-page of *Robinson Crusoe*. This feature too attracted censure: 'the Title of *Crusoe's Adventures* may pass for a Table of Contents', one journalist austerely protested, and paid 'low court to the Vulgar' in its sensational tone.[22] But extended titles paid off as a promotional device, and were to become a miniature art form in Defoe's later novels: the heroine of *Moll Flanders* is 'Twelve Year a *Whore*, Five Times a *Wife* (whereof once to her own Brother)'; the hero of *Colonel Jack*—in an inspired moment of typographical havoc—'married Four Wives, and Five of them prov'd *Whores*'. In the case of *Robinson Crusoe*, the title stops short of advertising the work's preoccupation with cannibalism (a bridge too far for Dampier, who had never encountered cannibals and doubted their existence), but otherwise offers an irresistible blend of shipwreck, piracy, and wonder. In similar vein, the nautical specificities and harrowing evocations of maritime crisis in Defoe's early pages show how closely he studied the voyage genre. The point is nicely caught by the satirist who, when Swift parodied Dampier's jargon of the sea in *Gulliver's Travels*, commented that the passages in question 'seem to have

---

[22] Matthew Concanen, 'Of the Frauds of Booksellers', *The Speculatist* (1730), 201, 200.

been added . . . by the Author of *Robinson Crusoe*, to enhance the Price'.[23]

Yet Defoe did much more than reproduce the Dampier format as he found it, and the extended title also clarifies his priorities as he adapted the conventions of the voyage, downplaying elements redundant to his purpose and intensifying others. His thinking can be glimpsed in an imaginary circumnavigation narrative that he wrote some years later, *A New Voyage round the World* (1724), which criticizes writers who allow the tedium of log-work and steerage to crowd out genuine action. 'The Stories of their Engagements, when they have had any Scuffle either with Natives, or *European* Enemies, are told superficially and by Halves', Defoe's narrator complains; 'the Storms and Difficulties at Sea or on Shore, have no where a full Relation'. The primary target here is Sir John Narbrough's relentlessly technical report of his South Seas explorations, post-humously published in 1711. But the implication is that even the more colourful works of Dampier and Rogers—both of whose narra-tives are inhibited in practice by the frequent illegality of their exploits—will be surpassed in the present text. 'A Seaman when he comes to the Press, is pretty much out of his Element', Defoe observes; in the alternative element of print—the element of his own personal mastery—he will rectify the usual imbalance.[24]

The method is already clear in *Robinson Crusoe*, with its turbulent evocations of shipwreck and storm and its battles with cannibals and mutineers. Here Defoe skilfully blends the rough directness of voyage narrative with features that distinguish his style elsewhere, notably a loose and flexible syntax that closely registers, in its impro-visatory form, effects of disorderly motion and random shock. A typical case arises on p. 40 when, pounded onto the island by waves, Crusoe recalls that

the Sea having hurried me along as before, landed me, or rather dash'd me against a Piece of a Rock, and that with such Force, as it left me senseless, and indeed helpless, as to my own Deliverance; for the Blow taking my Side and Breast, beat the Breath as it were quite out of my Body; and had it returned again immediately, I must have been strangled in the Water . . .

This sentence continues for a hundred more words, and mediates its

---

[23] *Gulliver Decypher'd* (1727?), 17; for Swift's parody, see *Gulliver's Travels*, ed. Claude Rawson and Ian Higgins (Oxford: Oxford World's Classics, 2005), esp. 75–6 (II. i).

[24] Daniel Defoe, *A New Voyage round the World* (1724), 2–3, 1.

representation of the storm entirely through the desperate senses of the half-drowned Crusoe. Yet it also balances the delirium of the moment with the clarity of later retrospection. The power of Crusoe's prose at this point flows from a deft combination of breath-less, disoriented syntax with studious verbal selection: the self-conscious modifications and elaborations ('landed me, or rather dash'd me'; 'senseless, and indeed helpless'); the quickfire alliterations ('taking . . . my Breast, beat the Breath'), the abrupt lexical surprises ('strangled in the water').

Elsewhere Defoe connects the turmoil of ocean and the turmoil of consciousness in the same shared terms—Crusoe 'drowns' his repentance after one crisis (p. 10); thoughts 'rowl' upon his mind in another (p. 132)—but on this occasion he sets up a different pattern in the text. In a passage of desolate calm that epitomized, for Virginia Woolf, the spare eloquence of the novel, Crusoe then goes on to recognize that all his comrades are dead, 'for, as for them, I never saw them afterwards, or any Sign of them, except three of their Hats, one Cap, and two Shoes that were not Fellows' (p. 41). In a novel where traces of life and signs of its absence are typically expressed as solitary footfalls, single footprints, or even (after the feast by cannibals on the shore) discarded and scattered feet, the unpaired shoes are a stroke of laconic genius.

Voyage narrative was not only an opportunity for outlandish adventure, however, or a launchpad for Defoe's virtuosity as a narra-tor of catastrophe. For all his disparagement of non-narrative con-tent, he also took care to absorb and develop more strictly descriptive features of the voyage genre. Dampier's text is one in which, some-times awkwardly, episodes of buccaneering and pillage exist along-side meticulous attempts to amass geographical information, record natural phenomena, and even approach what we might now call ethnography. In these ways, voyage writers not only assessed their destinations as candidates for colonial exploitation; they also re-sponded, more or less consciously, to the calls of Royal Society scientists that voyagers should contribute to knowledge through systematic observation and description of natural history in all its branches. Crusoe's table of climatic patterns and his call on 'the Naturalists' to explain a physical phenomenon that leaves him baffled (pp. 91, 159) are two conspicuous instances of a pervasive tendency in the text. Here Defoe not only builds on the norms of voyage

narrative but also pursues the affinity with Baconian empirical and
experimental science that marks his canon as a whole. Among the
clearest examples are *The Storm* (1704), which documents a freak
hurricane that had devastated England a few months beforehand,
and *A General History of Discoveries and Improvements* (1725–7), a
historical account of ancient and modern innovations in commerce,
industry, and exploration. As well as observing and recording nature,
Crusoe pursues the Baconian project of turning nature to practical
advantage through experiment and technological innovation, with
meticulous write-up of the results. Some of his attempts to become
'Master of every mechanick Art' (p. 59) are more promising than
others. But all, from his ingenious fabrication of pots and baskets to
his ill-advised tobacco therapy ('I . . . held my Nose close over the
Smoke of it as long as I could bear it' (p. 80)), display a commitment
to scientific advance rivalling that of the most diligent voyage narrator. As Ilse Vickers puts it, *Robinson Crusoe* expresses 'the characteristic Baconian belief in man's duty to study, alter and improve nature
to his various uses'; its focus on Crusoe's discoveries and applications makes the novel 'an allegory of the advancement of learning: a
model of initiative and invention'.[25]

At another level, Crusoe's close observation of rainfall and tides,
and his assiduous experiments in farming and manufacture, express
survival skills of very much the kind dramatized in some of the most
celebrated episodes of voyage narrative. Several voyages record tales
of castaways or maroons, the best known being the Scots mariner
Alexander Selkirk, a figure long assumed to have been the primary
model for Crusoe. Marooned after a dispute with his captain on
the island of Más a Tierra in the south Pacific archipelago of Juan
Fernández,[26] Selkirk survived alone for more than four years. His
rescue came in February 1709, when Woodes Rogers put in at the
island to find it inhabited by 'a Man clothed in Goat-Skins, who
look'd wilder than the first Owners of them'.[27] After voyaging further

[25] Ilse Vickers, *Defoe and the New Sciences* (Cambridge: Cambridge University Press,
1996), 99, 105.
[26] The island, a dominion of Chile, has now been entrepreneurially renamed Isla
Robinson Crusoe, though Defoe clearly strands his hero in the south Caribbean—
where, as Derek Walcott dryly observes, 'he has become the property of the Trinidad
and Tobago Tourist board' ('Figure of Crusoe', 35).
[27] Woodes Rogers, *A Cruising Voyage round the World*, 2nd edn. (1718), 125. Subsequent quotations are from pp. 125–9 of this edition.

with Rogers, Selkirk returned to Britain to become a reluctant celebrity in the following decade, and the pages devoted by Rogers to his case may indeed have set Defoe's mind to work. As well as appearing in *A Cruising Voyage*, Rogers's account was separately published in pamphlet form, with a title that heralds Defoe's dual emphasis on divine superintendence and strange adventure: *Providence Display'd, or a very Surprizing Account of one Mr. Alexander Selkirk, Master of a Merchant-Man call'd the Cinque-Ports; who Dreaming that the Ship would soon after be lost, he desired to be left on a Desolate-Island in the South-Seas, where he liv'd Four Years and Four Months, without seeing the Face of Man, the Ship being afterwards cast away as he Dreamed* (1712).

In Rogers's account, Selkirk survives an early period of despair, in which 'for the first eight months [he] had much ado to bear up against Melancholy, and the Terror of being left alone in such a desolate place'. Central to his recovery are his efforts to impose meaning on adversity by literally inscribing his identity on the island and structuring the vacancies of time. As Crusoe carves the record of his shipwreck on a post and notches each passing day, so Selkirk asserts his presence 'by cutting his Name on the Trees, and the Time of his being left, and Continuance there'. Other details of Selkirk's isolation look forward to *Robinson Crusoe*. He sustains himself spiritually through daily religious exercise, singing psalms and reciting scripture, and survives in practice by ingeniously adapting his basic stock of equipment: 'a Firelock, some Powder, Bullets, and Tobacco, a Hatchet, a Knife, a Kettle, a Bible, some practical Pieces, and his Mathematical Instruments and Books'. He hunts goats on foot when his gunpowder runs out, and, with Crusoe-like zeal for tabulating experience, 'kept an Account of 500 that he killed while there'. Like Crusoe again, who domesticates kids and holds whimsical banquets with his parrot and dog, Selkirk 'tam'd some Kids, and to divert himself would now and then sing and dance with them and his Cats'. He builds two huts from trees and grass, assigning separate purposes to each, and stitches together goatskins for clothes and bedding; he hides in a tree from marauding Spaniards 'because he apprehended they would murder him, or make a Slave of him in the Mines'.

Parallels with Defoe's hero are also suggested by other published accounts of Selkirk's ordeal, including an essay of 1713 by a rival

Whig journalist, Richard Steele. Concluding his essay, Steele anticipates Crusoe's disenchantment with the prosperity of his post-island
life—'I had more Care upon my Head now, than I had in my silent
State of Life in the Island' (p. 240)—by placing a similar paradox
in Selkirk's mouth. '*I am now worth 800 Pounds*', Steele has Selkirk
lament, '*but shall never be so happy, as when I was not worth a
Farthing.*'[28]

Selkirk was by no means the only available model, however. In
A Cruising Voyage, Rogers compares him with a previous inhabitant
of Más a Tierra, a Moskito Indian named Will, who had been
marooned from 1681 to 1684 until rescued by Dampier's crew.
Dampier devotes several pages to Will's formidable survival skills,
again with emphasis on his improvisatory use of the small supply
of tools and firearms available to him on the island. Dampier also
describes a ritual greeting between Will and the first rescuer to reach
him that anticipates Friday's encounter with Crusoe and later reunion
with his father. In Dampier's somewhat cumbersome account, the
rescuer is a fellow Moskito named Robin, who 'first leap'd ashore,
and running to his Brother *Moskito* Man, threw himself flat on his
face at his feet, who helping him up, and embracing him, fell flat
with his face on the Ground at *Robin*'s feet, and was by him taken up
also.'[29] At one level, Friday's comparable gesture in *Robinson Crusoe*
becomes a fantasy of colonial mastery—'this it seems was in token of
swearing to be my Slave for ever', Crusoe eagerly assumes (p. 172)—
but it may also be a borrowed reflection of actual Carib custom. Something similar may be true of the naming scene, where Crusoe appears
to ignore or erase Friday's native identity and name. 'By renaming
this handsome, twenty-six-year-old savage, Crusoe assumes possession of him in the same way that Columbus assumed possession of
the land by his namings,' writes one critic; another protests that
'Crusoe . . . never over the years inquires as to "Friday's" real
name'.[30] The assertion of ownership is unmistakable, but Defoe's
point about the naming (which, in a masterstroke of irony, Crusoe

[28] Richard Steele, *The Englishman* (1714), 173 (No. 26, 3 Dec. 1713).

[29] William Dampier, *A New Voyage round the World*, 5th edn. (1703), 86.

[30] Maximillian E. Novak, 'Friday: or, The Power of Naming', in Albert J. Rivero
(ed.), *Augustan Subjects: Essays in Honor of Martin C. Battestin* (Newark: University of
Delaware Press, 1997), 117; Patrick J. Keane, 'Slavery and the Slave Trade: Crusoe
as Defoe's Representative', in Roger D. Lund (ed.), *Critical Essays on Daniel Defoe*
(New York: G. K. Hall, 1997), 115.

botches, having already lost count of his calendar by a day) may be slightly different. Personal naming is alien to the culture inhabited by Will and Robin, Dampier claims: 'They take it as a great favour to be named by any of us, and will complain for want of it, if we do not appoint them some name when they are with us: saying of themselves they are poor Men, and have no Name' (*New Voyage*, 86–7).

Other castaways have been disinterred in a long-running quest to uncover the 'original' Crusoe—a quest in which points of comparison routinely drift into assertions of direct influence. Among the earliest candidates to emerge was the protagonist of a twelfth-century Hispano-Arabian text, the *Philosophus autodidactus* of Abu ibn al-Tufail, which existed in at least two English translations in Defoe's lifetime, including Simon Ockley's *The Improvement of Human-Reason, Exhibited in the Life of Hai Ebn Yokdan* (1711). This work tells of a child of nature who grows to maturity and wisdom in isolation from society, and it reappeared again in a loose adaptation soon after *Robinson Crusoe*. The original text 'has certainly been known to some few of our Countrymen', the preface to this adaptation declares, and 'the late History of *Robinson Crusoe* . . . plainly shows its Author had his first Hints from hence'.[31] Much more recently, Portuguese candidates have been proposed in a monograph based on similarities between *Robinson Crusoe* and various Renaissance travelogues, including the story of Fernão Lopes, who in the sixteenth century was stranded on St Helena for a decade with a Friday-like Javanese servant. Defoe is unlikely to have known the detail of this case, but he may indeed have seen passing mentions in translated histories of '*Ferdinando Lopez*, who to do Pennance for his Sins, voluntarily staid with a Black in the Island St. *Helena*, where he . . . began to sow that Island'.[32]

Closer to home is the castaway narrative of Henry Pitman, a surgeon and pharmacist with distant biographical links to Defoe. Like Defoe, Pitman had been involved in the Monmouth rebellion of 1685, and he survived to publish an account of his misfortunes with the bookseller John Taylor, whose son William was to publish *Robinson Crusoe* thirty years later. Sentenced to transportation, Pitman escaped with a group of fellow fugitives from the rising, only to be

[31] *The Life and Surprizing Adventures of Don Juliani de Trezz* (c. 1722), Preface.

[32] Manuel de Faria e Sousa, *The Portugues Asia* (1695), 187; see also Fernanda Durão Ferreira, *The Portuguese Origins of Robinson Crusoe* (London: Minerva Press, 2000).

cast away in 1687 on the Caribbean island of Tortuga. He returned
after the Glorious Revolution to record his experience in *A Relation
of the Great Sufferings and Strange Adventures of Henry Pitman,
Chyrurgion to the Late Duke of Monmouth* (1689). Among the salient
details of Pitman's narrative are his recurrent fears of falling prey to
cannibals or 'inhumane *Man-eaters*', his dogged but failed attempts
to make pottery 'by tempering the finest Sand with the Yolks of
Turtles Eggs and Goats Hair', and his admiration for the hunting
skills of 'my *Indian*' (a native he buys from buccaneers for thirty
pieces of eight), 'at which he was dextrous, that with his Bow and
Arrow he would shoot a small Fish at a great distance'. Eventually, in
an episode loosely resembling Crusoe's escape, the fugitives make off
by ambushing a gang of mutineers who drop anchor off Tortuga,
sailing away and leaving the mutineers stranded on 'this desolate and
disconsolate Island'.[33]

No single castaway narrative anticipates more than sporadic elements of Defoe's novel, however, and collectively they reveal nothing
so much as the creative surplus generated in *Robinson Crusoe*. It is
fair to assume that Defoe looked for raw material—environmental
details, survival techniques, even psychological insights—in stories
of figures like Selkirk, but the most telling overlaps show that he was
in the business of transformation, not imitation. Indeed, the most
striking thing about Crusoe's narrative is its reversal of the standard
trajectory of castaway tales, which involve not the construction of
a miniaturized civilization but extremes of degradation or even
derangement: more *Lord of the Flies* than *Robinson Crusoe*. Where
Crusoe flourishes in his little kingdom, progresses from wickedness
to regeneration, and grows in expressive fluency after decades alone,
Selkirk looks wilder than a goat when rescued, and 'had so much
forgot his Language for want of Use, that we could scarce understand him, for he seem'd to speak his words by halves' (*Cruising
Voyage*, 129). Ian Watt notes other cases of degeneration, including
that of a castaway on Mauritius driven mad by a diet of raw turtle,
and another on St Helena who puts to sea in the coffin of a buried
comrade.[34]

[33] *A Relation of the Great Sufferings and Strange Adventures of Henry Pitman* (1689),
18, 25, 24, 26; see also Tim Severin, 'Did Defoe's Publisher Know a "Real" Robinson
Crusoe?', *Notes and Queries*, 50.2 (2003), 201–2.
[34] Ian Watt, '*Robinson Crusoe* as a Myth', *Essays in Criticism*, 1.2 (1951), 107.

At such points, if Defoe is indeed writing with historical cases in mind, his activity is one of radical remodelling, even pointed viola-tion, of the expected pattern. By stranding Crusoe on the island and having him triumph over adversity, he offered his readers a gratify-ing fantasy of personal achievement, and one expressing the cluster of ideas contained in one of the most resonant terms of his personal lexicon, 'improvement'. From the raw material of the castaway tales, in which Crusoe's supposed models rarely move much beyond a state of low-level endurance, Defoe could produce a thematically concentrated study of inventiveness, industry, and improvement in its multiple senses. There are the practical lessons and spiritual growth that Crusoe draws from experience, 'improv[ing]' himself in 'all the mechanick Exercises which my Necessities put me upon' (p. 122) and making 'a just Improvement' of providential signs for the sake of religious consolation (p. 113). Then there are the achievements of manufacture and agriculture that mark his sojourn on the island, from domestic utensils—'in my Wicker Ware also I improved much' (p. 122)—to the cornfields, plantations, and enclosures—'my Works and Improvements' (p. 153)—that threaten to betray his presence when the cannibals land. Even Crusoe's audi-ence must join in the process by approaching his narrative with an eye to '*the Improvement of it*' in their own lives (p. 3).

In the largest sense, *Robinson Crusoe* thus contrives a narrative of human domination over raw nature in tune with the Whig ideology of progress that Defoe expresses more directly elsewhere. The theme is at its most pronounced in his last works, notably his celebrations of burgeoning industry and commerce in *A Tour thro' the Whole Island of Great Britain* (1724–6) and his insistence elsewhere that the English must truly become 'that industrious, applying, improving People that we pretend to be, and that we ought to be, and might be'.[35] Crusoe provides a model of just this endeavour, a character driven by the quest for improvement, and one who dedicates himself to productive labour, conversion of raw materials and resources into goods for consumption and investment, and rigorous account-ancy of profit and loss in material and spiritual concerns. From here flows the remarkable afterlife of Defoe's creation, especially via the German Robinsonades, in the history of economics. Crusoe is still an illustrative focus for analysis of such topics in economic theory

[35] Daniel Defoe, *An Humble Proposal to the People of England* (1729), 4.

xxvi   *Introduction*

as marginal utility, commodity exchange, and the labour theory of value, while the absence of women and the subordination of Friday in the island economy have spurred debate in feminist and postcolonial economics.[36]

Yet the status of Defoe's hero as 'the complacent apologist of nascent industrial capitalism', as Watt puts it in an extreme statement of this approach (*'Robinson Crusoe* as a Myth', 106), is always tenuous. As many factors make clear, including his boredom with the profitable Brazilian plantation and his disinclination to go beyond self-sufficiency, Crusoe is a peculiarly feckless and short-sighted capitalist. He is also one whose ill-focused cupidity is quietly mocked in the novel. Coleridge famously applauded the moment where Crusoe suspends his religious reflections on money—'O Drug! said I aloud, what art thou good for . . . However, upon second Thoughts, I took it away' (p. 50)—and the irony lingers throughout the work. Repeatedly, Crusoe disparages his gold—' 'Twas to me as the Dirt under my Feet' (p. 163)—even while counting and hoarding it with obsessive care. In *Farther Adventures*, he frankly acknowledges his temperamental unfitness for the rigours of capitalist venture, as though Defoe foresaw the violence that would be done to the original work, with all its complicating ironies and hints. Invited to join a commercial voyage to China, Crusoe now makes clear that he accepts from mere restlessness, for 'if Trade was not my Element, Rambling was'. As for the dignity of work and the accumulation of commodities for profit, he insists that his labour on the island was for survival alone, with no further purpose in, or application to, the world beyond. Rather than modelling the condition of economic man, he simply escapes it, and he evokes the treadmill of commercial modernity in tones that are almost tragic:

I saw the World busy round me, one Part labouring for Bread, and the other Part squandring in vile Excesses or empty Pleasures, equally miserable, because the End they propos'd still fled from them; for the Man of Pleasure every Day surfeited of his Vice, and heap'd up Work for Sorrow and Repentance; and the M[e]n of Labour spent their Strength in daily

---

[36] For a survey, see M. V. White, 'Robinson Crusoe', in John Eatwell, Murray Milgate, and Peter Newman (eds.), *The New Palgrave: A Dictionary of Economics*, 4 vols. (New York: Stockton Press, 1987), iv. 217–18; for recent developments, see Ulla Grapard and Gillian Hewitson (eds.), *Robinson Crusoe: The Construction and Deconstruction of Economic Man* (London: Routledge, 2007).

Strugglings for Bread to maintain the vital Strength they labour'd with, so living in a daily Circulation of Sorrow, living but to work, and working but to live, as if daily Bread were the only End of wearisome Life, and a wearisome Life the only Occasion of daily Bread.[37]

Religion and politics

Elsewhere in the sequel, Defoe's answer to readers who approached *Robinson Crusoe* in secular terms, scanning the text for errors in geography or inconsistencies of action, was to point to his religious seriousness. The abridgements had injured him not only by breaching copyright, he protests in the preface to *Farther Adventures*, but also by representing the original work as mere adventure: 'They strip it of all those Reflections, as well religious as moral, which . . . are calculated for the infinite Advantage of the Reader'. Claims to didactic probity in fiction were almost obligatory at the time, and need to be handled with care elsewhere in Defoe. But the religious dimension of *Robinson Crusoe* goes beyond incidental moralizing, and informs the whole shape of the text. As J. Paul Hunter puts it in one of two landmark accounts of religious traditions in Defoe, '*Robinson Crusoe* is structured on the basis of a familiar Christian pattern of disobedience–punishment–repentance–deliverance, a pattern set up in the first few pages of the book'.[38] From this point of view, castaways like Selkirk look less significant than the biblical exemplars who sometimes break the narrative surface: Jonah, punished for his disobedience by a storm at sea but providentially brought to land; Job, tested by unthinkable adversity but rewarded at his latter end; the reckless but repentant prodigal son of Luke 15. Also in play are the traditions of conversion narrative and diary-keeping outlined in G. A. Starr's classic study *Defoe and Spiritual Autobiography* (1965), associated in particular with the Puritan culture in which Defoe was raised. In spiritual autobiography, the individual life gains shape and meaning from the moment of repentance or conversion, but this moment rarely turns out to be secure, jeopardized as it is by recurrent backsliding, and demanding constant struggle. Focused to the exclusion of material conditions or secular

[37] Daniel Defoe, *The Farther Adventures of Robinson Crusoe* (1719), 248–9; 8–9.
[38] J. Paul Hunter, *The Reluctant Pilgrim: Defoe's Emblematic Method and Quest for Form in Robinson Crusoe* (Baltimore: Johns Hopkins Press, 1966), 19.

concerns on the fluctuating state of the soul, spiritual autobiography records the ongoing battle of inward grace with outward temptation, and demonstrates the author's efforts to achieve redemption while also inscribing the process for personal or shared contemplation.

With his anxious self-reproaches on religious grounds, and his determination to understand his life in terms of sin and grace, Crusoe organizes his narrative in a form that is clearly continuous with this tradition. Like Bunyan in *Grace Abounding* (1666), he snatches spurts of spiritual growth from chance fragments of scripture, and imposes meaning on the chaos of self and experience by progressively discovering, and constantly reasserting, providential pattern and meaning. Here the coexistence of journal and memoir in Crusoe's text is an important device for highlighting spiritual change. The early journal suggests the unmediated 'Discomposure of Mind' (p. 60) that afflicts Crusoe in his unregenerate condition; conversion then makes possible the orderly interpretation and communication of an otherwise 'unaccountable Life' (p. 153). In both cases, the result is strangely claustrophobic, the rigour of Crusoe's focus on spiritual inwardness tending to distance everything outside the self (though this is a fluctuating effect, part of Defoe's point about Crusoe being the inconsistency of his spiritual progress). As in Defoe's fiction as a whole, though with peculiar appropriateness in the case of this island novel, the consciousness of the narrator comes across as supremely alone and aloof, imprisoned in self-absorption even as the island becomes peopled. The first-person form perfectly embodies the philosophical solipsism articulated in *Serious Reflections*: the view that 'Life in general is . . . but one universal Act of Solitude', in which 'Every Thing revolves in our Minds by innumerable circular Motions, all centring in our selves' (*Serious Reflections*, 2).

It is a standard move to associate the obsessive self-analysis of spiritual autobiographers with the emergence, via Defoe and others, of a modern novel dedicated to inward experience and complex psychological representation. That is not to say, however, that Crusoe always comes across as rigorous or reliable when invoking spiritual or providential causes and effects. Although *Serious Reflections* censures those who cite reliance on Providence to excuse their own weakness or neglect, there are points in the novel where Crusoe does exactly that himself. When he fires at random into a group of mutineers,

only two of whom are his targets, his casual excuse that he thereby
puts it 'wholly upon God's Providence to direct the Shot' (p. 215)
inspires little confidence in his invocations of Providence elsewhere.
At other points—when the barley grows for miraculous or natural
reasons; when Crusoe is cured by scripture or tobacco—alternative
determinants remain delicately in play, with no firm adjudication
between secular and religious explanation. It is easy to see why, for
Gildon, the religious glosses of Crusoe's narrative were no more
than irrelevant cant, padding put gratuitously in 'to swell the Bulk of
your Treatise up to a five Shilling Book' (*Life . . . of Mr. D—— De
F—*, 30–1). Instead, the real explanation of the novel lay in the
resemblance between Crusoe's character—including his religious
hypocrisy—and that of Defoe himself. In their unscrupulous motiva-
tion and erratic progress, Crusoe's adventures could be mapped
directly onto the wayward career of their author. 'You are the true
Allegorick Image of thy tender Father *D——l*', Gildon has Defoe
tell Crusoe in a dramatized part of the pamphlet: 'I drew thee from
the Consideration of my own Mind; I have been all my Life that
Rambling, Inconsistent Creature, which I have made thee' (p. x).

Somewhat surprisingly, this was a charge that Defoe was prepared
to embrace. His preface to *Serious Reflections* is a masterly exercise
in ambiguity, written in a voice that associates, without ever quite
equating, Crusoe's perspective with his own. Irresistibly, however,
this preface implies the validity of an approach to *Robinson Crusoe*
as displaced autobiography, either because Defoe had consciously
encoded his own misfortunes in Crusoe's, or because Gildon had
alerted him to symbolic patterns that were unconscious at the time
of writing. Throughout his life, the language of storm and shipwreck
came instinctively to Defoe with reference to his own career, and his
favourite metaphor for debt was one of drowning: 'The Gulph is too
Large for me to Get ashore again', he laments in a typical letter.[39] In
Serious Reflections, he builds on his earlier public self-representations
by inviting readers to find autobiographical hints in the disasters
suffered by Crusoe. He even uses the term 'Allegorick History' to
redefine the novel no longer as literal truth (the official pose of the
original text) but as something teasingly poised between fact and
fiction. Now *Robinson Crusoe* is an 'imaginary Story', but one that in

[39] *Letters of Daniel Defoe*, ed. George Harris Healey (Oxford: Clarendon Press, 1955),
16 (to Robert Harley, May–June 1704?).

its circumstances reflects the real-life trials of its author: a man who has endured 'a Life of Wonders in continu'd Storms . . . been in Slavery worse than *Turkish* . . . been taken up at Sea in Distress, rais'd again and depress'd again, and that oftner perhaps in one Man's Life than ever was known before; Shipwreck'd often, tho' more by Land than by Sea . . .' (Appendix 1, pp. 266–7). Most strikingly of all, this new account of *Robinson Crusoe* as figurative autobiography turns the castaway experience that dominates the novel into a great emblem of incarceration. In a passage from *Serious Reflections* that was to be adopted by Albert Camus as an epigraph to *La Peste* (1947), Defoe writes enigmatically of 'a State of forc'd Confinement, which in my real History is represented by a confin'd Retreat in an Island'; the entire novel thus expresses 'one kind of Imprisonment by another' (Appendix 1, p. 267).

It would be misguided, of course, to attempt systematic correlation between the plot of *Robinson Crusoe* and its author's life. Occasionally, the hard outlines of *Pilgrim's Progress*-style allegory look to be in prospect, as when Crusoe writes of arriving at '*the Island of Despair*' (p. 60). But for the most part the significant connections are to do with psychological, emotional, and spiritual states, or with general patterns of oscillation between good and bad fortune. That said, Defoe's talk of the island as symbolic of other confinement inevitably suggests his own past as a political prisoner, and the link is reinforced by the cry Crusoe teaches his parrot— '*Poor* Robin Crusoe . . . *Where have you been? How come you here?*' (p. 121)—which echoes Defoe's own public lament after his punishment for seditious libel: 'Alas, *Poor De Foe!* What hast thou been doing, and for what hast thou suffer'd?'[40] More generally, Camus may have intuited something important when using Defoe's words from *Serious Reflections* to invite a political reading of his own novel (an allegory of oppression in which plague connotes Nazi occupation). It is important to remember here that Defoe's imprisonment for writing *The Shortest Way* was not only a matter of personal misfortune. It was also, in his own eyes, the symptom of a larger, communal persecution, resurgent after 1702 but severest under the restored Stuart monarchy of 1660–88, which is also almost exactly the span of Crusoe's ordeal on the island. This was a period of

---

[40] Daniel Defoe, *A Second Volume of the Writings of the Author of The True-Born Englishman* (1705), 313.

'Trampling on *Laws*, Oppressing of *Subjects*, Invading *Property*, Persecuting for *Conscience*, and Suspending the *Laws*', as Defoe characterized it decades later; the crisis comes with Charles II's death in 1685 and the failure of the Monmouth rising, when 'the Fury of *Civil-War* it self began to revive in the Popish and Tyrannical Government of King *James* II' (*Present State of the Parties*, 4).

The celebrated passage in which Crusoe refers to his island exile as 'my Reign, or my Captivity, which you please' (p. 117) usefully indicates the equal and opposite political echoes sounded by his situation and language. Chronological correspondence is crucial here, and the pointed simultaneity between Crusoe's time on the island and the reign at home of the restored Stuarts suggests a related thematic correspondence, linking Crusoe's captivity and reign with the predicament of England, or of Dissenters in particular, throughout the Restoration years. Crusoe is shipwrecked and stranded on 30 September 1659, just as the collapse of the Puritan republic was becoming inevitable, and a few months before Milton theatrically uttered, in *The Ready and Easy Way to Establish a Free Commonwealth* (1660), 'the last words of our expiring liberty'.[41] But the exact day and month are also important, in keeping with Defoe's emphasis in *Serious Reflections* and elsewhere on the providential significance of dates and their recurrence in history. The day of Crusoe's shipwreck heralds three key moments, for Defoe, in the extended national crisis surrounding James II's reign: James's marriage to Mary of Modena on 30 September 1673, an event inseparable in the public mind from his conversion to Catholicism; the execution at Taunton of several prominent Monmouth rebels, including Defoe's schoolfellows Benjamin Hewling and William Jenkyn, on 30 September 1685; William of Orange's Declaration of 30 September 1688, announcing his intention to intervene against James. The date of Crusoe's return to England is no less significant. He reaches his homeland on 11 June 1687, two years to the day after Monmouth had landed at Lyme to raise his ill-fated rebellion. But this is also a more auspicious time, when an increasingly formidable and concerted opposition to James were already negotiating with William, the aim being (in Defoe's words elsewhere) 'to restore the Liberties of the People, which the arbitrary Proceedings of that King had ruin'd and

[41] *John Milton: The Major Works*, ed. Stephen Orgel and Jonathan Goldberg (Oxford: Oxford University Press, 1991), 353.

subverted'.[42] As Michael Seidel writes in the first serious attempt
to correlate the time scheme of *Robinson Crusoe* with English political history, 'Crusoe endures an exile that parallels what Defoe saw as
a condition of the home island's regressive turn toward more and
more oppressive home rule . . . and he returns just as his land is
about to regain a legitimate status, or return to its senses'.[43]

   Several indications point up the relationship between Crusoe's
afflictions on one hand and Stuart despotism on the other. It may be
speculative to associate the summer storms on Crusoe's island with
the rain-drenched rout at Sedgemoor, as Tom Paulin does in his
bravura account of *Robinson Crusoe* as a novel of survivor's guilt, or
to hear the jeering of Judge Jeffreys at the Bloody Assizes in the
'cruel bloody Entertainment' of the cannibals on the shore (p. 142).[44]
But it is hard not to think of Defoe's friends and fellow rebels
when considering the incongruous imagery of judicial sentencing,
death by hanging, and sudden reprieve that haunts the novel, while
Crusoe's Job-like patience in his captivity neatly registers the spirit
of pious endurance sustaining Dissenters during the Restoration
years. One of Defoe's most direct political hints comes when Crusoe
compares his landing on the island to a stay of execution, and quotes
a rare line of verse: 'For sudden *Joys*, like *Griefs*, confound at first.'
The source of this quotation was not identified in scholarship until
1998, but would have been recognized by many early readers as
a controversial broadside of 1672 by Robert Wild, a Dissenting minister and satirical poet, entitled *Dr. Wild's Humble Thanks for His
Majesties Gracious Declaration for Liberty of Conscience*.[45] The poem
voices the mingled hopes and fears of Dissenters on the vexed issue
of religious toleration, and by citing it Defoe connects Crusoe's
island ordeal with the Puritan condition of jeopardy and alienation
under Stuart rule. By referring in particular to the 'sudden joys'
provoked by this promise of religious rights, he also sounds an ironic
note, given the well-founded suspicion that later emerged that Stuart
policies on toleration were largely a ploy to strengthen the position

---

[42] Daniel Defoe, *Jure Divino* (1706), x.

[43] Michael Seidel, 'Crusoe in Exile', *PMLA* 96 (1981), 366.

[44] Tom Paulin, 'Fugitive Crusoe', *London Review of Books*, 23.14 (19 July 2001),
15–20; a revised version is in Paulin's *Crusoe's Secret: The Aesthetics of Dissent* (London:
Faber, 2005).

[45] Robert Wild, *A Letter from Dr. Robert Wild . . . Together with His Poetica Licentia*
(1709), 13; see also Explanatory Note to p. 41.

of an implacable Catholic interest. As Defoe robustly put it years later (glancing at the fate of Huguenots in Catholic France), 'I told the *Dissenters*, I had rather the Church of *England* should pull our Cloaths off by Fines and Forfeitures, than the Papists should fall both upon the *Church*, and the *Dissenters*, and pull our Skins off by Fire and Fagot.'[46] Crusoe's perils, like those of his co-religionists, are only beginning at this point.

Yet there is no allegorical equivalence here, nor even the clarity of a number of other intertexts suggested by Crusoe's situation. In Andrew Marvell's poem 'Bermudas', the Puritan oarsmen who flee the Laudian persecutions of the 1630s rejoice as they approach 'an Isle so long unknown | And yet far kinder than our own', and the political meaning becomes unmistakable as they disembark 'on a grassy Stage; | Safe from the Storms, and Prelat's rage'.[47] In Henry Pitman's narrative of his ordeal on Tortuga, the status of the cast-aways as 'Sufferers on the account of the Duke of *Monmouth*' is never forgotten, and the Caribbean as a whole turns out to be awash with Monmouth sympathizers, even among James II's navy (*Relation of Henry Pitman*, 15; see also 19, 27). No such explicit indications are available in *Robinson Crusoe*, and the messages we get are more interestingly mixed. If on some occasions Crusoe suggests the posture of Puritan martyrology, reflecting the tone and stance of the defeated Milton or the imprisoned Bunyan, he also intermittently assumes a more ironic guise. Scholars have struggled to reconcile Crusoe's language of divine-right absolutism with Defoe's own Lockean politics, which, as expressed in texts such as *The Original Power*, firmly resists the claim of monarchical authority to be grounded in anything other than the assent of the people, contractually established and liable to withdrawal when power is abused. Yet the tone is clearly whimsical, even parodic, when Crusoe talks of being 'King and Lord of all this Country indefeasibly' (p. 85). This is not Crusoe's only attempt to define his relationship to the island and its inhabitants with reference to an ideology of divine right that Defoe alternately satirizes and denounces elsewhere. Later, Crusoe's voice is that of an absolute monarch who has 'none to dispute Sovereignty or Command with me' (p. 109), or who, in a

[46] Daniel Defoe, *An Appeal to Honour and Justice* (1715), 52; Defoe refers specifically here to James II's two Declarations of 1687–8.
[47] Andrew Marvell, 'Bermudas', lines 7–8, 11–12.

more sinister formulation, 'could hang, draw, give Liberty, and take it away, and no Rebels among all my Subjects' (p. 125). As the island begins to be peopled (Crusoe's earliest claims to sovereignty, absurdly, are over goats and cats), he even mimics the treacherous Stuart pose of religious toleration. Now the inhabitants of the island are 'perfectly subjected' to Crusoe as 'absolute Lord and Law-giver', while he exerts his power with the spurious magnanimity of the Declarations of Indulgence. 'My Man *Friday* was a Protestant, his Father was a *Pagan* and a *Cannibal*, and the *Spaniard* was a Papist', he observes: 'However, I allow'd Liberty of Conscience throughout my Dominions' (p. 203). Here Crusoe's condition is more a burlesque of Stuart autocracy than an allegory of Puritan exile; this indeed is reign and captivity at once.

The parodic nature of Crusoe's claims to absolute dominion and indefeasible right over the island also has a bearing on postcolonial criticism, in which *Robinson Crusoe* has a reputation no more enviable than that of *The Tempest*: a megatext of complacent Eurocentrism, an aggressive myth of supremacy, a rationale for imperial domination. But does this tell the whole story about a work that also articulates, in Walcott's words, 'the anguish of authority, of the conscience of empire' ('Figure of Crusoe', 36)? It is certainly the case that Crusoe's situation on the island, and its specific location, connect directly with Defoe's keen advocacy of colonial expansion, especially in South America, a continent he thought 'infinitely beyond the Plantations of *New England, Virginia*, &c. in the Fruitfulness of the Soil, Kind of Production, and other Advantages'. In the year of *Robinson Crusoe*, Defoe was probably the author of an article promoting a proposed South Sea Company venture near the mouth of the Orinoco (in other words, the mainland nearest Crusoe's island), where a new colony would serve 'to carry on a Trade there equal to that of the Portuguese in the Brazils, and to bring home an equal quantity of Gold, as well as to cause a prodigious Consumption of our British Manufactures'. He voices similar ambitions elsewhere for this region, which promises, with its abundant riches of people and gold, 'an infinite consumption of our Woollen Manufactures . . . and a Return of that most desirable of all Returns ready Money'.[48] At

[48] *Review*, 8 (No. 58, 7 Aug. 1711), 235; *Mist's Weekly Journal*, 7 Feb. 1719, quoted by Maximillian E. Novak, *Daniel Defoe: Master of Fictions* (Oxford: Oxford University Press, 2001), 546; *An Historical Account of the Voyages and Adventures of Sir Walter*

these and other points, Defoe's vision is clearly that of the 'first' British empire, a maritime and commercial empire of settlement as opposed to an empire of conquest founded on territorial expansion, economic exploitation, and racial subjection. But it was also one in which Defoe accepted the Atlantic slave trade and the use of slave labour on American and West Indian plantations as essential components of the project.[49] The serious qualms voiced in his religious works, notably *The Family Instructor* (1715), are comfortably trumped in his writings on trade, which justify the institution of slavery in terms of economic self-interest and competition with rival powers.

Yet in his imaginative writing, and especially his fiction, Defoe was able to think beyond the hard-edged certainties of his mercantilist tracts. In some respects, indeed, he keeps a step ahead of his postcolonial critics, including the first and greatest of them, James Joyce, whose account of Crusoe as a prophet of empire smacks of an essentialism about race—'the whole Anglo-Saxon spirit is in Crusoe' ('Daniel Defoe', 24)—that Defoe presciently debunks. As he writes in *The True-Born Englishman* (1701), ethnic purity is a mere mirage, and national identity derives from an enriching confluence, over the centuries, of diverse, mobile populations: 'A True-Born Englishman's a contradiction, | In speech an irony, in fact a fiction' (*True-Born Englishman and Other Writings*, 36). Something of this attitude conditions the sequel to *Robinson Crusoe*, which contrasts the fruitful English settlement on the island, with its indigenous wives and Anglo-Carib children, with the barren settlement of the Spaniards nearby, who 'did not like Women that were not Christians; and . . . would not touch one of them' (*Farther Adventures*, 88). A community arises on the island in which unregulated hybridization, in cultural as well as mere racial terms, displaces anything remotely akin to colonial replication of the homeland.

Spain is similarly a foil in the original novel, where Crusoe's urge to massacre the cannibals is checked by, among other religious and

Raleigh (1719), 41, a 'probable' attribution quoted by J. A. Downie, 'Defoe, Imperialism, and the Travel Books Reconsidered', in Lund (ed.), *Critical Essays*, 87.

[49] On the distinction (and overlaps) between the 'first' and 'second' British empires, one typified by Atlantic settlement and trade before the American revolution, the other by subcontinental conquest and annexation afterwards, see David Armitage, *The Ideological Origins of the British Empire* (Cambridge: Cambridge University Press, 2000), 2–3.

prudential factors, the memory of conquistador genocide. Elsewhere Defoe cites an early critique of the conquest of the Americas by Bartolomé de Las Casas, and Crusoe's dim awareness of the depredations recorded by Las Casas (who puts the number of victims at forty million) destabilizes the distinction between civilized and savage on which his self-image depends.

Also shaping Defoe's thinking at this point is Montaigne's alarming suggestion, at the height of the sixteenth-century wars of religion, that cannibals may be called barbarous 'in respect to the Rules of Reason: but not in respect to our selves, who in all Sorts of Barbarity exceed them'. Where cannibals roast enemies slain in battle as a ritual of revenge, Europeans roast their fellow-countrymen alive 'under Colour of Piety and Religion'; and this grim paradox plays constantly beneath the surface of *Robinson Crusoe*.[50] Several passages disrupt or overturn the assumed moral hierarchy between European and Carib, among them Crusoe's fear that the priests of the Spanish Inquisition will prove more barbarous than the savages (p. 206), and the clever reversal of perspectives involved when Friday perceives the English mutineers as potential cannibals (p. 211). By the time of the sequel, native barbarity has ceased to hold as a rationale for annexation, and Crusoe steps back from his whimsical pose as 'Governour' or 'Generalissimo' of an English colony. Revisiting the island, he reverts to a language of Lockean political relations that clearly exposes the parodic nature of his claims to divine-right sovereignty in the original novel: 'I never so much as pretended to plant in the Name of any Government or Nation . . . or to call my People Subjects to any one Nation more than another; nay, I never so much as gave the Place a Name; but left it as I found it, belonging to no Man; and the People under no Discipline or Government but my own; who . . . had no Authority or Power, to Act or Command one way or other, farther than voluntary Consent mov'd them to comply' (*Farther Adventures*, 216–17).

Slavery is the most intriguing question of all, though not one to which Crusoe himself gives very much thought. He exploits slave labour on his Brazilian plantation, undertakes three slaving voyages,

---

[50] *Essays of Michael Seigneur de Montaigne*, trans. Charles Cotton, 4th edn., 3 vols. (1711), i. 294–5; for Las Casas, see below, 145 and n. On the impact of both authors, see Claude Rawson, *God, Gulliver and Genocide: Barbarism and the European Imagination, 1492–1945* (Oxford: Oxford University Press, 2001), 17–91.

and talks about slavery as a given. Nothing indicates that when he laments the wickedness of his seafaring life he has in mind his activities as a slaver, and when he talks of having 'done wrong' by selling Xury into slavery (p. 31), or again by leaving his plantation 'to turn *Supra-Cargo* to *Guinea*, to fetch Negroes' (p. 164), he does so on grounds that are strictly pragmatic. Nor can this moral indifference be explained away with reference to the standards of the time. It is true that *Robinson Crusoe* pre-dates the abolitionist movement, and that an unequivocal position against slavery is nowhere found in fiction until the later eighteenth century, despite moves in that direction from Aphra Behn's *Oroonoko* (1688) onwards. Opposition to slavery had been mounted by Quakers as early as the 1670s, however, and in *Captain Singleton* Defoe reflects this fact by having Quaker William denounce the slave trade as contrary to nature and 'the highest Injustice'.[51] In this context, the oddness of Crusoe's inability to see his slaving activities as even potentially controversial is not only a modern perception. Writing within months of publication, Gildon expresses astonishment that Defoe seemed to have set up, but then failed to follow through, a moral fable in which Crusoe is punished specifically for his crimes as a slaver. ' 'Tho he afterwards proves so scrupulous about falling upon the Cannibals or Men-Eaters', Gildon protests of Crusoe's narrative, 'yet he neither then nor afterwards found any check of Conscience in that infamous Trade of buying and selling of Men for Slaves; else one would have expected him to have attributed his *Shipwreck* to this very Cause' (*Life . . . of Mr. D—— De F—*, 14).

Gildon does not entertain the possibility here that Crusoe's failure to recognize the most obvious rationale for his punishment is only the largest of the many ironies running through the text. Yet it is far from clear, for all the closeness of perspective between narrator and author in general, that the irrelevance of slave-trading in Crusoe's mind demonstrates its irrelevance in Defoe's. Though intermittent and fragmentary as an explicit topic, slavery is no less crucial as a submerged theme in *Robinson Crusoe* than in the comparable case, a century later, of Jane Austen's *Mansfield Park*. Both are novels in which little is said about slave traffic or slave labour but much is authorially implied, and in which the silence of characters complicit

[51] Daniel Defoe, *Captain Singleton*, ed. Shiv K. Kumar, introd. Penelope Wilson (Oxford: Oxford World's Classics, 1990), 157.

in the trade is itself an eloquent fact. Crusoe's own blind spot is obvious enough, but Defoe puts slavery at the very centre of his plot, which prefigures Crusoe's confinement on the island by his two-year enslavement on the Barbary Coast (an occupational hazard for European mariners at the time), and forces us to recognize that it is a slaving voyage, however irrelevant Crusoe thinks it, that lands him in his island prison. Moreover, Crusoe's inability to see any pattern here does not prevent him from making it visible to the reader. Enslaved to his Turkish master, he blurs the crucial point when deploring 'this surprising Change of my Circumstances from a Merchant to a miserable Slave' (p. 18), but not before reminding us that his special line as a merchant was as 'a *Guiney* Trader' (p. 17); the change of circumstance, in other words, is specifically from slaver to slave. He then defines his Turkish enslavement as 'but a Taste of the Misery I was to go thro'' (p. 18), thus indicating, while not quite grasping himself, the important sense in which his later experience on the island is also one of enslavement. Condemned to decades of hard labour, toiling on plantations an ocean from home, Crusoe endures an ordeal that uncannily reflects the fate of his intended cargo. He suffers a punishment that fits his crime even more perfectly than before.

Nor are the ironies lurking in Crusoe's story structural only. There is no need to go as far as Coleridge, who in point of style thought Defoe a finer ironist than Swift, to find in the episode of Xury's sale some calculated jarring notes. Having restrained the urge to drown Xury as they escape from their Turkish master, Crusoe then promises to make him 'a great Man', and credits him with qualities of affection and loyalty 'that made me love him ever after' (pp. 22, 24). But his tone abruptly changes when the Portuguese captain offers sixty pieces of eight—double the most famous of all temptations to betrayal—for ownership of Xury, with a vague promise to release the boy after ten years as a slave. 'I was very loath to sell the poor Boy's Liberty', Crusoe scrupulously notes, 'who had assisted me so faithfully in procuring my own. However . . . upon this, and *Xury* saying he was willing to go to him, I let the Captain have him' (p. 30). As so often in Defoe, the unheralded 'however', used not to modify but simply to erase the moral reflection that precedes it, is unmistakably incriminating in effect. In retrospect, moreover, it is hard not to hear the connection with Crusoe's empty renunciation of money some pages later: 'However, upon second Thoughts, I took it away' (p. 50; quoted above, p. xxvi). In both cases, Defoe exposes the dubious sincerity of his narrator, and his conscience-conquering reflexes of greed, by the same little shock of style.

Similar ironies return on the appearance of Friday, where Crusoe's first reaction, which is to look forward to having 'a Companion' on the island (p. 171), is rapidly sidelined by his inveterate solitariness and his impulse to dominate. Interpreting Friday's gestures of obligation in the most gratifying possible terms, and with an alliterative relish that underlines his acquisitive instincts, he reports that Friday 'made all the Signs to me of Subjection, Servitude, and Submission' (p. 174), and reads these signs as constituting a commitment to slavery for life. For all his subsequent benevolence in practice, Crusoe asserts over Friday a relationship of absolute power and possession that is then subtly connected by Defoe with the political theme of his novel. As the 'absolute Lord' to whom Friday is 'perfectly subjected' (p. 203), Crusoe establishes a hierarchy of domination that is no less extreme or arbitrary than the sovereignty claimed by James II, and enforced by his hitman Judge Jeffreys, over the people of England. When Defoe goes on to write in *Serious Reflections* of having personally lived under 'Slavery worse than *Turkish*', he seals this link between acts of enslavement in the novel and political oppression in the nation, and it is not a link that works wholly to Crusoe's advantage. As a prisoner who reigns and a slave who enslaves, Crusoe occupies the peculiarly conflicted position, at different levels, of tyrannized and tyrant at once. Perhaps Defoe's control of this paradox is no more secure than that of the slave-owning libertarians from whom, as Johnson famously wrote during the American Revolution more than fifty years later, 'we hear the loudest yelps for liberty among the drivers of negroes'.[52] But it would be hard to argue that he endorses Crusoe's position in all its aspects, or that he fails to expose the contradiction between slavery as a practice and the ideology of liberty for which his novel stands as a whole.

---

[52] Samuel Johnson, *Political Writings*, ed. Donald J. Greene (New Haven: Yale University Press, 1977), 454.

NOTE ON THE TEXT

Robinson Crusoe was entered in the Stationers' Register on 23 April 1719 and advertised as published 'this day' in the *Post Boy* and the *St James's Evening Post* for 23–5 April and the *Daily Courant* of 25 April. Seven numbered editions were published in Defoe's lifetime, the first four of these within four months, and the existence of entirely separate double printings of both the 'third' and 'fourth' editions brings to nine the true number of lifetime editions.[1] There were also various piracies, abridgements, and serializations. Defoe produced two sequels: *The Farther Adventures of Robinson Crusoe* on 20 August 1719 and *Serious Reflections During the Life and Surprising Adventures of Robinson Crusoe* on 6 August 1720.

The original publisher of *Robinson Crusoe* was William Taylor, printer and bookseller, who was said to have cleared £1,000 profit from the venture. The print-run of each edition appears to have been about 1,000, and the price of early editions was five shillings. Defoe's authorship was first asserted in September 1719 by Charles Gildon, who in *The Life and Strange Surprizing Adventures of Mr D—— De F—, of London, Hosier* (1719) indicates the commercial success of the novel with his jibe that 'there is not an old Woman that can go to the Price of it, but buys thy Life and Adventures' (pp. ix–x).

The Oxford World's Classics edition of *Robinson Crusoe* is based on the first-edition text established by J. Donald Crowley for the Oxford English Novels edition of 1972, to which we have made a handful of corrections and emendations. Substantive variants abound in other lifetime editions, but Crowley's painstaking collation of these editions (up to and including the posthumous 'eighth' of 1736 but excluding the alternative 'third' and 'fourth' editions, of which he was unaware) reveals no internal evidence of authorial revision; nor is there external evidence to this effect. Defoe's manuscript of the novel does not survive, but the obstacles faced by his compositors are indicated by other examples of his hurried

[1] K. I. D. Maslen, 'The Printers of *Robinson Crusoe*, 1719', *The Library*, 7 (1952), 124–31; Maslen, 'Edition Quantities for *Robinson Crusoe*, 1719', *The Library*, 24 (1969), 145–50; D. F. Foxon, 'More on *Robinson Crusoe*, 1719', *The Library*, 25 (1970), 57–8.

handwriting, with its close and indistinct characters, sketchy punctuation, crowded substitutions and revisions, and confusing shorthand contractions. Numerous corrections are made in later editions, but new errors also enter the text on each new setting of type, the overall number of textual variants running into many thousands.

Crowley's treatment of his copy text (the Bodleian Library copy of the first edition, shelfmark Don. E. 442) is conservative, and he confines his emendations to silent correction of substantive misprints and adjustment of accidentals where meaning is garbled or disrupted by the original punctuation. The 'errata' instructions listed at the end of the copy text have been observed. Otherwise, spelling, italicization, and punctuation remain unaltered from the first edition, which offers, for all its evident flaws, the closest available approach to the original style and rhythm of Defoe's prose. Crowley's Textual Notes are retained in the present edition as illustrations, necessarily selective, of the kinds of alteration unsystematically introduced in later editions, notably after 1726, when copyright of *Robinson Crusoe* passed to new booksellers, William Mears and Thomas Woodward, following Taylor's death in 1724.

SELECT BIBLIOGRAPHY

Bibliography and Reference

Blewett, David, *The Illustrations of Robinson Crusoe, 1719–1920* (Gerrards Cross: Colin Smythe, 1995).

Furbank, P. N., and W. R. Owens, *A Critical Bibliography of Daniel Defoe* (London: Pickering and Chatto, 1998).

Hutchins, Henry Clinton, *Robinson Crusoe and Its Printing, 1719–1731: A Bibliographical Study* (New York: Columbia University Press, 1925).

Kelly, James, 'Defoe's Library', *Library*, 3.3 (2002), 284–301.

Lovett, Robert W., *Robinson Crusoe: A Bibliographical Checklist of English Language Editions (1719–1979)* (New York: Greenwood, 1991).

Maslen, K. I. D., 'Edition Quantities for *Robinson Crusoe*, 1719', *Library*, 24 (1969), 145–50.

—— 'The Printers of *Robinson Crusoe*', *Library*, 7 (1952), 124–31.

Novak, Maximillian E., and Carl Fisher (ed.), *Approaches to Teaching Defoe's Robinson Crusoe* (New York: MLA, 2005).

Peterson, Spiro, *Daniel Defoe: A Reference Guide, 1731–1924* (Boston: G. K. Hall, 1987).

Rothman, Irving N., 'Coleridge on the Semi-Colon in *Robinson Crusoe*: Problems in Editing Defoe', *Studies in the Novel*, 27.3 (1995), 320–40.

Spackman, I. J., W. R. Owens, and P. N. Furbank, *A KWIC Concordance to Daniel Defoe's Robinson Crusoe* (New York: Garland, 1987).

Stoler, John A., *Daniel Defoe: An Annotated Bibliography of Modern Criticism, 1900–1980* (New York: Garland, 1984); entries for *Robinson Crusoe* are on pp. 123–80.

Biography

Backscheider, Paula R., *Daniel Defoe: His Life* (Baltimore: Johns Hopkins University Press, 1989).

Bastian, Frank, *Defoe's Early Life* (London: Macmillan, 1981).

Defoe, Daniel, *An Appeal to Honour and Justice . . . Being a True Account of His Conduct in Publick Affairs* (1715).

Novak, Maximillian E., *Daniel Defoe: Master of Fictions* (Oxford: Oxford University Press, 2001).

Richetti, John J., *The Life of Daniel Defoe: A Critical Biography* (Oxford: Blackwell, 2005).

Sources and Early Reception

Bastian, Frank, 'Crusoe's Derbyshire Caves', *Notes and Queries*, 35.2 (1988), 177–81.

Fausett, David, *The Strange Surprizing Sources of Robinson Crusoe* (Amsterdam: Rodopi, 1994).

Gildon, Charles, *The Life and Strange Surprizing Adventures of Mr. D——De F—, of London, Hosier* (1719); reprinted as *Robinson Crusoe Examin'd and Criticis'd*, ed. Paul Dottin (London: J. M. Dent, 1923).

Manguel, Alberto, 'The Library of Robinson Crusoe', *American Scholar*, 70.1 (2001), 61–70.

Rogers, Pat (ed.), *Daniel Defoe: The Critical Heritage* (London: Routledge, 1972).

Severin, Tim, 'Did Defoe's Publisher Know a "Real" Robinson Crusoe?', *Notes and Queries*, 50.2 (2003), 201–2.

Sill, Geoffrey, 'The Source of Robinson Crusoe's "Sudden Joys" ', *Notes and Queries*, 45.1 (1998), 67–8.

General Criticism

Alkon, Paul, *Defoe and Fictional Time* (Athens: University of Georgia Press, 1979).

Bell, Ian A., *Defoe's Fiction* (London: Croom Helm, 1985).

Bender, John, *Imagining the Penitentiary: Fiction and the Architecture of Mind in Eighteenth-Century England* (Chicago: University of Chicago Press, 1987), esp. ch. 2, 'The Novel and the Rise of the Penitentiary: *Robinson Crusoe*'.

Boardman, Michael M., *Defoe and the Uses of Narrative* (New Brunswick: Rutgers University Press, 1983).

Damrosch, Leopold, *God's Plots and Man's Stories: Studies in the Fictional Imagination from Milton to Fielding* (Chicago: University of Chicago Press, 1985), esp. ch. 5, 'Myth and Fiction in *Robinson Crusoe*'.

Downie, J. A., 'Defoe, Imperialism, and the Travel Books Reconsidered', *Yearbook of English Studies*, 13 (1983), 66–83.

Faller, Lincoln, 'Captain Misson's Failed Utopia, Crusoe's Failed Colony: Race and Identity in New, Not Quite Imaginable Worlds', *Eighteenth Century: Theory and Interpretation*, 43.1 (2002), 1–17.

Flynn, Carol Houlihan, *The Body in Swift and Defoe* (Cambridge: Cambridge University Press, 1990), esp. ch. 7, 'Consumptive Fictions: Cannibalism and Defoe'.

Hunter, J. Paul, *Before Novels: The Cultural Contexts of Eighteenth-Century English Fiction* (New York: Norton, 1990).

Lund, Roger D. (ed.), *Critical Essays on Daniel Defoe* (New York: G. K. Hall, 1997).

McKeon, Michael, *The Origins of the English Novel, 1600–1740* (Baltimore: Johns Hopkins University Press, 1987), esp. ch. 9, 'Parables of the Younger Son (1): Defoe and the Naturalization of Desire'.

Novak, Maximillian E., *Defoe and the Nature of Man* (Oxford: Clarendon Press, 1963).

—— *Economics and the Fiction of Daniel Defoe* (Berkeley: University of California Press, 1962).

—— *Realism, Myth and History in Defoe's Fiction* (Lincoln, Neb.: University of Nebraska Press, 1963).

Richetti, John J., *Daniel Defoe* (Boston: Twayne, 1987).

—— *Defoe's Narratives: Situations and Structures* (Oxford: Clarendon Press, 1975).

Starr, G. A., *Defoe and Casuistry* (Princeton: Princeton University Press, 1971).

—— *Defoe and Spiritual Autobiography* (Princeton: Princeton University Press, 1965).

—— 'Defoe's Prose Style: The Language of Interpretation', *Modern Philology*, 71.3 (1974), 277–94.

Vickers, Ilse, *Defoe and the New Sciences* (Cambridge: Cambridge University Press, 1996).

Watt, Ian, *The Rise of the Novel: Studies in Defoe, Richardson, and Fielding* (London: Chatto and Windus, 1957).

—— *Myths of Modern Individualism: Faust, Don Quixote, Don Juan, Robinson Crusoe* (Cambridge: Cambridge University Press, 1997), esp. ch. 5, '*Robinson Crusoe*'; ch. 6, 'Crusoe, Ideology, and Theory'.

Zimmerman, Everett, *Defoe and the Novel* (Berkeley and Los Angeles: University of California Press, 1975).

Robinson Crusoe

Armstrong, Dianne, 'The Myth of Cronus: Cannibal and Sign in *Robinson Crusoe*', *Eighteenth-Century Fiction*, 4.3 (1992), 207–20.

Ayers, Robert W., '*Robinson Crusoe*: Allusive Allegorick History', *PMLA* 82.5 (1967), 399–407.

Bell, Ian A., 'King Crusoe: Locke's Political Theory in *Robinson Crusoe*', *English Studies*, 69.1 (1988), 27–36.

Blackburn, Timothy, 'Friday's Religion: Its Nature and Importance in *Robinson Crusoe*', *Eighteenth-Century Studies*, 18.3 (1985), 360–82.

Donoghue, Frank, 'Inevitable Politics: Rulership and Identity in *Robinson Crusoe*', *Studies in the Novel*, 27.1 (1995), 1–11.

Ellis, Frank H. (ed.), *Twentieth Century Interpretations of Robinson Crusoe: A Collection of Critical Essays* (Englewood Cliffs, NJ: Prentice-Hall, 1969).

Hopes, Jeffrey, 'Real and Imaginary Stories: *Robinson Crusoe* and the *Serious Reflections*', *Eighteenth-Century Fiction*, 8.3 (1996), 313–28.

Hunter, J. Paul, *The Reluctant Pilgrim: Defoe's Emblematic Method and Quest for Form in Robinson Crusoe* (Baltimore: Johns Hopkins Press, 1966).

Jager, Eric, 'The Parrot's Voice: Language and the Self in *Robinson Crusoe*', *Eighteenth-Century Studies*, 21.3 (1988), 316–33.

Kavanagh, Thomas M., 'Unraveling Robinson: The Divided Self in Defoe's *Robinson Crusoe*', *Texas Studies in Language and Literature*, 20 (1978), 416–32.

McInelly, Brett C., 'Expanding Empires, Expanding Selves: Colonialism, the Novel, and *Robinson Crusoe*', *Studies in the Novel*, 35.1 (2003), 1–21.

Marshall, David, 'Autobiographical Acts in *Robinson Crusoe*', *ELH* 71.4 (2004), 899–920.

Morrissey, Lee, 'Robinson Crusoe and the South Sea Trade, 1710–1720', in John Louis DiGaetani (ed.), *Money, Lure, Lore, and Literature* (Westport, Conn.: Greenwood Press, 1994), 209–15.

Paulin, Tom, 'Fugitive Crusoe', *London Review of Books*, 23.14 (19 July 2001), 15–20; reprinted in *Crusoe's Secret: The Aesthetics of Dissent* (London: Faber, 2005).

Pearlman, E., 'Robinson Crusoe and the Cannibals', *Mosaic*, 10.1 (1976), 39–55.

Rogers, Pat, *Robinson Crusoe* (London: Allen and Unwin, 1979).

Schmidgen, Wolfram, 'Robinson Crusoe, Enumeration, and the Mercantile Fetish', *Eighteenth-Century Studies*, 35.1 (2001), 19–39.

Schonhorn, Manuel, *Defoe's Politics: Parliament, Power, Kingship, and Robinson Crusoe* (Cambridge: Cambridge University Press, 1991).

Seidel, Michael, 'Crusoe in Exile', *PMLA* 96 (1981), 363–74.

—— *Robinson Crusoe: Island Myths and the Novel* (Boston: Twayne, 1991).

Sill, Geoffrey, 'Crusoe in the Cave: Defoe and the Semiotics of Desire', *Eighteenth-Century Fiction*, 6.3 (1994), 215–32.

Sim, Stuart, 'Interrogating an Ideology: Defoe's *Robinson Crusoe*', *British Journal for Eighteenth-Century Studies*, 10.2 (1987), 163–73.

Spaas, Lieve, and Brian Stimpson (eds.), *Robinson Crusoe: Myths and Metamorphoses* (Basingstoke: Macmillan, 1996).

Watt, Ian, '*Robinson Crusoe* as a Myth', *Essays in Criticism*, 1.2 (1951), 95–119.

Wheeler, Roxann, ' "My Savage", "My Man": Racial Multiplicity in *Robinson Crusoe*', *ELH* 62.4 (1995), 821–61.

Zimmerman, Everett, '*Robinson Crusoe* and No Man's Land', *Journal of English and Germanic Philology*, 102.4 (2003), 506–29.

Further Reading in Oxford World's Classics

Defoe, Daniel, *A Journal of the Plague Year*, ed. Louis Landa, introduction by David Roberts.
—— *Moll Flanders*, ed. G. A. Starr.
—— *Roxana*, ed. John Mullan.

A CHRONOLOGY OF DANIEL DEFOE

	Life and works	Historical events
1660	Autumn: Daniel Defoe, son of James Foe, a prosperous tallow chandler, born in St Giles, Cripplegate.	Restoration of the Stuart monarchy with the arrival and coronation of Charles II in London.
1662	Samuel Annesley ejected from his living at St Giles, Cripplegate. The Foes follow him out of the Anglican church, becoming Nonconformists or Dissenters.	Act of Uniformity requires the use of all rites and ceremonies from the Book of Common Prayer in Anglican services.
1665	The Foes probably leave London during the outbreak of plague.	Start of the second Anglo–Dutch War. Plague in London kills 68,000.
1668	Defoe's mother, Ann Foe, dies some time between 1668 and 1671.	England, Sweden, and the United Provinces form the Triple Alliance against France.
1670		Charles agrees Treaty of Dover with Louis XIV, promising to restore England to Catholicism in return for subsidies.
1672	Defoe probably attends boarding school of James Fisher, an Independent clergyman, in Dorking, Surrey, at about this time.	Charles II issues Declaration of Indulgence, permitting licensed worship by Dissenters.
1673		First Test Act excludes Catholics and Dissenters from public office.
1674	Defoe enters Charles Morton's academy in Newington Green, where he trains for the Presbyterian ministry.	Parliament proposes to place new limitations on future Catholic rulers. Third Anglo–Dutch war ends with the Treaty of Westminster.
1678		Onset of the Exclusion Crisis: allegations of a Jesuit plot to kill Charles II and replace him with his Catholic brother, James, precipitate sustained attempts to exclude James from the succession.

	Life and works	*Historical events*
1681	Defoe decides against the ministry and becomes a wholesale hosier.	Parliament passes second Exclusion Bill against James.
1683	Defoe established as a hosier, living in Cornhill.	Rye House Plot to assassinate Charles II.
1684	Defoe marries Mary Tuffley, with a dowry of £3,700; the marriage produces six daughters and two sons.	Pope Innocent XI forms a Holy League to evict the Turks from Europe.
1685	Defoe is among the Monmouth rebels routed at the Battle of Sedgemoor in Somerset, but escapes the subsequent 'Bloody Assizes'.	Accession of James II. Rebellion raised by James Scott, Duke of Monmouth, bastard son of Charles II, defeated at Sedgemoor. Louis XIV revokes Edict of Nantes, ending toleration for Protestants in France.
1687	Defoe becomes a liveryman of the Butchers' Company. His name appears in the General Pardon issued for Monmouth rebels.	James II issues his first Declaration of Indulgence, suspending laws against Catholics and Dissenters.
1688	Defoe publishes his first pamphlet, *A Letter to a Dissenter from His Friend at the Hague*, alleging the insincerity of James II's offer of religious toleration.	Second Declaration of Indulgence. William of Orange lands at Torbay, precipitating 'Glorious Revolution' and flight of James to France. England joins War of the League of Augsburg against France.
1689	Defoe joins a 'Royal Regiment of Volunteer Horse', led by Monmouth's son, in parade honouring William III at the Lord Mayor's Show.	Parliament offers crown to William and passes Bill of Rights, limiting power of the monarchy. James II lands in Ireland. Toleration Act grants Dissenters rights of religious assembly, but not civil equality.
1690	Throughout this period, Defoe invests in shipping and an import/export business trading in tobacco, timber, wines and spirits, and hosiery.	James II decisively defeated by William III at the Battle of the Boyne, near Drogheda, Ireland.
1692	Defoe goes bankrupt for £17,000, and is committed to the Fleet and later the King's Bench Prison.	Massacre at Glencoe against the MacDonald clan, who had delayed pledging allegiance to William III.
1694	Establishes brick and tile factory at Tilbury, Essex. House of Lords rejects Bill to relieve named merchants (including Defoe) of part of their outstanding debt.	William makes a succession of political appointments, creating 'Whig Junto'. Bank of England established.

Life and works	*Historical events*
1695 Defoe becomes an accountant to the commissioners of the window tax. He now styles himself 'De Foe'.	Window tax imposed in England. Licensing Act lapses, suspending formal censorship of the press.
1697 Defoe publishes first major work, *An Essay upon Projects*.	Treaty of Ryswick ends War of the League of Augsburg. Louis XIV recognizes William III as king of England.
1698 *Lex Talionis; or, An Enquiry into the most Proper Ways to Prevent the Persecution of the Protestants in France*.	Launch of Darien scheme, an unsuccessful attempt by Scotland to establish a colony on the isthmus of Panama.
1701 Defoe becomes a household name with publication of *The True-Born Englishman*, a verse satire defending William III.	James II dies in exile. Louis XIV declares his grandson king of Spain, invades the Spanish Netherlands, and recognizes James II's son as James III.
1702 *The Shortest Way with the Dissenters*, a satire on the extremism of High Church Tories such as the preacher Henry Sacheverell, leads to issue of a warrant for Defoe's arrest.	Death of William III and accession of Queen Anne. Outbreak of War of Spanish Succession, fought by a European coalition, including England, to prevent the Bourbon dynasty inheriting the Spanish throne.
1703 Defoe imprisoned and pilloried for his authorship of *The Shortest Way*, released after intervention by Robert Harley, Speaker of the House of Commons and Secretary of State, but now financially ruined.	Southern England battered by the great storm of 26–7 November.
1704 Harley recruits Defoe as a political agent. Defoe publishes *The Storm* and launches the *Review*, a periodical on politics, trade, and religion (1704–13).	Whigs secure electoral victories, bringing the Whig Junto to power. British Forces capture Gibraltar and defeat the French at the Battle of Blenheim.
1706 Defoe publishes *Jure Divino*, a verse satire on arbitrary rule. Second bankruptcy. Sent to Scotland to advance the interests of political union with England, and publishes vigorously in this cause until 1710.	English, Dutch, and German troops defeat the French at the Battle of Ramillies. French fleet destroyed in Toulon.

	Life and works	*Historical events*
1707	Defoe is closely involved in political manoeuvres and negotiations leading to the Union.	Act of Union between England and Scotland creates the unitary state of Great Britain.
1708	Defoe reports to London on elections in Scotland, and serves the new ministry under Sidney Godolphin until 1710.	Attempted Jacobite landing at the Firth of Forth. General election brings in a moderate Whig and Tory administration.
1709	Publishes *The History of the Union of Great Britain*.	Copyright Act establishes limited protection of literary property.
1710	Defoe returns to Scotland to calm fears over High Church Tory extremism in England. He serves Robert Harley's ministry 1710–14.	Impeachment trial of Sacheverell. Whigs lose their majority in parliament. Harley becomes Chancellor of the Exchequer and starts secret peace talks with France.
1711	Defoe makes his final visit to Scotland. Publishes *An Essay on the History of Parties*, reviewing past legislation against Dissenters and attacking the Bill against Occasional Conformity.	South Sea Company established. Occasional Conformity Act prevents Dissenters and Catholics from taking occasional Anglican communion to qualify for public office.
1713	Defoe suffers further arrests for debt and, following publication of *Reasons against the Succession of the House of Hanover* and two other ironic tracts, seditious libel; successfully petitions Queen Anne for pardon.	Treaty of Utrecht ends War of the Spanish Succession. Britain secures the Asiento, the monopoly on trading slaves to Spanish America. General election results in a massive Tory victory.
1714	Defoe writes in defence of his patron, Harley, against charges of high treason.	Schism Act requires all teachers to conform to Church of England. Death of Anne and accession of George I, inaugurating Whig political supremacy until 1760.
1715	Defoe's career as a hired party writer drawing to a close. Publishes volume i of *The Family Instructor*, his first conduct manual, and a partly autobiographical text, *An Appeal to Honour and Justice*.	Major Jacobite rebellion in Scotland. With Henry St John, Viscount Bolingbroke, Robert Harley is impeached for treason. Bolingbroke flees to France.
1716	Defoe edits *Mercurius Politicus* (1716–20), a moderate Tory monthly journal.	Upsurge in piracy on the eastern seaboard of North America at about this time.

	Life and works	*Historical events*
1717	Defoe writes for Nathaniel Mist's Tory *Weekly Journal* (1717–19).	Failure of the impeachment trial against Harley.
1718	Publishes *A Continuation of Letters Written by a Turkish Spy at Paris* and volume ii of *The Family Instructor*.	Austria, Britain, France, and the United Provinces launch War of the Quadruple Alliance (to 1720) to halt Spain's territorial ambitions in Italy.
1719	Defoe founds Whig journal the *Manufacturer*, which runs from January to September. Publishes *Robinson Crusoe* (April) and *The Farther Adventures of Robinson Crusoe* (August).	Scheme for colonizing the mouth of the Orinoco is published in *Mist's Weekly Journal*. British troops defeat a Jacobite force at Glen Shiel. Occasional Conformity and Schism Acts repealed.
1720	Defoe pursues his career as novelist with *Memoirs of a Cavalier, Captain Singleton, Serious Reflections . . . of Robinson Crusoe*; 18–22 August: *The Farther Adventures of Robinson Crusoe*.	South Sea Bubble provokes stock market collapse and financial scandal. Quarantine to stop spread of plague from Marseilles, where 40,000–60,000 die.
1721–2	Defoe is now earning an estimated £1,000 or more per annum from his activities with various political journals.	Atterbury Plot, a Jacobite conspiracy involving Francis Atterbury, Bishop of Rochester.
1722	Defoe leases several hundred acres near Colchester, Essex. Publishes *Moll Flanders, Religious Courtship, A Journal of the Plague Year, Colonel Jack*.	Robert Walpole becomes de facto Prime Minister, using revelation of the Atterbury Plot to discredit the Tories and consolidate his grip on power.
1723	Defoe starts an abortive plan to establish a tile works.	Bolingbroke returns from exile. Waltham Black Act adds fifty capital offences to penal code.
1724	Defoe publishes *Roxana, A New Voyage round the World*, and volume i of *A Tour thro' the Whole Island of Great Britain* (volume ii, 1725; volume iii, 1726).	Thomas Longman purchases the stock and household goods of William Taylor, publisher of *Robinson Crusoe*, for £2,282 9s. 6d.
1725	Defoe undergoes a successful operation to remove bladder stones. Publishes volume i of *The Complete English Tradesman* (volume ii, 1727).	Treaty of Vienna: Austria pledges to assist Spain in recovering Gibraltar from Britain. League of Hanover: Britain, France, and Holland form alliance against Spain.

Chronology

	Life and works	Historical events
1727	*A General History of the Principal Discoveries and Improvements in Useful Arts* (published in four parts); *The Political History of the Devil* (two parts).	Accession of George II. War breaks out against Spain.
1728	Defoe is engaged in legal rows over his Colchester property, now heavily mortgaged and unprofitable. 21–3 March: *A Plan of English Commerce*.	Truce between England and Spain. Penal codes against Irish Catholics, commencing in 1695, culminate in a law withdrawing voting rights.
1729	Defoe commences *The Complete English Gentleman* (posthumously published in 1890).	Treaty of Seville formalizes peace between England and Spain.
1731	24 April: Defoe dies of a stroke in Rope Makers' Alley close to his birthplace, hiding from creditors.	Captain Robert Jenkins, a British seaman, is captured off Cuba and mistreated by the Spanish authorities, leading to War of Jenkins' Ear in 1739.

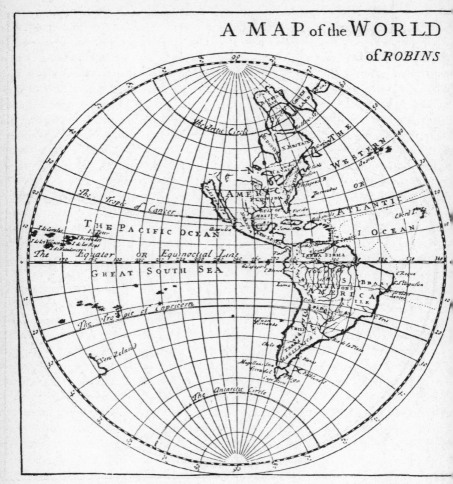

This map was first printed in the fourth edition of *Robinson Crusoe* and in the first edition of Defoe's continuation, *The Farther Adventures of Robinson Crusoe*, both published in August 1719. Dotted lines describe Crusoe's voyages in the sequel as well as in the original novel.

'R. Crusoe's I.' is shown near the mouth of the 'R Oronoque' off the northern coast of South America.

,on wch is Delineated the Voyages

ON CRUSO

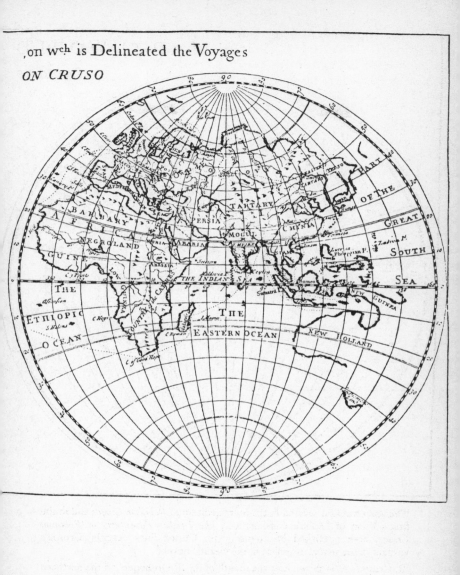

THE
LIFE
AND
Strange Surprizing
ADVENTURES
OF
ROBINSON CRUSOE,
Of *YORK*, Mariner:

Who lived Eight and Twenty Years,
all alone in an un-inhabited Island on the
Coast of AMERICA, near the Mouth of
the Great River of OROONOQUE;

Having been cast on Shore by Shipwreck, wherein all the Men perished but himself.

WITH

An Account how he was at last as strangely deliver'd by PYRATES.

Written by Himself.

LONDON:
Printed for W. TAYLOR at the *Ship* in *Pater-Noster-
Row.* MDCCXIX.

THE PREFACE.

IF ever the Story of any private Man's Adventures in the World were worth making Publick, and were acceptable when Publish'd, the Editor of this Account thinks this will be so.

The Wonders of this Man's Life exceed all that (he thinks) is to be found extant;* the Life of one Man being scarce capable of a greater Variety.

The Story is told with Modesty, with Seriousness, and with a religious Application of Events to the Uses to which wise Men always apply them (viz.) to the Instruction of others by this Example, and to justify and honour the Wisdom of Providence in all the Variety of our Circumstances, let them happen how they will.

The Editor believes the thing to be a just History of Fact;* neither is there any Appearance of Fiction in it: And however thinks, because all such things are dispatch'd,* that the Improvement of it, as well to the Diversion, as to the Instruction of the Reader, will be the same; and as such, he thinks, without farther Compliment to the World, he does them a great Service in the Publication.

THE LIFE
AND ADVENTURES OF
ROBINSON CRUSOE, &c.

I Was born in the Year 1632, in the City of *York*,* of a good Family, tho' not of that Country, my Father being a Foreigner of *Bremen*,* who settled first at *Hull:** He got a good Estate by Merchandise, and leaving off his Trade, lived afterward at *York*, from whence he had married my Mother, whose Relations were named *Robinson*, a very good Family in that Country, and from whom I was called *Robinson Kreutznaer*; but by the usual Corruption of Words in *England*, we are now called, nay we call our selves, and write our Name *Crusoe*,* and so my Companions always call'd me.

I had two elder Brothers, one of which was Lieutenant Collonel to an *English* Regiment of Foot in *Flanders*, formerly commanded by the famous Coll. *Lockhart*, and was killed at the Battle near *Dunkirk* against the *Spaniards:** What became of my second Brother I never knew any more than my Father or Mother did know what was become of me.

Being the third Son of the Family, and not bred to any Trade, my Head began to be fill'd very early with rambling Thoughts: My Father, who was very ancient, had given me a competent Share of Learning, as far as House-Education, and a Country Free-School generally goes, and design'd me for the Law; but I would be satisfied with nothing but going to Sea, and my Inclination to this led me so strongly against the Will, nay the Commands of my Father, and against all the Entreaties and Perswasions of my Mother and other Friends, that there seem'd to be something fatal in that Propension of Nature tending directly to the Life of Misery which was to befal me.

My Father, a wise and grave Man, gave me serious and excellent Counsel against what he foresaw was my Design. He call'd me one Morning into his Chamber, where he was confined by the Gout, and expostulated very warmly with me upon this Subject: He ask'd me what Reasons more than a meer wandring Inclination I had for leaving my Father's House and my native Country, where I might be well introduced, and had a Prospect of raising my Fortunes by Application and Industry, with a Life of Ease and Pleasure. He told me it was for Men of desperate Fortunes on one Hand, or of aspiring, superior Fortunes on the other, who went abroad upon Adventures, to rise by Enterprize, and make themselves famous in Undertakings of a Nature out of the common Road; that these things were all either too far above me, or too far below me; that mine was the middle State, or what might be called the upper Station of *Low Life*, which he had found by long Experience was the best State in the World, the most suited to human Happiness, not exposed to the Miseries and Hardships, the Labour and Sufferings of the mechanick Part of Mankind, and not embarass'd with the Pride, Luxury, Ambition and Envy of the upper Part of Mankind. He told me, I might judge of the Happiness of this State, by this one thing, *viz.* That this was the State of Life which all other People envied, that Kings have frequently lamented the miserable Consequences of being born to great things, and wish'd they had been placed in the Middle of the two Extremes, between the Mean and the Great; that the wise Man gave his Testimony to this as the just Standard of true Felicity, when he prayed to have neither Poverty or Riches.*

He bid me observe it, and I should always find, that the Calamities of Life were shared among the upper and lower Part of Mankind; but that the middle Station had the fewest Disasters, and was not expos'd to so many Vicissitudes as the higher or lower Part of Mankind; nay, they were not subjected to so many Distempers and Uneasinesses either of Body or Mind, as those were who, by vicious Living, Luxury and Extravagancies on one Hand, or by hard Labour, Want of Necessaries, and mean or insufficient Diet on the other Hand, bring Distempers upon themselves by the natural Consequences of their Way of Living; *That* the middle Station of Life was calculated for all kind of Vertues and all kinds of Enjoyments; that Peace and Plenty were the Hand-maids of a middle Fortune; that Temperance, Moderation, Quietness, Health, Society, all agreeable Diversions, and all desirable Pleasures, were the Blessings attending the middle Station of Life; that this Way Men went silently and smoothly thro' the World, and comfortably out of it, not embarass'd with the Labours of the Hands or of the Head, not sold to the Life of Slavery for daily Bread, or harrast with perplex'd Circumstances, which rob the Soul of Peace, and the Body of Rest;

not enrag'd with the Passion of Envy, or secret burning Lust of Ambition for great things; but in easy Circumstances sliding gently thro' the World, and sensibly tasting the Sweets of living, without the bitter, feeling that they are happy, and learning by every Day's Experience to know it more sensibly.

After this, he press'd me earnestly, and in the most affectionate manner, not to play the young Man, not to precipitate my self into Miseries which Nature and the Station of Life I was born in, seem'd to have provided against; that I was under no Necessity of seeking my Bread; that he would do well for me, and endeavour to enter me fairly into the Station of Life which he had been just recommending to me; and that if I was not very easy and happy in the World, it must be my meer Fate or Fault that must hinder it, and that he should have nothing to answer for, having thus discharg'd his Duty in warning me against Measures which he knew would be to my Hurt: In a word, that as he would do very kind things for me if I would stay and settle at Home as he directed, so he would not have so much Hand in my Misfortunes, as to give me any Encouragement to go away: And to close all, he told me I had my elder Brother for an Example, to whom he had used the same earnest Perswasions to keep him from going into the Low Country Wars, but could not prevail, his young Desires prompting him to run into the Army where he was kill'd;* and tho' he said he would not cease to pray for me, yet he would venture to say to me, that if I did take this foolish Step, God would not bless me, and I would have Leisure hereafter to reflect upon having neglected his Counsel when there might be none to assist in my Recovery.

I observed in this last Part of his Discourse, which was truly Prophetick, tho' I suppose my Father did not know it to be so himself; I say, I observed the Tears run down his Face very plentifully, and especially when he spoke of my Brother who was kill'd; and that when he spoke of my having Leisure to repent, and none to assist me, he was so mov'd, that he broke off the Discourse, and told me, his Heart was so full he could say no more to me.

I was sincerely affected with this Discourse, as indeed who could be otherwise?* and I resolv'd not to think of going abroad any more, but to settle at home according to my Father's Desire. But alas! a few Days wore it all off; and in short, to prevent any of my Father's farther Importunities, in a few Weeks after, I resolv'd to run quite away from him. However, I did not act so hastily neither as my first Heat of Resolution prompted, but I took my Mother, at a time when I thought her a little pleasanter than ordinary, and told her, that my Thoughts were so entirely bent upon seeing the World, that I should never settle to any thing with Resolution enough to go through with it, and my Father had better give me his Consent than force me to go without it; that I was now Eighteen Years old, which was too late to go Apprentice to a Trade, or Clerk to an Attorney; that I was sure if I did, I should never serve out my time, and I should certainly run away from my Master before my Time was out, and go to Sea; and if she would speak to my Father to let me go but one Voyage abroad, if I came home again and did not like it, I would go no more, and I would promise by a double Diligence to recover that Time I had lost.

This put my Mother into a great Passion: She told me, she knew it would be to no Purpose to speak to my Father upon any such Subject; that he knew too well what was my Interest to give his Consent to any thing so much for my Hurt, and that she wondered how I could think of any such thing after such a Discourse as I had had with my Father, and such kind and tender Expressions as she knew my Father had us'd to me; and that in short, if I would ruine my self there was no Help for me; but I might depend I should never have their Consent to it: That for her Part she would not have so much Hand in my Destruction; and I should never have it to say, that my Mother was willing when my Father was not.

Tho' my Mother refused to move it to my Father, yet as I have heard afterwards, she reported all the Discourse to him, and that my Father, after shewing a great Concern at it, said to her with a Sigh, That Boy might be happy if he would stay at home, but if he goes abroad he will be the miserablest Wretch that was ever born: I can give no Consent to it.

It was not till almost a Year after this that I broke loose, tho' in the mean time I continued obstinately deaf to all Proposals of settling to Business, and frequently expostulating with my Father and Mother, about their being so positively determin'd against what they knew my Inclinations prompted me to. But being one Day at *Hull*, where I went casually, and without any Purpose of making an Elopement that time; but I say, being there, and one of my Companions being going by Sea to *London*, in his Father's Ship, and prompting me to go with them, with the common Allurement of Seafaring Men, *viz* That it should cost me nothing for my Passage, I consulted neither Father or Mother any more, nor so much as sent them Word of it; but leaving them to hear of it as they might, without asking God's Blessing, or my Father's, without any Consideration of Circumstances or Consequences, and in an ill Hour, God knows. On the first of *September* 1651* I went on Board a Ship bound for *London*; never any young Adventurer's Misfortunes, I believe, began sooner, or continued longer than mine. The Ship was no sooner gotten out of the *Humber*, but the Wind began to blow, and the Waves to rise* in a most frightful manner; and as I had never been at Sea before, I was most inexpressibly sick in Body, and terrify'd in my Mind: I began now seriously to reflect upon what I had done, and how justly I was overtaken by the Judgment of Heaven for my wicked leaving my Father's House, and abandoning my Duty; all the good Counsel of my Parents, my Father's Tears and my Mother's Entreaties came now fresh into my Mind, and my Conscience, which was not yet come to the Pitch of Hardness to which it has been since, reproach'd me with the Contempt of Advice, and the Breach of my Duty to God and my Father.

All this while the Storm encreas'd, and the Sea, which I had never been upon before, went very high, tho' nothing like what I have seen many times since; no, nor like what I saw a few Days after: But it was enough to affect me then, who was but a young Sailor, and had never known any thing of the matter. I expected every Wave would have swallowed us up, and that every time the Ship fell down, as I thought, in the Trough or Hollow of the Sea, we should never rise more; and in this Agony of Mind, I made many Vows and Resolutions,* that if it would please God here to spare my Life this one Voyage, if ever I got once my Foot upon dry Land again, I would go directly home to my Father, and never set it into a Ship again while I liv'd; that I would take his Advice, and never run my self into such Miseries as these any more. Now I saw plainly the Goodness of his Observations about the middle Station of Life, how easy, how comfortably he had liv'd all his Days, and never had been expos'd to Tempests at Sea, or Troubles on Shore; and I resolv'd that I would, like a true repenting Prodigal,* go home to my Father.

These wise and sober Thoughts continued all the while the Storm continued, and indeed some time after; but the next Day the Wind was abated and the Sea calmer, and I began to be a little inur'd to it: However I was very grave for all that Day, being also a little Sea sick still; but towards Night the Weather clear'd up, the Wind was quite over, and a charming fine Evening follow'd; the Sun went down perfectly clear and rose so the next Morning; and having little or no Wind and a smooth Sea, the Sun shining upon it, the Sight was, as I thought, the most delightful that ever I saw.

I had slept well in the Night, and was now no more Sea sick but very chearful, looking with Wonder upon the Sea that was so rough and terrible the Day before, and could be so calm and so pleasant in so little time after. And now least my good Resolutions should continue, my Companion, who had indeed entic'd me away, comes to me, *Well* Bob, says he, clapping me on the Shoulder, *How do you do after it? I warrant you were frighted, wa'n't you, last Night, when it blew but a Cap full of Wind? A Cap full d'you call it?* said I, *'twas a terrible Storm: A Storm, you Fool you*, replies he, *do you call that a Storm, why it was nothing at all; give us but a good Ship and Sea Room, and we think nothing of such a Squal of Wind as that; but you're but a fresh Water Sailor*, Bob; *come let us make a Bowl of Punch and we'll forget all that, d'ye see what charming Weather 'tis now.* To make short this sad Part of my Story, we went the old way of all Sailors, the Punch was made, and I was made drunk with it, and in that one Night's Wickedness I drowned all my Repentance, all my Reflections upon my past Conduct, and all my Resolutions for my future. In a word, as the Sea was returned to its Smoothness of Surface and settled Calmness by the Abatement of that Storm, so the Hurry of my Thoughts being over, my Fears and Apprehensions of being swallow'd up by the Sea being forgotten, and the Current of my former Desires return'd, I entirely forgot the Vows and Promises that I made in my Distress. I found indeed some Intervals of Reflection, and the serious Thoughts did, as it were endeavour to return again sometimes, but I shook them off, and rouz'd my self from them as it were from a Distemper, and applying my self to Drink and Company, soon master'd the Return of those Fits, for so I call'd them, and I had in five or six Days got as compleat a Victory over Conscience as any young Fellow that resolv'd not to be troubled with it, could desire: But I was to have another Trial for it still; and Providence,* as in such Cases generally it does, resolv'd to leave me entirely without Excuse. For if I would not take this for a Deliverance, the next was to be such a one as the worst and most harden'd Wretch among us would confess both the Danger and the Mercy.

The sixth Day of our being at Sea we came into *Yarmouth* Roads; the Wind having been contrary, and the Weather calm, we had made but little Way since the Storm. Here we were obliged to come to an Anchor, and here we lay, the Wind continuing contrary, *viz.* at South-west, for seven or eight Days, during which time a great many Ships from *Newcastle* came into the same Roads, as the common Harbour where the Ships might wait for a Wind for the River.

We had not however rid here so long, but should have Tided it up the River, but that the Wind blew too fresh; and after we had lain four or five Days, blew very hard. However, the Roads being reckoned as good as a Harbour, the Anchorage good, and our Ground-Tackle very strong, our Men were unconcerned, and not in the least apprehensive of Danger, but spent the Time in Rest and Mirth, after the manner of the Sea; but the eighth Day in the Morning, the Wind increased, and we had all Hands at Work to strike our Top-Masts, and make every thing snug and close, that the Ship might ride as easy as possible. By Noon the Sea went very high indeed, and our Ship rid *Forecastle in,* shipp'd several Seas, and we thought once or twice our Anchor had come home; upon which our Master order'd out the Sheet Anchor; so that we rode with two Anchors a-Head, and the Cables vered out to the better End.*

By this Time it blew a terrible Storm indeed, and now I began to see Terror and Amazement in the Faces even of the Seamen themselves. The Master, tho' vigilant to the Business of preserving the Ship, yet as he went in and out of his Cabbin by me, I could hear him softly to himself say several times, *Lord be merciful to us, we shall be all lost, we shall be all undone*; and the like. During these first Hurries, I was stupid, lying still in my Cabbin, which was in the Steerage, and cannot describe my Temper: I could ill reassume the first Penitence, which I had so apparently trampled upon, and harden'd my self against: I thought the Bitterness of Death had been past, and that this would be nothing too like the first. But when the Master himself came by me, as I said just now, and said we should be all lost, I was dreadfully frighted: I got up out of my Cabbin, and look'd out; but such a dismal Sight I never saw: The Sea went Mountains high, and broke upon us every three or four Minutes: When I could look about, I could see nothing but Distress round us: Two Ships that rid near us we found had cut their Masts by the Board,* being deep loaden; and our Men cry'd out, that a Ship which rid about a Mile a-Head of us was foundered. Two more Ships being driven from their Anchors, were run out of the Roads to Sea at all Adventures, and that was not a Mast standing. The light Ships fared the best, as not so much labouring in the Sea; but two or three of them drove, and came close by us, running away with only their Sprit-sail out before the Wind.

Towards Evening the Mate and Boat-Swain begg'd the Master of our Ship to let them cut away the Foremast, which he was very unwilling to: But the Boat-Swain protesting to him, that if he did not, the Ship would founder, he consented; and when they had cut away the Foremast, the Main-Mast stood so loose, and shook the Ship so much, they were obliged to cut her away also, and make a clear Deck.

Any one may judge what a Condition I must be in at all this, who was but a young Sailor, and who had been in such a Fright before at but a little. But if I can express at this Distance the Thoughts I had about me at that time, I was in tenfold more Horror of Mind upon Account of my former Convictions, and the having returned from them to the Resolutions I had wickedly taken at first, than I was at Death it self; and these added to the Terror of the Storm, put me into such a Condition, that I can by no Words describe it. But the worst was not come yet, the Storm continued with such Fury, that the Seamen themselves acknowledged they had never known a worse. We had a good Ship, but she was deep loaden, and wallowed in the Sea, that the Seamen every now and then cried out, she would founder. It was my Advantage in one respect, that I did not know what they meant by Founder, till I enquir'd. However, the Storm was so violent, that I saw what is not often seen, the Master, the Boat-Swain, and some others more sensible than the rest, at their Prayers, and expecting every Moment when the Ship would go to the Bottom. In the Middle of the Night, and under all the rest of our Distresses, one of the Men that had been down on Purpose to see, cried out we had sprung a Leak; another said there was four Foot Water in the Hold. Then all Hands were called to the Pump. At that very Word my Heart, as I thought, died within me, and I fell backwards upon the Side of my Bed where I sat, into the Cabbin. However, the Men roused me, and told me, that I that was able to do nothing before, was as well able to pump as another; at which I stirr'd up, and went to the Pump and work'd very heartily. While this was doing, the Master seeing some light Colliers, who not able to ride out the Storm, were oblig'd to slip* and run away to Sea, and would come near us, ordered to fire a Gun as a Signal of Distress. I who knew nothing what that meant, was so surprised, that I thought the Ship had broke, or some dreadful thing had happen'd. In a word, I was so surprised, that I fell down in a Swoon. As this was a time when every Body had his own Life to think of, no Body minded me, or what was become of me; but another Man stept up the Pump, and thrusting me aside with his Foot, let me lye, thinking I had been dead; and it was a great while before I came to my self.

We work'd on, but the Water encreasing in the Hold, it was apparent that the Ship would founder, and tho' the Storm began to abate a little, yet as it was not possible she could swim till we might run into a Port, so the Master continued firing Guns for Help; and a light Ship who had rid it out just a Head of us ventured a Boat out to help us. It was with the utmost Hazard the Boat came near us, but it was impossible for us to get on Board, or for the Boat to lie near the Ship Side, till at last the Men rowing very heartily, and venturing their Lives to save ours, our Men cast them a Rope over the Stern with a Buoy to it, and then vered it out a great Length, which they after great Labour and Hazard took hold of and we hall'd them close under our Stern and got all into their Boat. It was to no Purpose for them or us after we were in the Boat to think of reaching to their own Ship, so all agreed to let her drive and only to pull her in towards Shore as much as we could, and our Master promised them, That if the Boat was stav'd upon Shore he would make it good to their Master, so partly rowing and partly driving our Boat went away to the Norward sloaping towards the Shore almost as far as *Winterton Ness.**

We were not much more than a quarter of an Hour out of our Ship but we saw her sink, and then I understood for the first time what was meant by a Ship foundering in the Sea; I must acknowledge I had hardly Eyes to look up when the Seamen told me she was sinking; for from that Moment they rather put me into the Boat than that I might be said to go in, my Heart was as it were dead within me, partly with Fright, partly with Horror of Mind and the Thoughts of what was yet before me.

While we were in this Condition, the Men yet labouring at the

Oar to bring the Boat near the Shore, we could see, when our Boat mounting the Waves, we were able to see the Shore, a great many People running along the Shore to assist us when we should come near, but we made but slow way towards the Shore, nor were we able to reach the Shore, till being past the Light-House at *Winterton*, the Shore falls off to the Westward towards *Cromer*, and so the Land broke off a little the Violence of the Wind:* Here we got in, and tho' not without much Difficulty got all safe on Shore and walk'd afterwards on Foot to *Yarmouth*, where, as unfortunate Men, we were used with great Humanity as well by the Magistrates of the Town, who assign'd us good Quarters, as by particular Merchants and Owners of Ships, and had Money given us sufficient to carry us either to *London* or back to *Hull*, as we thought fit.

Had I now had the Sense to have gone back to *Hull*, and have gone home, I had been happy, and my Father, an Emblem of our Blessed Saviour's Parable,* had even kill'd the fatted Calf for me; for hearing the Ship I went away in was cast away in *Yarmouth* Road, it was a great while before he had any Assurance that I was not drown'd.

But my ill Fate push'd me on now with an Obstinacy that nothing could resist; and tho' I had several times loud Calls from my Reason and my more composed Judgment to go home, yet I had no Power to do it. I know not what to call this, nor will I urge, that it is a secret over-ruling Decree that hurries us on to be the Instruments of our own Destruction, even tho' it be before us, and that we rush upon it with our Eyes open. Certainly nothing but some such decreed unavoidable Misery attending, and which it was impossible for me to escape, could have push'd me forward against the calm Reasonings and Perswasions of my most retired Thoughts, and against two such visible Instructions as I had met with in my first Attempt.

My Comrade, who had help'd to harden me before, and who was the Master's Son, was now less forward than I; the first time he spoke to me after we were at *Yarmouth*, which was not till two or three Days, for we were separated in the Town to several Quarters; I say, the first time he saw me, it appear'd his Tone was alter'd, and looking very melancholy and shaking his Head, ask'd me how I did, and telling his Father who I was, and how I had come this Voyage only for a Trial in order to go farther abroad; his Father turning to me with a very grave and concern'd Tone, *Young Man*, says he, *you ought never to go to Sea any more, you ought to take this for a plain and* *visible Token that you are not to be a Seafaring Man.* Why, Sir, said I, will you go to Sea no more? *That is another Case*, said he, *it is my Calling, and therefore my Duty; but as you made this Voyage for a Trial, you see what a Taste Heaven has given you of what you are to expect if you persist; perhaps this is all befallen us on your Account, like* Jonah *in the Ship of* Tarshish.* *Pray*, continues he, *what are you? and on what Account did you go to Sea?* Upon that I told him some of my Story; at the End of which he burst out with a strange kind of Passion, What had I done, says he, that such an unhappy Wretch should come into my Ship? I would not set my Foot in the same Ship with thee again for a Thousand Pounds. This indeed was, as I said, an Excursion of his Spirits which were yet agitated by the Sense of his Loss, and was farther than he could have Authority to go. However he afterwards talk'd very gravely to me, exhorted me to go back to my Father, and not tempt Providence to my Ruine; told me I might see a visible Hand of Heaven against me, *And young Man*, said he, *depend upon it, if you do not go back, where-ever you go, you will meet with nothing but Disasters and Disappointments till your Father's Words are fulfilled upon you.*

We parted soon after; for I made him little Answer, and I saw him no more; which way he went, I know not. As for me, having some Money in my Pocket, I travelled to *London* by Land; and there, as well as on the Road, had many Struggles with my self, what Course of Life I should take, and whether I should go Home, or go to Sea.

As to going Home, Shame opposed the best Motions that offered to my Thoughts; and it immediately occurr'd to me how I should be laugh'd at among the Neighbours, and should be asham'd to see, not my Father and Mother only, but even every Body else; from whence I have since often observed, how incongruous and irrational the common Temper of Mankind is, especially of Youth, to that Reason which ought to guide them in such Cases, *viz.* That they are not asham'd to sin, and yet are asham'd to repent; not asham'd of the Action for which they ought justly to be esteemed Fools, but are asham'd of the returning, which only can make them be esteem'd wise Men.

In this State of Life however I remained some time, uncertain what Measures to take, and what Course of Life to lead. An irresistible Reluctance continu'd to going Home; and as I stay'd a while, the Remembrance of the Distress I had been in wore off; and as that

abated, the little Motion I had in my Desires to a Return wore off
with it, till at last I quite lay'd aside the Thoughts of it, and lookt out
for a Voyage.

That evil Influence which carryed me first away from my Father's
House, that hurried me into the wild and indigested Notion of raising my Fortune; and that imprest those Conceits so forcibly upon
me, as to make me deaf to all good Advice, and to the Entreaties and
even Command of my Father: I say the same Influence, whatever it
was, presented the most unfortunate of all Enterprises to my View;
and I went on board a Vessel bound to the Coast of *Africa*; or, as our
Sailors vulgarly call it, a Voyage to *Guinea*.*

It was my great Misfortune that in all these Adventures I did not
ship my self as a Sailor; whereby, tho' I might indeed have workt a
little harder than ordinary, yet at the same time I had learn'd the
Duty and Office of a Fore-mast Man; and in time might have quallified my self for a Mate or Lieutenant, if not for a Master: But as it
was always my Fate to choose for the worse, so I did here; for having
Money in my Pocket, and good Cloaths upon my Back, I would
always go on board in the Habit of a Gentleman; and so I neither had
any Business in the Ship, or learn'd to do any.

It was my Lot first of all to fall into pretty good Company in
London, which does not always happen to such loose and unguided
young Fellows as I then was; the Devil generally not omitting to lay
some Snare for them very early: But it was not so with me, I first fell
acquainted with the Master of a Ship who had been on the Coast of
Guinea; and who having had very good Success there, was resolved
to go again; and who taking a Fancy to my Conversation, which was
not at all disagreeable at that time, hearing me say I had a mind to see
the World, told me if I wou'd go the Voyage with him I should be at
no Expence; I should be his Mess-mate and his Companion, and if I
could carry any thing with me, I should have all the Advantage of it
that the Trade would admit; and perhaps I might meet with some
Encouragement.

I embrac'd the Offer, and entring into a strict Friendship with this
Captain, who was an honest and plain-dealing Man, I went the Voyage with him, and carried a small Adventure with me, which by the
disinterested Honesty of my Friend the Captain, I increased very
considerably; for I carried about 40 *l*. in such Toys and Trifles as the
Captain directed me to buy. This 40 *l*. I had mustered together by

the Assistance of some of my Relations whom I corresponded with, and who, I believe, got my Father, or at least my Mother, to contribute so much as that to my first Adventure.

This was the only Voyage which I may say was successful in all my Adventures, and which I owe to the Integrity and Honesty of my Friend the Captain, under whom also I got a competent Knowledge of the Mathematicks and the Rules of Navigation,* learn'd how to keep an Account of the Ship's Course, take an Observation;* and in short, to understand some things that were needful to be understood by a Sailor: For, as he took Delight to introduce me, I took Delight to learn; and, in a word, this Voyage made me both a Sailor and a Merchant: for I brought Home *L.* 5. 9 *Ounces** of Gold Dust for my Adventure, which yielded me in *London* at my Return, almost 300 *l.* and this fill'd me with those aspiring Thoughts which have since so compleated my Ruin.

Yet even in this Voyage I had my Misfortunes too; particularly, that I was continually sick, being thrown into a violent Calenture by the excessive Heat of the Climate; our principal Trading being upon the Coast, from the Latitude of 15 Degrees, North even to the Line* it self.

I was now set up for a *Guiney* Trader; and my Friend, to my great Misfortune, dying soon after his Arrival, I resolved to go the same Voyage again, and I embark'd in the same Vessel with one who was his Mate in the former Voyage, and had now got the Command of the Ship. This was the unhappiest Voyage that ever Man made; for tho' I did not carry quite 100 *l.* of my new gain'd Wealth, so that I had 200 left, and which I lodg'd with my Friend's Widow, who was very just to me, yet I fell into terrible Misfortunes in this Voyage; and the first was this, *viz.* Our Ship making her Course towards the *Canary* Islands, or rather between those Islands and the *African* Shore, was surprised in the Grey of the Morning, by a *Turkish* Rover of *Sallee*,* who gave Chase to us with all the Sail she could make. We crowded also as much Canvas as our Yards would spread, or our Masts carry, to have got clear; but finding the Pirate gain'd upon us, and would certainly come up with us in a few Hours, we prepar'd to fight; our Ship having 12 Guns, and the Rogue 18. About three in the Afternoon he came up with us, and bringing to by Mistake, just athwart our Quarter,* instead of athwart our Stern, as he intended, we brought 8 of our Guns to bear on that Side, and pour'd in a

Broadside upon him, which made him sheer off again, after returning our Fire, and pouring in also his small Shot from near 200 Men
which he had on Board. However, we had not a Man touch'd, all our
Men keeping close. He prepar'd to attack us again, and we to defend
our selves; but laying us on Board* the next time upon our other
Quarter, he entred 60 Men upon our Decks, who immediately fell to
cutting and hacking the Decks and Rigging. We ply'd them with
Small-shot, Half-Pikes, Powder-Chests, and such like, and clear'd
our Deck of them twice. However, to cut short this melancholly Part
of our Story, our Ship being disabled, and three of our Men kill'd,
and eight wounded, we were obliged to yield, and were carry'd all
Prisoners into *Sallee*, a Port belonging to the *Moors*.

The Usage I had there was not so dreadful as at first I apprehended, nor was I carried up the Country to the Emperor's Court, as
the rest of our Men were, but was kept by the Captain of the Rover,
as his proper Prize, and made his Slave, being young and nimble, and
fit for his Business. At this surprising Change of my Circumstances
from a Merchant to a miserable Slave, I was perfectly overwhelmed;
and now I look'd back upon my Father's prophetick Discourse to
me, that I should be miserable, and have none to relieve me, which I
thought was now so effectually brought to pass, that it could not be
worse; that now the Hand of Heaven had overtaken me, and I was
undone without Redemption. But alas! this was but a Taste of the
Misery I was to go thro', as will appear in the Sequel of this Story.

As my new Patron or Master had taken me Home to his House, so
I was in hopes that he would take me with him when he went to Sea
again, believing that it would some time or other be his Fate to be
taken by a *Spanish* or *Portugal* Man of War; and that then I should be
set at Liberty. But this Hope of mine was soon taken away; for when
he went to Sea, he left me on Shoar to look after his little Garden,
and do the common Drudgery of Slaves about his House; and when
he came home again from his Cruise, he order'd me to lye in the
Cabbin to look after the Ship.

Here I meditated nothing but my Escape; and what Method I
might take to effect it, but found no Way that had the least Probability in it: Nothing presented to make the Supposition of it
rational; for I had no Body to communicate it to, that would embark
with me; no Fellow-Slave, no *Englishman*, *Irishman*, or *Scotsman*
there but my self; so that for two Years, tho' I often pleased my self

with the Imagination, yet I never had the least encouraging Prospect of putting it in Practice.

After about two Years an odd Circumstance presented it self, which put the old Thought of making some Attempt for my Liberty, again in my Head: My Patron lying at Home longer than usual, without fitting out his Ship, which, as I heard, was for want of Money; he used constantly, once or twice a Week, sometimes oftner, if the Weather was fair, to take the Ship's Pinnace, and go out into the Road a-fishing; and as he always took me and a young *Maresco** with him to row the Boat, we made him very merry, and I prov'd very dexterous in catching Fish; insomuch that sometimes he would send me with a *Moor,* one of his Kinsmen, and the Youth the *Maresco,* as they call'd him, to catch a Dish of Fish for him.

It happen'd one time, that going a fishing in a stark calm Morning, a Fog rose so thick, that tho' we were not half a League from the Shoar we lost Sight of it; and rowing we knew not whither or which way, we labour'd all Day and all the next Night, and when the Morning came we found we had pull'd off to Sea instead of pulling in for the Shoar; and that we were at least two Leagues from the Shoar: However we got well in again, tho' with a great deal of Labour, and some Danger; for the Wind began to blow pretty fresh in the Morning; but particularly we were all very hungry.

But our Patron warn'd by this Disaster, resolved to take more Care of himself for the future; and having lying by him the Long-boat of our *English* Ship we had taken, he resolved he would not go a fishing any more without a Compass and some Provision; so he ordered the Carpenter of his Ship, who also was an *English* Slave, to build a little State-room or Cabin in the middle of the Long Boat, like that of a Barge, with a Place to stand behind it to steer and hale home the Main-sheet,* and Room before for a hand or two to stand and work the Sails; she sail'd with that we call a Shoulder of Mutton Sail; and the Boom gib'd over the Top of the Cabbin, which lay very snug and low, and had in it Room for him to lye, with a Slave or two,* and a Table to eat on, with some small Lockers to put in some Bottles of such Liquor as he thought fit to drink in; particularly his Bread, Rice and Coffee.

We went frequently out with this Boat a fishing, and as I was most dextrous to catch fish for him, he never went without me: It happen'd that he had appointed to go out in this Boat, either for

Pleasure or for Fish, with two or three *Moors* of some Distinction in that Place, and for whom he had provided extraordinarily; and had therefore sent on board the Boat over Night, a larger Store of Provisions than ordinary; and had order'd me to get ready three Fuzees with Powder and Shot, which were on board his Ship; for that* they design'd some Sport of Fowling as well as Fishing.

I got all things ready as he had directed, and waited the next Morning with the Boat, washed clean, her Antient and Pendants out, and every thing to accomodate his Guests; when by and by my Patroon came on board alone, and told me his Guests had put off going, upon some Business that fell out, and order'd me with the Man and Boy, as usual, to go out with the Boat and catch them some Fish, for that his Friends were to sup at his House; and commanded that as soon as I had got some Fish I should bring it home to his House; all which I prepar'd to do.

This Moment my former Notions of Deliverance darted into my Thoughts, for now I found I was like to have a little Ship at my Command; and my Master being gone, I prepar'd to furnish my self, not for a fishing Business but for a Voyage; tho' I knew not, neither did I so much as consider whither I should steer; for any where to get out of that Place was my Way.

My first Contrivance was to make a Pretence to speak to this *Moor,* to get something for our Subsistance on board; for I told him we must not presume to eat of our Patroon's Bread, he said that was true; so he brought a large Basket of Rusk or Bisket of their kind, and three Jarrs with fresh Water into the Boat; I knew where my Patroon's Case of Bottles stood, which it was evident by the make were taken out of some *English* Prize; and I convey'd them into the Boat while the *Moor* was on Shoar, as if they had been there before, for our Master: I convey'd also a great Lump of Bees-Wax into the Boat, which weighed above half a Hundred Weight, with a Parcel of Twine or Thread, a Hatchet, a Saw and a Hammer, all which were of great Use to us afterwards; especially the Wax to make Candles. Another Trick I try'd upon him, which he innocently came into also; his Name was *Ismael*, who they call *Muly* or *Moely*, so I call'd to him, *Moely* said I, our Patroon's Guns are on board the Boat, can you not get a little Powder and Shot, it may be we may kill some *Alcamies* (a Fowl like our *Curlieus*) for our selves, for I know he keeps the Gunner's Stores in the Ship? Yes, *says he*, I'll bring some, and accordingly he brought a great Leather Pouch which held about a Pound and half of Powder, or rather more; and another with Shot, that had five or six Pound, with some Bullets; and put all into the Boat: At the same time I had found some Powder of my Master's in the Great Cabbin, with which I fill'd one of the large Bottles in the Case, which was almost empty; pouring what was in it into another: and thus furnished with every thing needful, we sail'd out of the Port to fish: The Castle which is at the Entrance of the Port knew who we were, and took no Notice of us; and we were not above a Mile out of the Port before we hal'd in our Sail, and set us down to fish: The Wind blew from the N.NE. which was contrary to my Desire; for had it blown southerly I had been sure to have made the Coast of *Spain*, and at least reacht to the Bay of *Cadiz*; but my Resolutions were, blow which way it would, I would be gone from that horrid Place where I was, and leave the rest to Fate.

After we had fisht some time and catcht nothing, for when I had Fish on my Hook, I would not pull them up, that he might not see them; I said to the *Moor*, this will not do, our Master will not be thus serv'd, we must stand farther off: He thinking no harm agreed, and being in the head of the Boat set the Sails; and as I had the Helm I run the Boat out near a League farther, and then brought her too as if I would fish; when giving the Boy the Helm, I stept forward to where the *Moor* was, and making as if I stoopt for something behind him, I took him by Surprize with my Arm under his Twist, and tost him clear over-board into the Sea; he rise* immediately, for he swam like a Cork, and call'd to me, begg'd to be taken in, told me he would go all over the World with me; he swam so strong after the Boat that he would have reacht me very quickly, there being but little Wind; upon which I stept into the Cabbin and fetching one of the Fowling-pieces, I presented it at him, and told him, I had done him no hurt, and if he would be quiet I would do him none; but said I, you swim well enough to reach to the Shoar, and the Sea is calm, make the best of your Way to Shoar and I will do you no harm, but if you come near the Boat I'll shoot you thro' the Head; for I am resolved to have my Liberty; so he turn'd himself about and swam for the Shoar, and I make no doubt but he reacht it with Ease, for he was an Excellent Swimmer.

I could ha' been content to ha' taken this *Moor* with me, and ha' drown'd the Boy, but there was no venturing to trust him: When he was gone I turn'd to the Boy, who they call'd *Xury*, and said to him, *Xury*, if you will be faithful to me I'll make you a great Man, but if you will not stroak your Face to be true to me, *that is*, *swear by* Mahomet *and his Father's Beard*, I must throw you into the Sea too; the Boy smil'd in my Face and spoke so innocently that I could not mistrust him; and swore to be faithful to me, and go all over the World with me.

While I was in View of the *Moor* that was swimming, I stood out directly to Sea with the Boat, rather stretching to Windward, that they might think me gone towards the *Straits*-mouth* (as indeed any one that had been in their Wits must ha' been supposed to do) for who would ha' suppos'd we were saild on to the southward to the truly *Barbarian* Coast,* where whole Nations of Negroes were sure to surround us with their Canoes, and destroy us; where we could ne'er once go on shoar but we should be devour'd by savage Beasts, or more merciless Savages of humane kind.*

But as soon as it grew dusk in the Evening, I chang'd my Course, and steer'd directly South and by East, bending my Course a little toward the East, that I might keep in with the Shoar; and having a fair fresh Gale of Wind, and a smooth quiet Sea, I made such Sail that I believe by the next Day at Three a Clock in the Afternoon, when I first made the Land, I could not be less than 150 Miles South of *Sallee*; quite beyond the Emperor of *Morocco's* Dominions, or indeed of any other King thereabouts, for we saw no People.

Yet such was the Fright I had taken at the *Moors*, and the dreadful Apprehensions I had of falling into their Hands, that I would not stop, or go on Shoar, or come to an Anchor; the Wind continuing fair, 'till I had sail'd in that manner five Days: And then the Wind shifting to the southward, I concluded also that if any of our Vessels were in Chase of me, they also would now give over; so I ventur'd to make to the Coast, and came to an Anchor in the Mouth of a little River, I knew not what, or where; neither what Latitude, what Country, what Nations, or what River: I neither saw, or desir'd to see any People, the principal thing I wanted was fresh Water: We came into this Creek in the Evening, resolving to swim on shoar as soon as it was dark, and discover the Country; but as soon as it was quite dark, we heard such dreadful Noises of the Barking, Roaring, and Howling of Wild Creatures, of we knew not what Kinds, that the poor Boy was ready to die with Fear, and beg'd of me not to go on shoar till

Day; well *Xury* said I, then I won't, but it may be we may see Men by Day, who will be as bad to us as those Lyons; *then we give them the shoot Gun* says *Xury* laughing, *make them run wey*; such *English Xury* spoke by conversing among us Slaves; however I was glad to see the Boy so cheerful, and I gave him a Dram (out of our Patroon's Case of Bottles) to chear him up: After all, *Xury's* Advice was good, and I took it, we dropt our little Anchor and lay still all Night; I say still, for we slept none! for in two or three Hours we saw vast great Creatures (we knew not what to call them) of many sorts, come down to the Sea-shoar and run into the Water, wallowing and washing themselves for the Pleasure of cooling themselves; and they made such hideous Howlings and Yellings, that I never indeed heard the like.

Xury was dreadfully frighted, and indeed so was I too; but we were both more frighted when we heard one of these mighty Crea-tures come swimming towards our Boat, we could not see him, but we might hear him by his blowing to be a monstrous, huge and furious Beast; *Xury* said it was a Lyon, and it might be so for ought I know; but poor *Xury* cryed to me to weigh the Anchor and row away; no says I, *Xury*, we can slip our Cable with the Buoy to it and go off to Sea, they cannot follow us far; I had no sooner said so, but I perceiv'd the Creature (whatever it was) within Two Oars Length, which something surprized me; however I immediately stept to the Cabbin-door, and taking up my Gun fir'd at him, upon which he immediately turn'd about and swam towards the Shoar again.

But it is impossible to describe the horrible Noises, and hideous Cryes and Howlings, that were raised as well upon the Edge of the Shoar, as higher within the Country; upon the Noise or Report of the Gun, a Thing I have some Reason to believe those Creatures had never heard before: This Convinc'd me that there was no going on Shoar for us in the Night upon that Coast, and how to venture on Shoar in the Day was another Question too; for to have fallen into the Hands of any of the Savages, had been as bad as to have fallen into the Hands of Lyons and Tygers; at least we were equally appre-hensive of the Danger of it.

Be that as it would, we were oblig'd to go on Shoar somewhere or other for Water, for we had not a Pint left in the Boat; when or where to get to it was the Point: *Xury* said, if I would let him go on Shoar with one of the Jarrs, he would find if there was any Water and bring some to me. I ask'd him why he would go? Why I should not go and he stay in the Boat? The Boy answer'd with so much Affection that made me love him ever after. Says he, *If wild Mans come, they eat me, you go wey*. Well, *Xury*, said I, we will both go, and if the wild Mans come we will kill them, they shall Eat neither of us; so I gave *Xury* a piece of Rusk-bread to Eat and a Dram out of our Patroon's Case of Bottles which I mentioned before; and we hal'd the Boat in as near the Shoar as we thought was proper, and so waded on Shoar, carrying nothing but our Arms and two Jarrs for Water.

I did not care to go out of Sight of the Boat, fearing the coming of Canoes with *Savages* down the River; but the Boy seeing a low Place about a Mile up the Country rambled to it; and by and by I saw him come running towards me, I thought he was pursued by some Savage, or frighted with some wild Beast, and I run forward towards him to help him, but when I came nearer to him, I saw something hanging over his Shoulders which was a Creature that he had shot, like a Hare but different in Colour, and longer Legs, however we were very glad of it, and it was very good Meat; but the great Joy that poor *Xury* came with, was to tell me he had found good Water and seen no wild Mans.

But we found afterwards that we need not take such Pains for Water, for a little higher up the Creek where we were, we found the Water fresh when the Tide was out, which flowed but a little way up; so we filled our Jarrs and feasted on the Hare we had killed, and prepared to go on our Way, having seen no Foot-steps of any humane Creature in that part of the Country.

As I had been one Voyage to this Coast before, I knew very well that the Islands of the *Canaries*, and the *Cape de Verd* Islands also, lay not far off from the Coast. But as I had no Instruments to take an Observation to know what Latitude we were in, and did not exactly know, or at least remember what Latitude they were in; I knew not where to look for them, or when to stand off to Sea towards them; otherwise I might now easily have found some of these Islands. But my hope was, that if I stood along this Coast till I came to that Part where the *English* Traded, I should find some of their Vessels upon their usual Design of Trade, that would relieve and take us in.

By the best of my Calculation, that Place where I now was, must be that Country, which lying between the Emperor of *Morocco's* Dominions and the *Negro's*, lies wast and uninhabited, except by wild Beasts; the *Negroes* having abandon'd it and gone farther South for fear of the *Moors*; and the *Moors* not thinking it worth inhabiting, by reason of its Barrenness; and indeed both forsaking it because of the prodigious Numbers of Tygers, Lyons, Leopards and other furious Creatures which harbour there; so that the *Moors* use it for their Hunting only, where they go like an Army, two or three thousand Men at a time; and indeed for near an hundred Miles together upon this Coast, we saw nothing but a wast uninhabited Country, by Day; and heard nothing but Howlings and Roaring of wild Beasts, by Night.

Once or twice in the Day time, I thought I saw the *Pico* of *Teneriffe*,* being the high top of the Mountain *Teneriffe* in the *Canaries;* and had a great mind to venture out in hopes of reaching thither; but having tried twice I was forced in again by contrary Winds, the Sea also going too high for my little Vessel, so I resolved to pursue my first Design and keep along the Shoar.

Several times I was obliged to land for fresh Water, after we had left this Place; and once in particular, being early in the Morning, we came to an Anchor under a little Point of Land which was pretty high, and the Tide beginning to flow, we lay still to go farther in; *Xury*, whose Eyes were more about him than it seems mine were, calls softly to me, and tells me that we had best go farther off the Shoar; for, says he, look yonder lies a dreadful Monster on the side of that Hillock fast asleep: I look'd where he pointed, and saw a dreadful Monster indeed, for it was a terrible great Lyon that lay on the Side of the Shoar, under the Shade of a Piece of the Hill that hung as it were a little over him. *Xury*, says I, you shall go on Shoar and kill him; *Xury* look'd frighted, and said, *Me kill! he eat me at one Mouth*; one Mouthful he meant; however, I said no more to the Boy, but bad him lye still, and I took our biggest Gun, which was almost Musquet-bore,* and loaded it with a good Charge of Powder, and with two Slugs, and laid it down; then I loaded another Gun with two Bullets, and the third, for we had three Pieces, I loaded with five smaller Bullets. I took the best aim I could with the first Piece to have shot him into the Head, but he lay so with his Leg rais'd a little above his Nose, that the Slugs hit his Leg about the Knee, and broke the Bone. He started up growling at first, but finding his Leg broke fell down again, and then got up upon three Legs and gave the most hideous Roar that ever I heard; I was a little suppriz'd that I had not

hit him on the Head; however I took up the second Piece immediately, and tho' he began to move off fir'd again, and shot him into the
Head, and had the Pleasure to see him drop, and make but little
Noise, but lay struggling for Life. Then *Xury* took Heart, and would
have me let him go on Shoar: Well, go said I, so the Boy jump'd into
the Water, and taking a little Gun in one Hand swam to Shoar with
the other Hand, and coming close to the Creature, put the Muzzle
of the Piece to his Ear, and shot him into the Head again which
dispatch'd him quite.*

This was Game indeed to us, but this was no Food, and I was very
sorry to lose three Charges of Powder and Shot upon a Creature that
was good for nothing to us. However *Xury* said he would have some
of him; so he comes on board, and ask'd me to give him the Hatchet;
for what, *Xury*, said I? *Me cut off his Head*, said he. However *Xury*
could not cut off his Head, but he cut off a Foot and brought it with
him, and it was a monstrous great one.

I bethought my self however, that perhaps the Skin of him might
one way or other be of some Value to us; and I resolved to take off his
Skin if I could. So *Xury* and I went to work with him; but *Xury* was
much the better Workman at it, for I knew very ill how to do it.
Indeed it took us up both the whole Day, but at last we got off the
Hide of him, and spreading it on the top of our Cabbin, the Sun
effectually dried it in two Days time, and it afterwards serv'd me to
lye upon.

After this Stop we made on to the Southward continually for ten
or twelve Days, living very sparing on our Provisions, which began
to abate very much, and going no oftner into the Shoar than we were
oblig'd to for fresh Water; my Design in this was to make the River
Gambia or *Sennegall*, that is to say, any where about the *Cape de Verd*,
where I was in hopes to meet with some *European* Ship, and if I did
not, I knew not what Course I had to take, but to seek out for the
Islands, or perish there among the *Negroes*. I knew that all the Ships
from *Europe*, which sail'd either to the Coast of *Guiney*, or to *Brasil*,
or to the *East-Indies*, made this *Cape* or those *Islands*; and in a word, I
put the whole of my Fortune upon this single Point, either that I
must meet with some Ship, or must perish.

When I had pursued this Resolution about ten Days longer, as I
have said, I began to see that the Land was inhabited, and in two or
three Places as we sailed by, we saw People stand upon the Shoar to

look at us, we could also perceive they were quite Black and Stark-naked. I was once inclin'd to ha' gone on Shoar to them; but *Xury* was my better Councellor, and said to me, *no go*, *no go*; however I hal'd in nearer the Shoar that I might talk to them, and I found they run along the Shoar by me a good way; I observ'd they had no Weapons in their Hands, except one who had a long slender Stick, which *Xury* said was a Lance, and that they would throw them a great way with good aim; so I kept at a distance, but talk'd with them by Signs as well as I could; and particularly made Signs for some thing to Eat, they beckon'd to me to stop my Boat, and that they would fetch me some Meat; upon this I lower'd the top of my Sail, and lay by,* and two of them run up into the Country, and in less than half an Hour came back and brought with them two Pieces of dry Flesh and some Corn, such as is the Produce of their Country, but we neither knew what the one or the other was; however we were willing to accept it, but how to come at it was our next Dispute, for I was not for venturing on Shore to them, and they were as much affraid of us; but they took a safe way for us all, for they brought it to the Shore and laid it down, and went and stood a great way off till we fetch'd it on Board, and then came close to us again.

We made Signs of Thanks to them, for we had nothing to make them amends; but an Opportunity offer'd that very Instant to oblige them wonderfully, for while we were lying by the Shore, came two mighty Creatures one pursuing the other, (as we took it) with great Fury, from the Mountains towards the Sea; whether it was the Male pursuing the Female, or whether they were in Sport or in Rage, we could not tell, any more than we could tell whether it was usual or strange, but I believe it was the latter; because in the first Place, those ravenous Creatures seldom appear but in the Night; and in the second Place, we found the People terribly frighted, especially the Women. The Man that had the Lance or Dart did not fly from them, but the rest did; however as the two Creatures ran directly into the Water, they did not seem to offer to fall upon any of the *Negroes*, but plung'd themselves into the Sea and swam about as if they had come for their Diversion; at last one of them began to come nearer our Boat than at first I expected, but I lay ready for him, for I had loaded my Gun with all possible Expedition, and bad *Xury* load both the other;* as soon as he came fairly within my reach, I fir'd, and shot him directly into the Head; immediately he sunk down into the Water, but rose instantly and plung'd up and down as if he was struggling for Life; and so indeed he was, he immediately made to the Shore, but between the Wound which was his mortal Hurt, and the strangling of the Water, he dyed just before he reach'd the Shore.

It is impossible to express the Astonishment of these poor Creatures at the Noise and the Fire of my Gun; some of them were even ready to dye for Fear, and fell down as Dead with the very Terror. But when they saw the Creature dead and sunk in the Water, and that I made Signs to them to come to the Shore; they took Heart and came to the Shore and began to search for the Creature, I found him by his Blood staining the Water, and by the help of a Rope which I flung round him and gave the *Negroes* to hawl, they drag'd him on Shore, and found that it was a most curious Leopard, spotted and fine to an admirable Degree, and the *Negroes* held up their Hands with Admiration to think what it was I had kill'd him with.

The other Creature frighted with the flash of Fire and the Noise of the Gun swam on Shore, and ran up directly to the Mountains from whence they came, nor could I at that Distance know what it was. I found quickly the *Negroes* were for eating the Flesh of this Creature, so I was willing to have them take it as a Favour from me, which when I made Signs to them that they might take him, they were very thankful for, immediately they fell to work with him, and tho' they had no Knife, yet with a sharpen'd Piece of Wood they took off his Skin as readily, and much more readily than we cou'd have done with a Knife; they offer'd me some of the Flesh, which I declined, making as if I would give it them, but made Signs for the Skin, which they gave me very freely, and brought me a great deal more of their Provision, which tho' I did not understand, yet I accepted; then I made Signs to them for some Water, and held out one of my Jarrs to them, turning it bottom upward, to shew that it was empty, and that I wanted to have it filled. They call'd immediately to some of their Friends, and there came two Women and brought a great Vessel made of Earth, and burnt as I suppose in the Sun; this they set down for me, as before, and I sent *Xury* on Shore with my Jarrs, and filled them all three: The Women were as stark Naked as the Men.

I was now furnished with Roots and Corn, such as it was, and Water, and leaving my friendly *Negroes*, I made forward for about eleven Days more without offering to go near the Shoar, till I saw the

Land run out a great Length into the Sea, at about the Distance of four or five Leagues before me, and the Sea being very calm I kept a large offing* to make this Point; at length, doubling the Point at about two Leagues from the Land, I saw plainly Land on the other Side to Seaward; then I concluded, as it was most certain indeed, that this was the *Cape de Verd*, and those the *Islands*, call'd from thence *Cape de Verd Islands*.* However they were at a great Distance, and I could not well tell what I had best to do, for if I should be taken with a Fresh of Wind I might neither reach one or other.

In this Dilemma, as I was very pensive, I stept into the Cabbin and sat me down, *Xury* having the Helm, when on a suddain the Boy cry'd out, *Master, Master, a Ship with a Sail*, and the foolish Boy was frighted out of his Wits, thinking it must needs be some of his Master's Ships sent to pursue us, when, I knew we were gotten far enough out of their reach. I jump'd out of the Cabbin, and immediately saw not only the Ship, but what she was, (*viz.*) that it was a *Portuguese* Ship, and as I thought was bound to the Coast of *Guinea* for *Negroes*. But when I observ'd the Course she steer'd, I was soon convinc'd they were bound some other way, and did not design to come any nearer to the Shoar; upon which I stretch'd out to Sea as much as I could, resolving to speak with them if possible.

With all the Sail I could make, I found I should not be able to come in their Way, but that they would be gone by, before I could make any Signal to them; but after I had crowded to the utmost,* and began to despair, they it seems saw me by the help of their Perspective-Glasses, and that it was some *European* Boat, which as they supposed must belong to some Ship that was lost, so they shortned Sail* to let me come up. I was encouraged with this, and as I had my Patroon's Antient on Board, I made a Waft of it* to them for a Signal of Distress, and fir'd a Gun, both which they saw, for they told me they saw the Smoke, tho' they did not hear the Gun; upon these Signals they very kindly brought too, and lay by for me, and in about three Hours time I came up with them.

They ask'd me what I was, in *Portuguese*, and in *Spanish*, and in *French*, but I understood none of them; but at last a *Scots* Sailor who was on board, call'd to me, and I answer'd him, and told him I was an *Englishman*, that I had made my escape out of Slavery from the *Moors* at *Sallee*; then they bad me come on board, and very kindly took me in, and all my Goods.

It was an inexpressible Joy to me, that any one will believe, that I was thus deliver'd, as I esteem'd it, from such a miserable and almost hopeless Condition as I was in, and I immediately offered all I had to the Captain of the Ship, as a Return for my Deliverance; but he generously told me, he would take nothing from me, but that all I had should be deliver'd safe to me when I came to the *Brasils*, for says he, *I have sav'd your Life on no other Terms than I would be glad to be saved my self, and it may one time or other be my Lot to be taken up in the same Condition; besides*, said he, *when I carry you to the* Brasils, *so great a way from your own Country, if I should take from you what you have, you will be starved there, and then I only take away that Life I have given. No, no, Seignor* Inglese, says he, *Mr.* Englishman, *I will carry you thither in Charity, and those things will help you to buy your Subsistance there and your Passage home again.*

As he was Charitable in his Proposal, so he was Just in the Performance to a tittle, for he ordered the Seamen that none should offer to touch any thing I had; then he took every thing into his own Possession, and gave me back an exact Inventory of them, that I might have them, even so much as my three Earthen Jarrs.

As to my Boat it was a very good one, and that he saw, and told me he would buy it of me for the Ship's use, and ask'd me what I would have for it?* I told him he had been so generous to me in every thing, that I could not offer to make any Price of the Boat, but left it entirely to him, upon which he told me he would give me a Note of his Hand to pay me 80 Pieces of Eight* for it at *Brasil*, and when it came there, if any one offer'd to give more he would make it up; he offer'd me also 60 Pieces of Eight more for my Boy *Xury*, which I was loath to take, not that I was not willing to let the Captain have him, but I was very loath to sell the poor Boy's Liberty,* who had assisted me so faithfully in procuring my own. However when I let him know my Reason, he own'd it to be just, and offer'd me this Medium, that he would give the Boy an Obligation to set him free in ten Years, if he turn'd Christian; upon this, and *Xury* saying he was willing to go to him, I let the Captain have him.

We had a very good Voyage to the *Brasils*, and arriv'd in the *Bay de Todos los Santos*, or *All-Saints Bay*,* in about Twenty-two Days after. And now I was once more deliver'd from the most miserable of all Conditions of Life, and what to do next with my self I was now to consider.

The generous Treatment the Captain gave me, I can never enough remember; he would take nothing of me for my Passage, gave me twenty Ducats for the Leopard's Skin, and forty for the Lyon's Skin which I had in my Boat, and caused every thing I had in the Ship to be punctually deliver'd me, and what I was willing to sell he bought, such as the Case of Bottles, two of my Guns, and a Piece of the Lump of Bees-wax, for I had made Candles of the rest; in a word, I made about 220 Pieces of Eight of all my Cargo, and with this Stock I went on Shoar in the *Brasils*.

I had not been long here, but being recommended to the House of a good honest Man like himself, who had an *Ingenio* as they call it; that is, a Plantation and a Sugar-House. I lived with him some time, and acquainted my self by that means with the Manner of their planting and making of Sugar; and seeing how well the Planters liv'd, and how they grew rich suddenly, I resolv'd, if I could get Licence to settle there, I would turn Planter among them, resolving in the mean time to find out some Way to get my Money which I had left in *London* remitted to me. To this Purpose getting a kind of a Letter of Naturalization, I purchased as much Land that was Uncur'd, as my Money would reach, and form'd a Plan for my Plantation and Settlement, and such a one as might be suitable to the Stock which I proposed to my self to receive from *England*.

I had a Neighbour, a *Portugueze* of *Lisbon*, but born of *English* Parents, whose Name was *Wells*, and in much such Circumstances as I was. I call him my Neighbour, because his Plantation lay next to mine, and we went on very sociably together. My Stock was but low as well as his; and we rather planted for Food than any thing else, for about two Years. However, we began to increase, and our Land began to come into Order; so that the third Year we planted some Tobacco, and made each of us a large Piece of Ground ready for planting Canes in the Year to come; but we both wanted Help, and now I found more than before, I had done wrong in parting with my Boy *Xury*.

But alas! for me to do wrong that never did right, was no great Wonder: I had no Remedy but to go on; I was gotten into an Employment quite remote to my Genius, and directly contrary to the Life I delighted in, and for which I forsook my Father's House, and broke thro' all his good Advice; nay, I was coming into the very Middle Station, or upper Degree of low Life, which my Father advised me to before; and which if I resolved to go on with, I might as well ha' staid at Home, and never have fatigu'd my self in the World as I had done; and I used often to say to my self, I could ha' done this as well in *England* among my Friends, as ha' gone 5000 Miles off to do it among Strangers and Salvages in a Wilderness, and at such a Distance, as never to hear from any Part of the World that had the least Knowledge of me.

In this manner I used to look upon my Condition with the utmost Regret. I had no body to converse with but now and then this Neighbour; no Work to be done, but by the Labour of my Hands; and I used to say, I liv'd just like a Man cast away upon some desolate Island, that had no body there but himself. But how just has it been, and how should all Men reflect, that when they compare their present Conditions with others that are worse, Heaven may oblige them to make the Exchange, and be convinc'd of their former Felicity by their Experience: I say, how just has it been, that the truly solitary Life I reflected on in an Island of meer Desolation should be my Lot, who had so often unjustly compar'd it with the Life which I then led, in which had I continued, I had in all Probability been exceeding prosperous and rich.

I was in some Degree settled in my Measures for carrying on the Plantation, before my kind Friend the Captain of the Ship that took me up at Sea, went back; for the Ship remained there in providing his Loading, and preparing for his Voyage, near three Months, when telling him what little Stock I had left behind me in *London*, he gave me this friendly and sincere Advice, *Seignior Inglese says he*, for so he always called me, if you will give me Letters, and a Procuration here in Form to me, with Orders to the Person who has your Money in *London*, to send your Effects to *Lisbon*, to such Persons as I shall direct, and in such Goods as are proper for this Country, I will bring you the Produce of them, God willing, at my Return; but since human Affairs are all subject to Changes and Disasters, I would have you give Orders but for One Hundred Pounds *Sterl.** which you say is Half your Stock, and let the Hazard be run for the first; so that if it come safe, you may order the rest the same Way; and if it miscarry, you may have the other Half to have Recourse to for your Supply.

This was so wholesom Advice, and look'd so friendly, that I could not but be convinc'd it was the best Course I could take; so I accordingly prepared Letters to the Gentlewoman with whom I had left my Money, and a Procuration to the *Portuguese* Captain, as he desired.

I wrote the *English* Captain's Widow a full Account of all my Adventures, my Slavery, Escape, and how I had met with the *Portugal* Captain at Sea, the Humanity of his Behaviour, and in what Condition I was now in, with all other necessary Directions for my Supply; and when this honest Captain came to *Lisbon*, he found means by some of the *English* Merchants there, to send over not the Order only, but a full Account of my Story to a Merchant at *London*, who represented it effectually to her; whereupon, she not only delivered the Money, but out of her own Pocket sent the *Portugal* Captain a very handsom Present for his Humanity and Charity to me.

The Merchant in *London* vesting this Hundred Pounds in *English* Goods, such as the Captain had writ for, sent them directly to him at *Lisbon*, and he brought them all safe to me to the *Brasils*, among which, without my Direction (for I was too young in my Business to think of them) he had taken Care to have all Sorts of Tools, Iron-Work, and Utensils necessary for my Plantation, and which were of great Use to me.

When this Cargo arrived, I thought my Fortunes made, for I was surprised with the Joy of it; and my good Steward the Captain had laid out the Five Pounds which my Friend had sent him for a Present for himself, to purchase, and bring me over a Servant under Bond for six Years Service, and would not accept of any Consideration, except a little Tobacco, which I would have him accept, being of my own Produce.

Neither was this all; but my Goods being all *English* Manufactures, such as Cloath, Stuffs, Bays, and things particularly valuable and desirable in the Country, I found means to sell them to a very great Advantage; so that I might say, I had more than four times the Value of my first Cargo, and was now infinitely beyond my poor Neighbour, I mean in the Advancement of my Plantation; for the first thing I did, I bought me a Negro Slave, and an *European* Servant also; I mean another besides that which the Captain brought me from *Lisbon*.

But as abus'd Prosperity is oftentimes made the very Means of our greatest Adversity, so was it with me. I went on the next Year with great Success in my Plantation: I raised fifty great Rolls of Tobacco on my own Ground, more than I had disposed of for Necessaries

among my Neighbours; and these fifty Rolls being each of above a
100 *Wt*.* were well cur'd and laid by against the Return of the Fleet
from *Lisbon*: and now increasing in Business and in Wealth, my Head
began to be full of Projects and Undertakings beyond my Reach;
such as are indeed often the Ruine of the best Heads in Business.

Had I continued in the Station I was now in, I had room for all the
happy things to have yet befallen me, for which my Father so earnestly recommended a quiet retired Life, and of which he had so
sensibly describ'd the middle Station of Life to be full of; but other
things attended me, and I was still to be the wilful Agent of all my
own Miseries; and particularly to encrease my Fault and double the
Reflections upon my self, which in my future Sorrows I should have
leisure to make; all these Miscarriages were procured by my apparent obstinate adhering to my foolish inclination of wandring abroad
and pursuing that Inclination, in contradiction to the clearest Views
of doing my self good in a fair and plain pursuit of those Prospects
and those measures of Life, which Nature and Providence concurred
to present me with, and to make my Duty.

As I had once done thus in my breaking away from my Parents, so
I could not be content now, but I must go and leave the happy View I
had of being a rich and thriving Man in my new Plantation, only to
pursue a rash and immoderate Desire of rising faster than the
Nature of the Thing admitted; and thus I cast my self down again
into the deepest Gulph of human Misery that ever Man fell into, or
perhaps could be consistent with Life and a State of Health in the
World.

To come then by the just Degrees, to the Particulars of this Part of
my Story; you may suppose, that having now lived almost four Years
in the *Brasils*, and beginning to thrive and prosper very well upon
my Plantation; I had not only learn'd the Language, but had contracted Acquaintance and Friendship among my Fellow-Planters, as
well as among the Merchants at St. *Salvadore*,* which was our Port;
and that in my Discourses among them, I had frequently given them
an Account of my two Voyages to the Coast of *Guinea*, the manner of
Trading with the *Negroes* there, and how easy it was to purchase
upon the Coast, for Trifles, such as Beads, Toys, Knives, Scissars,
Hatchets, bits of Glass, and the like; not only Gold Dust, *Guinea*
Grains,* Elephants Teeth, &*c*. but *Negroes* for the Service of the
Brasils, in great Numbers.

They listened always very attentively to my Discourses on these Heads, but especially to that Part which related to the buying *Negroes*, which was a Trade at that time not only not far entred into, but as far as it was, had been carried on by the Assiento's,* or Permission of the Kings of *Spain* and *Portugal*, and engross'd in the Publick, so that few *Negroes* were brought, and those excessive dear.*

It happen'd, being in Company with some Merchants and Planters of my Acquaintance, and talking of those things very earnestly, three of them came to me the next Morning, and told me they had been musing very much upon what I had discoursed with them of, the last Night, and they came to make a secret Proposal to me; and after enjoining me Secrecy, they told me, that they had a mind to fit out a Ship to go to *Guinea*, that they had all Plantations as well as I, and were straiten'd for nothing so much as Servants; that as it was a Trade that could not be carried on, because they could not publickly sell the *Negroes* when they came home, so they desired to make but one Voyage, to bring the *Negroes* on Shoar privately, and divide them among their own Plantations; and in a Word, the Question was, whether I would go their Super-Cargo in the Ship to manage the Trading Part upon the Coast of *Guinea*? And they offer'd me that I should have my equal Share of the *Negroes* without providing any Part of the Stock.

This was a fair Proposal it must be confess'd, had it been made to any one that had not had a Settlement and Plantation of his own to look after, which was in a fair way of coming to be very Considerable, and with a good Stock upon it. But for me that was thus entered and established, and had nothing to do but go on as I had begun for three or four Years more, and to have sent for the other hundred Pound from *England*, and who in that time, and with that little Addition, could scarce ha' fail'd of being worth three or four thousand Pounds Sterling, and that encreasing too; for me to think of such a Voyage, was the most preposterous Thing that ever Man in such Circumstances could be guilty of.

But I that was born to be my own Destroyer, could no more resist the Offer than I could restrain my first rambling Designs, when my Father's good Counsel was lost upon me. In a word, I told them I would go with all my Heart, if they would undertake to look after my Plantation in my Absence, and would dispose of it to such as I should direct if I miscarry'd. This they all engag'd to do, and entred into Writings or Covenants to do so; and I made a formal Will, disposing of my Plantation and Effects, in Case of my Death, making the Captain of the Ship that had sav'd my Life as before, my universal Heir, but obliging him to dispose of my Effects as I had directed in my Will, one half of the Produce being to himself, and the other to be ship'd to *England*.

In short, I took all possible Caution to preserve my Effects, and keep up my Plantation; had I used half as much Prudence to have look'd into my own Intrest, and have made a Judgment of what I ought to have done, and not to have done, I had certainly never gone away from so prosperous an Undertaking, leaving all the probable Views of a thriving Circumstance, and gone upon a Voyage to Sea, attended with all its common Hazards; to say nothing of the Reasons I had to expect particular Misfortunes to my self.

But I was hurried on, and obey'd blindly the Dictates of my Fancy rather than my Reason; and accordingly the Ship being fitted out, and the Cargo furnished, and all things done as by Agreement, by my Partners in the Voyage, I went on Board in an evil Hour, the 1st of *Sept.* 1659,* being the same Day eight Year that I went from my Father and Mother at *Hull*, in order to act the Rebel to their Authority, and the Fool to my own Interest.

Our Ship was about 120 Tun Burthen,* carried 6 Guns, and 14 Men, besides the Master, his Boy, and my self; we had on board no large Cargo of Goods, except of such Toys as were fit for our Trade with the *Negroes*, such as Beads, bits of Glass, Shells, and odd Trifles, especially little Looking-Glasses, Knives, Scissars, Hatchets, and the like.

The same Day I went on board we set sail, standing away to the Northward upon our own Coast, with Design to stretch over for the *Affrican* Coast, when they came about 10 or 12 Degrees of Northern Latitude, which it seems was the manner of their Course in those Days. We had very good Weather, only excessive hot, all the way upon our own Coast, till we came the Height of *Cape* St. *Augustino*,* from whence keeping farther off at Sea we lost Sight of Land, and steer'd as if we was bound for the Isle *Fernand de Noronha** holding our Course *N.E.* by *N.* and leaving those Isles on the East; in this Course we past the Line in about 12 Days time, and were by our last Observation in 7 Degrees 22 Min. Northern Latitude, when a violent Tournado or Hurricane took us quite out of our Knowledge; it began from the South-East, came about to the North-West, and then settled into the North-East, from whence it blew in such a terrible manner, that for twelve Days together we could do nothing but drive, and scudding away before it, let it carry us whither ever Fate and the Fury of the Winds directed; and during these twelve Days, I need not say, that I expected every Day to be swallowed up, nor indeed did any in the Ship expect to save their Lives.

In this Distress, we had besides the Terror of the Storm, one of our Men dyed of the Calenture, and one Man and the Boy wash'd over board; about the 12th Day the Weather abating a little, the Master made an Observation as well as he could,* and found that he was in about 11 Degrees North Latitude, but that he was 22 Degrees of Longitude difference West from *Cape* St. *Augustino*; so that he found he was gotten upon the Coast of *Guiana*,* or the North Part of *Brasil*, beyond the River *Amazones*, toward that of the River *Oronoque*, commonly call'd the *Great River*, and began to consult with me what Course he should take, for the Ship was leaky and very much disabled, and he was going directly back to the Coast of *Brasil*.

I was positively against that, and looking over the Charts of the Sea-Coast of *America* with him, we concluded there was no inhabited Country for us to have recourse to, till we came within the Circle of the *Carribbe-Islands*, and therefore resolved to stand away for *Barbadoes*, which by keeping off at Sea, to avoid the Indraft of the Bay or Gulph of *Mexico*, we might easily perform, as we hoped, in about fifteen Days Sail; whereas we could not possibly make our Voyage to the Coast of *Affrica* without some Assistance, both to our Ship and to our selves.

With this Design we chang'd our Course and steer'd away *N.W. by W.* in order to reach some of our *English* Islands, where I hoped for Relief; but our Voyage was otherwise determined, for being in the Latitude of 12 Deg. 18 Min.* a second Storm came upon us, which carry'd us away with the same Impetuosity Westward, and drove us so out of the very Way of all humane Commerce, that had all our Lives been saved, as to the Sea, we were rather in Danger of being devoured by Savages than ever returning to our own Country.

In this Distress, the Wind still blowing very hard, one of our Men early in the Morning, cry'd out, *Land*; and we had no sooner run out of the Cabbin to look out in hopes of seeing where abouts in the World we were; but the Ship struck upon a Sand, and in a moment her Motion being so stopp'd, the Sea broke over her in such a manner, that we expected we should all have perish'd immediately, and we were immediately driven into our close Quarters to shelter us from the very Foam and Sprye of the Sea.

It is not easy for any one, who has not been in the like Condition, to describe or conceive the Consternation of Men in such Circumstances; we knew nothing where we were, or upon what Land it was we were driven, whether an Island or the Main, whether inhabited or not inhabited; and as the Rage of the Wind was still great, tho' rather less than at first, we could not so much as hope to have the Ship hold many Minutes without breaking in Pieces, unless the Winds by a kind of Miracle should turn immediately about. In a word, we sat looking upon one another, and expecting Death every Moment, and every Man acting accordingly, as preparing for another World, for there was little or nothing more for us to do in this; that which was our present Comfort, and all the Comfort we had, was, that contrary to our Expectation the Ship did not break yet, and that the Master said the Wind began to abate.

Now tho' we thought that the Wind did a little abate, yet the Ship having thus struck upon the Sand, and sticking too fast for us to expect her getting off, we were in a dreadful Condition indeed, and had nothing to do but to think of saving our Lives as well as we could; we had a Boat at our Stern just before the Storm, but she was first stav'd by dashing against the Ship's Rudder, and in the next Place she broke away, and either sunk or was driven off to Sea, so there was no hope from her; we had another Boat on board, but how to get her off into the Sea, was a doubtful thing; however there was no room to debate, for we fancy'd the Ship would break in Pieces every Minute, and some told us she was actually broken already.

In this Distress the Mate of our Vessel lays hold of the Boat, and with the help of the rest of the Men, they got her flung over the Ship's-side, and getting all into her, let go, and committed our selves being Eleven in Number, to God's Mercy, and the wild Sea; for tho' the Storm was abated considerably, yet the Sea went dreadful high upon the Shore, and might well be call'd, *Den wild Zee*, as the *Dutch* call the Sea in a Storm.

And now our Case was very dismal indeed; for we all saw plainly, that the Sea went so high, that the Boat could not live, and that we should be inevitably drowned. As to making Sail, we had none, nor, if we had, could we ha' done any thing with it; so we work'd at the

Oar towards the Land, tho' with heavy Hearts, like Men going to
Execution; for we all knew, that when the Boat came nearer the
Shore, she would be dash'd in a Thousand Pieces by the Breach of
the Sea.* However, we committed our Souls to God in the most
earnest Manner, and the Wind driving us towards the Shore, we
hasten'd our Destruction with our own Hands, pulling as well as we
could towards Land.

What the Shore was, whether Rock or Sand, whether Steep or
Shoal, we knew not; the only Hope that could rationally give us the
least Shadow of Expectation, was, if we might happen into some Bay
or Gulph, or the Mouth of some River, where by great Chance we
might have run our Boat in, or got under the Lee of the Land,* and
perhaps made smooth Water. But there was nothing of this appeared;
but as we made nearer and nearer the Shore, the Land look'd more
frightful than the Sea.

After we had row'd, or rather driven about a League and a Half, as
we reckon'd it, a raging Wave, Mountain-like, came rowling a-stern
of us, and plainly bad us expect the *Coup de Grace*. In a word, it took
us with such a Fury, that it overset the Boat at once; and separating
us as well from the Boat, as from one another, gave us not time
hardly to say, O God! for we were all swallowed up in a Moment.

Nothing can describe the Confusion of Thought which I felt
when I sunk into the Water; for tho' I swam very well, yet I could not
deliver my self from the Waves so as to draw Breath, till that Wave
having driven me, or rather carried me a vast Way on towards the
Shore, and having spent it self, went back, and left me upon the
Land almost dry, but half-dead with the Water I took in. I had so
much Presence of Mind as well as Breath left, that seeing my self
nearer the main Land than I expected, I got upon my Feet, and
endeavoured to make on towards the Land as fast as I could, before
another Wave should return, and take me up again. But I soon found
it was impossible to avoid it; for I saw the Sea come after me as high
as a great Hill, and as furious as an Enemy which I had no Means or
Strength to contend with; my Business was to hold my Breath, and
raise my self upon the Water, if I could; and so by swimming to
preserve my Breathing, and Pilot my self towards the Shore, if possible; my greatest Concern now being, that the Sea, as it would carry
me a great Way towards the Shore when it came on, might not carry
me back again with it when it gave back towards the Sea.

The Wave that came upon me again, buried me at once 20 or 30 Foot deep in its own Body; and I could feel my self carried with a mighty Force and Swiftness towards the Shore a very great Way; but I held my Breath, and assisted my self to swim still forward with all my Might. I was ready to burst with holding my Breath, when, as I felt my self rising up, so to my immediate Relief, I found my Head and Hands shoot out above the Surface of the Water; and tho' it was not two Seconds of Time that I could keep my self so, yet it reliev'd me greatly, gave me Breath and new Courage. I was covered again with Water a good while, but not so long but I held it out; and finding the Water had spent it self, and began to return, I strook forward against the Return of the Waves, and felt Ground again with my Feet. I stood still a few Moments to recover Breath, and till the Water went from me, and then took to my Heels, and run with what Strength I had farther towards the Shore. But neither would this deliver me from the Fury of the Sea, which came pouring in after me again, and twice more I was lifted up by the Waves, and carried forwards as before, the Shore being very flat.

The last Time of these two had well near been fatal to me; for the Sea having hurried me along as before, landed me, or rather dash'd me against a Piece of a Rock, and that with such Force, as it left me senseless, and indeed helpless, as to my own Deliverance; for the Blow taking my Side and Breast, beat the Breath as it were quite out of my Body; and had it returned again immediately, I must have been strangled in the Water; but I recover'd a little before the return of the Waves, and seeing I should be cover'd again with the Water, I resolv'd to hold fast by a Piece of the Rock, and so to hold my Breath, if possible, till the Wave went back; now as the Waves were not so high as at first, being nearer Land, I held my Hold till the Wave abated, and then fetch'd another Run, which brought me so near the Shore, that the next Wave, tho' it went over me, yet did not so swallow me up as to carry me away, and the next run I took, I got to the main Land, where, to my great Comfort, I clamber'd up the Clifts of the Shore, and sat me down upon the Grass, free from Danger, and quite out of the Reach of the Water.

I was now landed, and safe on Shore, and began to look up and thank God that my Life was sav'd in a Case wherein there was some Minutes before scarce any room to hope. I believe it is impossible to express to the Life what the Extasies and Transports of the Soul are, when it is so sav'd, as I may say, out of the very Grave; and I do not wonder now at that Custom, *viz*. That when a Malefactor who has the Halter about his Neck, is tyed up, and just going to be turn'd off,* and has a Reprieve brought to him: I say, I do not wonder that they bring a Surgeon with it, to let him Blood that very Moment they tell him of it, that the Surprise may not drive the Animal Spirits from the Heart, and overwhelm him:

*For sudden Joys, like Griefs, confound at first.**

I walk'd about on the Shore, lifting up my Hands, and my whole Being, as I may say, wrapt up in the Contemplation of my Deliverance, making a Thousand Gestures and Motions which I cannot describe, reflecting upon all my Comerades that were drown'd, and that there should not be one Soul sav'd but my self; for, as for them, I never saw them afterwards, or any Sign of them, except three of their Hats, one Cap, and two Shoes that were not Fellows.

I cast my Eyes to the stranded Vessel, when the Breach and Froth of the Sea being so big, I could hardly see it, it lay so far off, and considered, Lord! how was it possible I could get on Shore?

After I had solac'd my Mind with the comfortable Part of my Condition, I began to look round me to see what kind of Place I was in, and what was next to be done, and I soon found my Comforts abate, and that in a word I had a dreadful Deliverance: For I was wet, had no Clothes to shift me, nor any thing either to eat or drink to comfort me, neither did I see any Prospect before me, but that of perishing with Hunger, or being devour'd by wild Beasts; and that which was particularly afflicting to me, was, that I had no Weapon either to hunt and kill any Creature for my Sustenance, or to defend my self against any other Creature that might desire to kill me for theirs: In a Word, I had nothing about me but a Knife, a Tobacco-pipe, and a little Tobacco in a Box, this was all my Provision, and this threw me into terrible Agonies of Mind, that for a while I run about like a Mad-man; Night coming upon me, I began with a heavy Heart to consider what would be my Lot if there were any ravenous Beasts in that Country, seeing at Night they always come abroad for their Prey.

All the Remedy that offer'd to my Thoughts at that Time, was, to get up into a thick bushy Tree like a Firr, but thorny, which grew near me, and where I resolv'd to set all Night, and consider the next

Day what Death I should dye, for as yet I saw no Prospect of Life; I
walk'd about a Furlong from the Shore, to see if I could find any
fresh Water to drink, which I did, to my great Joy; and having drank
and put a little Tobacco in my Mouth to prevent Hunger, I went to
the Tree, and getting up into it, endeavour'd to place my self so, as
that if I should sleep I might not fall; and having cut me a short
Stick, like a Truncheon, for my Defence, I took up my Lodging, and
having been excessively fatigu'd, I fell fast asleep, and slept as comfortably as, I believe, few could have done in my Condition, and
found my self the most refresh'd with it, that I think I ever was on
such an Occasion.

When I wak'd it was broad Day, the Weather clear, and the Storm
abated, so that the Sea did not rage and swell as before: But that
which surpris'd me most, was, that the Ship was lifted off in the
Night from the Sand where she lay, by the Swelling of the Tyde, and
was driven up almost as far as the Rock which I first mention'd,
where I had been so bruis'd by the dashing me against it; this being
within about a Mile from the Shore where I was, and the Ship
seeming to stand upright still, I wish'd my self on board, that, at
least, I might save some necessary things for my use.

When I came down from my Appartment in the Tree, I look'd
about me again, and the first thing I found was the Boat, which lay as
the Wind and the Sea had toss'd her up upon the Land, about two
Miles on my right Hand. I walk'd as far as I could upon the Shore to
have got to her, but found a Neck or Inlet of Water between me and
the Boat, which was about half a Mile broad, so I came back for the
present, being more intent upon getting at the Ship, where I hop'd to
find something for my present Subsistence.

A little after Noon I found the Sea very calm, and the Tyde ebb'd
so far out, that I could come within a Quarter of a Mile of the Ship;
and here I found a fresh renewing of my Grief, for I saw evidently,
that if we had kept on board, we had been all safe, that is to say, we
had all got safe on Shore, and I had not been so miserable as to be left
entirely destitute of all Comfort and Company, as I now was; this
forc'd Tears from my Eyes again, but as there was little Relief in
that, I resolv'd, if possible, to get to the Ship, so I pull'd off my
Clothes, for the Weather was hot to Extremity, and took the Water,
but when I came to the Ship, my Difficulty was still greater to know
how to get on board, for as she lay a ground, and high out of the

Water, there was nothing within my Reach to lay hold of; I swam round her twice, and the second Time I spy'd a small Piece of a Rope, which I wonder'd I did not see at first, hang down by the Fore-Chains so low, as that with great Difficulty I got hold of it, and by the help of that Rope, got up into the Forecastle of the Ship; here I found that the Ship was bulg'd, and had a great deal of Water in her Hold, but that she lay so on the Side of a Bank of hard Sand, or rather Earth, that her Stern lay lifted up upon the Bank, and her Head low almost to the Water; by this Means all her Quarter was free, and all that was in that Part was dry; for you may be sure my first Work was to search and to see what was spoil'd and what was free; and first I found that all the Ship's Provisions were dry and untouch'd by the Water, and being very well dispos'd to eat, I went to the Bread-room and fill'd my Pockets with Bisket,* and eat it as I went about other things, for I had no time to lose; I also found some Rum in the great Cabbin, of which I took a large Dram, and which I had indeed need enough of to spirit me for what was before me: Now I wanted nothing but a Boat to furnish my self with many things which I forsaw would be very necessary to me.

It was in vain to sit still and wish for what was not to be had, and this Extremity rouz'd my Application; we had several spare Yards, and two or three large sparrs of Wood, and a spare Top-mast or two in the Ship; I resolv'd to fall to work with these, and I flung as many of them over board as I could manage for their Weight, tying every one with a Rope that they might not drive away; when this was done I went down the Ship's Side, and pulling them to me, I ty'd four of them fast together at both Ends as well as I could, in the Form of a Raft, and laying two or three short Pieces of Plank upon them cross-ways, I found I could walk upon it very well, but that it was not able to bear any great Weight, the Pieces being too light; so I went to work, and with the Carpenter's Saw I cut a spare Top-mast into three Lengths, and added them to my Raft, with a great deal of Labour and Pains, but hope of furnishing my self with Necessaries, encourag'd me to go beyond what I should have been able to have done upon another Occasion.

My Raft was now strong enough to bear any reasonable Weight; my next Care was what to load it with, and how to preserve what I laid upon it from the Surf of the Sea; But I was not long considering this, I first laid all the Plank or Boards upon it that I could get, and

having consider'd well what I most wanted, I first got three of the
Seamens Chests, which I had broken open and empty'd, and lower'd
them down upon my Raft; the first of these I fill'd with Provision,
viz. Bread, Rice, three Dutch Cheeses, five Pieces of dry'd Goat's
Flesh, which we liv'd much upon, and a little Remainder of
European Corn which had been laid by for some Fowls which we
brought to Sea with us, but the Fowls were kill'd; there had been
some Barly and Wheat together, but, to my great Disappointment, I
found afterwards that the Rats had eaten or spoil'd it all; as for
Liquors, I found several Cases of Bottles belonging to our Skipper,
in which were some Cordial Waters, and in all about five or six
Gallons of Rack, these I stow'd by themselves, there being no need
to put them into the Chest, nor no room for them. While I was doing
this, I found the Tyde began to flow, tho' very calm, and I had the
Mortification to see my Coat, Shirt, and Wast-coat which I had left
on Shore upon the Sand, swim away; as for my Breeches which were
only Linnen and open knee'd, I swam on board in them and my
Stockings: However this put me upon rummaging for Clothes, of
which I found enough, but took no more than I wanted for present
use, for I had other things which my Eye was more upon, as first
Tools to work with on Shore, and it was after long searching that I
found out the Carpenter's Chest, which was indeed a very useful
Prize to me, and much more valuable than a Ship Loading of Gold
would have been at that time; I got it down to my Raft, even whole as
it was, without losing time to look into it, for I knew in general what
it contain'd.

My next Care was for some Ammunition and Arms; there were
two very good Fowling-pieces in the great Cabbin, and two Pistols,
these I secur'd first, with some Powder-horns, and a small Bag of
Shot, and two old rusty Swords; I knew there were three Barrels of
Powder in the Ship, but knew not where our Gunner had stow'd
them, but with much search I found them, two of them dry and
good, the third had taken Water, those two I got to my Raft, with the
Arms, and now I thought my self pretty well freighted, and began to
think how I should get to Shore with them, having neither Sail, Oar,
or Rudder, and the least Cap full of Wind would have overset all my
Navigation.

I had three Encouragements, 1. A smooth calm Sea, 2. The Tide
rising and setting in to the Shore, 3. What little Wind there was blew

me towards the Land; and thus, having found two or three broken
Oars belonging to the Boat, and besides the Tools which were in the
Chest, I found two Saws, an Axe, and a Hammer, and with this
Cargo I put to Sea; For a Mile, or thereabouts, my Raft went very
well, only that I found it drive a little distant from the Place where I
had landed before, by which I perceiv'd that there was some Indraft
of the Water, and consequently I hop'd to find some Creek or River
there, which I might make use of as a Port to get to Land with my
Cargo.

As I imagin'd, so it was, there appear'd before me a little opening
of the Land, and I found a strong Current of the Tide set into it, so I
guided my Raft as well as I could to keep in the Middle of the
Stream: But here I had like to have suffer'd a second Shipwreck,
which, if I had, I think verily would have broke my Heart, for knowing nothing of the Coast, my Raft run a-ground at one End of it
upon a Shoal, and not being a-ground at the other End, it wanted
but a little that all my Cargo had slip'd off towards that End that was
a-float, and so fall'n into the Water: I did my utmost by setting my
Back against the Chests, to keep them in their Places, but could not
thrust off the Raft with all my Strength, neither durst I stir from the
Posture I was in, but holding up the Chests with all my Might, stood
in that Manner near half an Hour, in which time the rising of
the Water brought me a little more upon a Level, and a little after, the
Water still rising, my Raft floated again, and I thrust her off with the
Oar I had, into the Channel, and then driving up higher, I at length
found my self in the Mouth of a little River, with Land on both Sides,
and a strong Current or Tide running up, I look'd on both Sides for
a proper Place to get to Shore, for I was not willing to be driven too
high up the River, hoping in time to see some Ship at Sea, and
therefore resolv'd to place my self as near the Coast as I could.

At length I spy'd a little Cove on the right Shore of the Creek, to
which with great Pain and Difficulty I guided my Raft, and at last
got so near, as that, reaching Ground with my Oar, I could thrust her
directly in, but here I had like to have dipt all my Cargo in the Sea
again; for that Shore lying pretty steep, that is to say sloping, there
was no Place to land, but where one End of my Float, if it run on
Shore, would lie so high, and the other sink lower as before, that it
would endanger my Cargo again: All that I could do, was to wait 'till
the Tide was at highest, keeping the Raft with my Oar like an

Anchor to hold the Side of it fast to the Shore, near a flat Piece of Ground, which I expected the Water would flow over; and so it did: As soon as I found Water enough, for my Raft drew about a Foot of Water,* I thrust her on upon that flat Piece of Ground, and there fasten'd or mor'd her by sticking my two broken Oars into the Ground; one on one Side near one End, and one on the other Side near the other End; and thus I lay 'till the Water ebb'd away, and left my Raft and all my Cargoe safe on Shore.

My next Work was to view the Country, and seek a proper Place for my Habitation, and where to stow my Goods to secure them from whatever might happen; where I was I yet knew not, whether on the Continent or on an Island, whether inhabited or not inhabited, whether in Danger of wild Beasts or not: There was a Hill not above a Mile from me, which rose up very steep and high, and which seem'd to over-top some other Hills which lay as in a Ridge from it northward; I took out one of the fowling Pieces, and one of the Pistols, and an Horn of Powder, and thus arm'd I travell'd for Discovery up to the Top of that Hill, where after I had with great Labour and Difficulty got to the Top, I saw my Fate to my great Affliction, (*viz.*) that I was in an Island environ'd every Way with the Sea, no Land to be seen, except some Rocks which lay a great Way off, and two small Islands less than this, which lay about three Leagues to the West.

I found also that the Island I was in was barren, and, as I saw good Reason to believe, un-inhabited, except by wild Beasts, of whom however I saw none, yet I saw Abundance of Fowls, but knew not their Kinds, neither when I kill'd them could I tell what was fit for Food, and what not; at my coming back, I shot at a great Bird which I saw sitting upon a Tree on the Side of a great Wood, I believe it was the first Gun that had been fir'd there since the Creation of the World; I had no sooner fir'd, but from all the Parts of the Wood there arose an innumerable Number of Fowls of many Sorts, making a confus'd Screaming, and crying every one according to his usual Note; but not one of them of any Kind that I knew: As for the Creature I kill'd, I took it to be a Kind of a Hawk, its Colour and Beak resembling it, but had no Talons or Claws more than common, its Flesh was Carrion, and fit for nothing.

Contented with this Discovery, I came back to my Raft, and fell to Work to bring my Cargoe on Shore, which took me up the rest of that Day, and what to do with my self at Night I knew not, nor indeed where to rest; for I was afraid to lie down on the Ground, not knowing but some wild Beast might devour me, tho', as I afterwards found, there was really no Need for those Fears.

However, as well as I could, I barricado'd my self round with the Chests and Boards that I had brought on Shore, and made a Kind of a Hut for that Night's Lodging; as for Food, I yet saw not which Way to supply my self, except that I had seen two or three Creatures like Hares run out of the Wood where I shot the Fowl.

I now began to consider, that I might yet get a great many Things out of the Ship, which would be useful to me, and particularly some of the Rigging, and Sails, and such other Things as might come to Land, and I resolv'd to make another Voyage on Board the Vessel, if possible; and as I knew that the first Storm that blew must necessarily break her all in Pieces, I resolv'd to set all other Things apart, 'till I got every Thing out of the Ship that I could get; then I call'd a Council, that is to say, in my Thoughts, whether I should take back the Raft, but this appear'd impracticable; so I resolv'd to go as before, when the Tide was down, and I did so, only that I stripp'd before I went from my Hut, having nothing on but a Chequer'd Shirt, and a Pair of Linnen Drawers, and a Pair of Pumps on my Feet.

I got on Board the Ship, as before, and prepar'd a second Raft, and having had Experience of the first, I neither made this so unweildy, nor loaded it so hard, but yet I brought away several Things very useful to me; as first, in the Carpenter's Stores I found two or three Bags full of Nails and Spikes, a great Skrew-Jack, a Dozen or two of Hatchets, and above all, that most useful Thing call'd a Grindstone; all these I secur'd together, with several Things belonging to the Gunner, particularly two or three Iron Crows, and two Barrels of Musquet Bullets, seven Musquets, and another fowling Piece, with some small Quantity of Powder more; a large Bag full of small Shot, and a great Roll of Sheet Lead: But this last was so heavy, I could not hoise* it up to get it over the Ship's Side.

Besides these Things, I took all the Mens Cloths that I could find, and a spare Fore-top-sail, a Hammock, and some Bedding; and with this I loaded my second Raft, and brought them all safe on Shore to my very great Comfort.

I was under some Apprehensions during my Absence from the Land, that at least my Provisions might be devour'd on Shore; but when I came back, I found no Sign of any Visitor, only there sat a Creature like a wild Cat upon one of the Chests, which when I came towards it, ran away a little Distance, and then stood still; she sat very compos'd, and unconcern'd, and look'd full in my Face, as if she had a Mind to be acquainted with me, I presented my Gun at her, but as she did not understand it, she was perfectly unconcern'd at it, nor did she offer to stir away; upon which I toss'd her a Bit of Bisket, tho' by the Way I was not very free of it, for my Store was not great: However, I spar'd her a Bit, I say, and she went to it, smell'd of it, and ate it, and look'd (as pleas'd) for more, but I thank'd her, and could spare no more; so she march'd off.

Having got my second Cargoe on Shore, tho' I was fain to open the Barrels of Powder, and bring them by Parcels, for they were too heavy, being large Casks, I went to work to make me a little Tent with the Sail and some Poles which I cut for that Purpose, and into this Tent I brought every Thing that I knew would spoil, either with Rain or Sun, and I piled all the empty Chests and Casks up in a Circle round the Tent, to fortify it from any sudden Attempt, either from Man or Beast.

When I had done this I block'd up the Door of the Tent with some Boards within, and an empty Chest set up an End* without, and spreading one of the Beds upon the Ground, laying my two Pistols just at my Head, and my Gun at Length by me, I went to Bed for the first Time, and slept very quietly all Night, for I was very weary and heavy, for the Night before I had slept little, and had labour'd very hard all Day, as well to fetch all those Things from the Ship, as to get them on Shore.

I had the biggest Magazine of all Kinds now that ever were laid up, I believe, for one Man, but I was not satisfy'd still; for while the Ship sat upright in that Posture, I thought I ought to get every Thing out of her that I could; so every Day at low Water I went on Board, and brought away some Thing or other: But particularly the third Time I went, I brought away as much of the Rigging as I could, as also all the small Ropes and Rope-twine I could get, with a Piece of spare Canvass, which was to mend the Sails upon Occasion, the Barrel of wet Gun-powder: In a Word, I brought away all the Sails first and last, only that I was fain to cut them in Pieces, and bring as much at a Time as I could; for they were no more useful to be Sails, but as meer Canvass only.

But that which comforted me more still was, that at last of all, after I had made five or six such Voyages as these, and thought I had nothing more to expect from the Ship that was worth my medling with, I say, after all this, I found a great Hogshead of Bread and three large Runlets of Rum or Spirits, and a Box of Sugar, and a Barrel of fine Flower; this was surprizing to me, because I had given over expecting any more Provisions, except what was spoil'd by the Water: I soon empty'd the Hogshead of that Bread, and wrapt it up Parcel by Parcel in Pieces of the Sails, which I cut out; and in a Word, I got all this safe on Shore also.

The next Day I made another Voyage; and now having plunder'd the Ship of what was portable and fit to hand out, I began with the Cables; and cutting the great Cable into Pieces, such as I could move, I got two Cables and a Hawser on Shore, with all the Iron Work I could get; and having cut down the Spritsail-yard, and the Missen-yard, and every Thing I could to make a large Raft, I loaded it with all those heavy Goods, and came away: But my good Luck began now to leave me; for this Raft was so unweildy, and so overloaden, that after I was enter'd the little Cove, where I had landed the rest of my Goods, not being able to guide it so handily as I did the other, it overset, and threw me and all my Cargoe into the Water; as for my self it was no great Harm, for I was near the Shore; but as to my Cargoe, it was great Part of it lost, especially the Iron, which I expected would have been of great Use to me: However, when the Tide was out, I got most of the Pieces of Cable ashore, and some of the Iron, tho' with infinite Labour; for I was fain to dip for it* into the Water, a Work which fatigu'd me very much: After this I went every Day on Board, and brought away what I could get.

I had been now thirteen Days on Shore, and had been eleven Times on Board the Ship;* in which Time I had brought away all that one Pair of Hands could well be suppos'd capable to bring, tho' I believe verily, had the calm Weather held, I should have brought away the whole Ship Piece by Piece: But preparing the 12th Time to go on Board, I found the Wind begin to rise; however at low Water I went on Board, and tho' I thought I had rumag'd the Cabbin so effectually, as that nothing more could be found, yet I discover'd a Locker with Drawers in it, in one of which I found two or three Razors, and one Pair of large Sizzers, with some ten or a Dozen of good Knives and Forks; in another I found about Thirty six Pounds value in Money, some *European* Coin, some *Brasil*, some Pieces of Eight, some Gold, some Silver.

I smil'd to my self at the Sight of this Money, O Drug! said I aloud, what art thou good for, Thou art not worth to me, no not the taking off of the Ground, one of those Knives is worth all this Heap, I have no Manner of use for thee,* e'en remain where thou art, and go to the Bottom as a Creature whose Life is not worth saving. However, upon Second Thoughts, I took it away, and wrapping all this in a Piece of Canvas, I began to think of making another Raft, but while I was preparing this, I found the Sky over-cast, and the Wind began to rise, and in a Quarter of an Hour it blew a fresh Gale from the Shore; it presently occur'd to me, that it was in vain to pretend to make a Raft with the Wind off Shore, and that it was my Business to be gone before the Tide of Flood began, otherwise I might not be able to reach the Shore at all: Accordingly I let my self down into the Water, and swam cross the Channel, which lay between the Ship and the Sands, and even that with Difficulty enough, partly with the Weight of the Things I had about me, and partly the Roughness of the Water, for the Wind rose very hastily, and before it was quite high Water, it blew a Storm.

But I was gotten home to my little Tent, where I lay with all my Wealth about me very secure. It blew very hard all that Night, and in the Morning when I look'd out, behold no more Ship was to be seen; I was a little surpriz'd, but recover'd my self with this satisfactory Reflection, *viz*. That I had lost no time, nor abated no Dilligence to get every thing out of her that could be useful to me, and that indeed there was little left in her that I was able to bring away if I had had more time.

I now gave over any more Thoughts of the Ship, or of any thing out of her, except what might drive on Shore from her Wreck, as indeed divers Pieces of her afterwards did; but those things were of small use to me.

My Thoughts were now wholly employ'd about securing my self against either Savages, if any should appear, or wild Beasts, if any were in the Island; and I had many Thoughts of the Method how to do this, and what kind of Dwelling to make, whether I should make me a Cave in the Earth, or a Tent upon the Earth: And, in short, I resolv'd upon both, the Manner and Discription of which, it may not be improper to give an Account of.

I soon found the Place I was in was not for my Settlement, particularly because it was upon a low moorish Ground near the Sea, and I believ'd would not be wholsome, and more particularly because there was no fresh Water near it, so I resolv'd to find a more healthy and more convenient Spot of Ground.

I consulted several Things in my Situation which I found would be proper for me, 1st. Health, and fresh Water I just now mention'd, 2dly. Shelter from the Heat of the Sun, 3dly. Security from ravenous Creatures, whether Men or Beasts, 4thly. a View to the Sea, that if God sent any Ship in Sight, I might not lose any Advantage for my Deliverance, of which I was not willing to banish all my Expectation yet.

In search of a Place proper for this, I found a little Plain on the Side of a rising Hill; whose Front towards this little Plain, was steep as a House-side, so that nothing could come down upon me from the Top; on the Side of this Rock there was a hollow Place worn a little way in like the Entrance or Door of a Cave, but there was not really any Cave or Way into the Rock at all.

On the Flat of the Green, just before this hollow Place, I resolv'd to pitch my Tent: This Plain was not above an Hundred Yards broad, and about twice as long, and lay like a Green before my Door, and at the End of it descended irregularly every Way down into the Low-grounds by the Sea-side. It was on the *N.N.W.* Side of the Hill, so that I was shelter'd from the Heat every Day, till it came to a *W.* and by *S.* Sun, or thereabouts, which in those Countries is near the Setting.

Before I set up my Tent, I drew a half Circle before the hollow Place, which took in about Ten Yards in its Semi-diameter from the Rock, and Twenty Yards in its Diameter, from its Beginning and Ending.

In this half Circle I pitch'd two Rows of strong Stakes, driving them into the Ground till they stood very firm like Piles, the biggest End being out of the Ground about Five Foot and a Half, and sharpen'd on the Top: The two Rows did not stand above Six Inches from one another.

Then I took the Pieces of Cable which I had cut in the Ship, and I laid them in Rows one upon another, within the Circle, between these two Rows of Stakes, up to the Top, placing other Stakes in the In-side, leaning against them, about two Foot and a half high, like a

Spurr to a Post,* and this Fence was so strong, that neither Man or Beast could get into it or over it: This cost me a great deal of Time and Labour, especially to cut the Piles in the Woods, bring them to the Place, and drive them into the Earth.

The Entrance into this Place I made to be not by a Door, but by a short Ladder to go over the Top, which Ladder, when I was in, I lifted over after me, and so I was compleatly fenc'd in, and fortify'd, as I thought, from all the World, and consequently slept secure in the Night, which otherwise I could not have done, tho', as it appear'd afterward, there was no need of all this Caution from the Enemies that I apprehended Danger from.

Into this Fence or Fortress, with infinite Labour, I carry'd all my Riches, all my Provisions, Ammunition and Stores, of which you have the Account above, and I made me a large Tent, which, to preserve me from the Rains that in one Part of the Year are very violent there, I made double, *viz.* One smaller Tent within, and one larger Tent above it, and cover'd the uppermost with a large Tarpaulin which I had sav'd among the Sails.

And now I lay no more for a while in the Bed which I had brought on Shore, but in a Hammock, which was indeed a very good one, and belong'd to the Mate of the Ship.

Into this Tent I brought all my Provisions, and every thing that would spoil by the Wet, and having thus enclos'd all my Goods, I made up the Entrance, which till now I had left open, and so pass'd and re-pass'd, as I said, by a short Ladder.

When I had done this, I began to work my Way into the Rock, and bringing all the Earth and Stones that I dug down out thro' my Tent, I laid 'em up within my Fence in the Nature of a Terras, that so* it rais'd the Ground within about a Foot and a Half; and thus I made me a Cave just behind my Tent, which serv'd me like a Cellar to my House.

It cost me much Labour, and many Days, before all these Things were brought to Perfection, and therefore I must go back to some other Things which took up some of my Thoughts. At the same time it happen'd after I had laid my Scheme for the setting up my Tent and making the Cave, that a Storm of Rain falling from a thick dark Cloud, a sudden Flash of Lightning happen'd, and after that a great Clap of Thunder, as is naturally the Effect of it; I was not so much surpris'd with the Lightning as I was with a Thought which darted into my Mind as swift as the Lightning it self: O my Powder! My very Heart sunk within me, when I thought, that at one Blast all my Powder might be destroy'd, on which, not my Defence only, but the providing me Food, as I thought, entirely depended; I was nothing near so anxious about my own Danger, tho' had the Powder took fire, I had never known who had hurt me.*

Such Impression did this make upon me, that after the Storm was over, I laid aside all my Works, my Building, and Fortifying, and apply'd my self to make Bags and Boxes to separate the Powder, and keep it a little and a little in a Parcel, in hope, that whatever might come, it might not all take Fire at once, and to keep it so apart that it should not be possible to make one part fire another: I finish'd this Work in about a Fortnight, and I think my Powder, which in all was about 240 l. weight was divided in not less than a Hundred Parcels; as to the Barrel that had been wet, I did not apprehend any Danger from that, so I plac'd it in my new Cave, which in my Fancy I call'd my Kitchin, and the rest I hid up and down in Holes among the Rocks, so that no wet might come to it, marking very carefully where I laid it.

In the Interval of time while this was doing I went out once at least every Day with my Gun, as well to divert my self, as to see if I could kill any thing fit for Food, and as near as I could to acquaint my self with what the Island produc'd. The first time I went out I presently discover'd that there were Goats in the Island,* which was a great Satisfaction to me; but then it was attended with this Misfortune to me, *viz.* That they were so shy, so subtile, and so swift of Foot, that it was the difficultest thing in the World to come at them: But I was not discourag'd at this, not doubting but I might now and then shoot one, as it soon happen'd, for after I had found their Haunts a little, I laid wait in this Manner for them: I observ'd if they saw me in the Valleys, tho' they were upon the Rocks, they would run away as in a terrible Fright; but if they were feeding in the Valleys, and I was upon the Rocks, they took no Notice of me, from whence I concluded, that by the Position of their Opticks, their Sight was so directed downward, that they did not readily see Objects that were above them; so afterward I took this Method, I always clim'd the Rocks first to get above them, and then had frequently a fair Mark. The first shot I made among these Creatures, I kill'd a She-Goat which had a little Kid by her which she gave Suck to, which griev'd me heartily; but when the Old one fell, the Kid stood stock still by her till I came and took her up, and not only so, but when I carry'd the Old one with me upon my Shoulders, the Kid follow'd me quite to my Enclosure, upon which I laid down the Dam, and took the Kid in my Arms, and carry'd it over my Pale, in hopes to have bred it up tame, but it would not eat, so I was forc'd to kill it and eat it my self; these two supply'd me with Flesh a great while, for I eat sparingly; and sav'd my Provisions (my Bread especially) as much as possibly I could.

Having now fix'd my Habitation, I found it absolutely necessary to provide a Place to make a Fire in, and Fewel to burn; and what I did for that, as also how I enlarg'd my Cave, and what Conveniencies I made, I shall give a full Account of in its Place: But I must first give some little Account of my self, and of my Thoughts about Living, which it may well be suppos'd were not a few.

I had a dismal Prospect of my Condition, for as I was not cast away upon that Island without being driven, as is said, by a violent Storm quite out of the Course of our intended Voyage, and a great Way, *viz.* some Hundreds of Leagues out of the ordinary Course of the Trade of Mankind, I had great Reason to consider it as a Determination of Heaven, that in this desolate Place, and in this desolate Manner I should end my Life; the Tears would run plenti-fully down my Face when I made these Reflections, and sometimes I would expostulate with my self, Why Providence should thus com-pleatly ruine its Creatures, and render them so absolutely miserable, so without Help abandon'd, so entirely depress'd, that it could hardly be rational to be thankful for such a Life.

But something always return'd swift upon me to check these Thoughts, and to reprove me; and particularly one Day walking with my Gun in my Hand by the Sea-side, I was very pensive upon the Subject of my present Condition, when Reason as it were expostu-lated with me t'other Way, thus: Well, you are in a desolate Condi-tion 'tis true, but pray remember, Where are the rest of you? Did not you come Eleven of you into the Boat, where are the Ten? Why were not they sav'd and you lost? Why were you singled out? Is it better to be here or there? and then I pointed to the Sea. All Evills are to be consider'd with the Good that is in them, and with what worse attends them.

Then it occurr'd to me again, how well I was furnish'd for my

Subsistence, and what would have been my Case if it had not
happen'd, *Which was an Hundred Thousand to one*, that the Ship
floated from the Place where she first struck and was driven so
near to the Shore that I had time to get all these Things out of her:
What would have been my Case, if I had been to have liv'd in the
Condition in which I at first came on Shore, without Necessaries of
Life, or Necessaries to supply and procure them? Particularly said
I aloud, (tho' to my self) what should I ha' done without a Gun,
without Ammunition, without any Tools to make any thing, or to
work with, without Clothes, Bedding, a Tent, or any manner of
Covering, and that now I had all these to a Sufficient Quantity, and
was in a fair way to provide my self in such a manner, as to live
without my Gun when my Ammunition was spent; so that I had a
tollerable View of subsisting without any Want as long as I liv'd; for
I consider'd from the beginning how I would provide for the
Accidents that might happen, and for the time that was to come,
even not only after my Ammunition should be spent, but even after
my Health or Strength should decay.

I confess I had not entertain'd any Notion of my Ammunition
being destroy'd at one Blast, I mean my Powder being blown up by
Lightning, and this made the Thoughts of it so surprising to me
when it lighten'd and thunder'd, as I observ'd just now.

And now being to enter into a melancholy Relation of a Scene of
silent Life, such perhaps as was never heard of in the World before, I
shall take it from its Beginning, and continue it in its Order. It was,
by my Account, the 30th. of *Sept.* when, in the Manner as above
said, I first set Foot upon this horrid Island, when the Sun being, to
us, in its Autumnal Equinox, was almost just over my Head, for I
reckon'd my self, by Observation, to be in the Latitude of 9 Degrees
22 Minutes North of the Line.*

After I had been there about Ten or Twelve Days, it came into my
Thoughts, that I should lose my Reckoning of Time for want of
Books and Pen and Ink, and should even forget the Sabbath Days
from the working Days; but to prevent this I cut it with my Knife
upon a large Post, in Capital Letters, and making it into a great Cross
I set it up on the Shore where I first landed, viz. *I came on Shore here
on the 30th of* Sept. 1659. Upon the Sides of this square Post I cut
every Day a Notch with my Knife, and every seventh Notch was as
long again as the rest, and every first Day of the Month as long again

as that long one, and thus I kept my Kalander, or weekly, monthly, and yearly reckoning of Time.

In the next place we are to observe, that among the many things which I brought out of the Ship in the several Voyages, which, as above mention'd, I made to it, I got several things of less Value, but not all* less useful to me, which I omitted setting down before; as in particular, Pens, Ink, and Paper, several Parcels in the Captain's, Mate's, Gunner's, and Carpenter's keeping, three or four Compasses, some Mathematical Instruments, Dials, Perspectives, Charts, and Books of Navigation, all which I huddel'd together, whether I might want them or no; also I found three very good Bibles which came to me in my Cargo from *England*, and which I had pack'd up among my things; some *Portugueze* Books also, and among them two or three Popish Prayer-Books, and several other Books, all which I carefully secur'd. And I must not forget, that we had in the Ship a Dog and two Cats, of whose eminent History I may have occasion to say something in its place; for I carry'd both the Cats with me, and as for the Dog, he jump'd out of the Ship of himself and swam on Shore to me the Day after I went on Shore with my first Cargo, and was a trusty Servant to me many Years; I wanted nothing that he could fetch me, nor any Company that he could make up to me, I only wanted to have him talk to me, but that would not do: As I observ'd before, I found Pen, Ink and Paper, and I husbanded them to the utmost, and I shall shew, that while my Ink lasted, I kept things very exact, but after that was gone I could not, for I could not make any Ink by any Means that I could devise.

And this put me in mind that I wanted many things, notwithstanding all that I had amass'd together, and of these, this of Ink was one, as also Spade, Pick-Axe, and Shovel to dig or remove the Earth, Needles, Pins, and Thread; as for Linnen, I soon learn'd to want that without much Difficulty.

This want of Tools made every Work I did go on heavily, and it was near a whole Year before I had entirely finish'd my little Pale or surrounded Habitation: The Piles or Stakes, which were as heavy as I could well lift, were a long time in cutting and preparing in the Woods, and more by far in bringing home, so that I spent some times two Days in cutting and bringing home one of those Posts, and a third Day in driving it into the Ground; for which Purpose I got a heavy Piece of Wood at first, but at last bethought my self of one of the Iron Crows, which however tho' I found it, yet it made driving those Posts or Piles very laborious and tedious Work.

But what need I ha' been concern'd at the Tediousness of any thing I had to do, seeing I had time enough to do it in, nor had I any other Employment if that had been over, at least, that I could foresee, except the ranging the Island to seek for Food, which I did more or less every Day.

I now began to consider seriously my Condition, and the Circumstance I was reduc'd to, and I drew up the State of my Affairs in Writing, not so much to leave them to any that were to come after me, for I was like to have but few Heirs, as to deliver my Thoughts from daily poring upon them, and afflicting my Mind; and as my Reason began now to master my Despondency, I began to comfort my self as well as I could, and to set the good against the Evil, that I might have something to distinguish my Case from worse, and I stated it very impartially, like Debtor and Creditor, the Comforts I enjoy'd, against the Miseries I suffer'd, Thus,

Evil.	Good.
I am cast upon a horrible desolate Island, void of all hope of Recovery.	*But I am alive, and not drown'd as all my Ship'd Company was.*
I am singl'd out and separated, as it were, from all the World to be miserable.	*But I am singl'd out too from all the Ship's Crew to be spar'd from Death; and he that miraculously sav'd me from Death, can deliver me from this Condition.*
I am divided from Mankind, a Solitaire, one banish'd from humane Society.	*But I am not starv'd and perishing on a barren Place, affording no Sustenance.*
I have not Clothes to cover me.	*But I am in a hot Climate, where if I had Clothes I could hardly wear them.*

<table>
<tr>
<td>I am without Defence or Means to resist any Violence of Man or Beast.</td>
<td>But I am cast on an Island, where I see no wild Beasts to hurt me, as I saw on the Coast of Africa: And what if I had been Ship-wreck'd there?</td>
</tr>
<tr>
<td>I have no Soul to speak to, or relieve me.</td>
<td>But God wonderfully sent the Ship in near enough to the Shore, that I have gotten out so many necessary things as will either supply my Wants, or enable me to supply my self even as long as I live.</td>
</tr>
</table>

Upon the whole, here was an undoubted Testimony, that there was scarce any Condition in the World so miserable, but there was something *Negative* or something *Positive* to be thankful for in it; and let this stand as a Direction from the Experience of the most miserable of all Conditions in this World, that we may always find in it something to comfort our selves from, and to set in the Description of Good and Evil, on the Credit Side of the Accompt.

Having now brought my Mind a little to relish my Condition, and given over looking out to Sea to see if I could spy a Ship, I say, giving over these things, I began to apply my self to accommodate my way of Living, and to make things as easy to me as I could.

I have already describ'd my Habitation, which was a Tent under the Side of a Rock, surrounded with a strong Pale of Posts and Cables, but I might now rather call it a Wall, for I rais'd a kind of Wall up against it of Turfs, about two Foot thick on the Out-side, and after some time, I think it was a Year and Half, I rais'd Rafters from it leaning to the Rock, and thatch'd or cover'd it with Bows of Trees, and such things as I could get to keep out the Rain, which I found at some times of the Year very violent.

I have already observ'd how I brought all my Goods into this Pale, and into the Cave which I had made behind me: But I must observe too, that at first this was a confus'd Heap of Goods, which as they lay in no Order, so they took up all my Place, I had no room to turn my self; so I set my self to enlarge my Cave and Works farther into the Earth, for it was a loose sandy Rock, which yielded easily to the Labour I bestow'd on it; and so when I found I was pretty safe as to Beasts of Prey, I work'd side-ways to the Right Hand into the Rock, and then turning to the Right again, work'd quite out and made me a Door to come out, on the Out-side of my Pale or Fortification.

This gave me not only Egress and Regress, as it were a back Way to my Tent and to my Storehouse, but gave me room to stow my Goods.

And now I began to apply my self to make such necessary things as I found I most wanted, as particularly a Chair and a Table, for without these I was not able to enjoy the few Comforts I had in the World, I could not write, or eat, or do several things with so much Pleasure without a Table.

So I went to work; and here I must needs observe, that as Reason is the Substance and Original of the Mathematicks, so by stating and squaring every thing by Reason, and by making the most rational Judgment of things, every Man may be in time Master of every mechanick Art. I had never handled a Tool in my Life, and yet in time by Labour, Application, and Contrivance, I found at last that I wanted nothing but I could have made it, especially if I had had Tools; however I made abundance of things, even without Tools, and some with no more Tools than an Adze and a Hatchet, which perhaps were never made that way before, and that with infinite Labour: For Example, If I wanted a Board, I had no other Way but to cut down a Tree, set it on an Edge before me, and hew it flat on either Side with my Axe, till I had brought it to be thin as a Plank, and then dubb it smooth with my Adze. It is true, by this Method I could make but one Board out of a whole Tree, but this I had no Remedy for but Patience, any more than I had for the prodigious deal of Time and Labour which it took me up to make a Plank or Board: But my Time or Labour was little worth, and so it was as well employ'd one way as another.

However, I made me a Table and a Chair, as I observ'd above, in the first Place, and this I did out of the short Pieces of Boards that I brought on my Raft from the Ship: But when I had wrought out some Boards, as above, I made large Shelves of the Breadth of a Foot and Half one over another, all along one Side of my Cave, to lay all my Tools, Nails, and Iron-work, and in a Word, to separate every thing at large in their Places, that I might come easily at them; I knock'd Pieces into the Wall of the Rock to hang my Guns and all things that would hang up.

So that had my Cave been to be seen, it look'd like a general Magazine of all Necessary things, and I had every thing so ready at my Hand, that it was a great Pleasure to me to see all my Goods in such Order, and especially to find my Stock of all Necessaries so great.

And now it was when I began to keep a Journal of every Day's Employment, for indeed at first I was in too much Hurry, and not only Hurry as to Labour, but in too much Discomposure of Mind, and my Journal would ha' been full of many dull things: For Example, I must have said thus. *Sept.* the 30th. After I got to Shore and had escap'd drowning, instead of being thankful to God for my Deliverance, having first vomited with the great Quantity of salt Water which was gotten into my Stomach, and recovering my self a little, I ran about the Shore, wringing my Hands and beating my Head and Face, exclaiming at my Misery, and crying out, I was undone, undone, till tyr'd and faint I was forc'd to lye down on the Ground to repose, but durst not sleep for fear of being devour'd.

Some Days after this, and after I had been on board the Ship, and got all that I could out of her, yet I could not forbear getting up to the Top of a little Mountain and looking out to Sea in hopes of seeing a Ship, then fancy at a vast Distance I spy'd a Sail, please my self with the Hopes of it, and then after looking steadily till I was almost blind, lose it quite, and sit down and weep like a Child, and thus encrease my Misery by my Folly.

But having gotten over these things in some Measure, and having settled my houshold Stuff and Habitation, made me a Table and a Chair, and all as handsome about me as I could, I began to keep my Journal, of which I shall here give you the Copy (tho' in it will be told all these Particulars over again)* as long as it lasted, for having no more Ink I was forc'd to leave it off.

The JOURNAL.

September 30, 1659. I poor miserable *Robinson Crusoe*, being shipwreck'd, during a dreadful Storm, in the offing, came on Shore on this dismal unfortunate Island, which I call'd *the Island of Despair*, all the rest of the Ship's Company being drown'd, and my self almost dead.

All the rest of that Day I spent in afflicting my self at the dismal Circumstances I was brought to, *viz.* I had neither Food, House, Clothes, Weapon, or Place to fly to, and in Despair of any Relief, saw nothing but Death before me, either that I should be devour'd by wild Beasts, murther'd by Savages, or starv'd to Death for Want of Food. At the Approach of Night, I slept in a Tree for fear of wild Creatures, but slept soundly tho' it rain'd all Night.

October 1. In the Morning I saw to my great Surprise the Ship had floated with the high Tide, and was driven on Shore again much nearer the Island, which as it was some Comfort on one hand, for seeing her sit upright, and not broken to Pieces, I hop'd, if the Wind abated, I might get on board, and get some Food and Necessaries out of her for my Relief; so on the other hand, it renew'd my Grief at the Loss of my Comrades, who I imagin'd if we had all staid on board might have sav'd the Ship, or at least that they would not have been all drown'd as they were; and that had the Men been sav'd, we might perhaps have built us a Boat out of the Ruins of the Ship, to have carried us to some other Part of the World. I spent great Part of this Day in perplexing my self on these things; but at length seeing the Ship almost dry, I went upon the Sand as near as I could, and then swam on board; this Day also it continu'd raining, tho' with no Wind at all.

From the 1st of *October*, to the 24th. All these Days entirely spent in many several Voyages to get all I could out of the Ship, which I brought on Shore, every Tide of Flood, upon Rafts. Much Rain also in these Days, tho' with some Intervals of fair Weather: But, it seems, this was the rainy Season.

Oct. 20. I overset my Raft, and all the Goods I had got upon it, but being in shoal Water, and the things being chiefly heavy, I recover'd many of them when the Tide was out.

Oct. 25. It rain'd all Night and all Day, with some Gusts of Wind, during which time the Ship broke in Pieces, the Wind blowing a little harder than before, and was no more to be seen, except the Wreck of her, and that only at low Water. I spent this Day in covering and securing the Goods which I had sav'd, that the Rain might not spoil them.

Oct. 26. I walk'd about the Shore almost all Day to find out a place to fix my Habitation, greatly concern'd to secure my self from an Attack in the Night, either from wild Beasts or Men. Towards Night I fix'd upon a proper Place under a Rock, and mark'd Out a Semi-Circle for my Encampment, which I resolv'd to strengthen with a Work, Wall, or Fortification made of double Piles, lin'd within with Cables, and without with Turf.

From the 26th. to the 30th. I work'd very hard in carrying all my Goods to my new Habitation, tho' some Part of the time it rain'd exceeding hard.

The 31st. in the Morning I went out into the Island with my Gun to see for some Food, and discover the Country, when I kill'd a She-Goat, and her Kid follow'd me home, which I afterwards kill'd also because it would not feed.

November 1. I set up my Tent under a Rock, and lay there for the first Night, making it as large as I could with Stakes driven in to swing my Hammock upon.

Nov. 2. I set up all my Chests and Boards, and the Pieces of Timber which made my Rafts, and with them form'd a Fence round me, a little within the Place I had mark'd out for my Fortification.

Nov. 3. I went out with my Gun and kill'd two Fowls like Ducks, which were very good Food. In the Afternoon went to work to make me a Table.

Nov. 4. This Morning I began to order my times of Work, of going out with my Gun, time of Sleep, and time of Diversion, *viz.* Every Morning I walk'd out with my Gun for two or three Hours if it did not rain, then employ'd my self to work till about Eleven a-Clock, then eat what I had to live on, and from Twelve to Two I lay down to sleep, the Weather being excessive hot, and then in the Evening to work again: The working Part of this Day and of the next were wholly employ'd in making my Table, for I was yet but a very sorry Workman, tho' Time and Necessity made me a compleat natural Mechanick soon after, as I believe it would do any one else.

Nov. 5. This Day went abroad with my Gun and my Dog, and kill'd a wild Cat, her Skin pretty soft, but her Flesh good for nothing: Every Creature I kill'd I took off the Skins and preserv'd them: Coming back by the Sea Shore, I saw many Sorts of Sea Fowls which I did not understand, but was surpris'd and almost frighted with two or three Seals,* which, while I was gazing at, not well knowing what they were, got into the Sea and escap'd me for that time.

Nov. 6. After my Morning Walk I went to work with my Table again, and finish'd it, tho' not to my liking; nor was it long before I learn'd to mend it.

Nov. 7. Now it began to be settled fair Weather. The 7th, 8th, 9th, 10th, and Part of the 12th. (for the 11th was Sunday) I took wholly up to make me a Chair, and with much ado brought it to a tolerable Shape, but never to please me, and even in the making I pull'd it in Pieces several times. *Note*, I soon neglected my keeping Sundays, for omitting my Mark for them on my Post, I forgot which was which.

Nov. 13. This Day it rain'd, which refresh'd me exceedingly, and cool'd the Earth, but it was accompany'd with terrible Thunder and Lightning, which frighted me dreadfully for fear of my Powder; as soon as it was over, I resolv'd to separate my Stock of Powder into as many little Parcels as possible, that it might not be in Danger.

Nov. 14, 15, 16. These three Days I spent in making little square Chests or Boxes, which might hold about a Pound or two Pound, at most, of Powder, and so putting the Powder in, I stow'd it in Places as secure and remote from one another as possible. On one of these three Days I kill'd a large Bird that was good to eat, but I know not what to call it.

Nov. 17. This Day I began to dig behind my Tent into the Rock to make room for my farther Conveniency: *Note*, Two Things I wanted exceedingly for this Work, *viz.* A Pick-axe, a Shovel, and a Wheel-barrow or Basket, so I desisted from my Work, and began to consider how to supply that Want and make me some Tools; as for a Pick-axe, I made use of the Iron Crows, which were proper enough, tho' heavy; but the next thing was a Shovel or Spade, this was so absolutely necessary, that indeed I could do nothing effectually without it, but what kind of one to make I knew not.

Nov. 18. The next Day in searching the Woods I found a Tree of that Wood, or like it, which, in the *Brasils* they call the *Iron Tree*,* for its exceeding Hardness, of this, with great Labour and almost spoiling my Axe, I cut a Piece, and brought it home too with Difficulty enough, for it was exceeding heavy.

The excessive Hardness of the Wood, and having no other Way, made me a long while upon this Machine, for I work'd it effectually by little and little into the Form of a Shovel or Spade, the Handle exactly shap'd like ours in *England*, only that the broad Part having no Iron shod upon it at Bottom, it would not last me so long, however it serv'd well enough for the uses which I had occasion to put it to; but never was a Shovel, I believe, made after that Fashion, or so long a making.

I was still deficient, for I wanted a Basket or a Wheel-barrow, a Basket I could not make by any Means, having no such things as Twigs that would bend to make Wicker Ware, at least none yet found out; and as to a Wheel-barrow, I fancy'd I could make all but the Wheel, but that I had no Notion of, neither did I know how to go about it; besides I had no possible Way to make the Iron Gudgeons for the Spindle or Axis of the Wheel to run in, so I gave it over, and so for carrying away the Earth which I dug out of the Cave, I made me a Thing like a Hodd, which the Labourers carry Morter in, when they serve the Bricklayers.

This was not so difficult to me as the making the Shovel; and yet this, and the Shovel, and the Attempt which I made in vain, to make a Wheel-Barrow, took me up no less than four Days, I mean always, excepting my Morning Walk with my Gun, which I seldom fail'd, and very seldom fail'd also bringing Home something fit to eat.

Nov. 23. My other Work having now stood still, because of my making these Tools; when they were finish'd, I went on, and working every Day, as my Strength and Time allow'd, I spent eighteen Days entirely in widening and deepening my Cave, that it might hold my Goods commodiously.

Note, During all this Time, I work'd to make this Room or Cave spacious enough to accommodate me as a Warehouse or Magazin, a Kitchen, a Dining-room, and a Cellar; as for my Lodging, I kept to the Tent, except that some Times in the wet Season of the Year, it rain'd so hard, that I could not keep my self dry, which caused me afterwards to cover all my Place within my Pale with long Poles in the Form of Rafters leaning against the Rock, and load them with Flaggs and large Leaves of Trees like a Thatch.

December 10th, I began now to think my Cave or Vault finished, when on a Sudden, (it seems I had made it too large) a great quantity of Earth fell down from the Top and one Side, so much, that in short it frighted me, and not without Reason too; for if I had been under it I had never wanted a Grave-Digger: Upon this Disaster I had a great deal of Work to do over again; for I had the loose Earth to carry out; and which was of more Importance, I had the Seiling to prop up, so that I might be sure no more would come down.

Dec. 11. This Day I went to Work with it accordingly, and got two Shores or Posts pitch'd upright to the Top, with two Pieces of Boards a-cross over each Post, this I finish'd the next Day; and setting more Posts up with Boards, in about a Week more I had the Roof secur'd; and the Posts standing in Rows, serv'd me for Partitions to part of my House.

Dec. 17. From this Day to the Twentieth I plac'd Shelves, and knock'd up Nails on the Posts to hang every Thing up that could be hung up, and now I began to be in some Order within Doors.

Dec. 20. Now I carry'd every Thing into the Cave, and began to furnish my House, and set up some Pieces of Boards, like a Dresser, to order my Victuals upon, but Boards began to be very scarce with me; also I made me another Table.

Dec. 24. Much Rain all Night and all Day, no stirring out.

Dec. 25. Rain all Day.

Dec. 26. No Rain, and the Earth much cooler than before, and pleasanter.

Dec. 27. Kill'd a young Goat, and lam'd another so as that I catch'd it, and led it Home in a String; when I had it Home, I bound and splinter'd up its Leg which was broke, *N.B.* I took such Care of it, that it liv'd, and the Leg grew well, and as strong as ever; but by my nursing it so long it grew tame, and fed upon the little Green at my Door, and would not go away: This was the first Time that I entertain'd a Thought of breeding up some tame Creatures, that I might have Food when my Powder and Shot was all spent.

Dec. 28, 29, 30. Great Heats and no Breeze; so that there was no Stirring abroad, except in the Evening for Food; this Time I spent in putting all my Things in Order within Doors.

January 1. Very hot still, but I went abroad early and late with my Gun, and lay still in the Middle of the Day; this Evening going farther into the Valleys which lay towards the Center of the Island, I found there was plenty of Goats, tho' exceeding shy and hard to come at, however I resolv'd to try if I could not bring my Dog to hunt them down.

Jan. 2. Accordingly, the next Day, I went out with my Dog, and set him upon the Goats; but I was mistaken, for they all fac'd about upon the Dog, and he knew his Danger too well, for he would not come near them.

Jan. 3. I began my Fence or Wall; which being still jealous of my being attack'd by some Body, I resolv'd to make very thick and strong.

N.B. *This Wall being describ'd before, I purposely omit what was said in the Journal; it is sufficient to observe, that I was no less Time than from the 3d of* January *to the* 14th *of* April, *working, finishing, and perfecting this Wall, tho' it was no more than about* 24 *Yards in Length, being a half Circle from one Place in the Rock to another Place about eight Yards from it, the Door of the Cave being in the Center behind it.*

All this Time I work'd very hard, the Rains hindering me many Days, nay sometimes Weeks together; but I thought I should never be perfectly secure 'till this Wall was finish'd; and it is scarce credible what inexpressible Labour every Thing was done with, especially the bringing Piles out of the Woods, and driving them into the Ground, for I made them much bigger than I need to have done.

When this Wall was finished, and the Out-side double fenc'd with a Turff-Wall rais'd up close to it, I perswaded my self, that if any People were to come on Shore there, they would not perceive any Thing like a Habitation; and it was very well I did so, as may be observ'd hereafter upon a very remarkable Occasion.*

During this Time, I made my Rounds in the Woods for Game every Day when the Rain admitted me, and made frequent Discoveries in these Walks of something or other to my Advantage; particularly I found a Kind of wild Pidgeons, who built not as Wood Pidgeons in a Tree, but rather as House Pidgeons, in the Holes of the Rocks; and taking some young ones, I endeavoured to breed them up tame, and did so; but when they grew older they flew all away, which perhaps was at first for Want of feeding them, for I had nothing to give them; however I frequently found their Nests, and got their young ones, which were very good Meat.

And now, in the managing my houshold Affairs, I found my self wanting in many Things, which I thought at first it was impossible for me to make, as indeed as to some of them it was; *for Instance*, I could never make a Cask to be hooped, I had a small Runlet or two, *as I observed before*, but I cou'd never arrive to the Capacity of making one by them, tho' I spent many Weeks about it; I could neither put in the Heads, or joint the Staves so true to one another, as to make them hold Water, so I gave that also over.

In the next Place, I was at a great Loss for Candle; so that as soon as ever it was dark, which was generally by Seven-a-Clock, I was oblig'd to go to Bed: I remembred the Lump of Bees-wax with which I made Candles in my *African* Adventure, but I had none of that now; the only Remedy I had was, that when I had kill'd a Goat, I sav'd the Tallow, and with a little Dish made of Clay, which I bak'd in the Sun, to which I added a Wick of some Oakum, I made me a Lamp; and this gave me Light, tho' not a clear steady Light like a Candle; in the Middle of all my Labours it happen'd, that rumaging my Things, I found a little Bag, which, as I hinted before, had been fill'd with Corn for the feeding of Poultry, not for this Voyage, but before, as I suppose, when the Ship came from *Lisbon*; what little Remainder of Corn had been in the Bag, was all devour'd with the Rats, and I saw nothing in the Bag but Husks and Dust; and being willing to have the Bag for some other Use, I think it was to put Powder in, when I divided it for Fear of the Lightning, or some such Use, I shook the Husks of Corn out of it on one Side of my Fortification under the Rock.

It was a little before the great Rains, just now mention'd, that I threw this Stuff away, taking no Notice of any Thing, and not so much as remembring that I had thrown any Thing there; when about a Month after, or thereabout, I saw some few Stalks of something green, shooting out of the Ground, which I fancy'd might be some Plant I had not seen, but I was surpriz'd and perfectly astonish'd, when, after a little longer Time, I saw about ten or twelve Ears come out, which were perfect green Barley of the same Kind as our *European*, nay, as our *English* Barley.

It is impossible to express the Astonishment and Confusion of my Thoughts on this Occasion; I had hitherto acted upon no religious Foundation at all, indeed I had very few Notions of Religion in my Head, or had* entertain'd any Sense of any Thing that had befallen me, otherwise than as a Chance, or, as we lightly say, what pleases God; without so much as enquiring into the End of Providence in these Things, or his Order in governing Events in the World: But after I saw Barley grow there, in a Climate which I know was not proper for Corn, and especially that I knew not how it came there, it startl'd me strangely, and I began to suggest, that God had miraculously caus'd this Grain to grow without any Help of Seed sown, and that it was so directed purely for my Sustenance, on that wild miserable Place.

This touch'd my Heart a little, and brought Tears out of my Eyes, and I began to bless my self, that such a Prodigy of Nature should happen upon my Account; and this was the more strange to me, because I saw near it still all along by the Side of the Rock, some other straggling Stalks, which prov'd to be Stalks of Ryce, and which I knew, because I had seen it grow in *Africa* when I was ashore there.

I not only thought these the pure Productions of Providence for my Support, but not doubting, but that there was more in the Place, I went all over that Part of the Island, where I had been before, peering in every Corner, and under every Rock, to see for more of it, but I could not find any; at last it occur'd to my Thoughts, that I had shook a Bag of Chickens Meat out in that Place, and then the Wonder began to cease; and I must confess, my religious Thankfulness to God's Providence began to abate too upon the Discovering that all this was nothing but what was common; tho' I ought to have been as thankful for so strange and unforseen Providence, as if it had been miraculous; for it was really the Work of Providence as to me, that should order or appoint, that 10 or 12 Grains of Corn should remain unspoil'd, (when the Rats had destroy'd all the rest,) as if it had been dropt from Heaven; as also, that I should throw it out in that particular Place, where it being in the Shade of a high Rock, it sprang up immediately; whereas, if I had thrown it anywhere else, at that Time, it had been burnt up and destroy'd.

I carefully sav'd the Ears of this Corn you may be sure in their Season, which was about the End of *June*; and laying up every Corn, I resolv'd to sow them all again, hoping in Time to have some Quantity sufficient to supply me with Bread; But it was not till the 4th Year that I could allow my self the least Grain of this Corn to eat, and even then but sparingly, as I shall say afterwards in its Order; for I lost all that I sow'd the first Season, by not observing the proper Time; for I sow'd it just before the dry Season, so that it never came up at all, at least, not as it would ha' done: Of which in its Place.*

Besides this Barley, there was, as above, 20 or 30 Stalks of Ryce, which I preserv'd with the same Care, and whose Use was of the same Kind or to the same Purpose, (*viz.*) to make me Bread, or rather Food; for I found Ways to cook it up without baking, tho' I did that also after some Time. But to return to my Journal,

I work'd excessive hard these three or four Months to get my Wall done; and the 14th of *April* I closed it up, contriving to go into it, not by a Door, but over the Wall by a Ladder, that there might be no Sign in the Out-side of my Habitation.

April 16. I finish'd the Ladder, so I went up with the Ladder to the Top, and then pull'd it up after me, and let it down in the In-side: This was a compleat Enclosure to me; for within I had Room enough, and nothing could come at me from without, unless it could first mount my Wall.

The very next Day after this Wall was finish'd, I had almost had all my Labour overthrown at once, and my self kill'd; the Case was thus, As I was busy in the Inside of it, behind my Tent, just in the Entrance into my Cave, I was terribly frighted with a most dreadful surprising Thing indeed; for all on a sudden I found the Earth come crumbling down from the Roof of my Cave, and from the Edge of the Hill over my Head, and two of the Posts I had set up in the Cave crack'd in a frightful Manner; I was heartily scar'd, but thought nothing* of what was really the Cause, only thinking that the Top of my Cave was falling in, as some of it had done before; and for Fear I shou'd be bury'd in it, I run foreward to my Ladder, and not think-ing my self safe there neither, I got over my Wall for Fear of the Pieces of the Hill which I expected might roll down upon me: I was no sooner stepp'd down upon the firm Ground, but I plainly saw it was a terrible Earthquake, for the Ground I stood on shook three Times at about eight Minutes Distance,* with three such Shocks, as would have overturn'd the strongest Building that could be suppos'd to have stood on the Earth, and a great Piece of the Top of a Rock, which stood about half a Mile from me next the Sea, fell down with such a terrible Noise, as I never heard in all my Life, I perceiv'd also, the very Sea was put into violent Motion by it; and I believe the Shocks were stronger under the Water than on the Island.

I was so amaz'd with the Thing it self, having never felt the like, or discours'd with any one that had, that I was like one dead or stupify'd; and the Motion of the Earth made my Stomach sick like one that was toss'd at Sea; but the Noise of the falling of the Rock awak'd me as it were, and rousing me from the stupify'd Condition I was in, fill'd me with Horror, and I thought of nothing then but the Hill falling upon my Tent and all my houshold Goods, and burying all at once; and this sunk my very Soul within me a second Time.

After the third Shock was over, and I felt no more for some Time, I began to take Courage, and yet I had not Heart enough to go over my Wall again, for Fear of being buried alive, but sat still upon the Ground, greatly cast down and disconsolate, not knowing what to do: All this while I had not the least serious religious Thought, nothing but the common, *Lord ha' Mercy upon me*; and when it was over, that went away too.

While I sat thus, I found the Air over-cast, and grow cloudy, as if it would Rain; soon after that the Wind rose by little and little, so that, in less than half an Hour, it blew a most dreadful Hurricane: The Sea was all on a Sudden cover'd over with Foam and Froth, the Shore was cover'd with the Breach of the Water, the Trees were torn up by the Roots, and a terrible Storm it was; and this held about three Hours, and then began to abate, and in two Hours more it was stark calm, and began to rain very hard.

All this while I sat upon the Ground very much terrify'd and dejected, when on a sudden it came into my thoughts, that these Winds and Rain being the Consequences of the Earthquake, the Earthquake it self was spent and over, and I might venture into my Cave again: With this Thought my Spirits began to revive, and the Rain also helping to perswade me, I went in and sat down in my Tent, but the Rain was so violent, that my Tent was ready to be beaten down with it, and I was forc'd to go into my Cave, tho' very much affraid and uneasy for fear it should fall on my Head.

This violent Rain forc'd me to a new Work, *viz.* To cut a Hole thro' my new Fortification like a Sink to let the Water go out, which would else have drown'd my Cave. After I had been in my Cave some time, and found still no more Shocks of the Earthquake follow, I began to be more compos'd; and now to support my Spirits, which indeed wanted it very much, I went to my little Store and took a small Sup of Rum, which however I did then and always very sparingly, knowing I could have no more when that was gone.

It continu'd raining all that Night, and great Part of the next Day, so that I could not stir abroad, but my Mind being more compos'd, I began to think of what I had best do, concluding that if the Island was subject to these Earthquakes, there would be no living for me in a Cave, but I must consider of building me some little Hut in an open Place which I might surround with a Wall as I had done here, and so make my self secure from wild Beasts or Men; but concluded, if I staid where I was, I should certainly, one time or other, be bury'd alive.

With these Thoughts I resolv'd to remove my Tent from the Place where it stood, which was just under the hanging Precipice of the Hill, and which, if it should be shaken again, would certainly fall upon my Tent: And I spent the two next Days, being the 19th and 20th of *April*, in contriving where and how to remove my Habitation.

The fear of being swallow'd up alive, made me that I never slept in quiet, and yet the Apprehensions of lying abroad without any Fence was almost equal to it; but still when I look'd about and saw how every thing was put in order, how pleasantly conceal'd I was, and how safe from Danger, it made me very loath to remove.

In the mean time it occur'd to me that it would require a vast deal of time for me to do this, and that I must be contented to run the Venture where I was, till I had form'd a Camp for my self, and had secur'd it so as to remove to it: So with this Resolution I compos'd my self for a time, and resolv'd that I would go to work with all Speed to build me a Wall with Piles and Cables, &c. in a Circle as before, and set my Tent up in it when it was finish'd, but that I would venture to stay where I was till it was finish'd and fit to remove to. This was the 21st.

April 22. The next Morning I began to consider of Means to put this Resolve in Execution, but I was at a great loss about my Tools; I had three large Axes and abundance of Hatchets, (for we carried the Hatchets for Traffick with the *Indians*) but with much chopping and cutting knotty hard Wood, they were all full of Notches and dull, and tho' I had a Grindstone, I could not turn it and grind my Tools too, this cost me as much Thought as a Statesman would have bestow'd upon a grand Point of Politicks, or a Judge upon the Life and Death of a Man. At length I contriv'd a Wheel with a String, to turn it with my Foot, that I might have both my Hands at Liberty: *Note*, I had never seen any such thing in *England*, or at least not to take Notice how it was done, tho' since I have observ'd it is very common there; besides that, my Grindstone was very large and heavy. This Machine cost me a full Week's Work to bring it to Perfection.

April 28, 29. These two whole Days I took up in grinding my Tools, my Machine for turning my Grindstone performing very well.

April 30. Having perceiv'd my Bread had been low a great while, now I took a Survey of it, and reduc'd my self to one Bisket-cake a Day, which made my Heart very heavy.

May 1. In the Morning looking towards the Sea-side, the Tide being low, I saw something lye on the Shore bigger than ordinary, and it look'd like a Cask; when I came to it, I found a small Barrel, and two or three Pieces of the Wreck of the Ship, which were driven on Shore by the late Hurricane, and looking towards the Wreck itself, I thought it seem'd to lye higher out of the Water than it us'd to do; I examin'd the Barrel which was driven on Shore, and soon found it was a Barrel of Gunpowder, but it had taken Water, and the Powder was cak'd as hard as a Stone; however I roll'd it farther on Shore for the present, and went on upon the Sands as near as I could to the Wreck of the Ship to look for more.

When I came down to the Ship I found it strangely remov'd, The Fore-castle which lay before bury'd in Sand, was heav'd up at least Six Foot, and the Stern which was broke to Pieces and parted from the rest by the Force of the Sea soon after I had left rummaging her, was toss'd, as it were, up, and cast on one Side, and the Sand was thrown so high on that Side next her Stern, that whereas there was a great Place of Water before, so that I could not come within a Quarter of a Mile of the Wreck without swimming, I could now walk quite up to her when the Tide was out; I was surpriz'd with this at first, but soon concluded it must be done by the Earthquake, and as by this Violence the Ship was more broken open than formerly, so many Things came daily on Shore, which the Sea had loosen'd, and which the Winds and Water rolled by Degrees to the Land.

This wholly diverted my Thoughts from the Design of removing my Habitation; and I busied my self mightily that Day especially, in searching whether I could make any Way into the Ship, but I found nothing was to be expected of that Kind, for that all the In-side of the Ship was choack'd up with Sand: However, as I had learn'd not to despair of any Thing, I resolv'd to pull every Thing to Pieces that I could of the Ship, concluding, that every Thing I could get from her would be of some Use or other to me.

May 3. I began with my Saw, and cut a Piece of a Beam thro', which I thought held some of the upper Part or Quarter-Deck together, and when I had cut it thro', I clear'd away the Sand as well as I could from the Side which lay highest; but the Tide coming in, I was oblig'd to give over for that Time.

May 4. I went a fishing, but caught not one Fish that I durst eat of, till I was weary of my Sport, when just going to leave off, I caught a young Dolphin. I had made me a long Line of some Rope Yarn, but I had no Hooks, yet I frequently caught Fish enough, as much as I car'd to eat; all which I dry'd in the Sun, and eat them dry.

May 5. Work'd on the Wreck, cut another Beam asunder, and brought three great Fir Planks off from the Decks, which I ty'd together, and made swim on Shore when the Tide of Flood came on.

May 6. Work'd on the Wreck, got several Iron Bolts out of her, and other Pieces of Iron Work, work'd very hard, and came Home very much tyr'd, and had Thoughts of giving it over.

May 7. Went to the Wreck again, but with an Intent not to work, but found the Weight of the Wreck had broke itself down, the Beams being cut, that several Pieces of the Ship seem'd to lie loose, and the In-side of the Hold lay so open, that I could see into it, but almost full of Water and Sand.

May 8. Went to the Wreck, and carry'd an Iron Crow to wrench up the Deck, which lay now quite clear of the Water or Sand; I wrench'd open two Planks, and brought them on Shore also with the Tide: I left the Iron Crow in the Wreck for next Day.

May 9. Went to the Wreck, and with the Crow made Way into the Body of the Wreck, and felt several Casks, and loosen'd them with the Crow, but could not break them up; I felt also the Roll of *English* Lead, and could stir it, but it was too heavy to remove.

May 10, 11, 12, 13, 14. Went every Day to the Wreck, and got a great deal of Pieces of Timber, and Boards, or Plank, and 2 or 300 Weight of Iron.

May 15. I carry'd two Hatchets to try if I could not cut a Piece off of the Roll of Lead, by placing the Edge of one Hatchet, and driving it with the other; but as it lay about a Foot and a half in the Water, I could not make any Blow to drive the Hatchet.

May 16. It had blow'd hard in the Night, and the Wreck appear'd more broken by the Force of the Water; but I stay'd so long in the Woods to get Pidgeons for Food, that the Tide prevented me going to the Wreck that Day.

May 17. I saw some Pieces of the Wreck blown on Shore, at a great Distance, near two Miles off me, but resolv'd to see what they were, and found it was a Piece of the Head, but too heavy for me to bring away.

May 24. Every Day to this Day I work'd on the Wreck, and with hard Labour I loosen'd some Things so much with the Crow, that the first blowing Tide several Casks floated out, and two of the Seamens Chests; but the Wind blowing from the Shore, nothing came to Land that Day, but Pieces of Timber, and a Hogshead which had some *Brazil* Pork in it, but the Salt-water and the Sand had spoil'd it.

I continu'd this Work every Day to the 15th of *June*, except the Time necessary to get Food, which I always appointed, during this Part of my Employment, to be when the Tide was up, that I might be ready when it was ebb'd out, and by this Time I had gotten Timber, and Plank, and Iron-Work enough, to have builded a good Boat, if I had known how; and also, I got at several Times, and in several Pieces, near 100 Weight of the Sheet-Lead.

June 16. Going down to the Sea-side, I found a large Tortoise or Turtle;* this was the first I had seen, which it seems was only my Misfortune, not any Defect of the Place, or Scarcity; for had I happen'd to be on the other Side of the Island, I might have had Hundreds of them every Day, as I found afterwards; but perhaps had paid dear enough for them.

June 17. I spent in cooking the Turtle; I found in her threescore Eggs; and her Flesh was to me at that Time the most savoury and pleasant that ever I tasted in my Life, having had no Flesh, but of Goats and Fowls, since I landed in this horrid Place.

June 18. Rain'd all Day, and I stay'd within. I thought at this Time the Rain felt Cold, and I was something chilly, which I knew was not usual in that Latitude.

June 19. Very ill, and shivering, as if the Weather had been cold.

June 20. No Rest all Night, violent Pains in my Head, and feaverish.

June 21. Very ill, frighted almost to Death with the Apprehensions of my sad Condition, to be sick, and no Help: Pray'd to GOD for the first Time since the Storm off of *Hull*, but scarce knew what I said, or why; my Thoughts being all confused.

June 22. A little better, but under dreadful Apprehensions of Sickness.

June 23. Very bad again, cold and shivering, and then a violent Head-ach.

June 24. Much better.

June 25. An Ague very violent; the Fit held me seven Hours, cold Fit and hot, with faint Sweats after it.

June 26. Better; and having no Victuals to eat, took my Gun, but found my self very weak; however I kill'd a She-Goat, and with much Difficulty got it Home, and broil'd some of it, and eat; I wou'd fain have stew'd it, and made some Broath, but had no Pot.

June 27. The Ague again so violent, that I lay a-Bed all Day, and neither eat or drank. I was ready to perish for Thirst, but so weak, I had not Strength to stand up, or to get my self any Water to drink: Pray'd to God again, but was light-headed, and when I was not, I was so ignorant, that I knew not what to say; only I lay and cry'd, *Lord look upon me, Lord pity me, Lord have Mercy upon me*: I suppose I did nothing else for two or three Hours, till the Fit wearing off, I fell asleep, and did not wake till far in the Night; when I wak'd, I found my self much refresh'd, but weak, and exceeding thirsty: However, as I had no Water in my whole Habitation, I was forc'd to lie till Morning, and went to sleep again: In this second Sleep, I had this terrible Dream.

I thought, that I was sitting on the Ground on the Out-side of my Wall, where I sat when the Storm blew after the Earthquake, and that I saw a Man descend from a great black Cloud, in a bright Flame of Fire, and light upon the Ground: He was all over as bright as a Flame, so that I could but just bear to look towards him; his Countenance was most inexpressibly dreadful, impossible for Words to describe; when he stepp'd upon the Ground with his Feet, I thought the Earth trembl'd, just as it had done before in the Earthquake, and all the Air look'd, to my Apprehension, as if it had been fill'd with Flashes of Fire.

He was no sooner landed upon the Earth, but he moved forward towards me, with a long Spear or Weapon in his Hand, to kill me; and when he came to a rising Ground, at some Distance, he spoke to me, or I heard a Voice so terrible, that it is impossible to express the Terror of it; all that I can say, I understood, was this, *Seeing all these Things have not brought thee to Repentance, now thou shalt die*: At which Words, I thought he lifted up the Spear that was in his Hand, to kill me.

No one, that shall ever read this Account, will expect that I should be able to describe the Horrors of my Soul at this terrible Vision, I mean, that even while it was a Dream, I even dreamed of those Horrors; nor is it any more possible to describe the Impression that remain'd upon my Mind when I awak'd and found it was but a Dream.

I had alas! no divine Knowledge; what I had received by the good Instruction of my Father was then worn out by an uninterrupted Series, for 8 Years, of Seafaring Wickedness, and a constant Conversation with nothing but such as were like my self, wicked and prophane to the last Degree: I do not remember that I had in all that Time one Thought that so much as tended either to looking upwards toward God, or inwards towards a Reflection upon my own Ways: But a certain Stupidity of Soul, without Desire of Good, or Conscience of Evil,* had entirely overwhelm'd me, and I was all that the most hardned, unthinking, wicked Creature among our common Sailors, can be supposed to be, not having the least Sense, either of the Fear of God in Danger, or of Thankfulness to God in Deliverances.

In the relating what is already past of my Story, this will be the more easily believ'd, when I shall add, that thro' all the Variety of Miseries that had to this Day befallen me, I never had so much as one Thought of it being the Hand of God, or that it was a just Punishment for my Sin; my rebellious Behaviour against my Father, or my present Sins which were great; or so much as a Punishment for the general Course of my wicked Life. When I was on the desperate Expedition on the desart Shores of *Africa*, I never had so much as one Thought of what would become of me; or one Wish to God to direct me whether I should go, or to keep me from the Danger which apparently surrounded me, as well from voracious Creatures as cruel Savages: But I was meerly thoughtless of a God,* or a Providence; acted like a meer Brute from the Principles of Nature, and by the Dictates of common Sense only, and indeed hardly that.

When I was deliver'd and taken up at Sea by the *Portugal* Captain, well us'd, and dealt justly and honourably with, as well as charitably, I had not the least Thankfulness on my Thoughts: When again I was shipwreck'd, ruin'd, and in Danger of drowning on this Island, I was as far from Remorse, or looking on it as a Judgment; I only said to my self often, that I was *an unfortunate Dog*, and born to be always miserable.

It is true, when I got on Shore first here, and found all my Ship's Crew drown'd, and my self spar'd, I was surpriz'd with a Kind of Extasie, and some Transports of Soul, which, had the Grace of God assisted, might have come up to true Thankfulness; but it ended where it begun, in a meer common Flight of Joy, or as I may say, *being glad I was alive*, without the least Reflection upon the distinguishing Goodness of the Hand which had preserv'd me, and had singled me out to be preserv'd, when all the rest were destroy'd; or an Enquiry why Providence had been thus merciful to me; even just the same common Sort of Joy which Seamen generally have after they are got safe ashore from a Ship-wreck, which they drown all in the next Bowl of Punch, and forget almost as soon as it is over, and all the rest of my Life was like it.

Even when I was afterwards, on due Consideration, made sensible of my Condition, how I was cast on this dreadful Place, out of the Reach of humane Kind, out of all Hope of Relief, or Prospect of Redemption, as soon as I saw but a Prospect of living, and that I should not starve and perish for Hunger, all the Sense of my Affliction wore off, and I begun to be very easy, apply'd my self to the Works proper for my Preservation and Supply, and was far enough from being afflicted at my Condition, as a Judgment from Heaven, or as the Hand of God against me; these were Thoughts which very seldom enter'd into my Head.

The growing up of the Corn, as is hinted in my Journal, had at first some little Influence upon me, and began to affect me with Seriousness, as long as I thought it had something miraculous in it; but as soon as ever that Part of the Thought was remov'd, all the Impression which was rais'd from it, wore off also, as I have noted already.

Even the Earthquake, tho' nothing could be more terrible in its Nature, or more immediately directing to the invisible Power which alone directs such Things, yet no sooner was the first Fright over, but the Impression it had made went off also. I had no more Sense of God or his Judgments, much less of the present Affliction of my Circumstances being from his Hand, than if I had been in the most prosperous Condition of Life.

But now when I began to be sick, and a leisurely View of the Miseries of Death came to place itself before me; when my Spirits began to sink under the Burthen of a strong Distemper, and Nature was exhausted with the Violence of the Feaver; Conscience that had slept so long, begun to awake, and I began to reproach my self with my past Life, in which I had so evidently, by uncommon

Wickedness, provok'd the Justice of God to lay me under uncommon Strokes, and to deal with me in so vindictive a Manner.

These Reflections oppress'd me for the second or third Day of my Distemper, and in the Violence, as well of the Feaver, as of the dreadful Reproaches of my Conscience, extorted some Words from me, like praying to God, tho' I cannot say they were either a Prayer attended with Desires or with Hopes; it was rather the Voice of meer Fright and Distress; my Thoughts were confus'd, the Convictions great upon my Mind, and the Horror of dying in such a miserable Condition rais'd Vapours into my Head with the meer Apprehensions; and in these Hurries of my Soul, I know not what my Tongue might express: but it was rather Exclamation, such as, Lord! what a miserable Creature am I? If I should be sick, I shall certainly die for Want of Help, and what will become of me! Then the Tears burst out of my Eyes, and I could say no more for a good while.

In this Interval, the good Advice of my Father came to my Mind, and presently his Prediction which I mention'd at the Beginning of this Story, *viz. That if I did take this foolish Step, God would not bless me, and I would have Leisure hereafter to reflect upon having neglected his Counsel, when there might be none to assist in my Recovery*.* Now, said I aloud, My dear Father's Words are come to pass: God's Justice has overtaken me, and I have none to help or hear me: I rejected the Voice of Providence, which had mercifully put me in a Posture or Station of Life, wherein I might have been happy and easy; but I would neither see it my self, or learn to know the Blessing of it from my Parents; I left them to mourn over my Folly, and now I am left to mourn under the Consequences of it: I refus'd their Help and Assistance who wou'd have lifted me into the World, and wou'd have made every Thing easy to me, and now I have Difficulties to struggle with, too great for even Nature itself to support, and no Assistance, no Help, no Comfort, no Advice; then I cry'd out, *Lord be my Help, for I am in great Distress*.

This was the first Prayer, if I may call it so, that I had made for many Years: But I return to my Journal.

June 28. Having been somewhat refresh'd with the Sleep I had had, and the Fit being entirely off, I got up; and tho' the Fright and Terror of my Dream was very great, yet I consider'd, that the Fit of the Ague wou'd return again the next Day, and now was my Time to get something to refresh and support my self when I should be ill;

and the first Thing I did, I fill'd a large square Case Bottle with Water, and set it upon my Table, in Reach of my Bed; and to take off the chill or aguish Disposition of the Water, I put about a Quarter of a Pint of Rum into it, and mix'd them together; then I got me a Piece of the Goat's Flesh, and broil'd it on the Coals, but could eat very little; I walk'd about, but was very weak, and withal very sad and heavy-hearted in the Sense of my miserable Condition; dreading the Return of my Distemper the next Day; at Night I made my Supper of three of the Turtle's Eggs, which I roasted in the Ashes, and eat, as we call it, in the Shell; and this was the first Bit of Meat I had ever ask'd God's Blessing to, even as I cou'd remember, in my whole Life.

After I had eaten, I try'd to walk, but found my self so weak, that I cou'd hardly carry the Gun, (for I never went out without that) so I went but a little Way, and sat down upon the Ground, looking out upon the Sea, which was just before me, and very calm and smooth: As I sat here, some such Thoughts as these occurred to me.

What is this Earth and Sea of which I have seen so much, whence is it produc'd, and what am I, and all the other Creatures, wild and tame, humane and brutal, whence are we?

Sure we are all made by some secret Power, who form'd the Earth and Sea, the Air and Sky; and who is that?

Then it follow'd most naturally, It is God that has made it all: Well, but then it came on strangely, if God has made all these Things, He guides and governs them all, and all Things that concern them; for the Power that could make all Things, must certainly have Power to guide and direct them.

If so, nothing can happen in the great Circuit of his Works, either without his Knowledge or Appointment.

And if nothing happens without his Knowledge, he knows that I am here, and am in this dreadful Condition; and if nothing happens without his Appointment, he has appointed all this to befal me.

Nothing occurr'd to my Thought to contradict any of these Conclusions; and therefore it rested upon me with the greater Force, that it must needs be, that God had appointed all this to befal me; that I was brought to this miserable Circumstance by his Direction, he having the sole Power, not of me only, but of every Thing that happen'd in the World. Immediately it follow'd,

Why has God done this to me? What have I done to be thus us'd?

My Conscience presently check'd me in that Enquiry, as if I had blasphem'd, and methought it spoke to me like a Voice; *WRETCH!* *dost thou ask what thou hast done!* look back upon a dreadful misspent Life, and ask thy self *what thou hast not done?* ask, Why is it *that thou wert not long ago destroy'd?* Why *wert thou not drown'd in* Yarmouth Roads? *Kill'd in the Fight when the Ship was taken by* the Sallee Man of War? *Devour'd by the wild Beasts on the* Coast of Africa? Or, *Drown'd HERE, when all the Crew perish'd but thy self?* Dost thou ask, *What have I done?*

I was struck dumb with these Reflections, as one astonish'd, and had not a Word to say, no not to answer to my self, but rise up pensive and sad, walk'd back to my Retreat, and went up over my Wall, as if I had been going to Bed, but my Thoughts were sadly disturb'd, and I had no Inclination to Sleep; so I sat down in my Chair, and lighted my Lamp, for it began to be dark: Now as the Apprehension of the Return of my Distemper terrify'd me very much, it occurr'd to my Thought, that the *Brasilians* take no Physick but their Tobacco, for almost all Distempers; and I had a Piece of a Roll of Tobacco in one of the Chests, which was quite cur'd, and some also that was green and not quite cur'd.

I went, directed by Heaven no doubt; for in this Chest I found a Cure, both for Soul and Body, I open'd the Chest, and found what I look'd for, *viz.* the Tobacco; and as the few Books, I had sav'd, lay there too, I took out one of the Bibles which I mention'd before, and which to this Time I had not found Leisure, or so much as Inclination to look into; I say, I took it out, and brought both that and the Tobacco with me to the Table.

What Use to make of the Tobacco,* I knew not, as to my Distemper, or whether it was good for it or no; but I try'd several Experiments with it, as if I was resolv'd it should hit one Way or other: I first took a Piece of a Leaf, and chew'd it in my Mouth, which indeed at first almost stupify'd my Brain, the Tobacco being green and strong, and that I had not been much us'd to it; then I took some and steeped it an Hour or two in some Rum, and resolv'd to take a Dose of it when I lay down; and lastly, I burnt some upon a Pan of Coals, and held my Nose close over the Smoke of it as long as I could bear it, as well for the Heat as almost for Suffocation.

In the Interval of this Operation, I took up the Bible and began to read, but my Head was too much disturb'd with the Tobacco to bear reading, at least that Time; only having open'd the Book casually, the first Words that occurr'd to me were these, *Call on me in the Day of Trouble, and I will deliver, and thou shalt glorify me.**

The Words were very apt to my Case, and made some Impression upon my Thoughts at the Time of reading them, tho' not so much as they did afterwards; for as for being deliver'd, the Word had no Sound, *as I may say*, to me; the Thing was so remote, so impossible in my Apprehension of Things, that I began to say as the Children of *Israel* did, when they were promis'd Flesh to eat, *Can God spread a Table in the Wilderness?** so I began to say, Can God himself deliver me from this Place? and as it was not for many Years that any Hope appear'd, this prevail'd very often upon my Thoughts: But however, the Words made a great Impression upon me, and I mused upon them very often. It grew now late, and the Tobacco had, as I said, doz'd my Head so much, that I inclin'd to sleep; so I left my Lamp burning in the Cave, least I should want any Thing in the Night, and went to Bed; but before I lay down, I did what I never had done in all my Life, I kneel'd down and pray'd to God to fulfil the Promise to me, that if I call'd upon him in the Day of Trouble, he would deliver me; after my broken and imperfect Prayer was over, I drunk the Rum in which I had steep'd the Tobacco, which was so strong and rank of the Tobacco, that indeed I could scarce get it down; immediately upon this I went to Bed, I found presently it flew up in my Head violently, but I fell into a sound Sleep, and wak'd no more 'till by the Sun it must necessarily be near Three a-Clock in the Afternoon the next Day; nay, to this Hour, I'm partly of the Opinion, that I slept all the next Day and Night, and 'till almost Three that Day after; for otherwise I knew not how I should lose a Day out of my Reckoning in the Days of the Week, as it appear'd some Years after I had done: for if I had lost it by crossing and re-crossing the Line,* I should have lost more than one Day: But certainly I lost a Day in my Accompt, and never knew which Way.

Be that however one Way or th' other, when I awak'd I found my self exceedingly refresh'd, and my Spirits lively and chearful; when I got up, I was stronger than I was the Day before, and my Stomach better, for I was hungry; and in short, I had no Fit the next Day, but continu'd much alter'd for the better; this was the 29th.

The 30th was my well Day of Course, and I went abroad with my Gun, but did not care to travel too far, I kill'd a Sea Fowl or two, something like a brand Goose,* and brought them Home, but was not very forward to eat them; so I ate some more of the Turtle's Eggs, which were very good: This Evening I renew'd the Medicine which I had suppos'd did me good the Day before, *viz.* the Tobacco steep'd in Rum, only I did not take so much as before, nor did I chew any of the Leaf, or hold my Head over the Smoke; however, I was not so well the next Day, which was the first of *July*, as I hop'd I shou'd have been; for I had a little Spice of the cold Fit, but it was not much.

July 2. I renew'd the Medicine all the three Ways, and doz'd my self with it as at first; and doubled the Quantity which I drank.

3. I miss'd the Fit for good and all, tho' I did not recover my full Strength for some Weeks after; while I was thus gathering Strength, my Thoughts run exceedingly upon this Scripture, *I will deliver thee*, and the Impossibility of my Deliverance lay much upon my Mind in Barr of* my ever expecting it: But as I was discouraging my self with such Thoughts, it occurr'd to my Mind, that I pored so much upon my Deliverance from the main Affliction, that I disregarded the Deliverance I had receiv'd; and I was, as it were, made to ask my self such Questions as these, *viz.* Have I not been deliver'd, and wonderfully too, from Sickness? from the most distress'd Condition that could be, and that was so frightful to me, and what Notice I had taken of it? Had I done my Part? *God had deliver'd me, but I had not glorify'd him*; that is to say, I had not own'd and been thankful for that as a Deliverance, and how cou'd I expect greater Deliverance?

This touch'd my Heart very much, and immediately I kneel'd down and gave God Thanks aloud, for my Recovery from my Sickness.

July 4. In the Morning I took the Bible, and beginning at the New Testament, I began seriously to read it, and impos'd upon my self to read a while every Morning and every Night, not tying my self to the Number of Chapters, but as long as my Thoughts shou'd engage me: It was not long after I set seriously to this Work, but* I found my Heart more deeply and sincerely affected with the Wickedness of my past Life: The Impression of my Dream reviv'd, and the Words, *All these Things have not brought thee to Repentance*, ran seriously in my Thought: I was earnestly begging of God to give me Repentance, when it happen'd providentially the very Day that reading the Scripture, I came to these Words, *He is exalted a Prince and a Saviour, to give Repentance, and to give Remission:** I threw down the Book, and with my Heart as well as my Hands lifted up to Heaven, in a Kind of

Extasy of Joy, I cry'd out aloud, *Jesus, thou Son of* David, *Jesus, thou exalted Prince and Saviour, give me Repentance!*

This was the first Time that I could say, in the true Sense of the Words, that I pray'd in all my Life; for now I pray'd with a Sense of my Condition, and with a true Scripture View of Hope founded on the Encouragement of the Word of God; and from this Time, I may say, I began to have Hope that God would hear me.

Now I began to construe the Words mentioned above, *Call on me, and I will deliver you*, in a different Sense from what I had ever done before; for then I had no Notion of any thing being call'd Deliverance, but my being deliver'd from the Captivity I was in; for tho' I was indeed at large in the Place, yet the Island was certainly a Prison to me,* and that in the worst Sense in the World; but now I learn'd to take it in another Sense: Now I look'd back upon my past Life with such Horrour, and my Sins appear'd so dreadful, that my Soul sought nothing of God, but Deliverance from the Load of Guilt that bore down all my Comfort: As for my solitary Life it was nothing; I did not so much as pray to be deliver'd from it, or think of it; It was all of no Consideration in Comparison to this: And I add this Part here, to hint to whoever shall read it, that whenever they come to a true Sense of things, they will find Deliverance from Sin a much greater Blessing, than Deliverance from Affliction.

But leaving this Part, I return to my Journal.

My Condition began now to be, tho' not less miserable as to my Way of living, yet much easier to my Mind; and my Thoughts being directed, by a constant reading the Scripture, and praying to God, to things of a higher Nature: I had a great deal of Comfort within, which till now I knew nothing of; also, as my Health and Strength returned, I bestirr'd my self to furnish my self with every thing that I wanted, and make my Way of living as regular as I could.

From the 4th of *July* to the 14th, I was chiefly employ'd in walking about with my Gun in my Hand, a little and a little, at a Time, as a Man that was gathering up his Strength after a Fit of Sickness: For it is hardly to be imagin'd, how low I was, and to what Weakness I was reduc'd. The Application which I made Use of was perfectly new, and perhaps what had never cur'd an Ague before, neither can I recommend it to any one to practise, by this Experiment; and tho' it did carry off the Fit, yet it rather contributed to weakening me; for I had frequent Convulsions in my Nerves and Limbs for some Time.

I learn'd from it also this in particular, that being abroad in the rainy Season was the most pernicious thing to my Health that could be, especially in those Rains which came attended with Storms and Hurricanes of Wind; for as the Rain which came in the dry Season was always most accompany'd with such Storms, so I found that Rain was much more dangerous than the Rain which fell in *September* and *October*.*

I had been now in this unhappy Island above 10 Months, all Possibility of Deliverance from this Condition, seem'd to be entirely taken from me; and I firmly believed, that no humane Shape had ever set Foot upon that Place:* Having now secur'd my Habitation, as I thought, fully to my Mind, I had a great Desire to make a more perfect Discovery of the Island, and to see what other Productions I might find, which I yet knew nothing of.

It was the 15th of *July* that I began to take a more particular Survey of the Island it self: I went up the Creek first, where, as I hinted, I brought my Rafts on Shore; I found after I came about two Miles up, that the Tide did not flow any higher, and that it was no more than a little Brook of running Water, and very fresh and good; but this being the dry Season, there was hardly any Water in some Parts of it, at least, not enough to run in any Stream, so as it could be perceiv'd.

On the Bank of this Brook I found many pleasant *Savana's*, or Meadows; plain, smooth, and cover'd with Grass; and on the rising Parts of them next to the higher Grounds, where the Water, as it might be supposed, never overflow'd, I found a great deal of Tobacco, green, and growing to a great and very strong Stalk; there were divers other Plants which I had no Notion of, or Understanding about, and might perhaps have Vertues of their own, which I could not find out.

I searched for the *Cassava* Root,* which the *Indians* in all that Climate make their Bread of, but I could find none. I saw large Plants of Alloes,* but did not then understand them. I saw several Sugar Canes, but wild, and for want of Cultivation, imperfect. I contented my self with these Discoveries for this Time, and came back musing with my self what Course I might take to know the Vertue and Goodness of any of the Fruits or Plants which I should discover; but could bring it to no Conclusion; for in short, I had made so little Observation while I was in the *Brasils*, that I knew little of the Plants in the Field, at least very little that might serve me to any Purpose now in my Distress.

The next Day, the 16th, I went up the same Way again, and after going something farther than I had gone the Day before, I found the Brook, and the *Savana's* began to cease, and the Country became more woody than before; in this Part I found different Fruits, and particularly I found Mellons upon the Ground in great Abundance, and Grapes upon the Trees; the Vines had spread indeed over the Trees, and the Clusters of Grapes were just now in their Prime, very ripe and rich: This was a surprising Discovery, and I was exceeding glad of them; but I was warn'd by my Experience to eat sparingly of them, remembring, that when I was ashore in *Barbary*, the eating of Grapes kill'd several of our *English* Men who were Slaves there, by throwing them into Fluxes and Feavers: But I found an excellent Use for these Grapes, and that was to cure or dry them in the Sun, and keep them as dry'd Grapes or Raisins are kept, which I thought would be, as indeed they were, as wholesom as agreeable to eat, when no Grapes might be to be had.

I spent all that Evening there, and went not back to my Habitation, which by the Way was the first Night, as I might say, I had lain from Home. In the Night I took my first Contrivance, and got up into a Tree, where I slept well, and the next Morning proceeded upon my Discovery, travelling near four Miles, as I might judge by the Length of the Valley, keeping still due North, with a Ridge of Hills on the South and North-side of me.

At the End of this March I came to an Opening, where the Country seem'd to descend to the West, and a little Spring of fresh Water which issued out of the Side of the Hill by me, run the other Way, that is due East; and the Country appear'd so fresh, so green, so flourishing, every thing being in a constant Verdure, or Flourish of *Spring*, that it looked like a planted Garden.

I descended a little on the Side of that delicious Vale, surveying it with a secret Kind of Pleasure, (tho' mixt with my other afflicting Thoughts) to think that this was all my own, that I was King and Lord of all this Country indefeasibly,* and had a Right of Possession; and if I could convey it, I might have it in Inheritance, as compleatly as any Lord of a Mannor in *England*. I saw here Abundance of Cocoa Trees, Orange, and Lemmon, and Citron Trees; but all wild, and very few bearing any Fruit, at least not then: However, the green

Limes that I gathered, were not only pleasant to eat, but very whole-some; and I mix'd their Juice afterwards with Water, which made it very wholesome, and very cool, and refreshing.

I found now I had Business enough to gather and carry Home; and I resolv'd to lay up a Store, as well of Grapes, as Limes and Lemons, to furnish my self for the wet Season, which I knew was approaching.

In Order to this, I gather'd a great Heap of Grapes in one Place, and a lesser Heap in another Place, and a great Parcel of Limes and Lemons in another Place; and taking a few of each with me, I trav-ell'd homeward, and resolv'd to come again, and bring a Bag or Sack, or what I could make to carry the rest Home.

Accordingly, having spent three Days in this Journey, I came Home; so I must now call my Tent and my Cave: But, before I got thither, the Grapes were spoil'd; the Richness of the Fruits, and the Weight of the Juice having broken them, and bruis'd them, they were good for little or nothing; as to the Limes, they were good, but I could bring but a few.

The next Day, being the 19th, I went back, having made me two small Bags to bring Home my Harvest: But I was surpriz'd, when coming to my Heap of Grapes, which were so rich and fine when I gather'd them, I found them all spread about, trod to Pieces, and dragg'd about, some here, some there, and Abundance eaten and devour'd: By this I concluded, there were some wild Creatures thereabouts, which had done this; but what they were, I knew not.

However, as I found there there was no laying them up on Heaps, and no carrying them away in a Sack, but that one Way they would be destroy'd, and the other Way they would be crush'd with their own Weight. I took another Course; for I gather'd a large Quantity of the Grapes, and hung them up upon the out Branches of the Trees, that they might cure and dry in the Sun; and as for the Limes and Lemons, I carry'd as many back as I could well stand under.

When I came Home from this Journey, I contemplated with great Pleasure the Fruitfulness of that Valley, and the Pleasantness of the Scituation, the Security from Storms on that Side the Water, and the Wood, and concluded, that I had pitch'd upon a Place to fix my Abode, which was by far the worst Part of the Country. Upon the Whole I began to consider of removing my Habitation; and to look out for a Place equally safe, as where I now was scituate, if possible, in that pleasant fruitful Part of the Island.

This Thought run long in my Head, and I was exceeding fond of it for some Time, the Pleasantness of the Place tempting me; but when I came to a nearer View of it, and to consider that I was now by the Sea-Side, where it was at least possible that something might happen to my Advantage, and by the same ill Fate that brought me hither, might bring some other unhappy Wretches to the same Place; and tho' it was scarce probable that any such Thing should ever happen, yet to enclose my self among the Hills and Woods, in the Center of the Island, was to anticipate my Bondage, and to render such an Affair not only Improbable, but Impossible; and that therefore I ought not by any Means to remove.

However, I was so Enamour'd of this Place, that I spent much of my Time there, for the whole remaining Part of the Month of *July*; and tho' upon second Thoughts I resolv'd as above, not to remove, yet I built me a little kind of a Bower, and surrounded it at a Distance with a strong Fence, being a double Hedge, as high as I could reach, well stak'd, and fill'd between with *Brushwood*; and here I lay very secure, sometimes two or three Nights together, always going over it with a Ladder, as before; so that I fancy'd now I had my Country-House, and my Sea-Coast-House: And this Work took me up to the Beginning of *August*.

I had but newly finish'd my Fence, and began to enjoy my Labour, but the Rains came on, and made me stick close to my first Habitation; for tho' I had made me a Tent like the other, with a Piece of a Sail, and spread it very well; yet I had not the Shelter of a Hill to keep me from Storms, nor a Cave behind me to retreat into, when the Rains were extraordinary.

About the Beginning of *August*, *as I said*, I had finish'd my Bower, and began to enjoy my self. The third of *August*, I found the Grapes I had hung up were perfectly dry'd, and indeed, were excellent good Raisins of the Sun; so I began to take them down from the Trees, and it was very happy that I did so; for the Rains which follow'd would have spoil'd them, and I had lost the best Part of my Winter Food; for I had above two hundred large Bunches of them. No sooner had I taken them all down, and carry'd most of them Home to my Cave, but it began to rain, and from hence, which was the fourteenth of *August*, it rain'd more or less, every Day, till the Middle of *October*;

and sometimes so violently, that I could not stir out of my Cave for several Days.

In this Season I was much surpriz'd with the Increase of my Family; I had been concern'd for the Loss of one of my Cats, who run away from me, or as I thought had been dead, and I heard no more Tale or Tidings of her, till to my Astonishment she came Home about the End of *August*, with three *Kittens*; this was the more strange to me, because tho' I had kill'd a wild Cat, as I call'd it, with my Gun; yet I thought it was a quite differing Kind from our *European* Cats; yet the young Cats were the same Kind of House breed like the old one; and both my Cats being Females, I thought it very strange: But from these three Cats, I afterwards came to be so pester'd with Cats, that I was forc'd to kill them like Vermine, or wild Beasts, and to drive them from my House as much as possible.

From the fourteenth of *August* to the twenty sixth, incessant Rain, so that I could not stir, and was now very careful not to be much wet. In this Confinement I began to be straitned for Food, but venturing out twice, I one Day kill'd a Goat, and the last Day, which was the twenty sixth, found a very large Tortoise, which was a Treat to me, and my Food was regulated thus; I eat a Bunch of Raisins for my Breakfast, a Piece of the Goat's Flesh, or of the Turtle for my Dinner broil'd; for to my great Misfortune, I had no Vessel to boil or stew any Thing; and two or three of the Turtle's Eggs for my Supper.

During this Confinement in my Cover, by the Rain, I work'd daily two or three Hours at enlarging my Cave, and by Degrees work'd it on towards one Side, till I came to the Out-Side of the Hill, and made a Door or Way out, which came beyond my Fence or Wall, and so I came in and out this Way; but I was not perfectly easy at lying so open; for as I had manag'd my self before, I was in a perfect Enclosure, whereas now I thought I lay expos'd, and open for any Thing to come in upon me; and yet I could not perceive that there was any living Thing to fear, the biggest Creature that I had yet seen upon the Island being a Goat.

September the thirtieth, I was now come to the unhappy Anniversary of my Landing. I cast up the Notches on my Post, and found I had been on Shore three hundred and sixty five Days. I kept this Day as a Solemn Fast, setting it apart to Religious Exercise, prostrating my self on the Ground with the most serious Humiliation, confessing my Sins to God, acknowledging his Righteous Judgments upon me, and praying to him to have Mercy on me, through Jesus Christ; and having not tasted the least Refreshment for twelve Hours, even till the going down of the Sun, I then eat a Bisket Cake, and a Bunch of Grapes, and went to Bed, finishing the Day as I began it.

I had all this Time observ'd no Sabbath-Day; for as at first I had no Sense of Religion upon my Mind, I had after some Time omitted to distinguish the Weeks, by making a longer Notch than ordinary for the Sabbath-Day, and so did not really know what any of the Days were; but now having cast up the Days, as above, I found I had been there a Year; so I divided it into Weeks, and set apart every seventh Day for a Sabbath; though I found at the End of my Account I had lost a Day or two in my Reckoning.

A little after this my Ink began to fail me, and so I contented my self to use it more sparingly, and to write down only the most remarkable Events of my Life, without continuing a daily *Memorandum* of other Things.

The rainy Season, and the dry Season, began now to appear regular to me, and I learn'd to divide them so, as to provide for them accordingly. But I bought all my Experience before I had it; and this I am going to relate, was one of the most discouraging Experiments that I made at all: I have mention'd that I had sav'd the few Ears of Barley and Rice, which I had so surprizingly found spring up, as I thought, of themselves, and believe there was about thirty Stalks of Rice, and about twenty of Barley; and now I thought it a proper Time to sow it after the Rains, the Sun being in its *Southern* Position going from me.

Accordingly I dug up a Piece of Ground as well as I could with my wooden Spade, and dividing it into two Parts, I sow'd my Grain; but as I was sowing, it casually occur'd to my Thoughts, That I would not sow it all at first, because I did not know when was the proper Time for it; so I sow'd about two Thirds of the Seed, leaving about a Handful of each.

It was a great Comfort to me afterwards, that I did so, for not one Grain of that I sow'd this Time came to any Thing; for the dry Months following, the Earth having had no Rain after the Seed was sown, it had no Moisture to assist its Growth, and never came up at all, till the wet Season had come again, and then it grew as if it had been but newly sown.

Finding my first Seed did not grow, which I easily imagin'd was by the Drought, I sought for a moister Piece of Ground to make another Trial in, and I dug up a Piece of Ground near my new Bower, and sow'd the rest of my Seed in *February*, a little before the *Vernal Equinox*; and this having the rainy Months of *March* and *April* to water it, sprung up very pleasantly, and yielded a very good Crop; but having Part of the Seed left only, and not daring to sow all that I had, I had but a small Quantity at last, my whole Crop not amounting to above half a Peck of each kind.

But by this Experiment I was made Master of my Business, and knew exactly when the proper Season was to sow; and that I might expect two Seed Times, and two Harvests every Year.

While this Corn was growing, I made a little Discovery which was of use to me afterwards: As soon as the Rains were over, and the Weather began to settle, which was about the Month of *November*, I made a Visit up the Country to my Bower, where though I had not been some Months, yet I found all Things just as I left them. The Circle or double Hedge that I had made, was not only firm and entire; but the Stakes which I had cut out of some Trees that grew thereabouts, were all shot out and grown with long Branches, as much as a Willow-Tree usually shoots the first Year after lopping its Head. I could not tell what Tree to call it, that these Stakes were cut from. I was surpriz'd, and yet very well pleas'd, to see the young Trees grow; and I prun'd them, and led them up to grow as much alike as I could; and it is scarce credible how beautiful a Figure they grew into in three Years; so that though the Hedge made a Circle of about twenty five Yards in Diameter, yet the Trees, for such I might now call them, soon cover'd it; and it was a compleat Shade, sufficient to lodge under all the dry Season.

This made me resolve to cut some more Stakes, and make me a Hedge like this in a Semicircle round my Wall; I mean that of my first Dwelling, which I did; and placing the Trees or Stakes in a double Row, at about eight Yards distance from my first Fence, they grew presently, and were at first a fine Cover to my Habitation, and afterward serv'd for a Defence also, as I shall observe in its Order.

I found now, That the Seasons of the Year might generally be divided, not into *Summer* and *Winter*, as in *Europe*; but into the Rainy Seasons, and the Dry Seasons, which were generally thus,*

Half *February*, *March*, Half *April*,	Rainy, the *Sun* being then on, or near the *Equinox*.
Half *April*, *May*, *June*, *July*, Half *August*,	Dry, the *Sun* being then to the *North* of the Line.
Half *August*, *September*, Half *October*,	Rainy, the *Sun* being then come back.
Half *October*, *November*, *December*, *January*, Half *February*,	Dry, the *Sun* being then to the *South* of the Line.

The Rainy Season sometimes held longer or shorter, as the Winds happen'd to blow; but this was the general Observation I made: After I had found by Experience, the ill Consequence of being abroad in the Rain. I took Care to furnish my self with Provisions before hand, that I might not be oblig'd to go out; and I sat within Doors as much as possible during the wet Months.

This Time I found much Employment, (and very suitable also to the Time) for I found great Occasion of many Things which I had no way to furnish my self with, but by hard Labour and constant Application; particularly, I try'd many Ways to make my self a Basket, but all the Twigs I could get for the Purpose prov'd so brittle, that they would do nothing. It prov'd of excellent Advantage to me now, That when I was a Boy, I used to take great Delight in standing at a *Basketmaker's*, in the Town where my Father liv'd, to see them make their *Wicker-ware*; and being as Boys usually are, very officious to help, and a great Observer of the Manner how they work'd those Things, and sometimes lending a Hand, I had by this Means full Knowledge of the Methods of it, that I wanted nothing but the Materials; when it came into my Mind, That the Twigs of that Tree from whence I cut my Stakes that grew, might possibly be as tough as the *Sallows*, and *Willows*, and *Osiers* in *England*, and I resolv'd to try.

Accordingly the next Day, I went to my Country-House, as I call'd
it, and cutting some of the smaller Twigs, I found them to my Purpose as much as I could desire; whereupon I came the next Time
prepar'd with a Hatchet to cut down a Quantity, which I soon found,
for there was great Plenty of them; these I set up to dry within my
Circle or Hedge, and when they were fit for Use, I carry'd them to
my Cave, and here during the next Season, I employ'd my self in
making, *as well as I could*, a great many Baskets, both to carry Earth,
or to carry or lay up any Thing as I had occasion; and tho' I did not
finish them very handsomly, yet I made them sufficiently serviceable
for my Purpose; and thus afterwards I took Care never to be without
them; and as my *Wicker-ware* decay'd, I made more, especially, I
made strong deep Baskets to place my Corn in, instead of Sacks,
when I should come to have any Quantity of it.

Having master'd this Difficulty, and employ'd a World of Time
about it, I bestirr'd my self to see if possible how to supply two
Wants: I had no Vessels to hold any Thing that was Liquid, except
two Runlets which were almost full of Rum, and some Glass-Bottles,
some of the common Size, and others which were Case-Bottles
square, for the holding of Waters, Spirits, &c. I had not so much as a
Pot to boil any Thing, except a great Kettle, which I sav'd out of the
Ship, and which was too big for such Use as I desir'd it, *viz.* To make
Broth, and stew a Bit of Meat by it self. The Second Thing I would
fain have had, was a Tobacco-Pipe; but it was impossible to me to
make one, however, I found a Contrivance for that too at last.*

I employ'd my self in Planting my Second Rows of Stakes or Piles
and in this *Wicker* working all the Summer, or dry Season, when
another Business took me up more Time than it could be imagin'd I
could spare.

I mention'd before, That I had a great Mind to see the whole
Island, and that I had travell'd up the Brook, and so on to where I
built my Bower, and where I had an Opening quite to the Sea on the
other Side of the Island; I now resolv'd to travel quite Cross to the
Sea-Shore on that Side; so taking my Gun, a Hatchet, and my Dog,
and a larger Quantity of Powder and Shot than usual, with two
Bisket Cakes, and a great Bunch of Raisins in my Pouch for my
Store, I began my Journey; when I had pass'd the Vale where my
Bower stood as above, I came within View of the Sea, to the *West*,
and it being a very clear Day, I fairly descry'd Land, whether an

Island or a Continent, I could not tell; but it lay very high, extending from the *West*, to the *W. S. W.* at a very great Distance; by my Guess it could not be less than Fifteen or Twenty Leagues off.

I could not tell what Part of the World this might be, otherwise than that I know it must be Part of *America*, and as I concluded by all my Observations, must be near the *Spanish* Dominions, and perhaps was all Inhabited by Savages, where if I should have landed, I had been in a worse Condition than I was now; and therefore I acquiesced in the Dispositions of Providence, which I began now to own, and to believe, order'd every Thing for the best; I say, I quieted my Mind with this, and left afflicting my self with Fruitless Wishes of being there.

Besides, after some Pause upon this Affair, I consider'd, that if this Land was the *Spanish* Coast, I should certainly, one Time or other, see some Vessel pass or re-pass one Way or other; but if not, then it was the *Savage* Coast between the *Spanish* Country and *Brasils*, which are indeed the worst of *Savages*; for they are Cannibals, or Men-eaters, and fail not to murther and devour all the humane Bodies that fall into their Hands.

With these Considerations I walk'd very leisurely forward, I found that Side of the Island where I now was, much pleasanter than mine, the open or *Savanna* Fields sweet, adorn'd with Flowers and Grass, and full of very fine Woods. I saw Abundance of Parrots, and fain I would have caught one, if possible to have kept it to be tame, and taught it to speak to me. I did, after some Pains taking, catch a young Parrot, for I knock'd it down with a Stick, and having recover'd it, I brought it home; but it was some Years before I could make him speak: However, at last I taught him to call me by my Name very familiarly: But the Accident that follow'd, tho' it be a Trifle, will be very diverting in its Place.

I was exceedingly diverted with this Journey: I found in the low Grounds Hares, as I thought them to be, and Foxes, but they differ'd greatly from all the other Kinds I had met with; nor could I satisfy my self to eat them, tho' I kill'd several: But I had no Need to be ventrous; for I had no Want of Food, and of that which was very good too; especially these three Sorts, *viz.* Goats, Pidgeons, and Turtle or Tortoise; which, added to my Grapes, *Leaden-hall* Market* could not have furnish'd a Table better than I, in Proportion to the Company; and tho' my Case was deplorable enough, yet I had great

Cause for Thankfulness, that I was not driven to any Extremities for Food; but rather Plenty, even to Dainties.

I never travell'd in this Journey above two Miles outright in a Day, or thereabouts; but I took so many Turns and Returns, to see what Discoveries I could make, that I came weary enough to the Place where I resolv'd to sit down for all Night; and then I either repos'd my self in a Tree, or surrounded my self with a Row of Stakes set upright in the Ground, either from one Tree to another, or so as no wild Creature could come at me, without waking me.

As soon as I came to the Sea Shore, I was surpriz'd to see that I had taken up my Lot on the worst Side of the Island; for here indeed the Shore was cover'd with innumerable Turtles, whereas on the other Side I had found but three in a Year and half. Here was also an infinite Number of Fowls, of many Kinds, some which I had seen, and some which I had not seen of before, and many of them very good Meat; but such as I knew not the Names of, except those call'd *Penguins*.*

I could have shot as many as I pleas'd, but was very sparing of my Powder and Shot; and therefore had more Mind to kill a she Goat, if I could, which I could better feed on; and though there were many Goats here more than on my Side the Island, yet it was with much more Difficulty that I could come near them, the Country being flat and even, and they saw me much sooner than when I was on the Hill.

I confess this Side of the Country was much pleasanter than mine, but yet I had not the least Inclination to remove; for as I was fix'd in my Habitation, it became natural to me, and I seem'd all the while I was here, to be as it were upon a Journey, and from Home: However, I travell'd along the Shore of the Sea, towards the *East*, I suppose about twelve Miles; and the setting up a great Pole upon the Shore for a Mark, I concluded I would go Home again; and that the next Journey I took should be on the other Side of the Island, *East* from my Dwelling, and so round till I came to my Post again: Of which in its Place.*

I took another Way to come back than that I went, thinking I could easily keep all the Island so much in my View, that I could not miss finding my first Dwelling by viewing the Country; but I found my self mistaken; for being come about two or three Miles, I found my self descended into a very large Valley; but so surrounded with Hills, and those Hills cover'd with Wood, that I could not see which was my Way by any Direction but that of the Sun, nor even then, unless I knew very well the Position of the Sun at that Time of the Day.

It happen'd to my farther Misfortune, That the Weather prov'd hazey for three or four Days, while I was in this Valley; and not being able to see the Sun, I wander'd about very uncomfortably, and at last was oblig'd to find out the Sea Side, look for my Post, and come back the same Way I went; and then by easy Journies I turn'd Homeward, the Weather being exceeding hot, and my Gun, Ammunition, Hatchet, and other Things very heavy.

In this Journey my Dog surpriz'd a young Kid, and seiz'd upon it, and I running in to take hold of it, caught it, and sav'd it alive from the Dog: I had a great Mind to bring it Home if I could; for I had often been musing, Whether it might not be possible to get a Kid or two, and so raise a Breed of tame Goats, which might supply me when my Powder and Shot should be all spent.

I made a Collar to this little Creature, and with a String which I made of some Rope-Yarn, which I always carry'd about me, I led him along, tho' with some Difficulty, till I came to my Bower, and there I enclos'd him, and left him; for I was very impatient to be at Home, from whence I had been absent above a Month.

I cannot express what a Satisfaction it was to me, to come into my old Hutch, and lye down in my Hamock-Bed: This little wandring Journey, without settled Place of Abode, had been so unpleasant to me, that my own House, as I call'd it to my self, was a perfect Settlement to me, compar'd to that; and it rendred every Thing about me so comfortable, that I resolv'd I would never go a great Way from it again, while it should be my Lot to stay on the Island.

I repos'd my self here a Week, to rest and regale my self after my long Journey; during which, most of the Time was taken up in the weighty Affair of making a Cage for my Poll, who began now to be a meer Domestick,* and to be mighty well acquainted with me. Then I began to think of the poor Kid, which I had penn'd in within my little Circle, and resolv'd to go and fetch it Home, or give it some Food; accordingly I went, and found it where I left it; for indeed it could not get out, but almost starv'd for want of Food: I went and cut Bows of Trees, and Branches of such Shrubs as I could find, and threw it over, and having fed it, I ty'd it as I did before, to lead it away; but it was so tame with being hungry, that I had no need to have ty'd it; for it follow'd me like a Dog; and as I continually fed it, the Creature became so loving, so gentle, and so fond, that it became from that Time one of my Domesticks also, and would never leave me afterwards.

The rainy Season of the *Autumnal Equinox* was now come, and I kept the 30th of *Sept.* in the same solemn Manner as before, being the Anniversary of my Landing on the Island, having now been there two Years, and no more Prospect of being deliver'd, than the first Day I came there. I spent the whole Day in humble and thankful Acknowledgments of the many wonderful Mercies which my Solitary Condition was attended with, and without which it might have been infinitely more miserable. I gave humble and hearty Thanks that God had been pleas'd to discover to me, even that it was possible I might be more happy in this Solitary Condition, than I should have been in a Liberty of Society, and in all the Pleasures of the World. That he could fully make up to me, the Deficiencies of my Solitary State, and the want of Humane Society by his Presence, and the Communications of his Grace to my Soul, supporting, comforting, and encouraging me to depend upon his Providence here, and hope for his Eternal Presence hereafter.

It was now that I began sensibly to feel how much more happy this Life I now led was, with all its miserable Circumstances, than the wicked, cursed, abominable Life I led all the past Part of my Days; and now I chang'd both my Sorrows and my Joys; my very Desires alter'd, my Affections chang'd their Gusts,* and my Delights were perfectly new, from what they were at my first Coming, or indeed for the two Years past.

Before, as I walk'd about, either on my Hunting, or for viewing the Country, the Anguish of my Soul at my Condition, would break out upon me on a sudden, and my very Heart would die within me, to think of the Woods, the Mountains, the Desarts I was in; and how I was a Prisoner lock'd up with the Eternal Bars and Bolts of the Ocean,* in an uninhabited Wilderness, without Redemption: In the midst of the greatest Composures of my Mind, this would break out upon me like a Storm, and make me wring my Hands, and weep like a Child: Sometimes it would take me in the middle of my Work, and I would immediately sit down and sigh, and look upon the Ground for an Hour or two together; and this was still worse to me; for if I could burst out into Tears, or vent my self by Words, it would go off, and the Grief having exhausted it self would abate.

But now I began to exercise my self with new Thoughts; I daily read the Word of God, and apply'd all the Comforts of it to my present State: One Morning being very sad, I open'd the Bible upon these Words, *I will never, never leave thee, nor forsake thee*;* immediately it occurr'd, That these Words were to me, Why else should they be directed in such a Manner, just at the Moment when I was mourning over my Condition, as one forsaken of God and Man? Well then, said I, if God does not forsake me, of what ill Consequence can it be, or what matters it, though the World should all forsake me, seeing on the other Hand, if I had all the World, and should lose the Favour and Blessing of God, there wou'd be no Comparison in the Loss.

From this Moment I began to conclude in my Mind, That it was possible for me to be more happy in this forsaken Solitary Condition, than it was probable I should ever have been in any other Particular State in the World; and with this Thought I was going to give Thanks to God for bringing me to this Place.

I know not what it was, but something shock'd my Mind at that Thought, and I durst not speak the Words: How canst thou be such a Hypocrite, (said I, even audibly) to pretend to be thankful for a Condition, which however thou may'st endeavour to be contented with, thou would'st rather pray heartily to be deliver'd from; so I stopp'd there: But though I could not say, I thank'd God for being there; yet I sincerely gave Thanks to God for opening my Eyes, by whatever afflicting Providences, to see the former Condition of my Life, and to mourn for my Wickedness, and repent. I never open'd the Bible, or shut it, but my very Soul within me, bless'd God for directing my Friend in *England*, without any Order of mine, to pack it up among my Goods; and for assisting me afterwards to save it out of the Wreck of the Ship.

Thus, and in this Disposition of Mind, I began my third Year: and tho' I have not given the Reader the Trouble of so particular Account of my Works this Year as the first; yet in General it may be observ'd, That I was very seldom idle; but having regularly divided my Time, according to the several daily Employments that were before me, such as, *First*, My Duty to God, and the Reading the Scriptures, which I constantly set apart some Time for thrice every Day. *Secondly*, The going Abroad with my Gun for Food, which generally took me up three Hours in every Morning, when it did not Rain.

Thirdly, The ordering, curing, preserving, and cooking what I had kill'd or catch'd for my Supply; these took up great Part of the Day; also it is to be considered that the middle of the Day when the Sun was in the *Zenith*, the Violence of the Heat was too great to stir out; so that about four Hours in the Evening was all the Time I could be suppos'd to work in; with this Exception, That sometimes I chang'd my Hours of Hunting and Working, and went to work in the Morning, and Abroad with my Gun in the Afternoon.

To this short Time allow'd for Labour, I desire may be added the exceeding Laboriousness of my Work; the many Hours which for want of Tools, want of Help, and want of Skill, every Thing I did, took up out of my Time: For Example, I was full two and forty Days making me a Board for a long Shelf, which I wanted in my Cave; whereas two Sawyers with their Tools, and a Saw-Pit, would have cut six of them out of the same Tree in half a Day.

My Case was this, It was to be a large Tree, which was to be cut down, because my Board was to be a broad one. This Tree I was three Days a cutting down, and two more cutting off the Bows, and reducing it to a Log, or Piece of Timber. With inexpressible hacking and hewing I reduc'd both the Sides of it into Chips, till it begun to be light enough to move; then I turn'd it, and made one Side of it smooth, and flat, as a Board from End to End; then turning that Side downward, cut the other Side, till I brought the Plank to be about three Inches thick, and smooth on both Sides. Any one may judge the Labour of my Hands in such a Piece of Work; but Labour and Patience carry'd me through that and many other Things: I only observe this in Particular, to shew, The Reason why so much of my Time went away with so little Work, *viz.* That what might be a little to be done with Help and Tools, was a vast Labour, and requir'd a prodigious Time to do alone, and by hand.

But notwithstanding this, with Patience and Labour I went through many Things; and indeed every Thing that my Circumstances made necessary to me to do, as will appear by what follows.

I was now, in the Months of *November* and *December*, expecting my Crop of Barley and Rice. The Ground I had manur'd or dug up for them was not great; for as I observ'd, my Seed of each was not above the Quantity of half a Peck; for I had lost one whole Crop by sowing in the dry Season; but now my Crop promis'd very well, when on a sudden I found I was in Danger of losing it all again by

Enemies of several Sorts, which it was scarce possible to keep from it; as First, The Goats, and wild Creatures which I call'd Hares, who tasting the Sweetness of the Blade, lay in it Night and Day, as soon as it came up, and eat it so close, that it could get no Time to shoot up into Stalk.

This I saw no Remedy for, but by making an Enclosure about it with a Hedge, which I did with a great deal of Toil; and the more, because it requir'd Speed. However, as my Arable Land was but small, suited to my Crop, I got it totally well fenc'd, in about three Weeks Time; and shooting some of the Creatures in the Day Time, I set my Dog to guard it in the Night, tying him up to a Stake at the Gate, where he would stand and bark all Night long; so in a little Time the Enemies forsook the Place, and the Corn grew very strong, and well, and began to ripen apace.

But as the Beasts ruined me before, while my Corn was in the Blade; so the Birds were as likely to ruin me now, when it was in the Ear; for going along by the Place to see how it throve, I saw my little Crop surrounded with Fowls of I know not how many sorts, who stood as it were watching till I should be gone: I immediately let fly among them (for I always had my Gun with me) I had no sooner shot, but there rose up a little Cloud of Fowls, which I had not seen at all, from among the Corn it self.

This touch'd me sensibly, for I foresaw, that in a few Days they would devour all my Hopes, that I should be starv'd, and never be able to raise a Crop at all, and what to do I could not tell: However I resolv'd not to loose my Corn, if possible, tho' I should watch it Night and Day. In the first Place, I went among it to see what Damage was already done, and found they had spoil'd a good deal of it, but that as it was yet too Green for them, the Loss was not so great, but that the Remainder was like to be a good Crop if it could be sav'd.

I staid by it to load my Gun, and then coming away I could easily see the Thieves sitting upon all the Trees about me, as if they only waited till I was gone away, and the Event proved it to be so; for as I walk'd off as if I was gone, I was no sooner out of their sight, but they dropt down one by one into the Corn again. I was so provok'd that I could not have Patience to stay till more came on, knowing that every Grain that they eat now, was, *as it might be said*, a Peck-loaf to me in the Consequence;* but coming up to the Hedge, I fir'd again, and kill'd three of them. This was what I wish'd for; so I took them up, and serv'd them as we serve notorious Thieves in *England*, (*viz.*) Hang'd them in Chains* for a Terror to others; it is impossible to imagine almost, that this should have such an Effect, as it had; for the Fowls wou'd not only not come at the Corn, but in short they forsook all that Part of the Island, and I could never see a Bird near the Place as long as my Scare-Crows hung there.

This I was very glad of, you may be sure, and about the latter end of *December*, which was our second Harvest of the Year, I reap'd my Crop.

I was sadly put to it for a Scythe or a Sicle to cut it down, and all I could do was to make one as well as I could out of one of the Broad Swords or Cutlasses, which I sav'd among the Arms out of the Ship. However, as my first Crop was but small I had no great Difficulty to cut it down; in short, I reap'd it my Way, for I cut nothing off but the Ears, and carry'd it away in a great Basket which I had made, and so rubb'd it out with my Hands; and at the End of all my Harvesting, I found that out of my half Peck of Seed, I had near two Bushels of Rice, and above two Bushels and half of Barley, *that is to say*, by my Guess, for I had no Measure at that time.

However, this was a great Encouragement to me, and I foresaw that in time, it wou'd please God to supply me with Bread: And yet here I was perplex'd again, for I neither knew how to grind or make Meal of my Corn, or indeed how to clean it and part it; nor if made into Meal, how to make Bread of it, and if how to make it, yet I knew not how to bake it; these things being added to my Desire of having a good Quantity for Store, and to secure a constant Supply, I resolv'd not to taste any of this Crop but to preserve it all for Seed against the next Season, and in the mean time to employ all my Study and Hours of Working to accomplish this great Work of Providing my self with Corn and Bread.

It might be truly said, that now I work'd for my Bread; 'tis a little wonderful, and what I believe few People have thought much upon, (*viz.*) the strange multitude of little Things necessary in the Providing, Producing, Curing, Dressing, Making and Finishing this one Article of Bread.

I that was reduced to a meer State of Nature, found this to my daily Discouragement, and was made more and more sensible of it every Hour, even after I had got the first Handful of Seed-Corn, which, as I have said, came up unexpectedly, and indeed to a surprize.

First, I had no Plow to turn up the Earth, no Spade or Shovel to dig it. Well, this I conquer'd, by making a wooden Spade, as I observ'd before; but this did my Work in but a wooden manner, and tho' it cost me a great many Days to make it, yet for want of Iron it not only wore out the sooner, but made my Work the harder, and made it be perform'd much worse.

However this I bore with, and was content to work it out with Patience, and bear with the badness of the Performance. When the Corn was sow'd, I had no Harrow, but was forced to go over it my self and drag a great heavy Bough of a Tree over it, to Scratch it, as it may be call'd, rather than Rake or Harrow it.

When it was growing and grown, I have observ'd already, how many things I wanted, to Fence it, Secure it, Mow or Reap it, Cure and Carry it Home, Thrash, Part it from the Chaff, and Save it. Then I wanted a Mill to Grind it, Sieves to Dress it, Yeast and Salt to make it into Bread, and an Oven to bake it, and yet all these things I did without, as shall be observ'd; and yet the Corn was an inestimable Comfort and Advantage to me too. All this, as I said, made every thing laborious and tedious to me, but that there was no help for; neither was my time so much Loss to me, because as I had divided it, a certain Part of it was every Day appointed to these Works; and as I resolv'd to use none of the Corn for Bread till I had a greater Quantity by me, I had the next six Months to apply my self wholly by Labour and Invention to furnish my self with Utensils proper for the performing all the Operations necessary for the making the Corn (when I had it) fit for my use.

But first, I was to prepare more Land, for I had now Seed enough to sow above an Acre of Ground. Before I did this, I had a Week's-work at least to make me a Spade, which when it was done was but a sorry one indeed, and very heavy, and requir'd double Labour to work with it; however I went thro' that, and sow'd my Seed in two large flat Pieces of Ground, as near my House as I could find them to my Mind, and fenc'd them in with a good Hedge, the Stakes of which were all cut of that Wood which I had set before, and knew it would grow, so that in one Year's time I knew I should have a Quick or Living-Hedge, that would want but little Repair. This Work was not so little as to take me up less than three Months, because great Part of that time was of the wet Season, when I could not go abroad.

Within Doors, *that is*, when it rained, and I could not go out, I found Employment on the following Occasions; always observing, that all the while I was at work I diverted my self with talking to my Parrot, and teaching him to Speak, and I quickly learn'd him to know his own Name, and at last to speak it out pretty loud P O L L, which was the first Word I ever heard spoken in the Island by any Mouth but my own. This therefore was not my Work, but an assist-ant to my Work, for now, as I said, I had a great Employment upon my Hands, as follows, (*viz.*) I had long study'd by some Means or other, to make my self some Earthen Vessels, which indeed I wanted sorely, but knew not where to come at them: However, considering the Heat of the Climate, I did not doubt but if I could find out any such Clay, I might botch up some such Pot, as might, being dry'd in the Sun, be hard enough, and strong enough to bear handling, and to hold any Thing that was dry, and requir'd to be kept so; and as this was necessary in the preparing Corn, Meal, &c. which was the Thing I was upon, I resolv'd to make some as large as I could, and fit only to stand like Jarrs to hold what should be put into them.

It would make the Reader pity me, or rather laugh at me, to tell how many awkward ways I took to raise this Paste, what odd mishap-en ugly things I made, how many of them fell in, and how many fell out, the Clay not being stiff enough to bear its own Weight; how many crack'd by the over violent Heat of the Sun, being set out too hastily; and how many fell in pieces with only removing, as well before as after they were dry'd; and in a word, how after having labour'd hard to find the Clay, to dig it, to temper it, to bring it home and work it; I could not make above two large earthern ugly things, I cannot call them Jarrs, in about two Months Labour.

However, as the Sun bak'd these Two, very dry and hard, I lifted them very gently up, and set them down again in two great Wicker-Baskets which I had made on purpose for them, that they might not break, and as between the Pot and the Basket there was a little room to spare, I stuff'd it full of the Rice and Barley Straw, and these two Pots being to stand always dry, I thought would hold my dry Corn, and perhaps the Meal, when the Corn was bruised.

Tho' I miscarried so much in my Design for large Pots, yet I made several smaller things with better Success, such as little round Pots, flat Dishes, Pitchers and Pipkins, and any things my Hand turn'd to, and the Heat of the Sun bak'd them strangely hard.

But all this would not answer my End, which was to get an earthen Pot to hold what was Liquid, and bear the Fire, which none of these could do. It happen'd after some time, making a pretty large Fire for cooking my Meat, when I went to put it out after I had done with it, I found a broken Piece of one of my Earthen-ware Vessels in the Fire, burnt as hard as a Stone, and red as a Tile. I was agreeably surpris'd to see it, and said to my self, that certainly they might be made to burn whole if they would burn broken.

This set me to studying how to order my Fire, so as to make it burn me some Pots. I had no Notion of a Kiln, such as the Potters burn in, or of glazing them with Lead, tho' I had some Lead to do it with; but I plac'd three large Pipkins, and two or three Pots in a Pile one upon another, and plac'd my Fire-wood all round it with a great Heap of Embers under them, I ply'd the Fire with fresh Fuel round the out-side, and upon the top, till I saw the Pots in the inside red hot quite thro', and observ'd that they did not crack at all; when I saw them clear red, I let them stand in that Heat about 5 or 6 Hours, till I found one of them, tho' it did not crack, did melt or run, for the Sand which was mixed with the Clay melted by the violence of the Heat, and would have run into Glass if I had gone on, so I slack'd my Fire gradually till the Pots began to abate of the red Colour, and watching them all Night, that I might not let the Fire abate too fast, in the Morning I had three very good, I will not say handsome Pipkins; and two other Earthen Pots, as hard burnt as cou'd be desir'd; and one of them perfectly glaz'd with the Running of the Sand.

After this Experiment, I need not say that I wanted no sort of Earthen Ware for my Use; but I must needs say, as to the Shapes of them, they were very indifferent, as any one may suppose, when I had no way of making them; but as the Children make Dirt-Pies, or as a Woman would make Pies, that never learn'd to raise Past.

No Joy at a Thing of so mean a Nature was ever equal to mine, when I found I had made an Earthen Pot that would bear the Fire; and I had hardly Patience to stay till they were cold, before I set one upon the Fire again, with some Water in it, to boil me some Meat, which it did admirably well; and with a Piece of a Kid, I made some very good Broth, though I wanted Oatmeal, and several other Ingredients, requisite to make it so good as I would have had it been.

My next Concern was, to get me a Stone Mortar, to stamp or beat some Corn in; for as to the Mill, there was no thought at arriving to that Perfection of Art, with one Pair of Hands. To supply this Want I was at a great Loss; for of all Trades in the World I was as perfectly unqualify'd for a Stone-cutter, as for any whatever; neither had I any Tools to go about it with. I spent many a Day to find out a great Stone big enough to cut hollow, and make fit for a Mortar, and could find none at all; except what was in the solid Rock, and which I had no way to dig or cut out; nor indeed were the Rocks in the Island of Hardness sufficient, but were all of a sandy crumbling Stone, which neither would bear the Weight of a heavy Pestle, or would break the Corn without filling it with Sand; so after a great deal of Time lost in searching for a Stone, I gave it over, and resolv'd to look out for a great Block of hard Wood, which I found indeed much easier; and getting one as big as I had Strength to stir, I rounded it, and form'd it in the Out-side with my Axe and Hatchet, and then with the Help of Fire, and infinite Labour, made a hollow Place in it, as the *Indians* in *Brasil* make their *Canoes*.* After this, I made a great heavy Pestle or Beater, of the Wood call'd the Iron-wood, and this I prepar'd and laid by against I had my next Crop of Corn, when I propos'd to my self, to grind, or rather pound my Corn into Meal to make my Bread.

My next Difficulty was to make a Sieve, or Search, to dress my Meal, and to part it from the Bran, and the Husk, without which I did not see it possible I could have any Bread. This was a most difficult Thing, so much as but to think on; for to be sure I had nothing like the necessary Thing to make it; I mean fine thin Canvas, or Stuff, to search the Meal through. And here I was at a full Stop for many Months; nor did I really know what to do; Linnen I had none left, but what was meer Rags; I had Goats Hair, but neither knew I how to weave it, or spin it; and had I known how, here was no Tools to work it with; all the Remedy that I found for this, was, That at last I did remember I had among the Seamens Cloaths which were sav'd out of the Ship, some Neckcloths of Callicoe, or Muslin; and with some Pieces of these, I made three small Sieves, but proper enough for the Work; and thus I made shift for some Years; how I did afterwards, I shall shew in its Place.*

The baking Part was the next Thing to be consider'd, and how I should make Bread when I came to have Corn; for first I had no Yeast; as to that Part, as there was no supplying the Want, so I did not concern my self much about it: But for an Oven, I was indeed in great Pain; at length I found out an Experiment for that also, which was this; I made some Earthen Vessels very broad, but not deep; that is to say, about two Foot Diameter, and not above nine Inches deep; these I burnt in the Fire, as I had done the other, and laid them by; and when I wanted to bake, I made a great Fire upon my Hearth, which I had pav'd with some square Tiles of my own making, and burning also; but I should not call them square.

When the Fire-wood was burnt pretty much into Embers, or live Coals, I drew them forward upon this Hearth, so as to cover it all over, and there I let them lye, till the Hearth was very hot, then sweeping away all the Embers, I set down my Loaf, or Loaves, and whelming down the Earthen Pot upon them, drew the Embers all round the Out-side of the Pot, to keep in, and add to the Heat; and thus, as well as in the best Oven in the World, I bak'd my Barley Loaves, and became in little Time a meer Pastry-Cook into the Bargain; for I made my self several Cakes of the Rice, and Puddings; indeed I made no Pies, neither had I any Thing to put into them, supposing I had, except the Flesh either of Fowls or Goats.

It need not be wondred at, if all these Things took me up most Part of the third Year of my Abode here; for it is to be observ'd, That in the Intervals of these Things, I had my new Harvest and Husbandry to manage; for I reap'd my Corn in its Season, and carry'd it Home as well as I could, and laid it up in the Ear, in my large Baskets, till I had Time to rub it out; for I had no Floor to thrash it on, or Instrument to thrash it with.

And now indeed my Stock of Corn increasing, I really wanted to build my Barns bigger. I wanted a Place to lay it up in; for the Increase of the Corn now yielded me so much, that I had of the Barley about twenty Bushels, and of the Rice as much, or more; insomuch, that now I resolv'd to begin to use it freely; for my Bread had been quite gone a great while; Also I resolved to see what quantity would be sufficient for me a whole Year, and to sow but once a Year.

Upon the whole, I found that the forty Bushels of Barley and Rice, was much more than I could consume in a Year; so I resolv'd to sow just the same Quantity every Year, that I sow'd the last, in Hopes that such a Quantity would fully provide me with Bread, &c.

All the while these Things were doing, you may be sure my

Thoughts run many times upon the Prospect of Land which I had seen from the other Side of the Island, and I was not without secret Wishes that I were on Shore there, fancying the seeing the main Land, and in an inhabited Country, I might find some Way or other to convey my self farther, and perhaps at last find some Means of Escape.

But all this while I made no Allowance for the Dangers of such a Condition, and how I might fall into the Hands of Savages, and perhaps such as I might have Reason to think far worse than the Lions and Tigers of *Africa*. That if I once came into their Power, I should run a Hazard more than a thousand to one of being kill'd, and perhaps of being eaten; for I had heard that the People of the *Carribean* Coast were Canibals, or Man-eaters; and I knew by the Latitude that I could not be far off from that Shore. That suppose they were not Canibals, yet that they might kill me, as many *Europeans* who had fallen into their Hands had been serv'd, even when they had been ten or twenty together; much more I that was but one, and could make little or no Defence: All these Things, I say, which I ought to have consider'd well of, and did cast up in my Thoughts afterwards, yet took up none of my Apprehensions at first; but my Head run mightily upon the Thought of getting over to the Shore.

Now I wish'd for my Boy *Xury*, and the long Boat, with the Shoulder of Mutton Sail, with which I sail'd above a thousand Miles on the Coast of *Africk*; but this was in vain. Then I thought I would go and look at our Ship's Boat, which, as I have said, was blown up upon the Shore, a great Way in the Storm, when we were first cast away. She lay almost where she did at first, but not quite; and was turn'd by the Force of the Waves and the Winds almost Bottom upward, against a high Ridge of Beachy rough Sand; but no Water about her as before.

If I had had Hands to have refitted her, and to have launch'd her into the Water, the Boat would have done well enough, and I might have gone back into the *Brasils* with her easily enough; but I might have foreseen, That I could no more turn her, and set her upright upon her Bottom, than I could remove the Island: However, I went to the Woods, and cut Levers and Rollers, and brought them to the Boat, resolv'd to try what I could do, suggesting to my self, That if I could but turn her down, I might easily repair the

Damage she had receiv'd, and she would be a very good Boat, and I might go to Sea in her very easily.

I spar'd no Pains indeed, in this Piece of fruitless Toil, and spent, I think, three or four Weeks about it; at last finding it impossible to heave it up with my little Strength, I fell to digging away the Sand, to undermine it, and so to make it fall down, setting Pieces of Wood to thrust and guide it right in the Fall.

But when I had done this, I was unable to stir it up again, or to get under it, much less to move it forward, towards the Water; so I was forc'd to give it over; and yet, though I gave over the Hopes of the Boat, my desire to venture over for the Main increased, rather than decreased, as the Means for it seem'd impossible.

This at length put me upon thinking, Whether it was not possible to make my self a *Canoe*, or *Periagua*, such as the Natives of those Climates make, even without Tools, or, as I might say, without Hands, *viz.* of the Trunk of a great Tree. This I not only thought possible, but easy, and pleas'd my self extreamly with the Thoughts of making it, and with my having much more Convenience for it than any of the *Negroes* or *Indians*; but not at all considering the particular Inconveniences which I lay under, more than the *Indians* did, *viz.* Want of Hands to move it, when it was made, into the Water, a Difficulty much harder for me to surmount, than all the Consequences of Want of Tools could be to them; for what was it to me, That when I had chosen a vast Tree in the Woods, I might with much Trouble cut it down, if after I might be able with my Tools to hew and dub the Out-side into the proper Shape of a Boat, and burn or cut out the In-side to make it hollow, so to make a Boat of it: If after all this, I must leave it just there where I found it, and was not able to launch it into the Water.

One would have thought, I could not have had the least Reflection upon my Mind of my Circumstance, while I was making this Boat; but I should have immediately thought how I should get it into the Sea; but my Thoughts were so intent upon my Voyage over the Sea in it, that I never once consider'd how I should get it off of the Land; and it was really in its own Nature more easy for me to guide it over forty five Miles of Sea, than about forty five Fathom of Land, where it lay, to set it a float in the Water.

I went to work upon this Boat, the most like a Fool, that ever Man did, who had any of his Senses awake. I pleas'd my self with the

Design, without determining whether I was ever able to undertake it; not but that the Difficulty of launching my Boat came often into my Head; but I put a stop to my own Enquiries into it, by this foolish Answer which I gave my self, *Let's first make it, I'll warrant I'll find some Way or other to get it along, when 'tis done.*

This was a most preposterous Method; but the Eagerness of my Fancy prevail'd, and to work I went. I fell'd a Cedar Tree: I question much whether *Solomon* ever had such a One for the Building of the Temple at *Jerusalem*.* It was five Foot ten Inches Diameter at the lower Part next the Stump, and four Foot eleven Inches Diameter at the End of twenty two Foot, after which it lessen'd for a while, and then parted into Branches: It was not without infinite Labour that I fell'd this Tree: I was twenty Days hacking and hewing at it at the Bottom. I was fourteen more getting the Branches and Limbs, and the vast spreading Head of it cut off, which I hack'd and hew'd through with Axe and Hatchet, and inexpressible Labour: After this, it cost me a Month to shape it, and dub it to a Proportion, and to something like the Bottom of a Boat, that it might swim upright as it ought to do. It cost me near three Months more to clear the In-side, and work it out so, as to make an exact Boat of it: This I did indeed without Fire, by meer Malett and Chissel, and by the dint of hard Labour, till I had brought it to be a very handsome *Periagua*, and big enough to have carry'd six and twenty Men, and consequently big enough to have carry'd me and all my Cargo.

When I had gone through this Work, I was extremely delighted with it. The Boat was really much bigger than I ever saw a *Canoe*, or *Periagua*, that was made of one Tree, in my Life. Many a weary Stroke it had cost, you may be sure; and there remain'd nothing but to get it into the Water; and had I gotten it into the Water, I make no question but I should have began the maddest Voyage, and the most unlikely to be perform'd, that ever was undertaken.

But all my Devices to get it into the Water fail'd me; tho' they cost me infinite Labour too. It lay about one hundred Yards from the Water, and not more: But the first Inconvenience was, it was up Hill towards the Creek; well, to take away this Discouragement, I resolv'd to dig into the Surface of the Earth, and so make a Declivity: This I begun, and it cost me a prodigious deal of Pains; but who grutches Pains, that have their Deliverance in View: But when this was work'd through, and this Difficulty manag'd, it was still much at one; for I could no more stir the *Canoe*, than I could the other Boat.

Then I measur'd the Distance of Ground, and resolv'd to cut a Dock, or Canal, to bring the Water up to the *Canoe*, seeing I could not bring the *Canoe* down to the Water: Well, I began this Work, and when I began to enter into it, and calculate how deep it was to be dug, how broad, how the Stuff to be thrown out, I found, That by the Number of Hands I had, being none but my own, it must have been ten or twelve Years before I should have gone through with it; for the Shore lay high, so that at the upper End, it must have been at least twenty Foot Deep; so at length, tho' with great Reluctancy, I gave this Attempt over also.

This griev'd me heartily, and now I saw, tho' too late, the Folly of beginning a Work before we count the Cost; and before we judge rightly of our own Strength to go through with it.

In the middle of this Work, I finish'd my fourth Year in this Place, and kept my Anniversary with the same Devotion, and with as much Comfort as ever before; for by a constant Study, and serious Application of the Word of God, and by the Assistance of his Grace, I gain'd a different Knowledge from what I had before. I entertain'd different Notions of Things. I look'd now upon the World as a Thing remote, which I had nothing to do with, no Expectation from, and indeed no Desires about: In a Word, I had nothing indeed to do with it, nor was ever like to have; so I thought it look'd as we may perhaps look upon it hereafter, *viz.* as a Place I had liv'd in, but was come out of it; and well might I say, as Father *Abraham* to *Dives*, *Between me and thee is a great Gulph fix'd.**

In the first Place, I was remov'd from all the Wickedness of the World here. I had neither the *Lust of the Flesh*, *the Lust of the Eye*, *or the Pride of Life*.* I had nothing to covet; for I had all that I was now capable of enjoying: I was Lord of the whole Mannor; or if I pleas'd, I might call my self King, or Emperor over the whole Country which I had Possession of. There were no Rivals. I had no Competitor, none to dispute Sovereignty or Command with me. I might have rais'd Ship Loadings of Corn; but I had no use for it; so I let as little grow as I thought enough for my Occasion. I had Tortoise or Turtles enough; but now and then one, was as much as I could put to any use. I had Timber enough to have built a Fleet of Ships. I had Grapes enough to have made Wine, or to have

cur'd into Raisins, to have loaded that Fleet, when they had been
built.

But all I could make use of, was, All that was valuable. I had
enough to eat, and to supply my Wants, and, what was all the rest to
me? If I kill'd more Flesh than I could eat, the Dog must eat it, or the
Vermin. If I sow'd more Corn than I could eat, it must be spoil'd.
The Trees that I cut down, were lying to rot on the Ground. I could
make no more use of them than for Fewel; and that I had no Occasion for, but to dress my Food.

In a Word, The Nature and Experience of Things dictated to me
upon just Reflection, That all the good Things of this World, are no
farther good to us, than they are for our Use; and that whatever we
may heap up indeed to give others, we enjoy just as much as we can
use, and no more. The most covetous griping Miser in the World
would have been cur'd of the Vice of Covetousness, if he had been in
my Case; for I possess'd infinitely more than I knew what to do with.
I had no room for Desire, except it was of Things which I had not,
and they were but Trifles, though indeed of great Use to me. I had,
as I hinted before, a Parcel of Money, as well Gold as Silver, about
thirty six Pounds Sterling: Alas! There the nasty sorry useless Stuff
lay; I had no manner of Business for it; and I often thought with my
self, That I would have given a Handful of it for a Gross of Tobacco-
Pipes, or for a Hand-Mill to grind my Corn; nay, I would have given
it all for Sixpenny-worth of *Turnip* and *Carrot* Seed out of *England*,
or for a Handful of *Pease* and *Beans*, and a Bottle of Ink: *As it was*, I
had not the least Advantage by it, or Benefit from it; but there it lay
in a Drawer, and grew mouldy with the Damp of the Cave, in the wet
Season; and if I had had the Drawer full of Diamonds, it had been
the same Case; and they had been of no manner of Value to me,
because of no Use.

I had now brought my State of Life to be much easier in it self
than it was at first, and much easier to my Mind, as well as to my
Body. I frequently sat down to my Meat with Thankfulness, and
admir'd the Hand of God's Providence, which had thus spread my
Table in the Wilderness. I learn'd to look more upon the bright
Side of my Condition, and less upon the dark Side; and to consider
what I enjoy'd, rather than what I wanted; and this gave me sometimes such secret Comforts, that I cannot express them; and which I
take Notice of here, to put those discontented People in Mind of it,

who cannot enjoy comfortably what God has given them; because they see, and covet something that he has not given them: All our Discontents about what we want, appear'd to me, to spring from the Want of Thankfulness for what we have.

Another Reflection was of great Use to me, and doubtless would be so to any one that should fall into such Distress as mine was; and this was, To compare my present Condition with what I at first expected it should be; nay, with what it would certainly have been, if the good Providence of God had not wonderfully order'd the Ship to be cast up nearer to the Shore, where I not only could come at her, but could bring what I got out of her to the Shore, for my Relief and Comfort; without which, I had wanted for Tools to work, Weapons for Defence, or Gun-Powder and Shot for getting my Food.

I spent whole Hours, I may say whole Days, in representing to my self in the most lively Colours, how I must have acted, if I had got nothing out of the Ship. How I could not have so much as got any Food, except Fish and Turtles; and that as it was long before I found any of them, I must have perish'd first. That I should have liv'd, if I had not perish'd, like a meer Savage. That if I had kill'd a Goat, or a Fowl, by any Contrivance, I had no way to flea or open them, or part the Flesh from the Skin, and the Bowels, or to cut it up; but must gnaw it with my Teeth, and pull it with my Claws like a Beast.

These Reflections made me very sensible of the Goodness of Providence to me, and very thankful for my present Condition, with all its Hardships and Misfortunes: And this Part also I cannot but recommend to the Reflection of those, who are apt in their Misery to say, *Is any Affliction like mine!* Let them consider, How much worse the Cases of some People are, and their Case might have been, if Providence had thought fit.

I had another Reflection which assisted me also to comfort my Mind with Hopes; and this was, comparing my present Condition with what I had deserv'd, and had therefore Reason to expect from the Hand of Providence. I had liv'd a dreadful Life, perfectly destitute of the Knowledge and Fear of God. I had been well instructed by Father and Mother; neither had they been wanting to me, in their early Endeavours, to infuse a religious Awe of God into my Mind, a Sense of my Duty, and of what the Nature and End of my Being, requir'd of me. But alas! falling early into the Seafaring Life, which of all the Lives is the most destitute of the Fear of God, though his

Terrors are always before them; I say, falling early into the Seafaring Life, and into Seafaring Company, all that little Sense of Religion which I had entertain'd, was laugh'd out of me by my Mess-Mates, by a harden'd despising of Dangers; and the Views of Death, which grew habitual to me; by my long Absence from all Manner of Opportunities to converse with any thing but what was like my self, or to hear any thing that was good, or tended towards it.

So void was I of every Thing that was good, or of the least Sense of what I was, or was to be, that in the greatest Deliverances I enjoy'd, such as my Escape from *Sallee*; my being taken up by the *Portuguese* Master of the Ship; my being planted so well in the *Brasils*; my receiving the Cargo from *England*, and the like; I never had once the Word *Thank God*, so much as on my Mind, or in my Mouth; nor in the greatest Distress, had I so much as a Thought to pray to him, or so much as to say, *Lord have Mercy upon me*; no nor to mention the Name of God, unless it was to swear by, and blaspheme it.

I had terrible Reflections upon my Mind for many Months, as I have already observ'd, on the Account of my wicked and hardned Life past; and when I look'd about me and considered what particular Providences had attended me since my coming into this Place, and how God had dealt bountifully with me; had not only punished me less than my Iniquity had deserv'd, but had so plentifully provided for me; this gave me great hopes that my Repentance was accepted, and that God had yet Mercy in store for me.

With these Reflections I work'd my Mind up, not only to Resignation to the Will of God in the present Disposition of my Circumstances; but even to a sincere Thankfulness for my Condition, and that I who was yet a living Man, ought not to complain, seeing I had not the due Punishment of my Sins; that I enjoy'd so many Mercies which I had no reason to have expected in that Place; that I ought never more to repine at my Condition but to rejoyce, and to give daily Thanks for that daily Bread, which nothing but a Croud of Wonders could have brought. That I ought to consider I had been fed even by Miracle, even as great as that of feeding *Elijah* by Ravens;* nay, by a long Series of Miracles, and that I could hardly have nam'd a Place in the unhabitable Part of the World where I could have been cast more to my Advantage: A Place, where as I had no Society, which was my Affliction on one Hand, so I found no ravenous Beast, no furious Wolves or Tygers to threaten my Life, no venomous Creatures or poisonous, which I might feed on to my Hurt, no Savages to murther and devour me.

In a word, as my Life was a Life of Sorrow, one way, so it was a Life of Mercy, another; and I wanted nothing to make it a Life of Comfort, but to be able to make my Sence of God's Goodness to me, and Care over me in this Condition, be my daily Consolation; and after I did make a just Improvement of these things, I went away and was no more sad.

I had now been here so long, that many Things which I brought on Shore for my Help, were either quite gone, or very much wasted and near spent.

My Ink, as I observed, had been gone some time, all but a very little, which I eek'd out with Water a little and a little, till it was so pale it scarce left any Appearance of black upon the Paper: As long as it lasted, I made use of it to minute down the Days of the Month on which any remarkable Thing happen'd to me, and first by casting up Times past: I remember that there was a strange Concurrence of Days, in the various Providences which befel me; and which, if I had been superstitiously inclin'd to observe Days as Fatal or Fortunate, I might have had Reason to have look'd upon with a great deal of Curiosity.*

First I had observed, that the same Day that I broke away from my Father and my Friends, and run away to *Hull*, in order to go to Sea; the same Day afterwards I was taken by the *Sallee* Man of War, and made a Slave.

The same Day of the Year that I escaped out of the Wreck of that Ship in *Yarmouth* Rodes, that same Day-Year afterwards I made my escape from *Sallee* in the Boat.

The same Day of the Year I was born on (*viz.*) the 30*th* of *September*, that same Day, I had my Life so miraculously saved 26 Year after,* when I was cast on Shore in this Island, so that my wicked Life, and my solitary Life begun both on a Day.

The next Thing to my Ink's being wasted, was that of my Bread, I mean the Bisket which I brought out of the Ship; this I had husbanded to the last degree, allowing my self but one Cake of Bread a Day for above a Year, and yet I was quite without Bread for near a Year before I got any Corn of my own, and great Reason I had to be thankful that I had any at all, the getting it being, as has been already observed, next to miraculous.

My Cloaths began to decay too mightily: As to Linnen, I had had none a good while, except some chequer'd Shirts which I found in the Chests of the other Seamen, and which I carefully preserved, because many times I could bear no other Cloaths on but a Shirt; and it was a very great help to me that I had among all the Men's Cloaths of the Ship almost three dozen of Shirts. There were also several thick Watch Coats of the Seamens, which were left indeed, but they were too hot to wear; and tho' it is true, that the Weather was so violent hot, that there was no need of Cloaths, yet I could not go quite naked; no, tho' I had been inclin'd to it, which I was not, nor could not abide the thoughts of it, tho' I was all alone.

The Reason why I could not go quite naked, was, I could not bear the heat of the Sun so well when quite naked, as with some Cloaths on; nay, the very Heat frequently blistered my Skin; whereas with a Shirt on, the Air itself made some Motion, and whistling under that Shirt was twofold cooler than without it; no more could I ever bring my self to go out in the heat of Sun, without a Cap or a Hat; the heat of the Sun beating with such Violence as it does in that Place, would give me the Head-ach presently, by darting so directly on my Head, without a Cap or Hat on, so that I could not bear it, whereas, if I put on my Hat, it would presently go away.

Upon those Views I began to consider about putting the few Rags I had, which I call'd Cloaths, into some Order; I had worn out all the Wast-coats I had, and my Business was now to try if I could not make Jackets out of the great Watch-Coats which I had by me, and with such other Materials as I had, so I set to Work a Taylering, or rather indeed a Botching, for I made most piteous Work of it. However, I made shift to make two or three new Wastcoats, which I hoped wou'd serve me a great while; as for Breeches or Drawers, I made but a very sorry shift indeed, till afterward.

I have mentioned that I saved the Skins of all the Creatures that I kill'd, I mean four-footed ones, and I had hung them up stretch'd out with Sticks in the Sun, by which means some of them were so dry and hard that they were fit for little, but others it seems were very useful. The first thing I made of these was a great Cap for my Head, with the Hair on the out Side to shoor off the Rain; and this I perform'd so well, that after this I made me a Suit of Cloaths wholly of these Skins, that is to say, a Wastcoat, and Breeches open at Knees, and both loose, for they were rather wanting to keep me cool than to keep me warm. I must not omit to acknowledge that they were wretchedly made; for if I was a bad *Carpenter*, I was a worse *Tayler*. However, they were such as I made very good shift with;* and when I was abroad, if it happen'd to rain, the Hair of my Wastcoat and Cap being outermost, I was kept very dry.

After this I spent a great deal of Time and Pains to make me an Umbrella; I was indeed in great want of one, and had a great Mind to make one; I had seen them made in the *Brasils*, where they are very useful in the great Heats which are there. And I felt the Heats every jot as great here, and greater too, being nearer the Equinox; besides, as I was oblig'd to be much abroad, it was a most useful thing to me, as well for the Rains as the Heats.* I took a world of Pains at it, and was a great while before I could make any thing likely to hold; nay, after I thought I had hit the Way, I spoil'd 2 or 3 before I made one to my Mind; but at last I made one that answer'd indifferently well: The main Difficulty I found was to make it to let down. I could make it to spread, but if it did not let down too, and draw in, it was not portable for me any Way but just over my Head, which wou'd not do. However, at last, as I said, I made one to answer, and covered it with Skins, the Hair upwards, so that it cast off the Rains like a Pent-house, and kept off the Sun so effectually, that I could walk out in the hottest of the Weather with greater Advantage than I could before in the coolest, and when I had no need of it, cou'd close it and carry it under my Arm.

Thus I liv'd mighty comfortably, my Mind being entirely composed by resigning to the Will of God, and throwing my self wholly upon the Disposal of his Providence. This made my Life better than sociable, for when I began to regret the want of Conversation, I would ask my self whether thus conversing mutually with my own Thoughts, and, as I hope I may say, with even God himself by Ejaculations, was not better than the utmost Enjoyment of humane Society in the World.

I cannot say that after this, for five Years, any extraordinary thing happened to me, but I liv'd on in the same Course, in the same Posture and Place, just as before; the chief things I was employ'd in, besides my yearly Labour of planting my Barley and Rice, and curing my Raisins, of both which I always kept up just enough to have sufficient Stock of one Year's Provisions beforehand. I say, besides this yearly Labour, and my daily Labour of going out with my Gun, I had one Labour to make me a Canoe, which at last I finished. So that by digging a Canal to it of six Foot wide, and four Foot deep, I brought it into the Creek, almost half a Mile. As for the first, which was so vastly big, as I made it without considering before-hand, as I ought to do, how I should be able to launch it; so never being able to bring it to the Water, or bring the Water to it, I was oblig'd to let it lye where it was, as a *Memorandum* to teach me to be wiser next Time: Indeed, the next Time, tho' I could not get a Tree proper for it, and in a Place where I could not get the Water to it, at any less Distance, than as I have said, near half a Mile; yet as I saw it was practicable at last, I never gave it over; and though I was near two Years about it, yet I never grutch'd my Labour, in Hopes of having a Boat to go off to Sea at last.

However, though my little *Periagua* was finish'd; yet the Size of it was not at all answerable to the Design which I had in View, when I made the first; I mean, Of venturing over to the *Terra Firma*, where it was above forty Miles broad; accordingly, the Smallness of my Boat assisted to put an End to that Design, and now I thought no more of it: But as I had a Boat, my next Design was to make a Tour round the Island; for as I had been on the other Side, in one Place, crossing as I have already describ'd it, over the Land; so the Discoveries I made in that little Journey, made me very eager to see other Parts of the Coast; and now I had a Boat, I thought of nothing but sailing round the Island.

For this Purpose, that I might do every Thing with Discretion and Consideration, I fitted up a little Mast to my Boat, and made a Sail to it, out of some of the Pieces of the Ship's Sail, which lay in store; and of which I had a great Stock by me.

Having fitted my Mast and Sail, and try'd the Boat, I found she would sail very well: Then I made little Lockers, or Boxes, at either End of my Boat, to put Provisions, Necessaries and Ammunition, &c. into, to be kept dry, either from Rain, or the Sprye of the Sea; and a little long hollow Place I cut in the In-side of the Boat, where I could lay my Gun, making a Flap to hang down over it to keep it dry.

I fix'd my Umbrella also in a Step at the Stern, like a Mast, to stand over my Head, and keep the Heat of the Sun off of me like an Auning; and thus I every now and then took a little Voyage upon the Sea, but never went far out, nor far from the little Creek; but at last being eager to view the Circumference of my little Kingdom, I resolv'd upon my Tour, and accordingly I victuall'd my Ship for the Voyage, putting in two Dozen of my Loaves (Cakes I should rather call them) of Barley Bread, an Earthen Pot full of parch'd Rice, a Food I eat a great deal of, a little Bottle of Rum, half a Goat, and Powder and Shot for killing more, and two large Watch-coats, of those which, as I mention'd before, I had sav'd out of the Seamen's Chests; these I took, one to lye upon, and the other to cover me in the Night.

It was the sixth of *November*, in the sixth Year of my Reign,* or my Captivity, which you please, That I set out on this Voyage, and I found it much longer than I expected; for though the Island it self was not very large, yet when I came to the *East* Side of it, I found a great Ledge of Rocks lye out above two Leagues into the Sea, some above Water, some under it; and beyond that, a Shoal of Sand, lying dry half a League more; so that I was oblig'd to go a great Way out to Sea to double the Point.

When first I discover'd them, I was going to give over my Enterprise, and come back again, not knowing how far it might oblige me to go out to Sea; and above all, doubting how I should get back again; so I came to an Anchor; for I had made me a kind of an Anchor with a Piece of a broken Graplin, which I got out of the Ship.

Having secur'd my Boat, I took my Gun, and went on Shore, climbing up upon a Hill, which seem'd to over-look that Point, where I saw the full extent of it, and resolv'd to venture.

In my viewing the Sea from that Hill where I stood, I perceiv'd a strong, and indeed, a most furious Current, which run to the *East*, and even came close to the Point; and I took the more Notice of it, because I saw there might be some Danger; that when I came into it, I might be carry'd out to Sea by the Strength of it, and not be able to make the Island again; and indeed, had I not gotten first up upon this Hill, I believe it would have been so; for there was the same Current on the other Side the Island, only, that it set off at a farther Distance; and I saw there was a strong Eddy under the Shore; so I had nothing to do but to get in out of the first Current, and I should presently be in an Eddy.

I lay here, however, two Days; because the Wind blowing pretty fresh at *E.S.E.* and that being just contrary to the said Current, made a great Breach of the Sea upon the Point; so that it was not safe for me to keep too close to the Shore for the Breach,* nor to go too far off because of the Stream.

The third Day in the Morning, the Wind having abated over Night, the Sea was calm, and I ventur'd; but I am a warning Piece* again, to all rash and ignorant Pilots; for no sooner was I come to the Point, when even I was not my Boat's Length from the Shore, but I found my self in a great Depth of Water, and a Current like the Sluice of a Mill: It carry'd my Boat a long with it with such Violence, That all I could do, could not keep her so much as on the Edge of it; but I found it hurry'd me farther and farther out from the Eddy, which was on my left Hand. There was no Wind stirring to help me, and all I could do with my Paddlers signify'd nothing, and now I began to give my self over for lost; for as the Current was on both Sides the Island, I knew in a few Leagues Distance they must joyn again, and then I was irrecoverably gone; nor did I see any Possibility of avoiding it; so that I had no Prospect before me but of Perishing; not by the Sea, for that was calm enough, but of starving for Hunger. I had indeed found a Tortoise on the Shore, as big almost as I could lift, and had toss'd it into the Boat; and I had a great Jar of fresh Water, that is to say, one of my Earthen Pots; but what was all this to being driven into the vast Ocean, where to be sure, there was no Shore, no main Land, or Island, for a thousand Leagues at least.

And now I saw how easy it was for the Providence of God to make the most miserable Condition Mankind could be in *worse*. Now I look'd back upon my desolate solitary Island, as the most pleasant Place in the World, and all the Happiness my Heart could wish for, was to be but there again. I stretch'd out my Hands to it with eager Wishes. O happy Desart, said I, I shall never see thee more. O miserable Creature, said I, whether am I going: Then I reproach'd my self with my unthankful Temper, and how I had repin'd at my solitary Condition; and now what would I give to be on Shore there again. Thus we never see the true State of our Condition, till it is illustrated to us by its Contraries; nor know how to value what we enjoy, but by the want of it. It is scarce possible to imagine the Consternation I was now in, being driven from my beloved Island (for so it appear'd to me now to be) into the wide Ocean, almost two Leagues, and in the utmost Despair of ever recovering it again. However, I work'd hard, till indeed my Strength was almost exhausted, and kept my Boat as much to the *Northward*, that is, towards the Side of the Current which the Eddy lay on, as possibly I could; when about Noon, as the Sun pass'd the Meridian, I thought I felt a little Breeze of Wind in my Face, springing up from the *S. S. E.* This chear'd my Heart a little, and especially when in about half an Hour more, it blew a pretty small gentle Gale. By this Time I was gotten at a frightful Distance from the Island, and had the least Cloud or haizy Weather interven'd, I had been undone another Way too; for I had no Compass on Board, and should never have known how to have steer'd towards the Island, if I had but once lost Sight of it; but the Weather continuing clear, I apply'd my self to get up my Mast again, spread my Sail, standing away to the *North*, as much as possible, to get out of the Current.

Just as I had set my Mast and Sail, and the Boat began to stretch away, I saw even by the Clearness of the Water, some Alteration of the Current was near; for where the Current was so strong, the Water was foul; but perceiving the Water clear, I found the Current abate, and presently I found to the *East*, at about half a Mile, a Breach of the Sea upon some Rocks; these Rocks I found caus'd the Current to part again, and as the main Stress of it ran away more *Southerly*, leaving the Rocks to the *North-East*; so the other return'd by the Repulse of the Rocks, and made a strong Eddy, which run back again to the *North-West*, with a very sharp Stream.

They who know what it is to have a Reprieve brought to them upon the Ladder, or to be rescued from Thieves just a going to murther them, or, who have been in such like Extremities, may guess what my present Surprise of Joy was, and how gladly I put my Boat into the Stream of this Eddy, and the Wind also freshning, how gladly I spread my Sail to it, running chearfully before the Wind, and with a strong Tide or Eddy under Foot.

This Eddy carryed me about a League in my Way back again directly towards the Island, but about two Leagues more to the Northward than the Current which carried me away at first; so that when I came near the Island, I found my self open to the Northern Shore of it, that is to say, the other End of the Island opposite to that which I went out from.

When I had made something more than a League of Way by the help of this Current or Eddy, I found it was spent and serv'd me no farther. However, I found that being between the two great Currents, (*viz.*) that on the South Side which had hurried me away, and that on the North which lay about a League on the other Side. I say between these two, in the wake of the Island, I found the Water at least still and running no Way, and having still a Breeze of Wind fair for me, I kept on steering directly for the Island, tho' not making such fresh Way as I did before.

About four a-Clock in the Evening, being then within about a League of the Island, I found the Point of the Rocks which occasioned this Disaster, stretching out as is describ'd before to the Southward, and casting off the Current more Southwardly, had of Course made another Eddy to the North, and this I found very strong, but not directly setting the Way my Course lay which was due West, but almost full North. However having a fresh Gale, I stretch'd a-cross this Eddy slanting North-west, and in about an Hour came within about a Mile of the Shore, where it being smooth Water, I soon got to Land.

When I was on Shore I fell on my Knees and gave God Thanks for my Deliverance, resolving to lay aside all Thoughts of my Deliverance by my Boat, and refreshing my self with such Things as I had, I brought my Boat close to the Shore in a little Cove that I had spy'd under some Trees, and lay'd me down to sleep, being quite spent with the Labour and Fatigue of the Voyage.

I was now at a great Loss which Way to get Home with my Boat, I had run so much Hazard, and knew too much the Case to think of attempting it by the Way I went out, and what might be at the other Side (I mean the West Side) I knew not, nor had I any Mind to run any more Ventures; so I only resolved in the Morning to make my Way Westward along the Shore and to see if there was no Creek where I might lay up my Frigate in Safety, so as to have her again if I wanted her; in about three Mile or thereabout coasting the Shore, I came to a very good Inlet or Bay about a Mile over, which narrowed till it came to a very little Rivulet or Brook, where I found a very convenient Harbour for my Boat and where she lay as if she had been in a little Dock made on Purpose for her. Here I put in, and having stow'd my Boat very safe, I went on Shore to look about me and see where I was.

I soon found I had but a little past by the Place where I had been before, when I travell'd on Foot to that Shore; so taking nothing out of my Boat, but my Gun and my Umbrella, for it was exceeding hot, I began my March: The Way was comfortable enough after such a Voyage as I had been upon, and I reach'd my old Bower in the Evening, where I found every thing standing as I left it; for I always kept it in good Order, being, as I said before, my Country House.

I got over the Fence, and laid me down in the Shade to rest my Limbs; for I was very weary, and fell asleep: But judge you, if you can, that read my Story, what a Surprize I must be in, when I was wak'd out of my Sleep by a Voice calling me by my Name several times, *Robin, Robin, Robin Crusoe*, poor *Robin Crusoe*, where are you *Robin Crusoe*? Where are you? Where have you been?*

I was so dead asleep at first, being fatigu'd with Rowing, or Paddling, as it is call'd, the first Part of the Day, and with walking the latter Part, that I did not wake thoroughly, but dozing between sleeping and waking, thought I dream'd that some Body spoke to me: But as the Voice continu'd to repeat *Robin Crusoe, Robin Crusoe*, at last I began to wake more perfectly, and was at first dreadfully frighted, and started up in the utmost Consternation: But no sooner were my Eyes open, but I saw my *Poll* sitting on the Top of the Hedge; and immediately knew that it was he that spoke to me; for just in such bemoaning Language I had used to talk to him, and teach him; and he had learn'd it so perfectly, that he would sit upon my Finger, and lay his Bill close to my Face, and cry, *Poor* Robin Crusoe, *Where are you? Where have you been? How come you here?* And such things as I had taught him.

However, even though I knew it was the Parrot, and that indeed it could be no Body else, it was a good while before I could compose my self: First, I was amazed how the Creature got thither, and then, how he should just keep about the Place, and no where else: But as I was well satisfied it could be no Body but honest *Poll*, I got it over; and holding out my Hand, and calling him by his Name *Poll*, the sociable Creature came to me, and sat upon my Thumb, as he used to do, and continu'd talking to me, *Poor* Robin Crusoe, and *how did I come here? and where had I been?* just as if he had been overjoy'd to see me again; and so I carry'd him Home along with me.

I had now had enough of rambling to Sea for some time, and had enough to do for many Days to sit still, and reflect upon the Danger I had been in: I would have been very glad to have had my Boat again on my Side of the Island; but I knew not how it was practicable to get it about as to the East Side of the Island, which I had gone round; I knew well enough there was no venturing that Way; my very heart would shrink, and my very Blood run chill but to think of it: And as to the other Side of the Island, I did not know how it might be there; but supposing the Current ran with the same Force against the

Shore at the East as it pass'd by it on the other, I might run the same Risk of being driven down the Stream, and carry'd by the Island, as I had been before, of being carry'd away from it; so with these Thoughts I contented my self to be without any Boat, though it had been the Product of so many Months Labour to make it, and of so many more to get it unto the Sea.

In this Government of my Temper, I remain'd near a Year, liv'd a very sedate retir'd Life, as you may well suppose; and my Thoughts being very much composed as to my Condition, and fully comforted in resigning my self to the Dispositions of Providence, I thought I liv'd really very happily in all things, except that of Society.

I improv'd my self in this time in all the mechanick Exercises which my Necessities put me upon applying my self to, and I believe cou'd, upon Occasion, make a very good *Carpenter*, especially considering how few Tools I had.

Besides this, I arriv'd at an unexpected Perfection in my Earthen Ware, and contriv'd well enough to make them with a Wheel, which I found infinitely easier and better; because I made things round and shapable, which before were filthy things indeed to look on. But I think I was never more vain of my own Performance, or more joyful for any thing I found out, than for my being able to make a Tobacco-Pipe. And tho' it was a very ugly clumsy thing, when it was done, and only burnt red like other Earthen Ware, yet as it was hard and firm, and would draw the Smoke, I was exceedingly comforted with it, for I had been always used to smoke, and there were Pipes in the Ship, but I forgot them at first, not knowing that there was Tobacco in the Island; and afterwards, when I search'd the Ship again, I could not come at any Pipes at all.

In my Wicker Ware also I improved much, and made abundance of necessary Baskets, as well as my Invention shew'd me, tho' not very handsome, yet they were such as were very handy and convenient for my laying things up in, or fetching things home in. For Example, if I kill'd a Goat abroad, I could hang it up in a Tree, flea it, and dress it, and cut it in Pieces, and bring it home in a Basket, and the like by a Turtle, I could cut it up, take out the Eggs, and a Piece or two of the Flesh, which was enough for me, and bring them home in a Basket, and leave the rest behind me. Also large deep Baskets were my Receivers for my Corn, which I always rubb'd out as soon as it was dry, and cured, and kept it in great Baskets.

I began now to perceive my Powder abated considerably, and this was a Want which it was impossible for me to supply, and I began seriously to consider what I must do when I should have no more Powder; that is to say, how I should do to kill any Goat. I had, as is observ'd in the third Year of my being here, kept a young Kid, and bred her up tame, and I was in hope of getting a He-Goat, but I could not by any Means bring it to pass, 'till my Kid grew an old Goat; and I could never find in my Heart to kill her, till she dy'd at last of meer Age.

But being now in the eleventh Year of my Residence, and, as I have said, my Ammunition growing low, I set my self to study some Art to trap and snare the Goats, to see whether I could not catch some of them alive, and particularly I wanted a She-Goat great with young.

To this Purpose I made Snares to hamper them, and I do believe they were more than once taken in them, but my Tackle was not good, for I had no Wire, and I always found them broken, and my Bait devoured.

At length I resolv'd to try a Pit-fall, so I dug several large Pits in the Earth, in Places where I had observ'd the Goats used to feed, and over these Pits I plac'd Hurdles of my own making too, with a great Weight upon them; and several times I put Ears of Barley, and dry Rice, without setting the Trap, and I could easily perceive that the Goats had gone in and eaten up the Corn, for I could see the Mark of their Feet. At length I set three Traps in one Night, and going the next Morning I found them all standing, and yet the Bait eaten and gone: This was very discouraging. However, I alter'd my Trap, and, not to trouble you with Particulars, going one Morning to see my Trap, I found in one of them a large old He-Goat, and in one of the other, three Kids, a Male and two Females.

As to the old one, I knew not what to do with him, he was so fierce I durst not go into the Pit to him; that is to say, to go about to bring him away alive, which was what I wanted. I could have kill'd him, but that was not my Business, nor would it answer my End. So I e'en let him out, and he ran away as if he had been frighted out of his Wits: But I had forgot then what I learn'd afterwards, that Hunger will tame a Lyon. If I had let him stay there three or four Days without Food, and then have carry'd him some Water to drink, and then a little Corn, he would have been as tame as one of the Kids, for they are mighty sagacious tractable Creatures where they are well used.

However, for the present I let him go, knowing no better at that time; then I went to the three Kids, and taking them one by one, I tyed them with Strings together, and with some Difficulty brought them all home.

It was a good while before they wou'd feed, but throwing them some sweet Corn, it tempted them and they began to be tame; and now I found that if I expected to supply my self with Goat-Flesh when I had no Powder or Shot left, breeding some up tame was my only way, when perhaps I might have them about my House like a Flock of Sheep.

But then it presently occurr'd to me, that I must keep the tame from the wild, or else they would always run wild when they grew up, and the only Way for this was to have some enclosed Piece of Ground, well fenc'd either with Hedge or Pale, to keep them in so effectually, that those within might not break out, or those without break in.

This was a great Undertaking for one Pair of Hands, yet as I saw there was an absolute Necessity of doing it, my first Piece of Work was to find out a proper Piece of Ground, *viz.* where there was likely to be Herbage for them to eat, Water for them to drink, and Cover to keep them from the Sun.

Those who understand such Enclosures will think I had very little Contrivance, when I pitch'd upon a Place very proper for all these, being a plain open Piece of Meadow-Land, or *Savanna*, (as our People call it in the Western Collonies,) which had two or three little Drills of fresh Water in it, and at one end was very woody. I say they will smile at my Forecast, when I shall tell them I began my enclosing of this Piece of Ground in such a manner, that my Hedge or Pale must have been at least two Mile about. Nor was the Madness of it so great as to the Compass, for if it was ten Mile about I was like to have time enough to do it in. But I did not consider that my Goats would be as wild in so much Compass as if they had had the whole Island, and I should have so much Room to chace them in, that I should never catch them.

My Hedge was begun and carry'd on, I believe, about fifty Yards, when this Thought occurr'd to me, so I presently stopt short, and for the first beginning I resolv'd to enclose a Piece of about 150 Yards in length, and 100 Yards in breadth, which as it would maintain as many as I should have in any reasonable time, so as my Flock encreased, I could add more Ground to my Enclosure.

This was acting with some Prudence, and I went to work with Courage. I was about three Months hedging in the first Piece, and till I had done it I tether'd the three Kids in the best part of it, and us'd* them to feed as near me as possible to make them familiar; and very often I would go and carry them some Ears of Barley, or a handful of Rice, and feed them out of my Hand; so that after my Enclosure was finished, and I let them loose, they would follow me up and down, bleating after me for a handful of Corn.

This answer'd my End, and in about a Year and half I had a Flock of about twelve Goats, Kids and all; and in two Years more I had three and forty, besides several that I took and kill'd for my Food. And after that I enclosed five several Pieces of Ground to feed them in, with little Pens to drive them into, to take them as I wanted, and Gates out of one Piece of Ground into another.

But this was not all, for now I not only had Goats Flesh to feed on when I pleas'd, but Milk too, a thing which indeed in my beginning I did not so much as think of, and which, when it came into my Thoughts, was really an agreeable Surprize. For now I set up my Dairy, and had sometimes a Gallon or two of Milk in a Day. And as Nature, who gives Supplies of Food to every Creature, dictates even naturally how to make use of it; so I that had never milk'd a Cow, much less a Goat, or seen Butter or Cheese made, very readily and handily, tho' after a great many Essays and Miscarriages, made me both Butter and Cheese at last, and never wanted it afterwards.

How mercifully can our great Creator treat his Creatures, even in those Conditions in which they seem'd to be overwhelm'd in Destruction. How can he sweeten the bitterest Providences, and give us Cause to praise him for Dungeons and Prisons. What a Table was here spread for me in a Wilderness, where I saw nothing at first but to perish for Hunger.*

It would have made a Stoick smile* to have seen, me and my little Family sit down to Dinner; there was my Majesty the Prince and Lord of the whole Island; I had the Lives of all my Subjects at my absolute Command. I could hang, draw, give Liberty, and take it away, and no Rebels among all my Subjects.

Then to see how like a King I din'd too all alone, attended by my Servants, *Poll*, as if he had been my Favourite, was the only Person permitted to talk to me. My Dog who was now grown very old and crazy, and had found no Species to multiply his Kind upon, sat always at my Right Hand, and two Cats, one on one Side the Table, and one on the other, expecting now and then a Bit from my Hand, as a Mark of special Favour.

But these were not the two Cats which I brought on Shore at first, for they were both of them dead, and had been interr'd near my Habitation by my own Hand; but one of them having multiply'd by I know not what Kind of Creature, these were two which I had preserv'd tame, whereas the rest run wild in the Woods, and became indeed troublesom to me at last; for they would often come into my House, and plunder me too, till at last I was obliged to shoot them, and did kill a great many; at length they left me with this Attendance, and in this plentiful Manner I lived; neither could I be said to want any thing but Society, and of that in some time after this, I was like to have too much.

I was something impatient, as I have observ'd, to have the Use of my Boat; though very loath to run any more Hazards; and therefore sometimes I sat contriving Ways to get her about the Island, and at other Times I sat my self down contented enough without her. But I had a strange Uneasiness in my Mind to go down to the Point of the Island, where, as I have said, in my last Ramble, I went up the Hill to see how the Shore lay, and how the Current set, that I might see what I had to do: This Inclination encreas'd upon me every Day, and at length I resolv'd to travel thither by Land, following the Edge of the Shore. I did so: But had any one in *England* been to meet such a Man as I was, it must either have frighted them, or rais'd a great deal of Laughter; and as I frequently stood still to look at my self, I could not but smile at the Notion of my travelling through *Yorkshire* with such an Equipage, and in such a Dress: Be pleas'd to take a Scetch of my Figure as follows.

I had a great high shapeless Cap, made of a Goat's Skin, with a Flap hanging down behind, as well to keep the Sun from me, as to shoot the Rain off from running into my Neck; nothing being so hurtful in these Climates, as the Rain upon the Flesh under the Cloaths.

I had a short Jacket of Goat-Skin, the Skirts coming down to about the middle of my Thighs; and a Pair of open-knee'd Breeches of the same, the Breeches were made of the Skin of an old *He-goat*, whose Hair hung down such a Length on either Side, that like *Pantaloons* it reach'd to the middle of my Legs; Stockings and Shoes I had none, but had made me a Pair of some-things, I scarce know what to call them, like Buskins to flap over my Legs, and lace on either Side like Spatter-dashes; but of a most barbarous Shape, as indeed were all the rest of my Cloaths.

I had on a broad Belt of Goat's-Skin dry'd, which I drew together with two Thongs of the same, instead of Buckles, and in a kind of a Frog on either Side of this. Instead of a Sword and a Dagger, hung a little Saw and a Hatchet, one on one Side, one on the other. I had another Belt not so broad, and fasten'd in the same Manner, which hung over my Shoulder; and at the End of it, under my left Arm, hung two Pouches, both made of Goat's-Skin too; in one of which hung my Powder, in the other my Shot: At my Back I carry'd my Basket, on my Shoulder my Gun, and over my Head a great clumsy ugly Goat-Skin Umbrella, but which, after all, was the most necessary Thing I had about me, next to my Gun: As for my Face, the Colour of it was really not so *Moletta*-like as one might expect from a Man not at all careful of it, and living within nine or ten Degrees of the *Equinox*.* My Beard I had once suffer'd to grow till it was about a quarter of a Yard long; but as I had both Scissars and Razors sufficient, I had cut it pretty short, except what grew on my upper Lip, which I had trimm'd into a large Pair of *Mahometan* Whiskers, such as I had seen worn by some *Turks*, who I saw at *Sallee*; for the *Moors* did not wear such, tho' the *Turks* did; of these Muschatoes or Whiskers, I will not say they were long enough to hang my Hat upon them; but they were of a Length and Shape monstrous enough, and such as in *England* would have pass'd for frightful.

But all this is by the by; for as to my Figure, I had so few to observe me, that it was of no manner of Consequence; so I say no more to that Part. In this kind of Figure I went my new Journey, and was out five or six Days. I travell'd first along the Sea Shore, directly to the Place where I first brought my Boat to an Anchor, to get up upon the Rocks; and having no Boat now to take care of, I went over the Land a nearer Way to the same Height that I was upon before, when looking forward to the Point of the Rocks which lay out, and which I was oblig'd to double with my Boat, as is said above: I was surpriz'd to see the Sea all smooth and quiet, no Ripling, no Motion, no Current, any more there than in other Places.

I was at a strange Loss to understand this, and resolv'd to spend some Time in the observing it, to see if nothing from the Sets of the Tide had occasion'd it; but I was presently convinc'd how it was, *viz.* That the Tide of Ebb setting from the *West*, and joyning with the Current of Waters from some great River on the Shore,* must be the Occasion of this Current; and that according as the Wind blew more forcibly from the *West*, or from the *North*, this Current came nearer, or went farther from the Shore; for waiting thereabouts till Evening, I went up to the Rock again, and then the Tide of Ebb being made, I plainly saw the Current again as before, only, that it run farther off, being near half a League from the Shore; whereas in my Case, it set close upon the Shore, and hurry'd me and my *Canoe* along with it, which at another Time it would not have done.

This Observation convinc'd me, That I had nothing to do but to observe the Ebbing and the Flowing of the Tide, and I might very easily bring my Boat about the Island again: But when I began to think of putting it in Practice, I had such a Terror upon my Spirits at the Remembrance of the Danger I had been in, that I could not think of it again with any Patience; but on the contrary, I took up another Resolution which was more safe, though more laborious; and this was, That I would build, or rather make me another *Periagua* or *Canoe*; and so have one for one Side of the Island, and one for the other.

You are to understand, that now I had, as I may call it, two Plant-ations in the Island; one my little Fortification or Tent, with the Wall about it under the Rock, with the Cave behind me, which by this Time I had enlarg'd into several Apartments, or Caves, one within another. One of these, which was the dryest, and largest, and had a Door out beyond my Wall or Fortification; that is to say, beyond where my Wall joyn'd to the Rock, was all fill'd up with the large Earthen Pots, of which I have given an Account, and with fourteen or fifteen great Baskets, which would hold five or six Bushels each, where I laid up my Stores of Provision, especially my Corn, some in the Ear cut off short from the Straw, and the other rubb'd out with my Hand.

As for my Wall made, *as before*, with long Stakes or Piles, those Piles grew all like Trees, and were by this Time grown so big, and spread so very much, that there was not the least Appearance to any one's View of any Habitation behind them.

Near this Dwelling of mine, but a little farther within the Land, and upon lower Ground, lay my two Pieces of Corn-Ground, which I kept duly cultivated and sow'd, and which duly yielded me their Harvest in its Season; and whenever I had occasion for more Corn, I had more Land adjoyning as fit as that.

Besides this, I had my Country Seat, and I had now a tollerable Plantation there also; for first, I had my little Bower, as I call'd it, which I kept in Repair; *that is to say*, I kept the Hedge which circled it in, constantly fitted up to its usual Height, the Ladder standing always in the Inside; I kept the Trees which at first were no more than my Stakes, but were now grown very firm and tall; I kept them always so cut, that they might spread and grow thick and wild, and make the more agreeable Shade, which they did effectually to my Mind. In the Middle of this I had my Tent always standing, being a piece of a Sail spread over Poles set up for that Purpose, and which never wanted any Repair or Renewing; and under this I had made me a Squab or Couch, with the Skins of the Creatures I had kill'd, and with other soft Things, and a Blanket laid on them, such as belong'd to our Sea-Bedding, which I had saved, and a great Watch-Coat to cover me; and here, whenever I had Occasion to be absent from my chief Seat, I took up my Country Habitation.

Adjoyning to this I had my Enclosures for my Cattle, that is to say, my Goats: And as I had taken an inconceivable deal of Pains to fence and enclose this Ground, so I was so uneasy to see it kept entire, lest the Goats should break thro', that I never left off till with infinite Labour I had stuck the Out-side of the Hedge so full of small Stakes, and so near to one another, that it was rather a Pale than a Hedge, and there was scarce Room to put a Hand thro' between them, which afterwards when those Stakes grew, as they all did in the next rainy Season, made the Enclosure strong like a Wall, indeed stronger than any Wall.

This will testify for me that I was not idle, and that I spared no Pains to bring to pass whatever appear'd necessary for my comfortable Support; for I consider'd the keeping up a Breed of tame Creatures thus at my Hand, would be a living Magazine of Flesh, Milk, Butter and Cheese, for me as long as I liv'd in the Place, if it were to be forty Years; and that keeping them in my Reach, depended entirely upon my perfecting my Enclosures to such a Degree, that I might be sure of keeping them together; which by this Method indeed I so effectually secur'd, that when these little Stakes began to grow, I had planted them so very thick, I was forced to pull some of them up again.

In this Place also I had my Grapes growing, which I principally depended on for my Winter Store of Raisins; and which I never fail'd to preserve very carefully, as the best and most agreeable Dainty of my whole Diet; and indeed they were not agreeable only, but physical, wholesome, nourishing, and refreshing to the last Degree.

As this was also about half Way between my other Habitation, and the Place where I had laid up my Boat, I generally stay'd, and lay here in my Way thither; for I used frequently to visit my Boat, and I kept all Things about or belonging to her in very good Order; sometimes I went out in her to divert my self, but no more hazardous Voyages would I go, nor scarce ever above a Stone's Cast or two from the Shore, I was so apprehensive of being hurry'd out of my Knowledge again by the Currents, or Winds, or any other Accident. But now I come to a new Scene of my Life.

It happen'd one Day about Noon going towards my Boat, I was exceedingly surpriz'd with the Print of a Man's naked Foot on the Shore, which was very plain to be seen in the Sand: I stood like one Thunder-struck, or as if I had seen an Apparition; I listen'd, I look'd round me, I could hear nothing, nor see any Thing, I went up to a rising Ground to look farther, I went up the Shore and down the Shore, but it was all one, I could see no other Impression but that one, I went to it again to see if there were any more, and to observe if it might not be my Fancy; but there was no Room for that, for there was exactly the very Print of a Foot, Toes, Heel, and every Part of a Foot; how it came thither, I knew not, nor could in the least imagine. But after innumerable fluttering Thoughts, like a Man perfectly confus'd and out of my self, I came Home to my Fortification, not feeling, as we say, the Ground I went on, but terrify'd to the last Degree, looking behind me at every two or three Steps, mistaking every Bush and Tree, and fancying every Stump at a Distance to be a Man; nor is it possible to describe how many various Shapes affrighted Imagination represented Things to me in, how many wild Ideas were found every Moment in my Fancy, and what strange unaccountable Whimsies came into my Thoughts by the Way.

When I came to my Castle, for so I think I call'd it ever after this, I fled into it like one pursued; whether I went over by the Ladder as first contriv'd, or went in at the Hole in the Rock, which I call'd a Door, I cannot remember; no, nor could I remember the next Morning, for never frighted Hare fled to Cover, or Fox to Earth, with more Terror of Mind than I to this Retreat.

I slept none that Night; the farther I was from the Occasion of my Fright, the greater my Apprehensions were, which is something contrary to the Nature of such Things, and especially to the usual Practice of all Creatures in Fear: But I was so embarrass'd with my own frightful Ideas of the Thing, that I form'd nothing but dismal Imaginations to my self, even tho' I was now a great way off of it. Sometimes I fancy'd it must be the Devil; and Reason joyn'd in with me upon this Supposition: For how should any other Thing in human Shape come into the Place? Where was the Vessel that brought them? What Marks was there of any other Footsteps? And how was it possible a Man should come there? But then to think that *Satan* should take human shape upon him in such a Place where there could be no manner of Occasion for it, but to leave the Print of his Foot behind him, and that even for no Purpose too, for he could not be sure I should see it; this was an Amusement the other Way; I consider'd that the Devil might have found out abundance of other Ways to have terrify'd me than this of the single Print of a Foot. That as I liv'd quite on the other Side of the Island, he would never have been so simple to leave a Mark in a Place where 'twas Ten Thousand to one whether I should ever see it or not, and in the Sand too, which the first Surge of the Sea upon a high Wind would have defac'd entirely: All this seem'd inconsistent with the Thing it self, and with all the Notions we usually entertain of the Subtilty of the Devil.

Abundance of such Things as these assisted to argue me out of all Apprehensions of its being the Devil: And I presently concluded then, that it must be some more dangerous Creature, (*viz.*) That it must be some of the Savages of the main Land over-against me, who had wander'd out to Sea in their *Canoes*; and either driven by the Currents, or by contrary Winds had made the Island; and had been on Shore, but were gone away again to Sea, being as loth, perhaps, to have stay'd in this desolate Island, as I would have been to have had them.

While these Reflections were rowling upon my Mind, I was very thankful in my Thoughts, that I was so happy as not to be thereabouts at that Time, or that they did not see my Boat, by which they would have concluded that some Inhabitants had been in the Place, and perhaps have search'd farther for me: Then terrible Thoughts rack'd my Imagination about their having found my Boat, and that there were People here; and that if so, I should certainly have them come again in greater Numbers, and devour me; that if it should happen so that they should not find me, yet they would find my Enclosure, destroy all my Corn, carry away all my Flock of tame Goats, and I should perish at last for meer Want.

Thus my Fear banish'd all my religious Hope; all that former Confidence in God which was founded upon such wonderful Experience as I had had of his Goodness, now vanished, as if he that had fed me by Miracle hitherto, could not preserve by his Power the Provision which he had made for me by his Goodness: I reproach'd my self with my Easiness, that would not sow any more Corn one Year than would just serve me till the next Season, as if no Accident could intervene to prevent my enjoying the Crop that was upon the Ground; and this I thought so just a Reproof, that I resolv'd for the future to have two or three Years Corn beforehand, so that whatever might come, I might not perish for want of Bread.

How strange a Chequer Work* of Providence is the Life of Man! and by what secret differing Springs are the Affections hurry'd about as differing Circumstances present! To Day we love what to Morrow we hate; to Day we seek what to Morrow we shun; to Day we desire what to Morrow we fear; nay even tremble at the Apprehensions of; this was exemplify'd in me at this Time in the most lively Manner imaginable; for I whose only Affliction was, that I seem'd banished from human Society, that I was alone, circumscrib'd by the boundless Ocean, cut off from Mankind, and condemn'd to what I call'd silent Life; that I was as one who Heaven thought not worthy to be number'd among the Living, or to appear among the rest of his Creatures; that to have seen one of my own Species, would have seem'd to me a Raising me from Death to Life, and the greatest Blessing that Heaven it self, next to the supreme Blessing of Salvation, could bestow; *I say*, that I should now tremble at the very Apprehensions of seeing a Man, and was ready to sink into the Ground at but the Shadow or silent Appearance of a Man's having set his Foot in the Island.

Such is the uneven State of human Life: And it afforded me a great many curious Speculations afterwards, when I had a little recover'd my first Surprize; I consider'd that this was the Station of Life the infinitely wise and good Providence of God had determin'd for me, that as I could not foresee what the Ends of Divine Wisdom might be in all this, so I was not to dispute his Sovereignty, who, as I was his Creature, had an undoubted Right by Creation to govern and dispose of me absolutely as he thought fit; and who, as I was a Creature who had offended him, had likewise a judicial Right to condemn me to what Punishment he thought fit; and that it was my Part to submit to bear his Indignation, because I had sinn'd against him.

I then reflected that God, who was not only Righteous but Omnipotent, as he had thought fit thus to punish and afflict me, so he was able to deliver me; that if he did not think fit to do it, 'twas my unquestion'd Duty to resign my self absolutely and entirely to his Will; and on the other Hand, it was my Duty also to hope in him, pray to him, and quietly to attend the Dictates and Directions of his daily Providence.

These Thoughts took me up many Hours, Days; nay, I may say, Weeks and Months; and one particular Effect of my Cogitations on this Occasion, I cannot omit, *viz.* One Morning early, lying in my Bed, and fill'd with Thought about my Danger from the Appearance of Savages, I found it discompos'd me very much, upon which those Words of the Scripture came into my Thoughts, *Call upon me in the Day of Trouble, and I will deliver, and thou shalt glorify me.**

Upon this, rising chearfully out of my Bed, my Heart was not only comforted, but I was guided and encourag'd to pray earnestly to God for Deliverance: When I had done praying, I took up my Bible, and opening it to read, the first Words that presented to me, were, *Wait on the Lord, and be of good Cheer, and he shall strengthen thy Heart; wait, I say, on the Lord:** It is impossible to express the Comfort this gave me. In Answer, I thankfully laid down the Book, and was no more sad, at least, not on that Occasion.

In the middle of these Cogitations, Apprehensions and Reflections, it came into my Thought one Day, that all this might be a meer Chimera of my own; and that this Foot might be the Print of my own

Foot, when I came on Shore from my Boat: This chear'd me up a little too, and I began to perswade my self it was all a Delusion; that it was nothing else but my own Foot, and why might not I come that way from the Boat, as well as I was going that way to the Boat; again, I consider'd also that I could by no Means tell for certain where I had trod, and where I had not; and that if at last this was only the Print of my own Foot, I had play'd the Part of those Fools, who strive to make stories of Spectres, and Apparitions; and then are frighted at them more than any body.

Now I began to take Courage, and to peep abroad again; for I had not stirr'd out of my Castle for three Days and Nights; so that I began to starve for Provision; for I had little or nothing within Doors, but some Barley Cakes and Water. Then I knew that my Goats wanted to be milk'd too, which usually was my Evening Diversion; and the poor Creatures were in great Pain and Inconvenience for want of it; and indeed, it almost spoil'd some of them, and almost dry'd up their Milk.

Heartning my self therefore with the Belief that this was nothing but the Print of one of my own Feet, and so I might be truly said to start at my own Shadow, I began to go abroad again, and went to my Country House, to milk my Flock; but to see with what Fear I went forward, how often I look'd behind me, how I was ready every now and then to lay down my Basket, and run for my Life, it would have made any one have thought I was haunted with an evil Conscience, or that I had been lately most terribly frighted, and so indeed I had.

However, as I went down thus two or three Days, and having seen nothing, I began to be a little bolder; and to think there was really nothing in it, but my own Imagination: But I cou'd not perswade my self fully of this, till I should go down to the Shore again, and see this Print of a Foot, and measure it by my own, and see if there was any Similitude or Fitness, that I might be assur'd it was my own Foot: But when I came to the Place, *First*, It appear'd evidently to me, that when I laid up my Boat, I could not possibly be on Shore any where there about. *Secondly*, When I came to measure the Mark with my own Foot, I found my Foot not so large by a great deal; both these Things fill'd my Head with new Imaginations, and gave me the Vapours again, to the highest Degree; so that I shook with cold, like one in an Ague: And I went Home again, fill'd with the Belief that some Man or Men had been on Shore there; or in short, that the Island was inhabited, and I might be surpriz'd before I was aware; and what course to take for my Security I knew not.

O what ridiculous Resolution Men take, when possess'd with Fear! It deprives them of the Use of those Means which Reason offers for their Relief. The first Thing I propos'd to my self, was, to throw down my Enclosures, and turn all my tame Cattle wild into the Woods, that the Enemy might not find them; and then frequent the Island in Prospect of the same, or the like Booty: Then to the simple Thing of Digging up my two Corn Fields, that they might not find such a Grain there, and still be prompted to frequent the Island; then to demolish my Bower, and Tent, that they might not see any Vestiges of Habitation, and be prompted to look farther, in order to find out the Persons inhabiting.

These were the Subject of the first Night's Cogitation, after I was come Home again, while the Apprehensions which had so over-run my Mind were fresh upon me, and my Head was full of Vapours, as above: Thus Fear of Danger is ten thousand Times more terrifying than Danger it self, when apparent to the Eyes; and we find the Burthen of Anxiety greater by much, than the Evil which we are anxious about; and which was worse than all this, I had not that Relief in this Trouble from the Resignation I used to practise, that I hop'd to have. I look'd, I thought, like *Saul*, who complain'd not only that the *Philistines* were upon him; but that God had forsaken him;* for I did not now take due Ways to compose my Mind, by crying to God in my Distress, and resting upon his Providence, as I had done before, for my Defence and Deliverance; which if I had done, I had, at least, been more cheerfully supported under this new Surprise, and perhaps carry'd through it with more Resolution.

This Confusion of my Thoughts kept me waking all Night; but in the Morning I fell asleep, and having by the Amusement of my Mind, been, as it were, tyr'd, and my Spirits exhausted; I slept very soundly, and wak'd much better compos'd than I had ever been before; and now I began to think sedately; and upon the utmost Debate with my self, I concluded, That this Island, which was so exceeding pleasant, fruitful, and no farther from the main Land than as I had seen, was not so entirely abandon'd as I might imagine: That altho' there were no stated Inhabitants who liv'd on the Spot; yet that there might sometimes come Boats off from the Shore, who either with Design, or perhaps never, but when they were driven by cross Winds, might come to this Place.

That I had liv'd here fifteen Years now, and had not met with the least Shadow or Figure of any People yet; and that if at any Time they should be driven here, it was probable they went away again as soon as ever they could, seeing they had never thought fit to fix there upon any Occasion, to this Time.

That the most I cou'd suggest any Danger from, was, from any such casual accidental Landing of straggling People from the Main, who, as it was likely if they were driven hither, were here against their Wills; so they made no stay here, but went off again with all possible Speed, seldom staying one Night on Shore, least they should not have the Help of the Tides, and Day-light back again; and that therefore I had nothing to do but to consider of some safe Retreat, in Case I should see any Savages land upon the Spot.

Now I began sorely to repent, that I had dug my Cave so large, as to bring a Door through again, which Door, as I said, came out beyond where my Fortification joyn'd to the Rock; upon maturely considering this therefore, I resolv'd to draw me a second Fortification, in the same Manner of a Semicircle, at a Distance from my Wall, just where I had planted a double Row of Trees, about twelve Years before, of which I made mention: These Trees having been planted so thick before, they wanted but a few Piles to be driven between them, that they should be thicker, and stronger, and my Wall would be soon finish'd.

So that I had now a double Wall, and my outer Wall was thickned with Pieces of Timber, old Cables, and every Thing I could think of, to make it strong; having in it seven little Holes, about as big as I might put my Arm out at: In the In-side of this, I thickned my Wall to above ten Foot thick, with continual bringing Earth out of my Cave, and laying it at the Foot of the Wall, and walking upon it; and through the seven Holes, I contriv'd to plant the Musquets, of which I took Notice, that I got seven on Shore out of the Ship; these, I say, I planted like my Cannon, and fitted them into Frames that held them like a Carriage, that so I could fire all the seven Guns in two Minutes Time: This Wall I was many a weary Month a finishing, and yet never thought my self safe till it was done.

When this was done, I stuck all the Ground without my Wall, for a great way every way, as full with Stakes or Sticks of the *Osier* like

Wood, which I found so apt to grow, as they could well stand; inso-much, that I believe I might set in near twenty thousand of them, leaving a pretty large Space between them and my Wall, that I might have room to see an Enemy, and they might have no shelter from the young Trees, if they attempted to approach my outer Wall.

Thus in two Years Time I had a thick Grove and in five or six Years Time I had a Wood before my Dwelling, growing so mon-strous thick and strong, that it was indeed perfectly impassable; and no Men of what kind soever, would ever imagine that there was any Thing beyond it, much less a Habitation: As for the Way which I propos'd to my self to go in and out, for I left no Avenue; it was by setting two Ladders, one to a Part of the Rock which was low, and then broke in, and left room to place another Ladder upon that; so when the two Ladders were taken down, no Man living could come down to me without mischieving himself; and if they had come down, they were still on the Out-side of my outer Wall.

Thus I took all the Measures humane Prudence could suggest for my own Preservation; and it will be seen at length, that they were not altogether without just Reason; though I foresaw nothing at that Time, more than my meer Fear suggested to me.

While this was doing, I was not altogether Careless of my other Affairs; for I had a great Concern upon me, for my little Herd of Goats; they were not only a present Supply to me upon every Occa-sion, and began to be sufficient to me, without the Expence of Pow-der and Shot; but also without the Fatigue of Hunting after the wild Ones, and I was loth to lose the Advantage of them, and to have them all to nurse up over again.

To this Purpose, after long Consideration, I could think of but two Ways to preserve them; one was to find another convenient Place to dig a Cave Under-ground, and to drive them into it every Night; and the other was to enclose two or three little Bits of Land, remote from one another and as much conceal'd as I could, where I might keep about half a Dozen young Goats in each Place: So that if any Disaster happen'd to the Flock in general, I might be able to raise them again with little Trouble and Time: And this, tho' it would require a great deal of Time and Labour, I thought was the most rational Design.

Accordingly I spent some Time to find out the most retir'd Parts of the Island; and I pitch'd upon one which was as private indeed as my Heart could wish for; it was a little damp Piece of Ground in the Middle of the hollow and thick Woods, where, as is observ'd, I almost lost my self once before, endeavouring to come back that Way from the Eastern Part of the Island: Here I found a clear Piece of Land near three Acres, so surrounded with Woods, that it was almost an Enclosure by Nature, at least it did not want near so much Labour to make it so, as the other Pieces of Ground I had work'd so hard at.

I immediately went to Work with this Piece of Ground, and in less than a Month's Time, I had so fenc'd it round, that my Flock or Herd, call it which you please, who were not so wild now as at first they might be supposed to be, were well enough secur'd in it. So, without any farther Delay, I removed ten young She-Goats and two He-Goats to this Piece; and when they were there, I continued to perfect the Fence till I had made it as secure as the other, which, however, I did at more Leisure, and it took me up more Time by a great deal.

All this Labour I was at the Expence of, purely from my Apprehensions on the Account of the Print of a Man's Foot which I had seen; for as yet I never saw any human Creature come near the Island, and I had now liv'd two Years under these Uneasinesses, which indeed made my Life much less comfortable than it was before; as may well be imagin'd by any who know what it is to live in the constant Snare of *the Fear of Man*; and this I must observe with Grief too, that the Discomposure of my Mind had too great Impressions also upon the religious Part of my Thoughts, for the Dread and Terror of falling into the Hands of Savages and Canibals, lay so upon my Spirits, that I seldom found my self in a due Temper for Application to my Maker, at least not with the sedate Calmness and Resignation of Soul which I was wont to do; I rather pray'd to God as under great Affliction and Pressure of Mind, surrounded with Danger, and in Expectation every Night of being murther'd and devour'd before Morning; and I must testify from my Experience, that a Temper of Peace, Thankfulness, Love and Affection, is much more the proper Frame for Prayer than that of Terror and Discomposure; and that under the Dread of Mischief impending, a Man is no more fit for a comforting Performance of the Duty of praying to God, than he is for Repentance on a sick Bed: For these Discomposures affect the Mind as the others do the Body; and the Discomposure of the Mind must necessarily be as great a Disability as that of the Body, and much greater, Praying to God being properly an Act of the Mind, not of the Body.

But to go on; After I had thus secur'd one Part of my little living Stock, I went about the whole Island, searching for another private Place, to make such another Deposit; when wandring more to the *West* Point of the Island, than I had ever done yet, and looking out to Sea, I thought I saw a Boat upon the Sea, at a great Distance; I had found a Prospective Glass, or two, in one of the Seamen's Chests, which I sav'd out of our Ship; but I had it not about me, and this was so remote, that I could not tell what to make of it; though I look'd at it till my Eyes were not able to hold to look any longer; whether it was a Boat, or not, I do not know; but as I descended from the Hill, I could see no more of it, so I gave it over; only I resolv'd to go no more out without a Prospective Glass in my Pocket.

When I was come down the Hill, to the End of the Island, where indeed I had never been before, I was presently convinc'd, that the seeing the Print of a Man's Foot, was not such a strange Thing in the Island as I imagin'd; and but that it was a special Providence that I was cast upon the Side of the Island, where the Savages never came: I should easily have known, that nothing was more frequent than for the *Canoes* from the Main, when they happen'd to be a little too far out at Sea, to shoot over to that Side of the Island for Harbour; likewise as they often met, and fought in their *Canoes*, the Victors having taken any Prisoners, would bring them over to this Shore, where according to their dreadful Customs, being all *Canibals*, they would kill and eat them; of which hereafter.

When I was come down the Hill, to the Shore, as I said above, being the *S. W.* Point of the Island, I was perfectly confounded and amaz'd; nor is it possible for me to express the Horror of my Mind, at seeing the Shore spread with Skulls, Hands, Feet, and other Bones of humane Bodies; and particularly I observ'd a Place where there had been a Fire made, and a Circle dug in the Earth, like a Cockpit, where it is suppos'd the Savage Wretches had sat down to their inhumane Feastings upon the Bodies of their Fellow-Creatures.

I was so astonish'd with the Sight of these Things, that I enter-tain'd no Notions of any Danger to my self from it for a long while; All my Apprehensions were bury'd in the Thoughts of such a Pitch of inhuman, hellish Brutality, and the Horror of the Degeneracy of Humane Nature; which though I had heard of often, yet I never had

so near a View of before; in short, I turn'd away my Face from the
horrid Spectacle; my Stomach grew sick, and I was just at the Point
of Fainting, when Nature discharg'd the Disorder from my Stomach; and having vomited with an uncommon Violence, I was a little
reliev'd; but cou'd not bear to stay in the Place a Moment; so I gat
me up the Hill again, with all the Speed I cou'd, and walk'd on
towards my own Habitation.

When I came a little out of that Part of the Island, I stood still a
while as amaz'd; and then recovering my self, I look'd up with the
utmost Affection of my Soul, and with a Flood of Tears in my Eyes,
gave God Thanks that had cast my first Lot in a Part of the World,
where I was distinguish'd from such dreadful Creatures as these; and
that though I had esteem'd my present Condition very miserable,
had yet given me so many Comforts in it, that I had still more to give
Thanks for than to complain of; and this above all, that I had even in
this miserable Condition been comforted with the Knowledge of
himself, and the Hope of his Blessing, which was a Felicity more
than sufficiently equivalent to all the Misery which I had suffer'd, or
could suffer.

In this Frame of Thankfulness, I went Home to my Castle, and
began to be much easier now, as to the Safety of my Circumstances,
than ever I was before; for I observ'd, that these Wretches never
came to this Island in search of what they could get; perhaps not
seeking, not wanting, or not expecting any Thing here; and having
often, no doubt, been up in the cover'd woody Part of it, without
finding any Thing to their Purpose. I knew I had been here now
almost eighteen Years, and never saw the least Foot-steps of Humane
Creature there before; and I might be here eighteen more, as entirely
conceal'd as I was now, if I did not discover my self to them, which I
had no manner of Occasion to do, it being my only Business to keep
my self entirely conceal'd where I was, unless I found a better sort of
Creatures than *Canibals* to make my self known to.

Yet I entertain'd such an Abhorrence of the Savage Wretches, that
I have been speaking of, and of the wretched inhuman Custom of
their devouring and eating one another up, that I continu'd pensive,
and sad, and kept close within my own Circle for almost two Years
after this: When I say my own Circle, I mean by it, my three Plantations, *viz.* my Castle, my Country Seat, which I call'd my Bower,
and my Enclosure in the Woods; nor did I look after this for any

other Use than as an Enclosure for my Goats; for the Aversion which Nature gave me to these hellish Wretches, was such, that I was fearful of seeing them, as of seeing the Devil himself; nor did I so much as go to look after my Boat, in all this Time; but began rather to think of making me another; for I cou'd not think of ever making any more Attempts, to bring the other Boat round the Island to me, least I should meet with some of these Creatures at Sea, in which, if I had happen'd to have fallen into their Hands, I knew what would have been my Lot.

Time however, and the Satisfaction I had, that I was in no Danger of being discover'd by these People, began to wear off my Uneasiness about them; and I began to live just in the same compos'd Manner as before; only with this Difference, that I used more Caution, and kept my Eyes more about me than I did before, least I should happen to be seen by any of them; and particularly, I was more cautious of firing my Gun, least any of them being on the Island, should happen to hear of it; and it was therefore a very good Providence to me,* that I had furnish'd my self with a tame Breed of Goats, that I needed not hunt any more about the Woods, or shoot at them; and if I did catch any of them after this, it was by Traps, and Snares, as I had done before; so that for two Years after this, I believe I never fir'd my Gun once off, though I never went out without it; and which was more, as I had sav'd three Pistols out of the Ship, I always carry'd them out with me, or at least two of them, sticking them in my Goat-skin Belt; also I furbish'd up one of the great Cutlashes, that I had out of the Ship, and made me a Belt to put it on also; so that I was now a most formidable Fellow to look at, when I went abroad, if you add to the former Description of my self, the Particular of two Pistols, and a great broad Sword, hanging at my Side in a Belt, but without a Scabbard.

Things going on thus, as I have said, for some Time; I seem'd, excepting these Cautions, to be reduc'd to my former calm, sedate Way of Living, all these Things tended to shewing me more and more how far my Condition was from being miserable, compar'd to some others; nay, to many other Particulars of Life, which it might have pleased God to have made my Lot. It put me upon reflecting, How little repining there would be among Mankind, at any Condition of Life, if People would rather compare their Condition with those that are worse, in order to be thankful, than be always comparing them with those which are better, to assist their Murmurings and Complainings.

As in my present Condition there were not really many Things which I wanted; so indeed I thought that the Frights I had been in about these Savage Wretches, and the Concern I had been in for my own Preservation, had taken off the Edge of my Invention for my own Conveniences; and I had dropp'd a good Design, which I had once bent my Thoughts too much upon; and that was, to try if I could not make some of my Barley into Malt, and then try to brew my self some Beer: This was really a whimsical Thought, and I reprov'd my self often for the Simplicity of it; for I presently saw there would be the want of several Things necessary to the making my Beer, that it would be impossible for me to supply; as First, Casks to preserve it in, which was a Thing, that as I have observ'd already, I cou'd never compass; no, though I spent not many Days, but Weeks, nay, Months in attempting it, but to no purpose. In the next Place, I had no Hops to make it keep, no Yeast to make it work, no Copper or Kettle to make it boil; and yet all these Things, notwithstanding, I verily believe, had not these Things interven'd, I mean the Frights and Terrors I was in about the Savages, I had undertaken it, and perhaps brought it to pass too; for I seldom gave any Thing over without accomplishing it, when I once had it in my Head enough to begin it.

But my Invention now run quite another Way; for Night and Day, I could think of nothing but how I might destroy some of these Monsters in their cruel bloody Entertainment, and if possible, save the Victim they should bring hither to destroy. It would take up a larger Volume than this whole Work is intended to be, to set down all the Contrivances I hatch'd, or rather brooded upon in my Thought, for the destroying these Creatures, or at least frighting them, so as to prevent their coming hither any more; but all was abortive, nothing could be possible to take effect, unless I was to be there to do it my self; and what could one Man do among them, when perhaps there might be twenty or thirty of them together, with their Darts, or their Bows and Arrows, with which they could shoot as true to a Mark, as I could with my Gun?

Sometimes I contriv'd to dig a Hole under the Place where they made their Fire, and put in five or six Pound of Gun-powder, which when they kindled their Fire, would consequently take Fire, and blow up all that was near it; but as in the first Place I should be very loth to wast so much Powder upon them, my Store being now within the Quantity of one Barrel; so neither could I be sure of its going off, at any certain Time, when it might surprise them, and at best, that it would do little more than just blow the Fire about their Ears and fright them, but not sufficient to make them forsake the Place; so I laid it aside, and then propos'd, that I would place my self in Ambush, in some convenient Place, with my three Guns, all double loaded; and in the middle of their bloody Ceremony, let fly at them, when I should be sure to kill or wound perhaps two or three at every shoot; and then falling in upon them with my three Pistols, and my Sword, I made no doubt, but that if there was twenty I should kill them all: This Fancy pleas'd my Thoughts for some Weeks, and I was so full of it, that I often dream'd of it; and sometimes that I was just going to let fly at them in my Sleep.

I went so far with it in my Imagination, that I employ'd my self several Days to find out proper Places to put my self in Ambuscade, as I said, to watch for them; and I went frequently to the Place it self, which was now grown more familiar to me; and especially while my Mind was thus fill'd with Thoughts of Revenge, and of a bloody putting twenty or thirty of them to the Sword, as I may call it, the Horror I had at the Place, and at the Signals of the barbarous Wretches devouring one another, abated my Malice.*

Well, at length I found a Place in the Side of the Hill, where I was satisfy'd I might securely wait, till I saw any of their Boats coming, and might then, even before they would be ready to come on Shore, convey my self unseen into Thickets of Trees, in one of which there was a Hollow large enough to conceal me entirely; and where I might sit, and observe all their bloody Doings, and take my full aim at their Heads, when they were so close together, as that it would be next to impossible that I should miss my Shoot, or that I could fail wounding three or four of them at the first Shoot.

In this Place then I resolv'd to fix my Design, and accordingly I prepar'd two Muskets, and my ordinary Fowling Piece. The two Muskets I loaded with a Brace of Slugs each, and four or five smaller Bullets, about the Size of Pistol Bullets; and the Fowling Piece I loaded with near a Handful of Swan-shot, of the largest Size; I also loaded my Pistols with about four Bullets each, and in this Posture, well provided with Ammunition for a second and third Charge, I prepar'd my self for my Expedition.

After I had thus laid the Scheme of my Design, and in my
Imagination put it in Practice, I continually made my Tour every
Morning up to the Top of the Hill, which was from my Castle, as I
call'd it, about three Miles, or more, to see if I cou'd observe any
Boats upon the Sea, coming near the Island, or standing over
towards it; but I began to tire of this hard Duty, after I had for two or
three Months constantly kept my Watch; but came always back
without any Discovery, there having not in all that Time been the
least Appearance, not only on, or near the Shore; but not on the
whole Ocean, so far as my Eyes or Glasses could reach every Way.

As long as I kept up my daily Tour to the Hill, to look out; so long
also I kept up the Vigour of my Design, and my Spirits seem'd to be
all the while in a suitable Form, for so outragious an Execution as the
killing twenty or thirty naked Savages, for an Offence which I had
not at all entred into a Discussion of in my Thoughts, any farther
than my Passions were at first fir'd by the Horror I conceiv'd at the
unnatural Custom of that People of the Country, who it seems had
been suffer'd by Providence in his wise Disposition of the World, to
have no other Guide than that of their own abominable and vitiated
Passions; and consequently were left, and perhaps had been so for
some Ages, to act such horrid Things, and receive such dreadful
Customs, as nothing but Nature entirely abandon'd of Heaven, and
acted by some hellish Degeneracy, could have run them into: But
now, when as I have said, I began to be weary of the fruitless Excursion, which I had made so long, and so far, every Morning in vain, so
my Opinion of the Action it self began to alter, and I began with
cooler and calmer Thoughts to consider what it was I was going to
engage in. What Authority, or Call I had, to pretend to be Judge and
Executioner upon these Men as Criminals, whom Heaven had
thought fit for so many Ages to suffer unpunish'd, to go on, and to be
as it were, the Executioners of his Judgments one upon another.
How far these People were Offenders against me, and what Right I
had to engage in the Quarrel of that Blood, which they shed pro-
miscuously one upon another. I debated this very often with my self
thus; How do I know what God himself judges in this particular
Case? it is certain these People either do not commit this as a Crime;
it is not against their own Consciences reproving, or their Light
reproaching them. They do not know it be an Offence, and then
commit it in Defiance of Divine Justice, as we do in almost all the

Sins we Commit. They think it no more a Crime to kill a Captive taken in War, than we do to kill an Ox; nor to eat humane Flesh, than we do to eat Mutton.

When I had consider'd this a little, it follow'd necessarily, that I was certainly in the Wrong in it, that these People were not Murtherers in the Sense that I had before condemn'd them, in my Thoughts; any more than those Christians were Murtherers, who often put to Death the Prisoners taken in Battle; or more frequently, upon many Occasions, put whole Troops of Men to the Sword, without giving Quarter, though they threw down their Arms and submitted.

In the next Place it occurr'd to me, that albeit the Usage they thus gave one another, was thus brutish and inhuman; yet it was really nothing to me: These People had done me no Injury. That if they attempted me,* or I saw it necessary for my immediate Preservation to fall upon them, something might be said for it; but that as I was yet out of their Power, and they had really no Knowledge of me, and consequently no Design upon me; and therefore it could not be just for me to fall upon them. That this would justify the Conduct of the *Spaniards* in all their Barbarities practis'd in *America*, and where they destroy'd Millions of these People, who however they were Idolaters and Barbarians, and had several bloody and barbarous Rites in their Customs, such as sacrificing human Bodies to their Idols, were yet, as to the *Spaniards*, very innocent People; and that the rooting them out of the Country, is spoken of with the utmost Abhorrence and Detestation, by even the *Spaniards* themselves, at this Time; and by all other Christian Nations of *Europe*, as a meer Butchery, a bloody and unnatural Piece of Cruelty, unjustifiable either to God or Man;* and such, as for which the very Name of a *Spaniard* is reckon'd to be frightful and terrible to all People of Humanity, or of Christian Compassion: As if the Kingdom of *Spain* were particularly Eminent for the Product of a Race of Men, who were without Principles of Tenderness, or the common Bowels of Pity* to the Miserable, which is reckon'd to be a Mark of generous Temper in the Mind.

These Considerations really put me to a Pause, and to a kind of a Full-stop; and I began by little and little to be off of my Design, and to conclude, I had taken wrong Measures in my Resolutions to attack the Savages; that it was not my Business to meddle with them, unless they first attack'd me, and this it was my Business if possible to prevent; but that if I were discover'd, and attack'd, then I knew my Duty.

On the other hand, I argu'd with my self, That this really was the way not to deliver my self, but entirely to ruin and destroy my self; for unless I was sure to kill every one that not only should be on Shore at that Time, but that should ever come on Shore afterwards, if but one of them escap'd, to tell their Country People what had happen'd, they would come over again by Thousands to revenge the Death of their Fellows, and I should only bring upon my self a certain Destruction, which at present I had no manner of occasion for.

Upon the whole I concluded, That neither in Principle or in Policy, I ought one way or other to concern my self in this Affair. That my Business was by all possible Means to conceal my self from them, and not to leave the least Signal to them to guess by, that there were any living Creatures upon the Island; I mean of humane Shape.

Religion joyn'd in with this Prudential, and I was convinc'd now many Ways, that I was perfectly out of my Duty, when I was laying all my bloody Schemes for the Destruction of innocent Creatures, I mean innocent as to me: As to the Crimes they were guilty of towards one another, I had nothing to do with them; they were National, and I ought to leave them to the Justice of God, who is the Governour of Nations, and knows how by National Punishments to make a just Retribution for National Offences; and to bring publick Judgments upon those who offend in a publick Manner, by such Ways as best pleases him.

This appear'd so clear to me now, that nothing was a greater Satisfaction to me, than that I had not been suffer'd to do a Thing which I now saw so much Reason to believe would have been no less a Sin, than that of wilful Murther, if I had committed it; and I gave most humble Thanks on my Knees to God, that had thus deliver'd me from Blood-Guiltiness; beseeching him to grant me the Protection of his Providence, that I might not fall into the Hands of the Barbarians; or that I might not lay my Hands upon them, unless I had a more clear Call from Heaven to do it, in Defence of my own Life.

In this Disposition I continu'd, for near a Year after this; and so far was I from desiring an Occasion for falling upon these Wretches, that in all that Time, I never once went up the Hill to see whether there were any of them in Sight, or to know whether any of them had been on Shore there, or not, that I might not be tempted to renew any of my Contrivances against them, or be provok'd by any Advantage which might present it self, to fall upon them; only this I did, I went and remov'd my Boat, which I had on the other Side the Island, and carry'd it down to the *East* End of the whole Island, where I ran it into a little Cove which I found under some high Rocks, and where I knew, by Reason of the Currents, the Savages durst not, at least would not come with their Boats, upon any Account whatsoever.

With my Boat I carry'd away every Thing that I had left there belonging to her, though not necessary for the bare going thither, *viz.* A Mast and Sail which I had made for her, and a Thing like an Anchor, but indeed which could not be call'd either Anchor or Grapling; however, it was the best I could make of its kind: All these I remov'd, that there might not be the least Shadow of any Discovery, or any Appearance of any Boat, or of any human Habitation upon the Island.

Besides this, I kept my self, as I said, more retir'd than ever, and seldom went from my Cell, other than upon my constant Employment, *viz.* To milk my She-goats, and manage my little Flock, in the Wood; which as it was quite on the other Part of the Island, was quite out of Danger; for certain it is, that these Savage People who sometimes haunted this Island, never came with any Thoughts of finding any Thing here; and consequently never wandred off from the Coast; and I doubt not, but they might have been several Times on Shore, after my Apprehensions of them had made me cautious as well as before; and indeed, I look'd back with some Horror upon the Thoughts of what my Condition would have been, if I had chop'd upon them, and been discover'd before that, when naked and unarm'd, except with one Gun, and that loaden often only with small Shot, I walk'd every where peeping, and peeping about the Island, to see what I could get; what a Surprise should I have been in, if when I discover'd the Print of a Man's Foot, I had instead of that, seen fifteen or twenty Savages, and found them pursuing me, and by the Swiftness of their Running, no Possibility of my escaping them.

The Thoughts of this sometimes sunk my very Soul within me, and distress'd my Mind so much, that I could not soon recover it, to think what I should have done, and how I not only should not have been able to resist them, but even should not have had Presence of

Mind enough to do what I might have done; much less, what now after so much Consideration and Preparation I might be able to do: Indeed, after serious thinking of these Things, I should be very Melancholly, and sometimes it would last a great while; but I resolv'd it at last all into Thankfulness to that Providence, which had deliver'd me from so many unseen Dangers, and had kept me from those Mischiefs which I could no way have been the Agent in delivering my self from; because I had not the least Notion of any such Thing depending, or the least Supposition of it being possible.

This renew'd a Contemplation, which often had come to my Thoughts in former Time, when first I began to see the merciful Dispositions of Heaven, in the Dangers we run through in this Life. How wonderfully we are deliver'd, when we know nothing of it. How when we are in (a *Quandary*, as we call it) a Doubt or Hesitation, whether to go this Way, or that Way, a secret Hint shall direct us this Way, when we intended to go that Way; nay, when Sense, our own Inclination, and perhaps Business has call'd to go the other Way, yet a strange Impression upon the Mind, from we know not what Springs, and by we know not what Power, shall over-rule us to go this Way; and it shall afterwards appear, that had we gone that Way which we should have gone, and even to our Imagination ought to have gone, we should have been ruin'd and lost: Upon these, and many like Reflections, I afterwards made it a certain Rule with me, That whenever I found those secret Hints, or pressings of my Mind, to doing, or not doing any Thing that presented; or to going this Way, or that Way, I never fail'd to obey the secret Dictate; though I knew no other Reason for it, than that such a Pressure, or such a Hint hung upon my Mind: I could give many Examples of the Success of this Conduct in the Course of my Life; but more especially in the latter Part of my inhabiting this unhappy Island; besides many Occasions which it is very likely I might have taken Notice of, if I had seen with the same Eyes then, that I saw with now: But 'tis never too late to be wise; and I cannot but advise all considering Men, whose Lives are attended with such extraordinary Incidents as mine, or even though not so extraordinary, not to slight such secret Intimations of Providence, let them come from what invisible Intelligence they will, that I shall not discuss,* and perhaps cannot account for; but certainly they are a Proof of the Converse of Spirits, and the secret Communication between those embody'd, and those unembody'd; and such a Proof as can never be withstood: Of which I shall have Occasion to give some very remarkable Instances, in the Remainder of my solitary Residence in this dismal Place.

I believe the Reader of this will not think strange, if I confess that these Anxieties, these constant Dangers I liv'd in, and the Concern that was now upon me, put an End to all Invention, and to all the Contrivances that I had laid for my future Accommodations and Conveniencies. I had the Care of my Safety more now upon my Hands, than that of my Food. I car'd not to drive a Nail, or chop a Stick of Wood now, for fear the Noise I should make should be heard; much less would I fire a Gun, for the same Reason; and above all, I was intollerably uneasy at making any Fire, least the Smoke which is visible at a great Distance in the Day should betray me; and for this Reason I remov'd that Part of my Business which requir'd Fire; such as burning of Pots, and Pipes, &c. into my new Apartment in the Woods, where after I had been some time, I found to my unspeakable Consolation, a meer natural Cave in the Earth, which went in a vast way, and where, I dare say, no Savage, had he been at the Mouth of it, would be so hardy as to venture in, nor indeed, would any Man else; but one who like me, wanted nothing so much as a safe Retreat.

The Mouth of this Hollow, was at the Bottom of a great Rock, where by meer accident, (I would say, if I did not see abundant Reason to ascribe all such Things now to Providence) I was cutting down some thick Branches of Trees, to make Charcoal; and before I go on, I must observe the Reason of my making this Charcoal; which was thus:

I was afraid of making a Smoke about my Habitation, as I said before; and yet I could not live there without baking my Bread, cooking my Meat, &c. so I contriv'd to burn some Wood here, as I had seen done in *England*, under Turf, till it became Chark, or dry Coal; and then putting the Fire out, I preserv'd the Coal to carry Home; and perform the other Services which Fire was wanting for at Home without Danger of Smoke.

But this is by the by: While I was cutting down some Wood here, I perceiv'd that behind a very thick Branch of low Brushwood, or Underwood, there was a kind of hollow Place; I was curious to look into it, and getting with Difficulty into the Mouth of it, I found it was pretty large; that is to say, sufficient for me to stand upright in it, and perhaps another with me; but I must confess to you, I made more hast out than I did in, when looking farther into the Place, and which was perfectly dark, I saw two broad shining Eyes of some Creature, whether Devil or Man I knew not, which twinkl'd like two Stars, the dim Light from the Cave's Mouth shining directly in and making the Reflection.

However, after some Pause, I recover'd my self, and began to call my self a thousand Fools, and tell my self, that he that was afraid to see the Devil, was not fit to live twenty Years in an Island all alone; and that I durst to believe there was nothing in this Cave that was more frightful than my self; upon this, plucking up my Courage, I took up a great Firebrand, and in I rush'd again, with the Stick flaming in my Hand; I had not gone three Steps in, but I was almost as much frighted as I was before; for I heard a very loud Sigh, like that of a Man in some Pain, and it was follow'd by a broken Noise, *as if* of Words half express'd, and then a deep Sigh again: I stepp'd back, and was indeed struck with such a Surprize, that it put me into a cold Sweat; and if I had had a Hat on my Head, I will not answer for it, that my Hair might not have lifted it off. But still plucking up my Spirits as well as I could, and encouraging my self a little with considering that the Power and Presence of God was every where, and was able to protect me; upon this I stepp'd forward again, and by the Light of the Firebrand, holding it up a little over my Head, I saw lying on the Ground a most monstrous frightful old He-goat, just making his Will, as we say, and gasping for Life, and dying indeed of meer old Age.*

I stirr'd him a little to see if I could get him out, and he essay'd to get up, but was not able to raise himself; and I thought with my self, he might even lie there; for if he had frighted me so, he would certainly fright any of the Savages, if any of them should be so hardy as to come in there, while he had any Life in him.

I was now recover'd from my Surprize, and began to look round me, when I found the Cave was but very small, that is to say, it might be about twelve Foot over, but in no manner of Shape, either round or square, no Hands having ever been employ'd in making it, but those of meer Nature: I observ'd also, that there was a Place at the farther Side of it, that went in farther, but was so low, that it requir'd me to creep upon my Hands and Knees to go into it, and whither I went I knew not; so having no Candle, I gave it over for some Time;

but resolv'd to come again the next Day, provided with Candles, and a Tinder-box, which I had made of the Lock of one of the Muskets, with some wild-fire in the Pan.*

Accordingly the next Day, I came provided with six large Candles of my own making; for I made very good Candles now of Goat's Tallow; and going into this low Place, I was oblig'd to creep upon all Fours, *as I have said*, almost ten Yards; which by the way, I thought was a Venture bold enough, considering that I knew not how far it might go, nor what was beyond it. When I was got through the Strait, I found the Roof rose higher up, I believe near twenty Foot; but never was such a glorious Sight seen in the Island, I dare say, as it was, to look round the Sides and Roof of this Vault, or Cave; the Walls reflected 100 thousand Lights to me from my two Candles; what it was in Rock, whether Diamonds, or any other precious Stones, or Gold, which I rather suppos'd it to be, I knew not.

The Place I was in, was a most delightful Cavity, or Grotto, of its kind, as could be expected, though perfectly dark; the Floor was dry and level, and had a sort of small lose Gravel upon it, so that there was no nauseous or venemous Creature to be seen, neither was there any damp, or wet, on the Sides or Roof: The only Difficulty in it was the Entrance, which however as it was a Place of Security, and such a Retreat as I wanted, I thought that was a Convenience; so that I was really rejoyc'd at the Discovery, and resolv'd without any Delay, to bring some of those Things which I was most anxious about, to this Place; particularly, I resolv'd to bring hither my Magazine of Powder, and all my spare Arms, *viz.* Two Fowling-Pieces, for I had three in all; and three Muskets, for of them I had eight in all; so I kept at my Castle only five, which stood ready mounted like Pieces of Cannon, on my out-most Fence; and were ready also to take out upon any Expedition.

Upon this Occasion of removing my Ammunition, I took occasion to open the Barrel of Powder which I took up out of the Sea, and which had been wet; and I found that the Water had penetrated about three or four Inches into the Powder, on every Side, which caking and growing hard, had preserv'd the inside like a Kernel in a Shell; so that I had near sixty Pound of very good Powder in the Center of the Cask, and this was an agreeable Discovery to me at that Time; so I carry'd all away thither, never keeping above two or three

Pound of Powder with me in my Castle, for fear of a Surprize of any kind: I also carry'd thither all the Lead I had left for Bullets.

I fancy'd my self now like one of the ancient Giants, which are said to live in Caves, and Holes, in the Rocks, where none could come at them; for I perswaded my self while I was here, if five hundred Savages were to hunt me, they could never find me out; or if they did, they would not venture to attack me here.

The old Goat who I found expiring, dy'd in the Mouth of the Cave, the next Day after I made this Discovery; and I found it much easier to dig a great Hole there, and throw him in, and cover him with Earth, than to drag him out; so I interr'd him there, to prevent the Offence to my Nose.

I was now in my twenty third Year of Residence in this Island, and was so naturaliz'd to the Place, and to the Manner of Living, that could I have but enjoy'd the Certainty that no Savages would come to the Place to disturb me, I could have been content to have capitulated for spending the rest of my Time there, even to the last Moment, till I had laid me down and dy'd, like the old Goat in the Cave. I had also arriv'd to some little Diversions and Amusements, which made the Time pass more pleasantly with me a great deal, than it did before; as First, I had taught my Poll, as I noted before, to speak; and he did it so familiarly, and talk'd so articulately and plain, that it was very pleasant to me; and he liv'd with me no less than six and twenty Years: How long he might live afterwards, I know not; though I know they have a Notion in the *Brasils*, that they live a hundred Years; perhaps poor Poll may be alive there still,* calling after *Poor Robin Crusoe* to this Day. I wish no *English* Man the ill Luck to come there and hear him; but if he did, he would certainly believe it was the Devil. My Dog was a very pleasant and loving Companion to me, for no less than sixteen Years of my Time, and then dy'd, of meer old Age; as for my Cats, they multiply'd as I have observ'd to that Degree, that I was oblig'd to shoot several of them at first, to keep them from devouring me, and all I had; but at length, when the two old Ones I brought with me were gone, and after some time continually driving them from me, and letting them have no Provision with me, they all ran wild into the Woods, except two or three Favourites, which I kept tame; and whose Young when they had any, I always drown'd; and these were part of my Family: Besides these, I always kept two or three houshold Kids about me, who I taught to feed out of my Hand; and I had two more Parrots which talk'd pretty well, and would all call *Robin Crusoe*; but none like my first; nor indeed did I take the Pains with any of them that I had done with him. I had also several tame Sea-Fowls, whose Names I know not, who I caught upon the Shore, and cut their Wings; and the little Stakes which I had planted before my Castle Wall being now grown up to a good thick Grove, these Fowls all liv'd among these low Trees, and bred there, which was very agreeable to me; so that as I said above, I began to be very well contented with the Life I led, if it might but have been secur'd from the dread of the Savages.

But it was otherwise directed; and it may not be amiss for all People who shall meet with my Story, to make this just Observation from it, *viz*. How frequently in the Course of our Lives, the Evil which in it self we seek most to shun, and which when we are fallen into it, is the most dreadful to us, is oftentimes the very Means or Door of our Deliverance, by which alone we can be rais'd again from the Affliction we are fallen into. I cou'd give many Examples of this in the Course of my unaccountable Life; but in nothing was it more particularly remarkable, than in the Circumstances of my last Years of solitary Residence in this Island.

It was now the Month of *December*, as I said above, in my twenty third Year; and this being the *Southern* Solstice,* for Winter I cannot call it, was the particular Time of my Harvest, and requir'd my being pretty much abroad in the Fields; when going out pretty early in the Morning, even before it was thorow Day-light, I was surpriz'd with seeing a Light of some Fire upon the Shore, at a Distance from me, of about two Mile towards the End of the Island, where I had observ'd some Savages had been as before; but not on the other Side; but to my great Affliction, it was on my Side of the Island.

I was indeed terribly surpriz'd at the Sight, and stepp'd short* within my Grove, not daring to go out, least I might be surpriz'd; and yet I had no more Peace within, from the Apprehensions I had, that if these Savages in rambling over the Island, should find my Corn standing, or cut, or any of my Works and Improvements, they would immediately conclude, that there were People in the Place, and would then never give over till they had found me out: In this Extremity I went back directly to my Castle, pull'd up the Ladder after me, and made all Things without look as wild and natural as I could.

Then I prepar'd my self within, putting my self in a Posture of

Defence; I loaded all my Cannon, as I call'd them; that is to say, my Muskets, which were mounted upon my new Fortification, and all my Pistols, and resolv'd to defend my self to the last Gasp, not forgetting seriously to commend my self to the Divine Protection, and earnestly to pray to God to deliver me out of the Hands of the Barbarians; and in this Posture I continu'd about two Hours; but began to be mighty impatient for Intelligence abroad, for I had no Spies to send out.

After sitting a while longer, and musing what I should do in this Case, I was not able to bear sitting in Ignorance any longer; so setting up my Ladder to the Side of the Hill, where there was a flat Place, as I observ'd before, and then pulling the Ladder up after me, I set it up again, and mounted to the Top of the Hill; and pulling out my Perspective Glass, which I had taken on Purpose, I laid me down flat on my Belly, on the Ground, and began to look for the Place; I presently found there was no less than nine naked Savages, sitting round a small Fire, they had made, not to warm them; for they had no need of that, the Weather being extreme hot; but as I suppos'd, to dress some of their barbarous Diet, of humane Flesh, which they had brought with them, whether alive or dead I could not know.

They had two *Canoes* with them, which they had haled up upon the Shore; and as it was then Tide of Ebb, they seem'd to me to wait for the Return of the Flood, to go away again; it is not easy to imagine what Confusion this Sight put me into, especially seeing them come on my Side the Island, and so near me too; but when I observ'd their coming must be always with the Current of the Ebb, I began afterwards to be more sedate in my Mind, being satisfy'd that I might go abroad with Safety all the Time of the Tide of Flood, if they were not on Shore before: And having made this Observation, I went abroad about my Harvest Work with the more Composure.

As I expected, so it prov'd; for as soon as the Tide made to the *Westward*, I saw them all take Boat, and row (or paddle as we call it) all away: I should have observ'd, that for an Hour and more before they went off, they went to dancing, and I could easily discern their Postures, and Gestures, by my Glasses: I could not perceive by my nicest Observation, but that they were stark naked, and had not the least covering upon them; but whether they were Men or Women, that I could not distinguish.

As soon as I saw them shipp'd, and gone, I took two Guns upon my Shoulders, and two Pistols at my Girdle, and my great Sword by my Side, without a Scabbard, and with all the Speed I was able to make, I went away to the Hill, where I had discover'd the first Appearance of all; and as soon as I gat thither, which was not less than two Hours (for I could not go apace, being so loaden with Arms as I was) I perceiv'd there had been three *Canoes* more of Savages on that Place; and looking out farther, I saw they were all at Sea together, making over for the Main.

This was a dreadful Sight to me, especially when going down to the Shore, I could see the Marks of Horror, which the dismal Work they had been about had left behind it, *viz*. The Blood, the Bones, and part of the Flesh of humane Bodies, eaten and devour'd by those Wretches, with Merriment and Sport: I was so fill'd with Indignation at the Sight, that I began now to premeditate the Destruction of the next that I saw there, let them be who, or how many soever.

It seem'd evident to me, that the Visits which they thus make to this Island, are not very frequent; for it was above fifteen Months before any more of them came on Shore there again; that is to say, I neither saw them, or any Footsteps, or Signals of them, in all that Time; for as to the rainy Seasons, then they are sure not to come abroad, at least not so far; yet all this while I liv'd uncomfortably, by reason of the constant Apprehensions I was in of their coming upon me by Surprize; from whence I observe, that the Expectation of Evil is more bitter than the Suffering, especially if there is no room to shake off that Expectation, or those Apprehensions.

During all this Time, I was in the murthering Humour; and took up most of my Hours, which should have been better employ'd, in contriving how to circumvent, and fall upon them, the very next Time I should see them; especially if they should be divided, as they were the last Time, into two Parties; nor did I consider at all, that if I kill'd one Party, suppose Ten, or a Dozen, I was still the next Day, or Week, or Month, to kill another, and so another, even *ad infinitum*, till I should be at length no less a Murtherer than they were in being Man-eaters; and perhaps much more so.

I spent my Days now in great Perplexity, and Anxiety of Mind, expecting that I should one Day or other fall into the Hands of these merciless Creatures; and if I did at any Time venture abroad, it was not without looking round me with the greatest Care and Caution imaginable; and now I found to my great Comfort, how happy it was that I provided for a tame Flock or Herd of Goats; for I durst not upon any account fire my Gun, especially near that Side of the Island where they usually came, least I should alarm the Savages; and if they had fled from me now, I was sure to have them come back again, with perhaps two or three hundred *Canoes* with them, in a few Days, and then I knew what to expect.

However, I wore out a Year and three Months more, before I ever saw any more of the Savages, and then I found them again, as I shall soon observe. It is true, they might have been there once, or twice; but either they made no stay, or at least I did not hear them; but in the Month of *May*, as near as I could calculate, and in my four and twentieth Year, I had a very strange Encounter with them, of which in its Place.

The Perturbation of my Mind, during this fifteen or sixteen Months Interval, was very great; I slept unquiet, dream'd always frightful Dreams, and often started out of my Sleep in the Night: In the Day great Troubles overwhelm'd my Mind, and in the Night I dream'd often of killing the Savages, and of the Reasons why I might justify the doing of it; but to wave all this for a while; it was in the middle of *May*, on the sixteenth Day I think, as well as my poor wooden Calendar would reckon; for I markt all upon the Post still; I say, it was the sixteenth of *May*, that it blew a very great Storm of Wind, all Day, with a great deal of Lightning, and Thunder, and a very foul Night it was after it; I know not what was the particular Occasion of it; but as I was reading in the Bible, and taken up with very serious Thoughts about my present Condition, I was surpriz'd with a Noise of a Gun as I thought fir'd at Sea.

This was to be sure a Surprize of a quite different Nature from any I had met with before; for the Notions this put into my Thoughts, were quite of another kind. I started up in the greatest hast imaginable, and in a trice clapt my Ladder to the middle Place of the Rock, and pull'd it after me, and mounting it the second Time, got to the Top of the Hill, the very Moment, that a Flash of Fire bid me listen for a second Gun, which accordingly, in about half a Minute I heard; and by the sound, knew that it was from that Part of the Sea where I was driven down the Current in my Boat.

I immediately consider'd that this must be some Ship in Distress, and that they had some Comrade, or some other Ship in Company, and fir'd these Guns for Signals of Distress, and to obtain Help: I had this Presence of Mind at that Minute, as to think that though I could not help them, it may be they might help me; so I brought together all the dry Wood I could get at hand, and making a good handsome Pile, I set it on Fire upon the Hill; the Wood was dry, and blaz'd freely; and though the Wind blew very hard, yet it burnt fairly out; that I was certain, if there was any such Thing as a Ship, they must needs see it, and no doubt they did; for as soon as ever my Fire blaz'd up, I heard another Gun, and after that several others, all from the same Quarter; I ply'd my Fire all Night long, till Day broke; and when it was broad Day, and the Air clear'd up, I saw something at a great Distance at Sea, full *East* of the Island, whether a Sail, or a Hull, I could not distinguish, no not with my Glasses, the Distance was so great, and the Weather still something haizy also; at least it was so out at Sea.

I look'd frequently at it all that Day, and soon perceiv'd that it did not move; so I presently concluded, that it was a Ship at an Anchor, and being eager, you may be sure, to be satisfy'd, I took my Gun in my Hand, and run toward the *South* Side of the Island, to the Rocks where I had formerly been carry'd away with the Current, and getting up there, the Weather by this Time being perfectly clear, I could plainly see to my great Sorrow, the Wreck of a Ship cast away in the Night, upon those concealed Rocks which I found, when I was out in my Boat; and which Rocks, as they check'd the Violence of the Stream, and made a kind of Counter-stream, or Eddy, were the Occasion of my recovering from the most desperate hopeless Condition that ever I had been in, in all my Life.

Thus what is one Man's Safety, is another Man's Destruction; for it seems these Men, whoever they were, being out of their Knowledge, and the Rocks being wholly under Water, had been driven upon them in the Night, the Wind blowing hard at *E.* and *E.N.E*: Had they seen the Island, as I must necessarily suppose they did not, they must, as I thought, have endeavour'd to have sav'd themselves on Shore by the Help of their Boat; but their firing of Guns for Help, especially when they saw, as I imagin'd, my Fire, fill'd me with many Thoughts: First, I imagin'd that upon seeing my Light, they might have put themselves into their Boat, and have endeavour'd to make the Shore; but that the Sea going very high, they might have been cast away; other Times I imagin'd, that they might have lost their Boat before, as might be the Case many Ways; as particularly by the

Breaking of the Sea upon their Ship, which many Times obliges Men to stave,* or take in Pieces their Boat; and sometimes to throw it over-board with their own Hands: Other Times I imagin'd, they had some other Ship, or Ships in Company, who upon the Signals of Distress they had made, had taken them up, and carry'd them off: Other whiles I fancy'd, they were all gone off to Sea in their Boat, and being hurry'd away by the Current that I had been formerly in, were carry'd out into the great Ocean, where there was nothing but Misery and Perishing; and that perhaps they might by this Time think of starving, and of being in a Condition to eat one another.

As all these were but Conjectures at best; so in the Condition I was in, I could do no more than look on upon the Misery of the poor Men, and pity them, which had still this good Effect on my Side, that it gave me more and more Cause to give Thanks to God who had so happily and comfortably provided for me in my desolate Condition; and that of two Ships Companies who were now cast away upon this part of the World, not one Life should be spar'd but mine: I learn'd here again to observe, that it is very rare that the Providence of God casts us into any Condition of Life so low, or any Misery so great, but we may see something or other to be thankful for; and may see others in worse Circumstances than our own.

Such certainly was the Case of these Men, of whom I could not so much as see room to suppose any of them were sav'd; nothing could make it rational, so much as to wish, or expect that they did not all perish there; except the Possibility only of their being taken up by another Ship in Company, and this was but meer Possibility indeed; for I saw not the least Signal or Appearance of any such Thing.

I cannot explain by any possible Energy of Words,* what a strange longing or hankering of Desires I felt in my Soul upon this Sight; breaking out sometimes thus; O that there had been but one or two; nay, or but one Soul sav'd out of this Ship, to have escap'd to me, that I might but have had one Companion, one Fellow-Creature to have spoken to me, and to have convers'd with! In all the Time of my solitary Life, I never felt so earnest, so strong a Desire after the Society of my Fellow-Creatures, or so deep a Regret at the want of it.

There are some secret moving Springs in the Affections, which when they are set a going by some Object in view, or be it some Object, though not in view, yet rendred present to the Mind by the

Power of Imagination, that Motion carries out the Soul* by its Impetuosity to such violent eager embracings of the Object, that the Absence of it is insupportable.

Such were these earnest Wishings, That but one Man had been sav'd! *O that it had been but One!* I believe I repeated the Words, *O that it had been but One!* A thousand Times; and the Desires were so mov'd by it, that when I spoke the Words, my Hands would clinch together, and my Fingers press the Palms of my Hands, that if I had had any soft Thing in my Hand, it wou'd have crusht it involuntarily; and my Teeth in my Head wou'd strike together, and set against one another so strong, that for some time I cou'd not part them again.

Let the Naturalists* explain these Things, and the Reason and Manner of them; all I can say to them, is, to describe the Fact, which was even surprising to me when I found it; though I knew not from what it should proceed; it was doubtless the effect of ardent Wishes, and of strong Ideas form'd in my Mind, realizing the Comfort, which the Conversation of one of my Fellow-Christians would have been to me.

But it was not to be; either their Fate or mine, or both, forbid it; for till the last Year of my being on this Island, I never knew whether any were saved out of that Ship or no; and had only the Affliction some Days after, to see the Corps of a drownded Boy come on Shore, at the End of the Island which was next the Shipwreck: He had on no Cloaths, but a Seaman's Wastcoat, a pair of open knee'd Linnen Drawers, and a blew Linnen Shirt; but nothing to direct me so much as to guess what Nation he was of: He had nothing in his Pocket, but two Pieces of Eight, and a Tobacco Pipe; the last was to me of ten times more value than the first.

It was now calm, and I had a great mind to venture out in my Boat, to this Wreck; not doubting but I might find something on board, that might be useful to me; but that did not altogether press me so much, as the Possibility that there might be yet some living Creature on board, whose Life I might not only save, but might by saving that Life, comfort my own to the last Degree; and this Thought clung so to my Heart, that I could not be quiet, Night or Day, but I must venture out in my Boat on board this Wreck; and committing the rest to God's Providence, I thought the Impression was so strong upon my Mind, that it could not be resisted, that it must come from some invisible Direction, and that I should be want-ing to my self if I did not go.

Under the Power of this Impression, I hasten'd back to my Castle, prepar'd every Thing for my Voyage, took a Quantity of Bread, a great Pot for fresh Water, a Compass to steer by, a Bottle of Rum; for I had still a great deal of that left; a Basket full of Raisins: And thus loading my self with every Thing necessary, I went down to my Boat, got the Water out of her, and got her afloat, loaded all my Cargo in her, and then went Home again for more; my second Cargo was a great Bag full of Rice, the Umbrella to set up over my Head for Shade; another large Pot full of fresh Water, and about two Dozen of my small Loaves, or Barley Cakes, more than before, with a Bottle of Goat's-Milk, and a Cheese; all which, with great Labour and Sweat, I brought to my Boat; and praying to God to direct my Voyage, I put out, and Rowing or Padling the Canoe along the Shore, I came at last to the utmost Point of the Island on that Side, (*viz.*) *N. E.* And now I was to launch out into the Ocean, and either to venture, or not to venture. I look'd on the rapid Currents which ran constantly on both Sides of the Island, at a Distance, and which were very terrible to me, from the Remembrance of the Hazard I had been in before, and my Heart began to fail me; for I foresaw that if I was driven into either of those Currents, I should be carry'd a vast Way out to Sea, and perhaps out of my Reach, or Sight of the Island again; and that then, as my Boat was but small, if any little Gale of Wind should rise, I should be inevitably lost.

These Thoughts so oppress'd my Mind, that I began to give over my Enterprize, and having haled my Boat into a little Creek on the Shore, I stept out, and sat me down upon a little rising bit of Ground, very pensive and anxious, between Fear and Desire about my Voyage; when as I was musing, I could perceive that the Tide was turn'd, and the Flood come on, upon which my going was for so many Hours impracticable; upon this presently it occurr'd to me, that I should go up to the highest Piece of Ground I could find, and observe, if I could, how the Sets of the Tide, or Currents lay, when the Flood came in, that I might judge whether if I was driven one way out, I might not expect to be driven another way home, with the same Rapidness of the Currents: This Thought was no sooner in my Head, but I cast my Eye upon a little Hill, which sufficiently over-look'd the Sea both ways, and from whence I had a clear view of the

Currents, or Sets of the Tide, and which way I was to guide my self in my Return; here I found, that as the Current of the Ebb set out close by the South Point of the Island; so the Current of the Flood set in close by the Shore of the North Side, and that I had nothing to do but to keep to the North of the Island in my Return, and I should do well enough.

Encourag'd with this Observation, I resolv'd the next Morning to set out with the first of the Tide; and reposing my self for the Night in the Canoe, under the great Watch-coat, I mention'd, I launched out: I made first a little out to Sea full North, till I began to feel the Benefit of the Current, which set Eastward, and which carry'd me at a great rate, and yet did not so hurry me as the Southern Side Current had done before, and so as to take from me all Government of the Boat; but having a strong Steerage with my Paddle, I went at a great rate, directly for the Wreck, and in less than two Hours I came up to it.

It was a dismal Sight to look at: The Ship, which by its building was *Spanish*, stuck fast, jaum'd* in between two Rocks; all the Stern and Quarter of her was beaten to pieces, with the Sea; and as her Forecastle, which stuck in the Rocks, had run on with great Violence, her Mainmast and Foremast were brought by the Board; that is to say, broken short off; but her Boltsprit was found, and the Head and Bow appear'd firm; when I came close to her, a Dog appear'd upon her, who seeing me coming, yelp'd, and cry'd; and as soon as I call'd him, jump'd into the Sea, to come to me, and I took him into the Boat; but found him almost dead for Hunger and Thirst: I gave him a Cake of my Bread, and he eat it like a ravenous Wolf, that had been starving a Fortnight in the Snow: I then gave the poor Creature some fresh Water, with which, if I would have let him, he would have burst himself.

After this I went on board; but the first Sight I met with, was two Men drown'd, in the Cookroom, or Forecastle of the Ship,* with their Arms fast about one another: I concluded, as is indeed probable, that when the Ship struck, it being in a Storm, the Sea broke so high, and so continually over her, that the Men were not able to bear it, and were strangled with the constant rushing in of the Water, as much as if they had been under Water. Besides the Dog, there was nothing left in the Ship that had Life; nor any Goods that I could see, but what were spoil'd by the Water. There were some Casks of

Liquor, whether Wine or Brandy, I knew not, which lay lower in the Hold; and which, the Water being ebb'd out, I could see; but they were too big to meddle with: I saw several Chests, which I believ'd belong'd to some of the Seamen; and I got two of them into the Boat, without examining what was in them.

Had the Stern of the Ship been fix'd, and the Forepart broken off, I am perswaded I might have made a good Voyage; for by what I found in these two Chests, I had room to suppose, the Ship had a great deal of Wealth on board; and if I may guess by the Course she steer'd, she must have been bound from the *Buenos Ayres*, or the *Rio de la Plata*, in the South Part of *America*, beyond the *Brasils*, to the *Havana*, in the Gulph of *Mexico*, and so perhaps to *Spain*:* She had no doubt a great Treasure in her; but of no use at that time to any body; and what became of the rest of her People, I then knew not.

I found besides these Chests, a little Cask full of Liquor, of about twenty Gallons, which I got into my Boat, with much Difficulty; there were several Muskets in a Cabin, and a great Powder-horn, with about 4 Pounds of Powder in it; as for the Muskets, I had no occasion for them;* so I left them, but took the Powder-horn: I took a Fire Shovel and Tongs, which I wanted extremely; as also two little Brass Kettles, a Copper Pot to make Chocolate, and a Gridiron; with this Cargo, and the Dog, I came away, the Tide beginning to make home again; and the same Evening, about an Hour within Night, I reach'd the Island again, weary and fatigu'd to the last Degree.

I repos'd that Night in the Boat, and in the Morning I resolved to harbour what I had gotten in my new Cave, not to carry it home to my Castle. After refreshing my self, I got all my Cargo on Shore, and began to examine the Particulars: The Cask of Liquor I found to be a kind of Rum, but not such as we had at the *Brasils*; and in a Word, not at all good; but when I came to open the Chests, I found several Things, of great use to me: For Example, I found in one, a fine Case of Bottles, of an extraordinary kind, and fill'd with Cordial Waters, fine, and very good; the Bottles held about three Pints each, and were tipp'd with Silver: I found two Pots of very good Succades, or Sweetmeats, so fastned also on top, that the Salt Water had not hurt them; and two more of the same, which the Water had spoil'd: I found some very good Shirts, which were very welcome to me; and about a dozen and half of Linnen white Hand-kerchiefs, and colour'd Neckcloths; the former were also very welcome, being exceeding refreshing to wipe my Face in a hot Day; besides this, when I came to the Till in the Chest, I found there three great Bags of Pieces of Eight, which held about eleven hundred Pieces in all; and in one of them, wrapt up in a Paper, six Doubloons of Gold, and some small Bars or Wedges of Gold; I suppose they might all weigh near a Pound.

The other Chest I found had some Cloaths in it, but of little Value; but by the Circumstances it must have belong'd to the Gunner's Mate; though there was no Powder in it; but about two Pound of fine glaz'd Powder, in three small Flasks, kept, I suppose, for charging their Fowling-Pieces on occasion: Upon the whole, I got very little by this Voyage, that was of any use to me; for as to the Money, I had no manner of occasion for it: 'Twas to me as the Dirt under my Feet; and I would have given it all for three or four pair of *English* Shoes and Stockings, which were Things I greatly wanted, but had not had on my Feet now for many Years: I had indeed gotten two pair of Shoes now, which I took off of the Feet of the two drown'd Men, who I saw in the Wreck; and I found two pair more in one of the Chests, which were very welcome to me; but they were not like our *English* Shoes, either for Ease, or Service; being rather what we call Pumps, than Shoes: I found in this Seaman's Chest, about fifty Pieces of Eight in Ryals, but no Gold; I suppose this belong'd to a poorer Man than the other, which seem'd to belong to some Officer.

Well, however, I lugg'd this Money home to my Cave, and laid it up, as I had done that before, which I brought from our own Ship; but it was great Pity as I said, that the other Part of this Ship had not come to my Share; for I am satisfy'd I might have loaded my *Canoe* several Times over with Money, which if I had ever escap'd to *England*, would have lain here safe enough, till I might have come again and fetch'd it.

Having now brought all my Things on Shore, and secur'd them, I went back to my Boat, and row'd, or paddled her along the Shore, to her old Harbour, where I laid her up, and made the best of my way to my old Habitation, where I found every thing safe and quiet; so I began to repose my self, live after my old fashion, and take care of my Family Affairs; and for a while, I liv'd easy enough; only that I was more vigilant than I us'd to be, look'd out oftner, and did not go abroad so much; and if at any time I did stir with any Freedom, it was always to the *East* Part of the Island, where I was pretty well satisfy'd the Savages never came, and where I could go without so many Precautions, and such a Load of Arms and Ammunition, as I always carry'd with me, if I went the other way.

I liv'd in this Condition near two Years more; but my unlucky Head, that was always to let me know it was born to make my Body miserable, was all this two Years fill'd with Projects and Designs, how, if it were possible, I might get away from this Island; for sometimes I was for making another Voyage to the Wreck, though my Reason told me that there was nothing left there, worth the Hazard of my Voyage: Sometimes for a Ramble one way, sometimes another; and I believe verily, if I had had the Boat that I went from *Sallee* in, I should have ventur'd to Sea, bound any where, I knew not whither.

I have been in all my Circumstances a *Memento* to those who are touch'd with the general Plague of Mankind, whence, for ought I know, one half of their Miseries flow; I mean, that of not being satisfy'd with the Station wherein God and Nature has plac'd them; for not to look back upon my primitive Condition, and the excellent Advice of my Father, the Opposition to which, was, *as I may call it*, my ORIGINAL SIN;* my subsequent Mistakes of the same kind had been the Means of my coming into this miserable Condition; for had that Providence, which so happily had seated me at the *Brasils*, as a Planter, bless'd me with confin'd Desires, and I could have been contented to have gone on gradually, I might have been by this Time; *I mean, in the Time of my being in this Island*, one of the most considerable Planters in the *Brasils*, nay, I am perswaded, that by the Improvements I had made, in that little Time I liv'd there, and the Encrease I should probably have made, if I had stay'd, I might have been worth an hundred thousand *Moydors*; and what Business had I to leave a settled Fortune, a well stock'd Plantation, improving and encreasing, to turn *Supra-Cargo* to *Guinea*, to fetch Negroes; when Patience and Time would have so encreas'd our Stock at Home, that we could have bought them at our own Door, from those whose Business it was to fetch them; and though it had cost us something more, yet the Difference of that Price was by no Means worth saving, at so great a Hazard.

But as this is ordinarily the Fate of young Heads, so Reflection upon the Folly of it, is as ordinarily the Exercise of more Years, or of the dear bought Experience of Time; and so it was with me now; and yet so deep had the Mistake taken root in my Temper, that I could not satisfy my self in my Station, but was continually poring upon the Means, and Possibility of my Escape from this Place; and that I may with the greater Pleasure to the Reader, bring on the remaining Part of my Story, it may not be improper, to give some Account of my first Conceptions on the Subject of this foolish Scheme, for my Escape; and how, and upon what Foundation I acted.

I am now to be suppos'd retir'd into my Castle, after my late Voyage to the Wreck, my Frigate laid up, and secur'd under Water, as usual, and my Condition restor'd to what it was before: I had more Wealth indeed than I had before, but was not at all the richer; for I had no more use for it, than the *Indians* of *Peru* had, before the *Spaniards* came there.

It was one of the Nights in the rainy Season in *March*, the four and twentieth Year of my first setting Foot in this Island of Solitariness; I was lying in my Bed, or Hammock, awake, very well in Health, had no Pain, no Distemper, no Uneasiness of Body; no, nor any Uneasiness of Mind, more than ordinary; but could by no means close my Eyes; that is, so as to sleep; no, not a Wink all Night long, otherwise than as follows:

It is as impossible, as needless, to set down the innumerable Crowd of Thoughts that whirl'd through that great thorow-fare of the Brain, the Memory, in this Night's Time: I run over the whole History of my Life in Miniature, or by Abridgment, *as I may call it*, to my coming to this Island; and also of the Part of my Life, since I came to this Island. In my Reflections upon the State of my Case, since I came on Shore on this Island, I was comparing the happy Posture of my Affairs, in the first Years of my Habitation here, compar'd to the Life of Anxiety, Fear and Care, which I had liv'd ever since I had seen the Print of a Foot in the Sand; not that I did not believe the Savages had frequented the Island even all the while, and might have been several Hundreds of them at Times on Shore there; but I had never known it, and was incapable of any Apprehensions about it; my Satisfaction was perfect, though my Danger was the same; and I was as happy in not knowing my Danger, as if I had never really been expos'd to it: This furnish'd my Thoughts with many very profitable Reflections, and particularly this one, How infinitely Good that Providence is, which has provided in its Government of Mankind, such narrow bounds to his Sight and

Knowledge of Things, and though he walks in the midst of so many thousand Dangers, the Sight of which, if discover'd to him, would distract his Mind, and sink his Spirits; he is kept serene, and calm, by having the Events of Things hid from his Eyes, and knowing nothing of the Dangers which surround him.

After these Thoughts had for some Time entertain'd me, I came to reflect seriously upon the real Danger I had been in, for so many Years, in this very Island; and how I had walk'd about in the greatest Security, and with all possible Tranquillity; even when perhaps nothing but a Brow of a Hill, a great Tree, or the casual Approach of Night, had been between me and the worst kind of Destruction, *viz.* That of falling into the Hands of Cannibals, and Savages, who would have seiz'd on me with the same View, as I did of a Goat, or a Turtle; and have thought it no more a Crime to kill and devour me, than I did of a Pidgeon, or a Curlieu:* I would unjustly slander my self, if I should say I was not sincerely thankful to my great Preserver, to whose singular Protection I acknowledg'd, with great Humility, that all these unknown Deliverances were due; and without which, I must inevitably have fallen into their merciless Hands.

When these Thoughts were over, my Head was for some time taken up in considering the Nature of these wretched Creatures; I mean, the Savages; and how it came to pass in the World, that the wise Governour of all Things should give up any of his Creatures to such Inhumanity; nay, to something so much below, even Brutality it self, as to devour its own kind; but as this ended in some (at that Time fruitless) Speculations, it occurr'd to me to enquire, what Part of the World these Wretches liv'd in; how far off the Coast was from whence they came; what they ventur'd over so far from home for; what kind of Boats they had; and why I might not order my self, and my Business so, that I might be as able to go over thither, as they were to come to me.

I never so much as troubl'd my self to consider what I should do with my self, when I came thither; what would become of me, if I fell into the Hands of the Savages; or how I should escape from them, if they attempted me; no, nor so much as how it was possible for me to reach the Coast, and not be attempted by some or other of them, without any Possibility of delivering my self; and if I should not fall into their Hands, what I should do for Provision, or whither I should bend my Course; none of these Thoughts, I say, so much as came in my way; but my Mind was wholly bent upon the Notion of my passing over in my Boat, to the Main Land: I look'd back upon my present Condition, as the most miserable that could possibly be, that I was not able to throw my self into any thing but Death, that could be call'd worse; that if I reached the Shore of the Main, I might perhaps meet with Relief, or I might coast along, as I did on the Shore of *Africk*, till I came to some inhabited Country, and where I might find some Relief; and after all perhaps, I might fall in with some Christian Ship, that might take me in; and if the worse came to the worst, I could but die, which would put an end to all these Miseries at once. Pray note, all this was the fruit of a disturb'd Mind, an impatient Temper, made as it were desperate by the long Continuance of my Troubles, and the Disappointments I had met in the Wreck, I had been on board of; and where I had been so near the obtaining what I so earnestly long'd for, *viz.* Some-body to speak to, and to learn some Knowledge from of the Place where I was, and of the probable Means of my Deliverance; I say, I was agitated wholly by these Thoughts: All my Calm of Mind in my Resignation to Providence, and waiting the Issue of the Dispositions of Heaven, seem'd to be suspended; and I had, as it were, no Power to turn my Thoughts to any thing, but to the Project of a Voyage to the Main, which came upon me with such Force, and such an Impetuosity of Desire, that it was not to be resisted.

When this had agitated my Thoughts for two Hours, or more, with such Violence, that it set my very Blood into a Ferment, and my Pulse beat as high as if I had been in a Feaver, meerly with the extraordinary Fervour of my Mind about it; Nature, as if I had been fatigued and exhausted with the very Thought of it, threw me into a sound Sleep; one would have thought, I should have dream'd of it: But I did not, nor of any Thing relating to it; but I dream'd, that as I was going out in the Morning as usual from my Castle, I saw upon the Shore, two *Canoes*, and eleven Savages coming to Land, and that they brought with them another Savage, who they were going to kill, in Order to eat him; when on a sudden, the Savage that they were going to kill, jumpt away, and ran for his Life; and I thought in my Sleep, that he came running into my little thick Grove, before my Fortification, to hide himself; and that I seeing him alone, and not perceiving that the other sought him that Way, show'd my self to him, and smiling upon him, encourag'd him; that he kneel'd down to

me, seeming to pray me to assist him; upon which I shew'd my
Ladder, made him go up, and carry'd him into my Cave, and he
became my Servant; and that as soon as I had gotten this Man, I said
to my self, now I may certainly venture to the main Land; for this
Fellow will serve me as a Pilot, and will tell me what to do, and
whether to go for Provisions; and whether not to go for fear of being
devoured, what Places to venture into, and what to escape: I wak'd
with this Thought, and was under such inexpressible Impressions of
Joy, at the Prospect of my Escape in my Dream, that the Disappointments which I felt upon coming to my self, and finding it was
no more than a Dream, were equally extravagant the other Way, and
threw me into a very great Dejection of Spirit.

Upon this however, I made this Conclusion, that my only Way to
go about an Attempt for an Escape, was, if possible, to get a Savage
into my Possession; and if possible, it should be one of their
Prisoners, who they had condemn'd to be eaten, and should bring
thither to kill; but these Thoughts still were attended with this Difficulty, that it was impossible to effect this, without attacking a whole
Caravan of them, and killing them all; and this was not only a very
desperate Attempt, and might miscarry; but on the other Hand, I
had greatly scrupled the Lawfulness of it to me; and my Heart
trembled at the thoughts of shedding so much Blood, tho' it was for
my Deliverance. I need not repeat the Arguments which occurr'd to
me against this, they being the same mention'd before; but tho' I had
other Reasons to offer now (*viz.*) that those Men were Enemies to
my Life, and would devour me, if they could; that it was Self-
preservation in the highest Degree, to deliver my self from this
Death of a Life, and was acting in my own Defence, as much as if
they were actually assaulting me, and the like. I say, tho' these
Things argued for it, yet the Thoughts of shedding Humane Blood
for my Deliverance, were very Terrible to me, and such as I could by
no Means reconcile my self to, a great while.

However at last, after many secret Disputes with my self, and after
great Perplexities about it, for all these Arguments one Way and
another struggl'd in my Head a long Time, the eager prevailing
Desire of Deliverance at length master'd all the rest; and I resolv'd,
if possible, to get one of those Savages into my Hands, cost what it
would. My next Thing then was to contrive how to do it, and this
indeed was very difficult to resolve on: But as I could pitch upon no

probable Means for it, so I resolv'd to put my self upon the Watch, to see them when they came on Shore, and leave the rest to the Event, taking such Measures as the Opportunity should present, let be what would be.

With these Resolutions in my Thoughts, I set my self upon the Scout, as often as possible, and indeed so often till I was heartily tir'd of it, for it was above a Year and Half that I waited, and for great part of that Time went out to the *West* End, and to the *South West* Corner of the Island, almost every Day, to see for Canoes, but none appear'd. This was very discouraging, and began to trouble me much, tho' I cannot say that it did in this Case, as it had done some time before that, (*viz.*) wear off the Edge of my Desire to the Thing. But the longer it seem'd to be delay'd, the more eager I was for it; in a Word, I was not at first so careful to shun the sight of these Savages, and avoid being seen by them, as I was now eager to be upon them.

Besides, I fancied my self able to manage One, nay, Two or Three Savages, if I had them so as to make them entirely Slaves to me, to do whatever I should direct them, and to prevent their being able at any time to do me any Hurt. It was a great while, that I pleas'd my self with this Affair, but nothing still presented; all my Fancies and Schemes came to nothing, for no Savages came near me for a great while.

About a Year and half after I had entertain'd these Notions, and by long musing, had as it were resolved them all into nothing, for want of an Occasion to put them in Execution, I was surpriz'd one Morning early, with seeing no less than five *Canoes* all on Shore together on my side the Island; and the People who belong'd to them all landed, and out of my sight: The Number of them broke all my Measures, for seeing so many, and knowing that they always came four or six, or sometimes more in a Boat, I could not tell what to think of it, or how to take my Measures, to attack Twenty or Thirty Men single handed; so I lay still in my Castle, perplex'd and discomforted: However I put my self into all the same Postures for an Attack that I had formerly provided, and was just ready for Action, if any Thing had presented; having waited a good while, listening to hear if they made any Noise; at length being very impatient, I set my Guns at the Foot of my Ladder, and clamber'd up to the Top of the Hill, by my two Stages as usual; standing so however that my Head did not appear above the Hill, so that they could not perceive me by any Means; here I observ'd by the help of my Perspective Glass, that they were no less than Thirty in Number, that they had a Fire kindled, that they had had Meat dress'd. How they had cook'd it, that I knew not, or what it was; but they were all Dancing in I know not how many barbarous Gestures and Figures, their own Way, round the Fire.

While I was thus looking on them, I perceived by my Perspective, two miserable Wretches dragg'd from the Boats, where it seems they were laid by, and were now brought out for the Slaughter. I perceived one of them immediately fell, being knock'd down, I suppose with a Club or Wooden Sword, for that was their way, and two or three others were at work immediately cutting him open for their Cookery, while the other Victim was left standing by himself, till they should be ready for him. In that very Moment this poor Wretch seeing himself a little at Liberty, Nature inspir'd him with Hopes of Life, and he started away from them, and ran with incredible Swiftness along the Sands directly towards me, I mean towards that part of the Coast, where my Habitation was.

I was dreadfully frighted, (that I must acknowledge) when I perceived him to run my Way; and especially, when as I thought I saw him pursued by the whole Body, and now I expected that part of my Dream was coming to pass, and that he would certainly take shelter in my Grove; but I could not depend by any means upon my Dream for the rest of it, (*viz.*) that the other Savages would not pursue him thither, and find him there. However I kept my Station, and my Spirits began to recover, when I found that there was not above three Men that follow'd him, and still more was I encourag'd, when I found that he outstrip'd them exceedingly in running, and gain'd Ground of them, so that if he could but hold it for half an Hour, I saw easily he would fairly get away from them all.

There was between them and my Castle, the Creek which I mention'd often at the first part of my Story, when I landed my Cargoes out of the Ship; and this I saw plainly, he must necessarily swim over, or the poor Wretch would be taken there: But when the Savage escaping came thither, he made nothing of it, tho' the Tide was then up, but plunging in, swam thro' in about Thirty Strokes or thereabouts, landed and ran on with exceeding Strength and Swiftness; when the Three Persons came to the Creek, I found that Two of them could Swim, but the Third cou'd not, and that standing on the other Side, he look'd at the other, but went no further; and soon after went softly back again, which as it happen'd, was very well for him in the main.

I observ'd, that the two who swam, were yet more than twice as long swimming over the Creek, as the Fellow was, that fled from them: It came now very warmly upon my Thoughts, and indeed irresistibly, that now was my Time to get me a Servant, and perhaps a Companion, or Assistant; and that I was call'd plainly by Providence to save this poor Creature's Life; I immediately run down the Ladders with all possible Expedition, fetches my two Guns, for they were both but at the Foot of the Ladders, as I observ'd above; and getting up again, with the same haste, to the Top of the Hill, I cross'd toward the Sea; and having a very short Cut, and all down Hill, clapp'd my self in the way, between the Pursuers, and the Pursu'd; hallowing aloud to him that fled, who looking back, was at first perhaps as much frighted at me, as at them; but I beckon'd with my Hand to him, to come back; and in the mean time, I slowly advanc'd towards the two that follow'd; then rushing at once upon the foremost, I knock'd him down with the Stock of my Piece; I was loath to fire, because I would not have the rest hear; though at that distance, it would not have been easily heard, and being out of Sight of the Smoke too, they wou'd not have easily known what to make of it: Having knock'd this Fellow down, the other who pursu'd with him stopp'd, as if he had been frighted; and I advanc'd a-pace towards him; but as I came nearer, I perceiv'd presently, he had a Bow and Arrow, and was fitting it to shoot at me; so I was then necessitated to shoot at him first, which I did, and kill'd him at the first Shoot; the poor Savage who fled, but had stopp'd; though he saw both his Enemies fallen, and kill'd, as he thought; yet was so frighted with the Fire, and Noise of my Piece, that he stood Stock still, and neither came forward or went backward, tho' he seem'd rather enclin'd to fly still, than to come on; I hollow'd again to him, and made Signs to come forward, which he easily understood, and came a little way, then stopp'd again, and then a little further, and stopp'd again, and I cou'd then perceive that he stood trembling, as if he had been taken Prisoner, and had just been to be kill'd,* as his two Enemies were; I beckon'd him again to come to me, and gave him all the Signs of Encouragement that I could think of, and he came nearer and nearer, kneeling down every Ten or Twelve steps in token of acknowledgement for my saving his Life: I smil'd at him, and look'd pleasantly, and beckon'd to him to come still nearer; at length he came close to me, and then he kneel'd down again, kiss'd the Ground, and laid his Head upon the Ground, and taking me by the Foot, set my Foot upon his Head; this it seems was in token of swearing to be my Slave for ever; I took him up, and made much of him, and encourag'd him all I could. But there was more work to do yet, for I perceived the Savage who I knock'd down, was not kill'd, but stunn'd with the blow, and began to come to himself; so I pointed to him, and showing him the Savage, that he was not dead; upon this he spoke some Words to me, and though I could not understand them, yet I thought they were pleasant to hear, for they were the first sound of a Man's Voice, that I had heard, *my own excepted*, for above Twenty Five Years. But there was no time for such Reflections now, the Savage who was knock'd down recover'd himself so far, as to sit up upon the Ground, and I perceived that my Savage began to be afraid; but when I saw that, I presented my other Piece at the Man, as if I would shoot him, upon this my Savage, *for so I call him now*, made a Motion to me to lend him my Sword, which hung naked in a Belt by my side; so I did: he no sooner had it, but he runs to his Enemy, and at one blow cut off his Head as cleaverly,* no Executioner in *Germany*,* could have done it sooner or better; which I thought very strange, for one who I had Reason to believe never saw a Sword in his Life before, except their own Wooden Swords; however it seems, as I learn'd afterwards, they make their Wooden Swords so sharp, so heavy, and the Wood is so hard, that they will cut off Heads even with them, ay and Arms, and that at one blow too; when he had done this, he comes laughing to me in Sign of Triumph, and brought me the Sword again, and with abundance of Gestures which I did not understand, laid it down with the Head of the Savage, that he had kill'd just before me.

But that which astonish'd him most, was to know how I had kill'd the other Indian so far off, so pointing to him, he made Signs to me to let him go to him, so I bad him go, as well as I could, when he came to him, he stood like one amaz'd, looking at him, turn'd him first on one side, then on t'other, look'd at the Wound the Bullet had made, which it seems was just in his Breast, where it had made a Hole, and no great quantity of Blood had follow'd, but he had bled inwardly, for he was quite dead; He took up his Bow, and Arrows, and came back, so I turn'd to go away, and beckon'd to him to follow me, making Signs to him, that more might come after them.

Upon this he sign'd to me, that he should bury them with Sand, that they might not be seen by the rest if they follow'd; and so I made Signs again to him to do so; he fell to Work, and in an instant he had scrap'd a Hole in the Sand, with his Hands, big enough to bury the first in, and then dragg'd him into it, and cover'd him, and did so also by the other; I believe he had bury'd them both in a Quarter of an Hour; then calling him away, I carry'd him not to my Castle, but quite away to my Cave, on the farther Part of the Island; so I did not let my Dream come to pass in that Part, *viz.* That he came into my Grove for shelter.

Here I gave him Bread, and a Bunch of Raisins to eat, and a Draught of Water, which I found he was indeed in great Distress for, by his Running; and having refresh'd him, I made Signs for him to go lie down and sleep; pointing to a Place where I had laid a great Parcel of Rice Straw, and a Blanket upon it, which I used to sleep upon my self sometimes; so the poor Creature laid down, and went to sleep.

He was a comely handsome Fellow, perfectly well made; with straight strong Limbs, not too large; tall and well shap'd, and as I reckon, about twenty six Years of Age. He had a very good Countenance, not a fierce and surly Aspect; but seem'd to have something very manly in his Face, and yet he had all the Sweetness and Softness of an *European* in his Countenance too, especially when he smil'd. His Hair was long and black, not curl'd like Wool; his Forehead very high, and large, and a great Vivacity and sparkling Sharpness in his Eyes. The Colour of his Skin was not quite black, but very tawny; and yet not of an ugly yellow nauseous tawny, as the *Brasilians*, and *Virginians*, and other Natives of *America* are; but of a bright kind of a dun olive Colour, that had in it something very agreeable; tho' not very easy to describe. His Face was round, and plump; his Nose small, not flat like the Negroes, a very good Mouth, thin Lips, and his fine Teeth well set, and white as Ivory.* After he had slumber'd, rather than slept, about half an Hour, he wak'd again, and comes out of the Cave to me; for I had been milking my Goats, which I had in the Enclosure just by: When he espy'd me, he came running to me, laying himself down again upon the Ground, with all the possible Signs of an humble thankful Disposition, making a many antick

Gestures to show it: At last he lays his Head flat upon the Ground, close to my Foot, and sets my other Foot upon his Head, as he had done before; and after this, made all the Signs to me of Subjection, Servitude, and Submission imaginable, to let me know, how he would serve me as long as he liv'd; I understood him in many Things, and let him know, I was very well pleas'd with him; in a little Time I began to speak to him, and teach him to speak to me; and first, I made him know his Name should be *Friday*,* which was the Day I sav'd his Life; I call'd him so for the Memory of the Time; I likewise taught him to say *Master*, and then let him know, that was to be my Name; I likewise taught him to say, YES, and NO, and to know the Meaning of them; I gave him some Milk, in an earthen Pot, and let him see me Drink it before him, and sop my Bread in it; and I gave him a Cake of Bread, to do the like, which he quickly comply'd with, and made Signs that it was very good for him.

I kept there with him all that Night; but as soon as it was Day, I beckon'd to him to come with me, and let him know, I would give him some Cloaths, at which he seem'd very glad, for he was stark naked: As we went by the Place where he had bury'd the two Men, he pointed exactly to the Place, and shew'd me the Marks that he had made to find them again, making Signs to me, that we should dig them up again, and eat them; at this I appear'd very angry, express'd my Abhorrence of it, made as if I would vomit at the Thoughts of it, and beckon'd with my Hand to him to come away, which he did immediately, with great Submission. I then led him up to the Top of the Hill, to see if his Enemies were gone; and pulling out my Glass, I look'd, and saw plainly the Place where they had been, but no appearance of them, or of their *Canoes*; so that it was plain they were gone, and had left their two Comrades behind them, without any search after them.

But I was not content with this Discovery; but having now more Courage, and consequently more Curiosity, I takes my Man *Friday* with me, giving him the Sword in his Hand, with the Bow and Arrows at his Back, which I found he could use very dextrously, making him carry one Gun for me, and I two for my self, and away we march'd to the Place, where these Creatures had been; for I had a Mind now to get some fuller Intelligence of them: When I came to the Place, my very Blood ran chill in my Veins, and my Heart sunk within me, at the Horror of the Spectacle: Indeed it was a dreadful

Sight, at least it was so to me; though *Friday* made nothing of it: The Place was cover'd with humane Bones, the Ground dy'd with their Blood, great Pieces of Flesh left here and there, half eaten, mangl'd and scorch'd; and in short, all the Tokens of the triumphant Feast they had been making there, after a Victory over their Enemies; I saw three Skulls, five Hands, and the Bones of three or four Legs and Feet, and abundance of other Parts of the Bodies; and *Friday*, by his Signs, made me understand, that they brought over four Prisoners to feast upon; that three of them were eaten up, and that he, pointing to himself, was the fourth: That there had been a great Battle between them, and their next King, whose Subjects it seems he had been one of; and that they had taken a great Number of Prisoners, all which were carry'd to several Places by those that had taken them in the Fight, in order to feast upon them, as was done here by these Wretches upon those they brought hither.

I caus'd *Friday* to gather all the Skulls, Bones, Flesh, and whatever remain'd, and lay them together on a Heap, and make a great Fire upon it, and burn them all to Ashes: I found *Friday* had still a hankering Stomach after some of the Flesh, and was still a Cannibal in his Nature; but I discover'd so much Abhorrence at the very Thoughts of it, and at the least Appearance of it, that he durst not discover it; for I had by some Means let him know, that I would kill him if he offer'd it.

When we had done this, we came back to our Castle, and there I fell to work for my Man *Friday*; and first of all, I gave him a pair of Linnen Drawers, which I had out of the poor Gunner's Chest I mention'd, and which I found in the Wreck; and which with a little Alteration fitted him very well; then I made him a Jerkin of Goat's-skin, as well as my Skill would allow; and I was now grown a tollerable good Taylor; and I gave him a Cap, which I had made of a Hare-skin, very convenient, and fashionable enough; and thus he was cloath'd for the present, tollerably well; and was mighty well pleas'd to see himself almost as well cloath'd as his Master: It is true, he went awkardly in these Things at first; wearing the Drawers was very awkard to him, and the Sleeves of the Wastcoat gall'd his Shoulders, and the inside of his Arms; but a little easing them where he complain'd they hurt him, and using himself to them, at length he took to them very well.

The next Day after I came home to my Hutch with him, I began to consider where I should lodge him, and that I might do well for him, and yet be perfectly easy my self; I made a little Tent for him in the vacant Place between my two Fortifications, in the inside of the last, and in the outside of the first; and as there was a Door, or Entrance there into my Cave, I made a formal fram'd Door Case, and a Door to it of Boards, and set it up in the Passage, a little within the Entrance; and causing the Door to open on the inside, I barr'd it up in the Night, taking in my Ladders too; so that *Friday* could no way come at me in the inside of my innermost Wall, without making so much Noise in getting over, that it must needs waken me; for my first Wall had now a compleat Roof over it of long Poles, covering all my Tent, and leaning up to the side of the Hill, which was again laid cross with smaller Sticks instead of Laths, and then thatch'd over a great Thickness, with the Rice Straw, which was strong like Reeds; and at the Hole or Place which was left to go in or out by the Ladder, I had plac'd a kind of Trap-door, which if it had been attempted on the outside, would not have open'd at all, but would have fallen down, and made a great Noise; and as to Weapons, I took them all in to my Side every Night.

But I needed none of all this Precaution; for never Man had a more faithful, loving, sincere Servant, than *Friday* was to me; without Passions, Sullenness or Designs, perfectly oblig'd and engag'd; his very Affections were ty'd to me, like those of a Child to a Father; and I dare say, he would have sacrific'd his Life for the saving mine, upon any occasion whatsoever; the many Testimonies he gave me of this, put it out of doubt, and soon convinc'd me, that I needed to use no Precautions, as to my Safety on his Account.

This frequently gave me occasion to observe, and that with wonder, that however it had pleas'd God, in his Providence, and in the Government of the Works of his Hands, to take from so great a Part of the World of his Creatures, the best uses to which their Faculties, and the Powers of their Souls are adapted; yet that he has bestow'd upon them the same Powers, the same Reason, the same Affections, the same Sentiments of Kindness and Obligation, the same Passions and Resentments of Wrongs, the same Sense of Gratitude, Sincerity, Fidelity, and all the Capacities of doing Good, and receiving Good, that he has given to us; and that when he pleases to offer to them Occasions of exerting these, they are as ready, nay, more ready to apply them to the right Uses for which they were bestow'd, than we are; and this made me very melancholly sometimes, in reflecting as the several Occasions presented, how mean a Use we make of all these, even though we have these Powers enlighten'd by the great Lamp of Instruction, the Spirit of God, and by the Knowledge of his Word, added to our Understanding; and why it has pleas'd God to hide the like saving Knowledge from so many Millions of Souls, who if I might judge by this poor Savage, would make a much better use of it than we did.

From hence, I sometimes was led too far to invade the Soveraignty of *Providence*, and as it were arraign the Justice of so arbitrary a Disposition of Things, that should hide that Light from some, and reveal it to others, and yet expect a like Duty from both: But I shut it up, and check'd my Thoughts with this Conclusion, (1st.) That we did not know by what Light and Law these should be Condemn'd; but that as God was necessarily, and by the Nature of his Being, infinitely Holy and Just, so it could not be, but that if these Creatures were all sentenc'd to Absence from himself, it was on account of sinning against that Light which, as the Scripture says, was a Law to themselves,* and by such Rules as their Consciences would acknowledge to be just, tho' the Foundation was not discover'd to us: And (2d.) that still as we are all the Clay in the Hand of the Potter, no Vessel could say to him, Why hast thou form'd me thus?*

But to return to my New Companion; I was greatly delighted with him, and made it my Business to teach him every Thing, that was proper to make him useful, handy, and helpful; but especially to make him speak, and understand me when I spake, and he was the aptest Schollar* that ever was, and particularly was so merry, so constantly diligent, and so pleased, when he cou'd but understand me, or make me understand him, that it was very pleasant to me to talk to him; and now my Life began to be so easy, that I began to say to my self, that could I but have been safe from more Savages, I cared not, if I was never to remove from the place while I lived.

After I had been two or three Days return'd to my Castle, I thought that, in order to bring *Friday* off from his horrid way of feeding, and from the Relish of a Cannibal's Stomach, I ought to let him taste other Flesh; so I took him out with me one Morning to the Woods: I went indeed intending to kill a Kid out of my own Flock, and bring him home and dress it. But as I was going, I saw a She

Goat lying down in the Shade, and two young Kids sitting by her; I catch'd hold of *Friday*, hold says I, stand still; and made Signs to him not to stir, immediately I presented my Piece, shot and kill'd one of the Kids. The poor Creature who had at a Distance indeed seen me kill the Savage his Enemy, but did not know, or could imagine how it was done, was sensibly surpriz'd, trembled, and shook, and look'd so amaz'd, that I thought he would have sunk down. He did not see the Kid I shot at, or perceive I had kill'd it, but ripp'd up his Wastcoat to feel if he was not wounded, and as I found, presently thought I was resolv'd to kill him; for he came and kneel'd down to me, and embraceing my Knees, said a great many Things I did not understand; but I could easily see that the meaning was to pray me not to kill him.

I soon found a way to convince him that I would do him no harm, and taking him up by the Hand laugh'd at him, and pointed to the Kid which I had kill'd, beckoned to him to run and fetch it, which he did; and while he was wondering and looking to see how the Creature was kill'd, I loaded my Gun again, and by and by I saw a great Fowl like a Hawk sit upon a Tree within Shot; so to let *Friday* understand a little what I would do, I call'd him to me again, pointed at the Fowl which was indeed a Parrot, tho' I thought it had been a Hawk, I say pointing to the Parrot, and to my Gun, and to the Ground under the Parrot, to let him see I would make it fall, I made him understand that I would shoot and kill that Bird; accordingly I fir'd and bad him look, and immediately he saw the Parrot fall, he stood like one frighted again, notwithstanding all I had said to him; and I found he was the more amaz'd, because he did not see me put any Thing into the Gun; but thought that there must be some wonderful Fund of Death and Destruction in that Thing, able to kill Man, Beast, Bird, or any Thing near, or far off; and the Astonishment this created in him was such, as could not wear off for a long Time; and I believe, if I would have let him, he would have worshipp'd me and my Gun: As for the Gun it self, he would not so much as touch it for several Days after; but would speak to it, and talk to it, as if it had answer'd him, when he was by himself; which, as I afterwards learn'd of him, was to desire it not to kill him.

Well, after his Astonishment was a little over at this, I pointed to him to run and fetch the Bird I had shot, which he did, but stay'd some Time; for the Parrot not being quite dead, was flutter'd away a good way off from the Place where she fell; however, he found her, took her up, and brought her to me; and as I had perceiv'd his Ignorance about the Gun before, I took this Advantage to charge the Gun again, and not let him see me do it, that I might be ready for any other Mark that might present; but nothing more offer'd at that Time; so I brought home the Kid, and the same Evening I took the Skin off, and cut it out as well as I could; and having a Pot for that purpose, I boil'd, or stew'd some of the Flesh, and made some very good Broth; and after I had begun to eat some, I gave some to my Man, who seem'd very glad of it, and lik'd it very well; but that which was strangest to him, was, to see me eat Salt with it; he made a Sign to me, that the Salt was not good to eat, and putting a little into his own Mouth, he seem'd to nauseate it, and would spit and sputter at it, washing his Mouth with fresh Water after it; on the other hand, I took some Meat in my Mouth without Salt, and I pretended to spit and sputter for want of Salt, as fast as he had done at the Salt; but it would not do, he would never care for Salt with his Meat, or in his Broth; at least not a great while,* and then but a very little.

Having thus fed him with boil'd Meat and Broth, I was resolv'd to feast him the next Day with roasting a Piece of the Kid; this I did by hanging it before the Fire, in a String, as I had seen many People do in *England*, setting two Poles up, one on each side the Fire, and one cross on the Top, and tying the String to the Cross-stick, letting the Meat turn continually: This *Friday* admir'd very much; but when he came to taste the Flesh, he took so many ways to tell me how well he lik'd it, that I could not but understand him; and at last he told me he would never eat Man's Flesh any more, which I was very glad to hear.

The next Day I set him to work to beating some Corn out, and sifting it in the manner I us'd to do, as I observ'd before, and he soon understood how to do it as well as I, especially after he had seen what the Meaning of it was, and that it was to make Bread of; for after that I let him see me make my Bread, and bake it too, and in a little Time *Friday* was able to do all the Work for me, as well as I could do it my self.

I begun now to consider, that having two Mouths to feed, instead of one, I must provide more Ground for my Harvest, and plant a larger quantity of Corn, than I us'd to do; so I mark'd out a larger Piece of Land, and began the Fence in the same Manner as before, in which *Friday* not only work'd very willingly, and very hard; but did it very chearfully, and I told him what it was for; that it was for Corn to make more Bread, because he was now with me, and that I might have enough for him, and my self too: He appear'd very sensible of that Part, and let me know, that he thought I had much more Labour upon me on his Account, than I had for my self; and that he would work the harder for me, if I would tell him what to do.

This was the pleasantest Year of all the Life I led in this Place; *Friday* began to talk pretty well, and understand the Names of almost every Thing I had occasion to call for, and of every Place I had to send him to, and talk'd a great deal to me; so that in short I began now to have some Use for my Tongue again, which indeed I had very little occasion for before; that is to say, *about Speech*; besides the Pleasure of talking to him, I had a singular Satisfaction in the Fellow himself; his simple unfeign'd Honesty, appear'd to me more and more every Day, and I began really to love the Creature; and on his Side, I believe he lov'd me more than it was possible for him ever to love any Thing before.

I had a Mind once to try if he had any hankering Inclination to his own Country again, and having learn'd him *English* so well that he could answer me almost any Questions, I ask'd him whether the Nation that he belong'd to never conquer'd in Battle, at which he smil'd; and said; yes, yes, we always fight the better; that is, he meant always get the better in Fight; and so we began the following Discourse: You always fight the better said I, How came you to be taken Prisoner then, *Friday*?

Friday, My Nation beat much, for all that.

Master, How beat; if your Nation beat them, how come you to be taken?

Friday, They more many than my Nation in the Place where me was; they take one, two, three, and me; my Nation over beat them in the yonder Place, where me no was; there my Nation take one, two, great Thousand.

Master, But why did not your Side recover you from the Hands of your Enemies then?

Friday, They run one, two, three, and me, and make go in the *Canoe*; my Nation have no *Canoe* that time.

Master, Well, *Friday*, and What does your Nation do with the Men they take, do they carry them away, and eat them, as these did?

Friday, Yes, my Nation eat Mans too, eat all up.

Master, Where do they carry them?

Friday, Go to other Place where they think.

Master, Do they come hither?

Friday, Yes, yes, they come hither; come other else Place.

Master, Have you been here with them?

Friday, Yes, I been here; [*points to the* N. W. *Side of the Island*, which it seems was their Side.]

By this I understood, that my Man *Friday* had formerly been among the Savages, who us'd to come on Shore on the farther Part of the Island, on the same Man eating Occasions that he was now brought for; and sometime after, when I took the Courage to carry him to that Side, being the same I formerly mention'd, he presently knew the Place, and told me, he was there once when they eat up twenty Men, two Women, and one Child; he could not tell Twenty in *English*; but he numbred them by laying so many Stones on a Row, and pointing to me to tell them over.

I have told this Passage, because it introduces what follows; that after I had had this Discourse with him, I ask'd him how far it was from our Island to the Shore, and whether the *Canoes* were not often lost; he told me, there was no Danger, no *Canoes* ever lost; but that after a little way out to the Sea, there was a Current, and Wind, always one way in the Morning, the other in the Afternoon.

This I understood to be no more than the Sets of the Tide, as going out, or coming in; but I afterwards understood, it was occasion'd by the great Draft and Reflux of the mighty River *Oroonooko*;* in the Mouth, or the Gulph of which River, as I found afterwards, our Island lay; and this Land which I perceiv'd to the *W.* and *N. W.* was the great Island *Trinidad*, on the *North* Point of the Mouth of the River: I ask'd *Friday* a thousand questions about the Country, the Inhabitants, the Sea, the Coast, and what Nation were near; he told me all he knew with the greatest Openness imaginable; I ask'd him the Names of the several Nations of his Sort of People; but could get no other Name than *Caribs*; from whence I easily understood, that these were the *Caribbees*,* which our Maps place on the Part of *America*, which reaches from the Mouth of the River *Oroonooko* to *Guiana*, and onwards to *St. Martha*:* He told me that up a great way beyond the Moon, that was, beyond the Setting of the Moon, which must be *W.* from their Country, there dwelt white bearded Men, like me; and pointed to my great Whiskers, which I mention'd before; and that they had kill'd *much Mans*, that was his Word; by all which I understood, he meant the *Spaniards*, whose Cruelties in *America* had been spread over the whole Countries, and was remember'd by all the Nations from Father to Son.

I enquir'd if he could tell me how I might come from this Island, and get among those white Men; he told me, yes, yes, I might go *in two Canoe*; I could not understand what he meant, or make him describe to me what he meant by *two Canoe*, till at last with great Difficulty, I found he meant it must be in a large great Boat, as big as *two Canoes*.

This Part of *Friday's* Discourse began to relish with me very well,* and from this Time I entertain'd some Hopes, that one Time or other, I might find an Opportunity to make my Escape from this Place; and that this poor Savage might be a Means to help me to do it.

During the long Time that *Friday* has now been with me, and that he began to speak to me, and understand me, I was not wanting to lay a Foundation of religious Knowledge in his Mind; particularly I ask'd him one Time who made him? The poor Creature did not understand me at all, but thought I had ask'd who was his Father; but I took it by another handle, and ask'd him who made the Sea, the Ground we walk'd on, and the Hills, and Woods; he told me it was one old *Benamuckee*, that liv'd beyond all: He could describe nothing of this great Person, but that he was very old; much older he said than the Sea, or the Land; than the Moon, or the Stars: I ask'd him then, if this old Person had made all Things, why did not all Things worship him; he look'd very grave, and with a perfect Look of Innocence, said, *All Things do say O to him*: I ask'd him if the People who die in his Country went away any where; he said, yes, they all went to *Benamuckee*; then I ask'd him whether these they eat up went thither too, he said yes.

From these Things, I began to instruct him in the Knowledge of the true God: I told him that the great Maker of all Things liv'd up there, pointing up towards Heaven: That he governs the World by the same Power and Providence by which he had made it: That he was omnipotent, could do every Thing for us, give every Thing to us, take every Thing from us; and thus by Degrees I open'd his Eyes. He listned with great Attention, and receiv'd with Pleasure the

Notion of *Jesus Christ* being sent to redeem us, and of the Manner of making our Prayers to God, and his being able to hear us, even into Heaven; he told me one Day, that if our God could hear us up beyond the Sun, he must needs be a greater God than their *Bena-muckee*, who liv'd but a little way off, and yet could not hear, till they went up to the great Mountains where he dwelt, to speak to him; I ask'd him if ever he went thither, to speak to him; he said no, they never went that were young Men; none went thither but the old Men, who he call'd their *Oowocakee*, that is, as I made him explain it to me, their Religious, or Clergy, and that they went to say *O*, (so he called saying Prayers) and then came back, and told them what *Benamuckee* said: By this I observ'd, That there is *Priestcraft*, even amongst the most blinded ignorant Pagans in the World; and the Policy of making a secret Religion, in order to preserve the Vener-ation of the People to the Clergy, is not only to be found in the *Roman*, but perhaps among all Religions in the World,* even among the most brutish and barbarous Savages.

I endeavour'd to clear up this Fraud, to my Man *Friday*, and told him, that the Pretence of their old Men going up the Mountains, to say *O* to their God *Benamuckee*, was a Cheat, and their bringing Word from thence what he said, was much more so; that if they met with any Answer, or spake with any one there, it must be with an evil Spirit: And then I entred into a long Discourse with him about the Devil, the Original of him, his Rebellion against God, his Enmity to Man, the Reason of it, his setting himself up in the dark Parts of the World to be Worship'd instead of God, and as God; and the many Stratagems he made use of to delude Mankind to his Ruine; how he had a secret access to our Passions, and to our Affections, to adapt his Snares so to our Inclinations, as to cause us even to be our own Tempters, and to run upon our Destruction by our own Choice.

I found it was not so easie to imprint right Notions in his Mind about the Devil, as it was about the Being of a God. Nature assisted all my Arguments to Evidence to him, even the Necessity of a great first Cause* and over-ruling governing Power; a secret directing Providence, and of the Equity, and Justice, of paying Homage to him that made us, and the like. But there appeared nothing of all this in the Notion of an evil Spirit; of his Original, his Being, his Nature, and above all of his Inclination to do Evil, and to draw us in to do so too; and the poor Creature puzzl'd me once in such a manner, by a

Question meerly natural and innocent, that I scarce knew what to say to him. I had been talking a great deal to him of the Power of God, his Omnipotence, his dreadful Nature to Sin,* his being a consuming Fire* to the Workers of Iniquity;* how, as he had made us all, he could destroy us and all the World in a Moment; and he listen'd with great Seriousness to me all the while.

After this, I had been telling him how the Devil was God's Enemy in the Hearts of Men, and used all his Malice and Skill to defeat the good Designs of Providence, and to ruine the Kingdom of Christ in the World; and the like. Well, says *Friday*, but you say, God is so strong, so great, is he not much strong, much might as the Devil? Yes, yes, says I, *Friday*, God is stronger than the Devil, God is above the Devil, and therefore we pray to God to tread him down* under our Feet, and enable us to resist his Temptations and quench his fiery Darts.* *But*, says he again, *if God much strong, much might as the Devil, why God no kill the Devil, so make him no more do wicked?*

I was strangely surpriz'd at his Question, and after all, tho' I was now an old Man, yet I was but a young Doctor, and ill enough quallified for a Casuist, or a Solver of Difficulties:* And at first I could not tell what to say, so I pretended not to hear him, and ask'd him what he said? But he was too earnest for an Answer to forget his Question; so that he repeated it in the very same broken Words, as above. By this time I had recovered my self a little, and I said, *God will at last punish him severely*; he is *reserv'd for the Judgment, and is to be cast into the Bottomless-Pit, to dwell with everlasting Fire.** This did not satisfie *Friday*, but he returns upon me, repeating my Words, RESERVE, AT LAST, *me no understand*; but, *Why not kill the Devil now, not kill great ago?* You may as well ask me, *said I*, Why God does not kill you and I, when we do wicked Things here that offend him? We are preserv'd to repent and be pardon'd: He muses a while at this; *well, well*, says he, mighty affectionately, *that well; so you, I, Devil, all wicked, all preserve, repent, God pardon all.* Here I was run down again by him to the last Degree, and it was a Testimony to me, how the meer Notions of Nature, though they will guide reasonable Creatures to the Knowledge of a God, and of a Worship or Homage due to the supreme Being, of God as the Consequence of our Nature; yet nothing but divine Revelation can form the Knowledge of *Jesus Christ*, and of a Redemption purchas'd for us, of a Mediator of the new Covenant,* and of an Intercessor, at the Foot-stool of God's

Throne;* I say, nothing but a Revelation from Heaven, can form
these in the Soul, and that therefore the Gospel of our Lord and
Saviour *Jesus Christ*; I mean, the Word of God, and the Spirit of
God promis'd for the Guide and Sanctifier of his People, are the
absolutely necessary Instructors of the Souls of Men, in the saving
Knowledge of God, and the Means of Salvation.

I therefore diverted the present Discourse between me and my
Man, rising up hastily, as upon some sudden Occasion of going out;
then sending him for something a good way off, I seriously pray'd to
God that he would enable me to instruct savingly this poor Savage,
assisting by his Spirit the Heart of the poor ignorant Creature, to
receive the Light of the Knowledge of God in *Christ*, reconciling
him to himself, and would guide me to speak so to him from the
Word of God, as his Conscience might be convinc'd, his Eyes
open'd, and his Soul sav'd. When he came again to me, I entred into
a long Discourse with him upon the Subject of the Redemption of
Man by the Saviour of the World, and of the Doctrine of the Gospel
preach'd from Heaven, *viz.* of Repentance towards God, and Faith
in our Blessed Lord Jesus. I then explain'd to him, as well as I could,
why our Blessed Redeemer took not on him the Nature of Angels,
but the Seed of *Abraham*,* and how for that Reason the fallen Angels
had no Share in the Redemption; that he came only to the lost Sheep
of the House of *Israel*,* and the like.

I had, *God knows*, more Sincerity than Knowledge, in all the
Methods I took for this poor Creature's Instruction, and must
acknowledge what I believe all that act upon the same Principle will
find, That in laying Things open to him, I really inform'd and
instructed my self in many Things, that either I did not know, or had
not fully consider'd before; but which occurr'd naturally to my
Mind, upon my searching into them, for the Information of this
poor Savage; and I had more Affection in my Enquiry after Things
upon this Occasion, than ever I felt before; so that whether this poor
wild Wretch was the better for me, or no, I had great Reason to be
thankful that ever he came to me: My Grief set lighter upon me, my
Habitation grew comfortable to me beyond Measure; and when I
reflected that in this solitary Life which I had been confin'd to, I had
not only been moved my self to look up to Heaven, and to seek to the
Hand that had brought me there; but was now to be made an
Instrument under Providence to save the Life, and *for ought I knew*,

the Soul of a poor Savage, and bring him to the true Knowledge of Religion, and of the Christian Doctrine, that he might know Christ Jesus, *to know whom is Life eternal*. I say, when I reflected upon all these Things, a secret Joy run through every Part of my Soul, and I frequently rejoyc'd that ever I was brought to this Place, which I had so often thought the most dreadful of all Afflictions that could possibly have befallen me.

In this thankful Frame I continu'd all the Remainder of my Time, and the Conversation which employ'd the Hours between *Friday* and I, was such, as made the three Years which we liv'd there together perfectly and compleatly happy, *if any such Thing as compleat Happiness can be form'd in a sublunary State*. The Savage was now a good Christian, a much better than I; though I have reason to hope, and bless God for it, that we were equally penitent, and comforted restor'd Penitents; we had here the Word of God to read, and no farther off from his Spirit to instruct,* than if we had been in *England*.

I always apply'd my self in Reading the Scripture, to let him know, as well as I could, the Meaning of what I read; and he again, by his serious Enquiries, and Questionings, made me, *as I said before*, a much better Scholar in the Scripture Knowledge, than I should ever have been by my own private meer Reading. Another thing I cannot refrain from observing here also from Experience, in this retir'd Part of my Life, *viz.* How infinite and inexpressible a Blessing it is, that the Knowledge of God, and of the Doctrine of Salvation by *Christ Jesus*, is so plainly laid down in the Word of God; so easy to be receiv'd and understood: That as the bare reading the Scripture made me capable of understanding enough of my Duty, to carry me directly on to the great Work of sincere Repentance for my Sins, and laying hold of a Saviour for Life and Salvation, to a stated Reformation in Practice, and Obedience to all God's Commands, and this without any Teacher or Instructer; I mean, humane; so the same plain Instruction sufficiently serv'd to the enlightning this Savage Creature, and bringing him to be such a Christian, as I have known few equal to him in my Life.

As to all the Disputes, Wranglings, Strife and Contention, which has happen'd in the World about Religion, whether Niceties in Doctrines, or Schemes of Church Government, they were all perfectly useless to us; as for ought I can yet see, they have been to all the rest of the World: We had the *sure Guide* to Heaven, *viz.* The Word of God; and we had, *blessed be God*, comfortable Views of the Spirit of God teaching and instructing us by his Word, *leading us into all Truth*,* and making us both willing and obedient to the Instruction of his Word; and I cannot see the least Use that the greatest Knowledge of the disputed Points in Religion which have made such Confusions in the World would have been to us, if we could have obtain'd it; but I must go on with the Historical Part of Things, and take every Part in its order.

After *Friday* and I became more intimately acquainted, and that he could understand almost all I said to him, and speak fluently, though in broken *English* to me; I acquainted him with my own Story, or at least so much of it as related to my coming into the Place, how I had liv'd there, and how long. I let him into the Mystery, for such it was to him, of Gunpowder, and Bullet, and taught him how to shoot: I gave him a Knife, which he was wonderfully delighted with, and I made him a Belt, with a Frog hanging to it, such as in *England* we wear Hangers in; and in the Frog, instead of a Hanger, I gave him a Hatchet, which was not only as good a Weapon in some Cases, but much more useful upon other Occasions.

I describ'd to him the Country of *Europe*, and particularly *England*, which I came from; how we liv'd, how we worshipp'd God, how we behav'd to one another; and how we traded in Ships to all Parts of the World: I gave him an Account of the Wreck which I had been on board of, and shew'd him as near as I could, the Place where she lay; but she was all beaten in Pieces before, and gone.

I shew'd him the Ruins of our Boat, which we lost when we escap'd, and which I could not stir with my whole Strength then; but was now fallen almost all to Pieces: Upon seeing this Boat, *Friday* stood musing a great while, and said nothing; I ask'd him what it was he study'd upon, at last says he, *me see such Boat like come to Place at my Nation.*

I did not understand him a good while; but at last, when I had examin'd farther into it, I understood by him, that a Boat, such as that had been, came on Shore upon the Country where he liv'd; that is, as he explain'd it, was driven thither by Stress of Weather: I presently imagin'd, that some *European* Ship must have been cast away upon their Coast, and the Boat might get loose, and drive a Shore; but was so dull, that I never once thought of Men making

escape from a Wreck thither, much less whence they might come; so
I only enquir'd after a Description of the Boat.

Friday describ'd the Boat to me well enough; but brought me
better to understand him, when he added with some Warmth, *we
save the white Mans from drown*: Then I presently ask'd him, if there
was any *white Mans*, as he call'd them, in the Boat; *yes*, he said, *the
Boat full white Mans*: I ask'd him how many; he told upon his Fingers seventeen: I ask'd him then what become of them; he told me,
they live, they dwell at my Nation.

This put new Thoughts into my Head; for I presently imagin'd,
that these might be the Men belonging to the Ship, that was cast
away in Sight of *my Island*, as I now call it; and who after the Ship
was struck on the Rock, and they saw her inevitably lost, had sav'd
themselves in their Boat, and were landed upon that wild Shore
among the Savages.

Upon this, I enquir'd of him more critically, What was become
of them? He assur'd me they lived still there; that they had been
there about four Years; that the Savages let them alone, and gave
them Victuals to live. I ask'd him, How it came to pass they did not
kill them and eat them? He said, *No, they make Brother with them;*
that is, as I understood him, a Truce: And then he added, *They no
eat Mans but when make the War fight;** that is to say, they never eat
any Men but such as come to fight with them, and are taken in
Battle.

It was after this some considerable Time, that being upon the Top
of the Hill, at the *East* Side of the Island, from whence as I have said,
I had in a clear Day discover'd the Main, or Continent of *America*;
Friday, the Weather being very serene, looks very earnestly towards
the Main Land, and in a kind of Surprise, falls a jumping and dancing, and calls out to me, for I was at some Distance from him: I
ask'd him, What was the Matter? *O joy!* Says he, *O glad! There see
my Country, there my Nation!*

I observ'd an extraordinary Sense of Pleasure appear'd in his Face,
and his Eyes sparkled, and his Countenance discover'd a strange
Eagerness, as if he had a Mind to be in his own Country again; and
this Observation of mine, put a great many Thoughts into me, which
made me at first not so easy about my new Man *Friday* as I was
before; and I made no doubt, but that if *Friday* could get back to his
own Nation again, he would not only forget all his Religion, but all

his Obligation to me; and would be forward enough to give his Countrymen an Account of me, and come back perhaps with a hundred or two of them, and make a Feast upon me, at which he might be as merry as he us'd to be with those of his Enemies, when they were taken in War.

But I wrong'd the poor honest Creature very much, for which I was very sorry afterwards. However as my Jealousy encreased, and held me some Weeks, I was a little more circumspect, and not so familiar and kind to him as before; in which I was certainly in the Wrong too, the honest grateful Creature having no thought about it, but what consisted with the best Principles, both as a religious Christian, and as a grateful Friend, as appeared afterwards to my full Satisfaction.

While my Jealousy of him lasted, you may be sure I was every Day pumping him to see if he would discover any of the new Thoughts, which I suspected were in him; but I found every thing he said was so Honest, and so Innocent, that I could find nothing to nourish my Suspicion; and in spight of all my Uneasiness he made me at last entirely his own again, nor did he in the least perceive that I was Uneasie, and therefore I could not suspect him of Deceit.

One Day walking up the same Hill, but the Weather being haizy at Sea, so that we could not see the Continent, I call'd to him, and said, *Friday*, do not you wish your self in your own Country, your own Nation? Yes, he said, *he be much O glad to be at his own Nation.* What would you do there said I, would you turn Wild again, eat Mens Flesh again, and be a Savage as you were before? He lookt full of Concern, and shaking his Head said, *No no*, Friday *tell them to live Good*, tell them *to pray God*, tell them *to eat Corn-bread, Cattle-flesh, Milk, no eat Man again*: Why then said I to him, *They will kill you.* He look'd grave at that, and then said, *No, they no kill me, they willing love learn*: He meant by this, they would be willing to learn. He added, they learn'd much of the Bearded-Mans that come in the Boat. Then I ask'd him if he would go back to them? He smil'd at that, and told me he could not swim so far. I told him I would make a *Canoe* for him. He told me, *he would go, if I would go with him.* I go! says I, why they will Eat me if I come there! No, no, says he, *me make they no Eat you; me make they much Love you*: He meant he would tell them how I had kill'd his Enemies, and sav'd his Life, and so he would make them love me; then he told me as well as he could, how kind they were to seventeen White-men, or Bearded-men, as he call'd them, who came on Shore there in Distress.

From this time I confess I had a Mind to venture over, and see if I could possibly joyn with these Bearded-men, who I made no doubt were *Spaniards* or *Portuguese*; not doubting but if I could we might find some Method to Escape from thence, being upon the Continent, and a good Company together, better than I could from an Island 40 Miles off the Shore, and alone without Help. So after some Days I took *Friday* to work again, by way of Discourse, and told him I would give him a Boat to go back to his own Nation; and accordingly I carry'd him to my Frigate which lay on the other Side of the Island, and having clear'd it of Water, for I always kept it sunk in the Water, I brought it out, shewed it him, and we both went into it.

I found he was a most dextrous Fellow at managing it, would make it go almost as swift and fast again as I could; so when he was in, I said to him, Well now, *Friday*, shall we go to your Nation? He look'd very dull at my saying so, which it seems was, because he thought the Boat too small to go so far. I told him then I had a bigger; so the next Day I went to the Place where the first Boat lay which I had made, but which I could not get into Water: He said that was big enough; but then as I had taken no Care of it, and it had lain two or three and twenty Years there, the Sun had split and dry'd it, that it was in a manner rotten. *Friday* told me such a Boat would do very well, and would carry *much enough Vittle, Drink, Bread*, that was his Way of Talking.

Upon the whole, I was by this Time so fix'd upon my Design of going over with him to the Continent, that I told him we would go and make one as big as that, and he should go home in it. He answer'd not one Word, but look'd very grave and sad: I ask'd him what was the matter with him? He ask'd me again thus; *Why, you angry mad with* Friday, *what me done?* I ask'd him what he meant; I told him I was not angry with him at all. *No angry! No angry!* says he, repeating the Words several Times, *Why send* Friday *home away to my Nation?* Why, (says I) *Friday*, did you not say you wish'd you were there? *Yes, yes*, says he, *wish be both there, no wish* Friday *there, no Master there*. In a Word, he would not think of going there without me; *I go there!* Friday, (says I) *what shall I do there?* He turn'd very quick upon me at this: *You do great deal much good*, says he, *you teach wild Mans be good sober tame Mans; you tell them know God, pray God, and live new Life*. Alas! Friday, (says I) *thou knowest not what thou *sayest, I am but an ignorant Man my self. Yes, yes*, says he, *you teachee me Good, you teachee them Good. No, no*, Friday, (says I) *you shall go without me, leave me here to live by my self as I did before.* He look'd confus'd again at that Word, and running to one of the Hatchets which he used to wear, he takes it up hastily, comes and gives it me, *What must I do with this?* says I to him. *You take, kill* Friday; (says he.) *What must I kill you for?* said I again. He returns very quick, *What you send* Friday *away for? take, kill* Friday, *no send* Friday *away.* This he spoke so earnestly, that I saw Tears stand in his Eyes: In a Word, I so plainly discover'd the utmost Affection in him to me, and a firm Resolution in him, that I told him then, and often after, that I would never send him away from me, if he was willing to stay with me.

Upon the whole, as I found by all his Discourse a settled Affection to me, and that nothing should part him from me, so I found all the Foundation of his Desire to go to his own Country, was laid in his ardent Affection to the People, and his Hopes of my doing them good; a Thing which as I had no Notion of my self, so I had not the least Thought or Intention, or Desire of undertaking it. But still I found a strong Inclination to my attempting an Escape as above, founded on the Supposition gather'd from the Discourse, (*viz.*) That there were seventeen bearded Men there; and therefore, without any more Delay, I went to Work with *Friday* to find out a great Tree proper to fell, and make a large Periagua or Canoe to undertake the Voyage. There were Trees enough in the Island to have built a little Fleet, not of Periagua's and Canoes, but even of good large Vessels. But the main Thing I look'd at, was to get one so near the Water that we might launch it when it was made, to avoid the Mistake I committed at first.

At last, *Friday* pitch'd upon a Tree, for I found he knew much better than I what kind of Wood was fittest for it, nor can I tell to this Day what Wood to call the Tree we cut down, except that it was very like the Tree we call *Fustic*,* or between that and the *Nicaragua* Wood,* for it was much of the same Colour and Smell. *Friday* was for burning the Hollow or Cavity of this Tree out to make it for a Boat. But I shew'd him how rather to cut it out with Tools, which, after I had shew'd him how to use, he did very handily, and in about a Month's hard Labour, we finished it, and made it very handsome, especially when with our Axes, which I shew'd him how to handle, we cut and hew'd the out-side into the true Shape of a Boat; after this, however, it cost us near a Fortnight's Time to get her along as it were Inch by Inch upon great Rowlers into the Water. But when she was in, she would have carry'd twenty Men with great Ease.

When she was in the Water, and tho' she was so big it amazed me to see with what Dexterity and how swift my Man *Friday* would manage her, turn her, and paddle her along; so I ask'd him if he would, and if we might venture over in her; *Yes*, he said, *he venture over in her very well, tho' great blow Wind.* However, I had a farther Design that he knew nothing of, and that was to make a Mast and Sail and to fit her with an Anchor and Cable: As to a Mast, that was easy enough to get; so I pitch'd upon a strait young Cedar-Tree, which I found near the Place, and which there was great Plenty of in the Island, and I set *Friday* to Work to cut it down, and gave him Directions how to shape and order it. But as to the Sail, that was my particular Care; I knew I had old Sails, or rather Pieces of old Sails enough; but as I had had them now six and twenty Years by me, and had not been very careful to preserve them, not imagining that I should ever have this kind of Use for them, I did not doubt but they were all rotten, and indeed most of them were so; however, I found two Pieces which appear'd pretty good, and with these I went to Work, and with a great deal of Pains, and awkward tedious stitching (you may be sure) for Want of Needles, I at length made a three Corner'd ugly Thing, like what we call in *England*, a Shoulder of Mutton Sail, to go with a Boom at bottom, and a little short Sprit at the Top, such as usually our Ships Long-Boats sail with, and such as I best knew how to manage; because it was such a one as I had to the Boat, in which I made my Escape from *Barbary*, as related in the first Part of my Story.

I was near two Months performing this last Work, *viz.* rigging and fitting my Mast and Sails; for I finish'd them very compleat, making a small Stay, and a Sail, or Foresail to it, to assist, if we should turn to Windward; and which was more than all, I fix'd a Rudder to the Stern of her, to steer with; and though I was but a bungling Ship-wright, yet as I knew the Usefulness, and even Necessity of such a Thing, I apply'd my self with so much Pains to do it, that at last I brought it to pass; though considering the many dull Contrivances I had for it that sail'd, I think it cost me almost as much Labour as making the Boat.

After all this was done too, I had my Man *Friday* to teach as to what belong'd to the Navigation of my Boat; for though he knew very well how to paddle a *Canoe*, he knew nothing what belong'd to a Sail, and a Rudder; and was the most amaz'd, when he saw me work the Boat too and again in the Sea by the Rudder, and how the Sail gyb'd, and fill'd this way, or that way, as the Course we sail'd chang'd; I say, when he saw this, he stood like one, astonish'd, and amaz'd: However, with a little Use, I made all these Things familiar to him; and he became an expert Sailor, except that as to the Compass, I could make him understand very little of that. On the other hand, as there was very little cloudy Weather, and seldom or never any Fogs in those Parts, there was the less occasion for a Compass, seeing the Stars were always to be seen by Night, and the Shore by Day, except in the rainy Seasons, and then no body car'd to stir abroad, either by Land or Sea.

I was now entred on the seven and twentieth Year of my Captivity in this Place; though the three last Years that I had this Creature with me, ought rather to be left out of the Account, my Habitation being quite of another kind than in all the rest of the Time. I kept the Anniversary of my Landing here with the same Thankfulness to God for his Mercies, as at first; and if I had such Cause of Acknowledgment at first, I had much more so now, having such additional Testimonies of the Care of Providence over me, and the great Hopes I had of being effectually, and speedily deliver'd; for I had an invincible Impression upon my Thoughts, that my Deliverance was at hand, and that I should not be another Year in this Place: However, I went on with my Husbandry, digging, planting, fencing, as usual; I gather'd and cur'd my Grapes, and did every necessary Thing as before.

The rainy Season was in the mean Time upon me, when I kept more within Doors than at other Times; so I had stow'd our new Vessel as secure as we could, bringing her up into the Creek, where as I said, in the Beginning I landed my Rafts from the Ship, and haling her up to the Shore, at high Water mark, I made my Man *Friday* dig a little Dock, just big enough to hold her, and just deep enough to give her Water enough to fleet in; and then when the Tide was out, we made a strong Dam cross the End of it, to keep the Water out; and so she lay dry, as to the Tide from the Sea; and to keep the Rain off, we laid a great many Boughs of Trees, so thick, that she was as well thatch'd as a House; and thus we waited for the Month of *November* and *December*, in which I design'd to make my Adventure.

When the settled Season began to come in, as the thought of my Design return'd with the fair Weather, I was preparing daily for the Voyage; and the first Thing I did, was to lay by a certain Quantity of Provisions, being the Stores for our Voyage; and intended in a Week or a Fortnight's Time, to open the Dock, and launch out our Boat. I was busy one Morning upon some Thing of this kind, when I call'd to *Friday*, and bid him go to the Sea Shore, and see if he could find a Turtle, or Tortoise, a Thing which we generally got once a Week, for the Sake of the Eggs, as well as the Flesh: *Friday* had not been long gone, when he came running back, and flew over my outer Wall, or Fence, like one that felt not the Ground, or the Steps he set his Feet on; and before I had time to speak to him, he cries out to me, *O Master! O Master! O Sorrow! O bad!* What's the Matter, *Friday?* says I; *O yonder, there,* says he, *one, two, three Canoe! one, two, three!* By his way of speaking, I concluded there were six; but on enquiry, I found it was but three: Well, *Friday,* says I, do not be frighted; so I heartned him up as well as I could: However, I saw the poor Fellow was most terribly scar'd; for nothing ran in his Head but that they were come to look for him, and would cut him in Pieces, and eat him; and the poor Fellow trembled so, that I scarce knew what to do with him: I comforted him as well as I could, and told him I was in as much Danger as he, and that they would eat me as well as him; *but,* says I, *Friday, we must resolve to fight them; Can you fight,* Friday? *Me shoot,* says he, *but there come many great Number.* No matter for that, said I again, our Guns will fright them that we do not kill; so I ask'd him, Whether if I resolv'd to defend him, he would defend me, and stand by me, and do just as I bid him? He said, *Me die, when you bid die, Master*; so I went and fetch'd a good Dram of Rum, and gave him; for I had been so good a Husband of my Rum, that I had a great deal left: When he had drank it, I made him take the two Fowling-Pieces, which we always carry'd, and load them with large Swan-Shot, as big as small Pistol Bullets; then I took four Muskets, and loaded them with two Slugs, and five small Bullets each; and my two Pistols I loaded with a Brace of Bullets each; I hung my great Sword as usual, naked by my Side, and gave *Friday* his Hatchet.

When I had thus prepar'd my self, I took my Perspective-Glass, and went up to the Side of the Hill, to see what I could discover; and I found quickly, by my Glass, that there were one and twenty Savages, three Prisoners, and three *Canoes*; and that their whole Business seem'd to be the triumphant Banquet upon these three humane Bodies, (a barbarous Feast indeed) but nothing more than as I had observ'd was usual with them.

I observ'd also, that they were landed not where they had done, when *Friday* made his Escape; but nearer to my Creek, where the Shore was low, and where a thick Wood came close almost down to the Sea: This, with the Abhorrence of the inhumane Errand these Wretches came about, fill'd me with such Indignation, that I came down again to *Friday*, and told him, I was resolv'd to go down to them, and kill them all; and ask'd him, If he would stand by me? He was now gotten over his Fright, and his Spirits being a little rais'd, with the Dram I had given him, he was very chearful, and told me, as before, *he would die, when I bid die.*

In this Fit of Fury, I took first and divided the Arms which I had charg'd, as before, between us; I gave *Friday* one Pistol to stick in his Girdle, and three Guns upon his Shoulder; and I took one Pistol, and the other three my self; and in this Posture we march'd out: I took a small Bottle of Rum in my Pocket, and gave *Friday* a large Bag, with more Powder and Bullet; and as to Orders, I charg'd him to keep close behind me, and not to stir, or shoot, or do any Thing, till I bid him; and in the mean Time, not to speak a Word: In this Posture I fetch'd a Compass* to my Right-Hand, of near a Mile, as well to get over the Creek, as to get into the Wood; so that I might come within shoot* of them, before I should be discover'd, which I had seen by my Glass, it was easy to do.

While I was making this March, my former Thoughts returning, I began to abate my Resolution; I do not mean, that I entertain'd any Fear of their Number; for as they were naked, unarm'd Wretches, 'tis certain I was superior to them; nay, though I had been alone; but it occurr'd to my Thoughts, What Call? What Occasion? much less, What Necessity I was in to go and dip my Hands in Blood, to attack People, who had neither done, or intended me any Wrong? Who as to me were innocent, and whose barbarous Customs were their own Disaster, being in them a Token indeed of God's having left them, with the other Nations of that Part of the World, to such Stupidity, and to such inhumane Courses; but did not call me to take upon me to be a Judge of their Actions, much less an Executioner of his Justice; that whenever he thought fit, he would take the Cause into his own Hands, and by national Vengeance punish them as a People, for national Crimes; but that in the mean time, it was none of my Business; that it was true, *Friday* might justify it, because he was a declar'd Enemy, and in a State of War with those very particular People; and it was lawful for him to attack them; but I could not say the same with respect to me: These Things were so warmly press'd upon my Thoughts, all the way as I went, that I resolv'd I would only go and place my self near them, that I might observe their barbarous Feast, and that I would act then as God should direct; but that unless something offer'd that was more a Call to me than yet I knew of, I would not meddle with them.

With this Resolution I enter'd the Wood, and with all possible Waryness and Silence, *Friday* following close at my Heels, I march'd till I came to the Skirt of the Wood, on the Side which was next to them; only that one Corner of the Wood lay between me and them; here I call'd softly to *Friday*, and shewing him a great Tree, which was just at the Corner of the Wood, I bad him go to the Tree, and bring me Word if he could see there plainly what they were doing; he did so, and came immediately back to me, and told me they might be plainly view'd there; that they were all about their Fire, eating the Flesh of one of their Prisoners; and that another lay bound upon the Sand, a little from them, which* he said they would kill next, and which fir'd all the very Soul within me; he told me it was not one of their Nation; but one of the bearded Men, who he had told me of, that came to their Country in the Boat: I was fill'd with Horror at the very naming the white-bearded Man, and going to the Tree, I saw plainly by my Glass, a white Man who lay upon the Beach of the Sea, with his Hands and his Feet ty'd, with Flags, or Things like Rushes; and that he was an *European*, and had Cloaths on.

There was another Tree, and a little Thicket beyond it, about fifty Yards nearer to them than the Place where I was, which by going a little way about, I saw I might come at undiscover'd, and that then I should be within half Shot of them;* so I with-held my Passion, though I was indeed enrag'd to the highest Degree, and going back about twenty Paces, I got behind some Bushes, which held all the way, till I came to the other Tree; and then I came to a little rising

Ground, which gave me a full View of them, at the Distance of about eighty Yards.

I had now not a Moment to loose;* for nineteen of the dreadful Wretches sat upon the Ground, all close huddled together, and had just sent the other two to butcher the poor *Christian*, and bring him perhaps Limb by Limb to their Fire, and they were stoop'd down to untie the Bands, at his Feet; I turn'd to *Friday*, now *Friday*, said I, do as I bid thee; *Friday* said he would; then *Friday*, says I, do exactly as you see me do, fail in nothing; so I set down one of the Muskets, and the Fowling-Piece, upon the Ground, and *Friday* did the like by his; and with the other Musket, I took my aim at the Savages, bidding him do the like; then asking him, If he was ready? He said, yes, then fire at them, said I; and the same Moment I fir'd also.

Friday took his Aim so much better than I, that on the Side that he shot, he kill'd two of them, and wounded three more; and on my Side, I kill'd one, and wounded two: They were, you may be sure, in a dreadful Consternation; and all of them, who were not hurt, jump'd up upon their Feet, but did not immediately know which way to run, or which way to look; for they knew not from whence their Destruction came: *Friday* kept his Eyes close upon me, that as I had bid him, he might observe what I did; so as soon as the first Shot was made, I threw down the Piece, and took up the Fowling-Piece, and *Friday* did the like; he see me cock, and present,* he did the same again; Are you ready, *Friday*? said I; yes, says he; let fly then, says I, in the Name of God, and with that I fir'd again among the amaz'd Wretches, and so did *Friday*; and as our Pieces were now loaden with what I call'd Swan-Shot, or small Pistol Bullets, we found only two drop; but so many were wounded, that they run about yelling, and skreaming, like mad Creatures, all bloody, and miserably wounded, most of them; whereof three more fell quickly after, though not quite dead.

Now *Friday*, says I, laying down the discharg'd Pieces, and taking up the Musket, which was yet loaden; follow me, says I, which he did, with a great deal of Courage; upon which I rush'd out of the Wood, and shew'd my self, and *Friday* close at my Foot; as soon as I per-ceiv'd they saw me, I shouted as loud as I could, and bad *Friday* do so too; and running as fast as I could, *which by the way, was not very fast, being loaden with Arms as I was*, I made directly towards the poor Victim, who was, as I said, lying upon the Beach, or Shore, between the Place where they sat, and the Sea; the two Butchers who were just going to work with him, had left him, at the Suprize of our first Fire, and fled in a terrible Fright, to the Sea Side, and had jump'd into a *Canoe*, and three more of the rest made the same way; I turn'd to *Friday*, and bid him step forwards, and fire at them; he understood me immediately, and running about forty Yards, to be near them, he shot at them, and I thought he had kill'd them all; for I see them all fall of a Heap into the Boat; though I saw two of them up again quickly: However, he kill'd two of them, and wounded the third; so that he lay down in the Bottom of the Boat, as if he had been dead.

While my Man *Friday* fir'd at them, I pull'd out my Knife, and cut the Flags that bound the poor Victim, and loosing his Hands, and Feet, I lifted him up, and ask'd him in the *Portuguese* Tongue, What he was? He answer'd in Latin,* *Christianus*; but was so weak, and faint, that he could scarce stand, or speak; I took my Bottle out of my Pocket, and gave it him, making Signs that he should drink, which he did; and I gave him a Piece of Bread, which he eat; then I ask'd him, What Countryman he was? And he said, *Espagniole*; and being a little recover'd, let me know by all the Signs he could possibly make, how much he was in my Debt for his Deliverance; *Seignior*, said I, with as much *Spanish* as I could make up, we will talk afterwards; but we must fight now; if you have any Strength left, take this Pistol, and Sword, and lay about you; he took them very thankfully, and no sooner had he the Arms in his Hands, but as if they had put new Vigour into him, he flew upon his Murtherers, like a Fury, and had cut two of them in Pieces, in an instant; for the Truth is, as the whole was a Surprize to them; so the poor Creatures were so much frighted with the Noise of our Pieces, that they fell down for meer Amazement, and Fear; and had no more Power to attempt their own Escape, than their Flesh had to resist our Shot; and that was the Case of those Five that *Friday* shot at in the Boat; for as three of them fell with the Hurt they receiv'd, so the other two fell with the Fright.

I kept my Piece in my Hand still, without firing, being willing to keep my Charge ready; because I had given the *Spaniard* my Pistol, and Sword; so I call'd to *Friday*, and bad him run up to the Tree, from whence we first fir'd, and fetch the Arms which lay there, that had been discharg'd, which he did with great Swiftness; and then giving him my Musket, I sat down my self to load all the rest again, and bad them come to me when they wanted: While I was loading these Pieces, there happen'd a fierce Engagement between the *Spaniard*, and one of the Savages, who made at him with one of their great wooden Swords, the same Weapon that was to have kill'd him before, if I had not prevented it: The *Spaniard*, who was as bold, and as brave as could be imagin'd, though weak, had fought this *Indian* a good while, and had cut him two great Wounds on his Head; but the Savage being a stout lusty Fellow, closing in with him, had thrown him down (being faint) and was wringing my Sword out of his Hand, when the *Spaniard*, tho' undermost, wisely quitting the Sword, drew the Pistol* from his Girdle, shot the Savage through the Body, and kill'd him upon the Spot; before I, who was running to help him, could come near him.

Friday being now left to his Liberty, pursu'd the flying Wretches with no Weapon in his Hand, but his Hatchet; and with that he dispatch'd those three, who, as I said before, were wounded at first and fallen, and all the rest he could come up with, and the *Spaniard* coming to me for a Gun, I gave him one of the Fowling-Pieces, with which he pursu'd two of the Savages, and wounded them both; but as he was not able to run, they both got from him into the Wood, where *Friday* pursu'd them, and kill'd one of them; but the other was too nimble for him, and though he was wounded, yet had plunged himself into the Sea, and swam with all his might off to those two who were left in the *Canoe*, which three in the *Canoe*, with one wounded, who we know not whether he dy'd or no, were all that escap'd our Hands of one and twenty: The Account of the Rest is as follows;

3 Kill'd at our first Shot from the Tree.
2 Kill'd at the next Shot.
2 Kill'd by *Friday* in the Boat.
2 Kill'd by *Ditto*, of those at first wounded.
1 Kill'd by *Ditto*, in the Wood.
3 Kill'd by the *Spaniard*.
4 Kill'd, being found dropp'd here and there of their Wounds, or kill'd by *Friday* in his Chase of them.
4 Escap'd in the Boat, whereof one wounded if not dead.
—
21 In all.
—

Those that were in the *Canoe*, work'd hard to get out of Gun-
Shot; and though *Friday* made two or three Shot at them, I did not
find that he hit any of them: *Friday* would fain have had me took
one of their *Canoes*, and pursu'd them; and indeed I was very
anxious about their Escape, least carrying the News home to their
People, they should come back perhaps with two or three hundred
of their *Canoes*, and devour us by meer Multitude; so I consented to
pursue them by Sea, and running to one of their *Canoes*, I jump'd
in, and bad *Friday* follow me; but when I was in the *Canoe*, I was
surpriz'd to find another poor Creature lye there alive, bound Hand
and Foot, as the *Spaniard* was, for the Slaughter, and almost dead
with Fear, not knowing what the Matter was; for he had not been
able to look up over the Side of the Boat, he was ty'd so hard, Neck
and Heels, and had been ty'd so long, that he had really but little
Life in him.

I immediately cut the twisted Flags, or Rushes, which they had
bound him with, and would have helped him up; but he could not
stand, or speak, but groan'd most piteously, believing it seems still
that he was only unbound in order to be kill'd.

When *Friday* came to him, I bad him speak to him, and tell him of
his Deliverance, and pulling out my Bottle, made him give the poor
Wretch a Dram, which, with the News of his being deliver'd, reviv'd
him, and he sat up in the Boat; but when *Friday* came to hear him
speak, and look in his Face, it would have mov'd any one to Tears, to
have seen how *Friday* kiss'd him, embrac'd him, hugg'd him, cry'd,
laugh'd, hollow'd, jump'd about, danc'd, sung, then cry'd again,
wrung his Hands, beat his own Face, and Head, and then sung, and
jump'd about again, like a distracted Creature: It was a good while
before I could make him speak to me, or tell me what was the Matter;
but when he came a little to himself, he told me, that it was his
Father.

It is not easy for me to express how it mov'd me to see what Extasy
and filial Affection had work'd in this poor *Savage*, at the Sight of
his Father,* and of his being deliver'd from Death; nor indeed can I
describe half the Extravagancies of his Affection after this; for he
went into the Boat and out of the Boat a great many times: When he
went in to him, he would sit down by him, open his Breast, and hold
his Father's Head close to his Bosom, half an Hour together, to
nourish it; then he took his Arms and Ankles, which were numb'd

and stiff with the Binding, and chaffed and rubbed them with his Hands; and I perceiving what the Case was, gave him some Rum out of my Bottle, to rub them with, which did them a great deal of Good.

This Action put an End to our Pursuit of the Canoe, with the other *Savages*, who were now gotten almost out of Sight; and it was happy for us that we did not; for it blew so hard within two Hours after, and before they could be gotten a Quarter of their Way, and continued blowing so hard all Night, and that from the *North-west*, which was against them, that I could not suppose their Boat could live, or that they ever reach'd to their own Coast.

But to return to *Friday*, he was so busy about his Father, that I could not find in my Heart to take him off for some time: But after I thought he could leave him a little, I call'd him to me, and he came jumping and laughing, and pleas'd to the highest Extream; then I ask'd him, If he had given his Father any Bread? He shook his Head, and said, *None: Ugly Dog eat all up self*; so I gave him a Cake of Bread out of a little Pouch I carry'd on Purpose; I also gave him a Dram for himself, but he would not taste it, but carry'd it to his Father: I had in my Pocket also two or three Bunches of my Raisins, so I gave him a Handful of them for his Father. He had no sooner given his Father these Raisins, but I saw him come out of the Boat, and run away, as if he had been bewitch'd, he run at such a Rate; for he was the swiftest Fellow of his Foot that ever I saw; I say, he run at such a Rate, that he was out of Sight, as it were, in an instant; and though I call'd, and hollow'd too, after him, it was all one, away he went, and in a Quarter of an Hour, I saw him come back again, though not so fast as he went; and as he came nearer, I found his Pace was slacker, because he had something in his Hand.

When he came up to me, I found he had been quite Home for an Earthen Jugg or Pot to bring his Father some fresh Water, and that he had got two more Cakes, or Loaves of Bread: The Bread he gave me, but the Water he carry'd to his Father: However, as I was very thirsty too, I took a little Sup of it. This Water reviv'd his Father more than all the Rum or Spirits I had given him; for he was just fainting with Thirst.

When his Father had drank, I call'd to him to know if there was any Water left; he said, yes; and I bad him give it to the poor *Spaniard*, who was in as much Want of it as his Father; and I sent one of the Cakes, that *Friday* brought, to the *Spaniard* too, who was indeed very weak, and was reposing himself upon a green Place under the Shade of a Tree; and whose Limbs were also very stiff, and very much swell'd with the rude Bandage he had been ty'd with. When I saw that upon *Friday's* coming to him with the Water, he sat up and drank, and took the Bread, and began to eat, I went to him, and gave him a Handful of Raisins; he look'd up in my Face with all the Tokens of Gratitude and Thankfulness, that could appear in any Countenance; but was so weak, notwithstanding he had so exerted himself in the Fight, that he could not stand up upon his Feet; he try'd to do it two or three times, but was really not able, his Ankles were so swell'd and so painful to him; so I bad him sit still, and caused *Friday* to rub his Ankles, and bathe them with Rum, as he had done his Father's.

I observ'd the poor affectionate Creature every two Minutes, or perhaps less, all the while he was here, turn'd his Head about, to see if his Father was in the same Place, and Posture, as he left him sitting; and at last he found he was not to be seen; at which he started up, and without speaking a Word, flew with that Swiftness to him, that one could scarce perceive his Feet to touch the Ground, as he went: But when he came, he only found he had laid himself down to ease his Limbs; so *Friday* came back to me presently, and I then spoke to the *Spaniard* to let *Friday* help him up if he could, and lead him to the Boat, and then he should carry him to our Dwelling, where I would take Care of him: But *Friday*, a lusty strong Fellow, took the *Spaniard* quite up upon his Back, and carry'd him away to the Boat, and set him down softly upon the Side or Gunnel of the Canoe, with his Feet in the inside of it, and then lifted him quite in, and set him close to his Father, and presently stepping out again, launched the Boat off, and paddled it along the Shore faster than I could walk, tho' the Wind blew pretty hard too; so he brought them both safe into our Creek; and leaving them in the Boat, runs away to fetch the other Canoe. As he pass'd me, I spoke to him, and ask'd him, whither he went, he told me, *Go fetch more Boat*; so away he went like the Wind; for sure never Man or Horse run like him, and he had the other Canoe in the Creek, almost as soon as I got to it by Land; so he wafted me over, and then went to help our new Guests out of the Boat, which he did; but they were neither of them able to walk; so that poor *Friday* knew not what to do.

To remedy this, I went to Work in my Thought, and calling to

Friday to bid them sit down on the Bank while he came to me, I soon made a Kind of Hand-Barrow to lay them on, and *Friday* and I carry'd them up both together upon it between us: But when we got them to the outside of our Wall or Fortification, we were at a worse Loss than before; for it was impossible to get them over; and I was resolv'd not to break it down: So I set to Work again; and *Friday* and I, in about 2 Hours time, made a very handsom Tent, cover'd with old Sails, and above that with Boughs of Trees, being in the Space without our outward Fence, and between that and the Grove of young Wood which I had planted: And here we made them two Beds of such things as I had (*viz.*) of good Rice-Straw, with Blankets laid upon it to lye on, and another to cover them on each Bed.

My Island was now peopled, and I thought my self very rich in Subjects; and it was a merry Reflection which I frequently made, How like a King I look'd. First of all, the whole Country was my own meer Property;* so that I had an undoubted Right of Dominion. 2*dly*, My People were perfectly subjected: I was absolute Lord and Law-giver; they all owed their Lives to me, and were ready to lay down their Lives, *if there had been Occasion of it*, for me. It was remarkable too, we had but three Subjects, and they were of three different Religions. My Man *Friday* was a Protestant, his Father was a *Pagan* and a *Cannibal*, and the *Spaniard* was a Papist: However, I allow'd Liberty of Conscience throughout my Dominions:* But this is by the Way.

As soon as I had secur'd my two weak rescued Prisoners, and given them Shelter, and a Place to rest them upon, I began to think of making some Provision for them: And the first thing I did, I order'd *Friday* to take a yearling Goat, betwixt a Kid and a Goat, out of my particular Flock, to be kill'd, when I cut off the hinder quarter, and chopping it into small Pieces, I set *Friday* to Work to boiling and stewing, and made them a very good Dish, I assure you, of Flesh and Broth, having put some Barley and Rice also into the Broth; and as I cook'd it without Doors, for I made no Fire within my inner Wall, so I carry'd it all into the new Tent; and having set a Table there for them, I sat down and eat my own Dinner also with them, and, as well as I could, chear'd them and encourag'd them; *Friday* being my Interpreter, especially to his Father, and indeed to the *Spaniard* too; for the *Spaniard* spoke the Language of the *Savages* pretty well.

After we had dined, or rather supped, I order'd *Friday* to take one of the Canoes, and go and fetch our Muskets and other Fire-Arms, which for Want of time we had left upon the Place of Battle, and the next Day I order'd him to go and bury the dead Bodies of the Savages, which lay open to the Sun, and would presently be offensive; and I also order'd him to bury the horrid Remains of their barbarous Feast, which I knew were pretty much, and which I could not think of doing my self; nay, I could not bear to see them, if I went that Way: All which he punctually performed, and defaced the very Appearance of the *Savages* being there; so that when I went again, I could scarce know where it was, otherwise than by the Corner of the Wood pointing to the Place.

I then began to enter into a little Conversation with my two new Subjects; and first I set *Friday* to enquire of his Father, what he thought of the Escape of the *Savages* in that Canoe, and whether we might expect a Return of them with a Power too great for us to resist: His first Opinion was, that the Savages in the Boat never could live out the Storm which blew that Night they went off, but must of Necessity be drowned or driven *South* to those other Shores where they were as sure to be devoured as they were to be drowned if they were cast away; but as to what they would do if they came safe on Shore, he said he knew not; but it was his Opinion that they were so dreadfully frighted with the Manner of their being attack'd, the Noise and the Fire, that he believed they would tell their People, they were all kill'd by Thunder and Lightning, not by the Hand of Man, and that the two which appear'd, (*viz.*) *Friday* and me, were two Heavenly Spirits or Furies, come down to destroy them, and not Men with Weapons: This he said he knew, because he heard them all cry out so in their Language to one another, for it was impossible to them to conceive that a Man could dart Fire, and speak Thunder, and kill at a Distance without lifting up the Hand, as was done now: And this old Savage was in the right; for, as I understood since by other Hands, the Savages never attempted to go over to the Island afterwards; they were so terrified with the Accounts given by those four Men, (for it seems they did escape the Sea) that they believ'd whoever went to that enchanted Island would be destroy'd with Fire from the Gods.

This however I knew not, and therefore was under continual Apprehensions for a good while, and kept always upon my Guard, me and all my Army; for as we were now four of us, I would have ventur'd upon a hundred of them fairly in the open Field at any Time.

In a little Time, however, no more Canoes appearing, the Fear of their Coming wore off, and I began to take my former Thoughts of a Voyage to the Main into Consideration, being likewise assur'd by *Friday's* Father, that I might depend upon good Usage from their Nation on his Account, if I would go.

But my Thoughts were a little suspended, when I had a serious Discourse with the *Spaniard*, and when I understood that there were sixteen more of his Countrymen and *Portuguese*, who having been cast away, and made their Escape to that Side, liv'd there at Peace indeed with the Savages, but were very sore put to it for Necessaries, and indeed for Life: I ask'd him all the Particulars of their Voyage, and found they were a *Spanish* Ship bound from the *Rio de la Plata* to the *Havana*,* being directed to leave their Loading there, which was chiefly Hides and Silver, and to bring back what *European* Goods they could meet with there; that they had five *Portuguese* Seamen on Board, who they took out of another Wreck; that five of their own Men were drowned when the first Ship was lost, and that these escaped thro' infinite Dangers and Hazards, and arriv'd almost starv'd on the *Cannibal* Coast, where they expected to have been devour'd every Moment.

He told me, they had some Arms with them, but they were perfectly useless, for that they had neither Powder or Ball, the Washing of the Sea having spoil'd all their Powder but a little, which they used at their first Landing to provide themselves some Food.

I ask'd him what he thought would become of them there, and if they had form'd no Design of making any Escape? He said, They had many Consultations about it, but that having neither Vessel, or Tools to build one, or Provisions of any kind, their Councils always ended in Tears and Despair.

I ask'd him how he thought they would receive a Proposal from me, which might tend towards an Escape? And whether, if they were all here, it might not be done? I told him with Freedom, I fear'd mostly their Treachery and ill Usage of me, if I put my Life in their Hands; for that Gratitude was no inherent Virtue in the Nature of Man;* nor did Men always square their Dealings by the Obligations they had receiv'd, so much as they did by the Advantages they expected. I told him it would be very hard, that I should be the

Instrument of their Deliverance, and that they should afterwards make me their Prisoner in *New Spain*, where an *English* Man was certain to be made a Sacrifice, what Necessity, or what Accident soever, brought him thither: And that I had rather be deliver'd up to the *Savages*, and be devour'd alive, than fall into the merciless Claws of the Priests, and be carry'd into the *Inquisition*.* I added, That otherwise I was perswaded, if they were all here, we might, with so many Hands, build a Bark large enough to carry us all away, either to the *Brasils* South-ward, or to the Islands or *Spanish* Coast North-ward: But that if in Requital they should, when I had put Weapons into their Hands, carry me by Force among their own People, I might be ill used for my Kindness to them, and make my Case worse than it was before.

He answer'd with a great deal of Candor and Ingenuity, That their Condition was so miserable, and they were so sensible of it, that he believed they would abhor the Thought of using any Man unkindly that should contribute to their Deliverance; and that, if I pleased, he would go to them with the old Man, and discourse with them about it, and return again, and bring me their Answer: That he would make Conditions with them upon their solemn Oath, That they should be absolutely under my Leading, as their Commander and Captain; and that they should swear upon the Holy Sacraments* and the Gospel, to be true to me, and to go to such Christian Coun-try, as that I should agree to, and no other; and to be directed wholly and absolutely by my Orders, 'till they were landed safely in such Country, as I intended; and that he would bring a Contract from them under their Hands for that Purpose.

Then he told me, he would first swear to me himself, That he would never stir from me as long as he liv'd, 'till I gave him Orders; and that he would take my Side to the last Drop of his Blood, if there should happen the least Breach of Faith among his Country-men.

He told me, they were all of them very civil honest Men, and they were under the greatest Distress imaginable, having neither Weapons or Cloaths, nor any Food, but at the Mercy and Discretion of the *Savages*; out of all Hopes of ever returning to their own Country; and that he was sure, if I would undertake their Relief, they would live and die by me.

Upon these Assurances, I resolv'd to venture to relieve them, if possible, and to send the old *Savage* and this *Spaniard* over to them to treat: But when we had gotten all things in a Readiness to go, the *Spaniard* himself started an Objection, which had so much Prudence in it on one hand, and so much Sincerity on the other hand, that I could not but be very well satisfy'd in it; and by his Advice, put off the Deliverance of his Comerades, for at least half a Year. The Case was thus:

He had been with us now about a Month; during which time, I had let him see in what Manner I had provided, with the Assistance of Providence, for my Support; and he saw evidently what Stock of Corn and Rice I had laid up; which as it was more than sufficient for my self, so it was not sufficient, at least without good Husbandry, for my Family; now it was encreas'd to Number four: But much less would it be sufficient, if his Country-men, who were, as he said, fourteen* still alive, should come over. And least of all should it be sufficient to victual our Vessel, if we should build one, for a Voyage to any of the Christian Colonies of *America*. So he told me, he thought it would be more advisable, to let him and the two other, dig and cultivate some more Land, as much as I could spare Seed to sow; and that we should wait another Harvest, that we might have a Supply of Corn for his Country-men when they should come; for Want might be a Temptation to them to disagree, or not to think themselves delivered, otherwise than out of one Difficulty into another. You know, says he, the Children of *Israel*, though they rejoyc'd at first for their being deliver'd out of *Egypt*, yet rebell'd even against God himself that deliver'd them, when they came to want Bread in the Wilderness.*

His Caution was so seasonable, and his Advice so good, that I could not but be very well pleased with his Proposal, as well as I was satisfy'd with his Fidelity. So we fell to digging all four of us, as well as the Wooden Tools we were furnish'd with permitted; and in about a Month's time, by the End of which it was Seed time, we had gotten as much Land cur'd and trim'd up,* as we sowed 22 Bushels of Barley on, and 16 Jarrs of Rice, which was in short all the Seed we had to spare; nor indeed did we leave our selves Barley sufficient for our own Food, for the six Months that we had to expect our Crop, that is to say, reckoning from the time we set our Seed aside for sowing; for it is not to be supposed it is six Months in the Ground in the Country.

Having now Society enough, and our Number being sufficient to put us out of Fear of the *Savages*, if they had come, unless their Number had been very great, we went freely all over the Island, where-ever we found Occasion; and as here we had our Escape or Deliverance upon our Thoughts, it was impossible, *at least for me*, to have the Means of it out of mine; to this Purpose, I mark'd out several Trees which I thought fit for our Work, and I set *Friday* and his Father to cutting them down; and then I caused the *Spaniard*, to whom I imparted my Thought on that Affair, to oversee and direct their Work. I shewed them with what indefatigable Pains I had hewed a large Tree into single Planks, and I caused them to do the like, till they had made about a Dozen large Planks of good Oak, near 2 Foot broad, 35 Foot long, and from 2 Inches to 4 Inches thick: What prodigious Labour it took up, any one may imagine.

At the same time I contriv'd to encrease my little Flock of tame Goats as much as I could; and to this Purpose, I made *Friday* and the *Spaniard* go out one Day, and my self with *Friday* the next Day; for we took our Turns: And by this Means we got above 20 young Kids to breed up with the rest; for when-ever we shot the Dam, we saved the Kids, and added them to our Flock: But above all, the Season for curing the Grapes coming on, I caused such a prodigious Quantity to be hung up in the Sun, that I believe, had we been at *Alicant*,* where the Raisins of the Sun are cur'd, we could have fill'd 60 or 80 Barrels; and these with our Bread was a great Part of our Food, and very good living too, I assure you; for it is an exceeding nourishing Food.

It was now Harvest, and our Crop in good Order; it was not the most plentiful Encrease I had seen in the Island, but however it was enough to answer our End; for from our 22 Bushels of Barley, we brought in and thrashed out above 220 Bushels; and the like in Proportion of the Rice, which was Store enough for our Food to the next Harvest, tho' all the 16 *Spaniards* had been on Shore with me; or if we had been ready for a Voyage, it would very plentifully have victualled our Ship, to have carry'd us to any Part of the World, that is to say, of *America*.

When we had thus hous'd and secur'd our Magazine of Corn, we fell to Work to make more Wicker Work, (*viz.*) great Baskets in which we kept it; and the *Spaniard* was very handy and dexterous at this Part, and often blam'd me that I did not make some things, for Defence, of this Kind of Work; but I saw no Need of it.

And now having a full Supply of Food for all the Guests I

expected, I gave the *Spaniard* Leave to go over to the *Main*, to see what he could do with those he had left behind him there. I gave him a strict Charge in Writing,* Not to bring any Man with him, who would not first swear in the Presence of himself and of the old *Savage*, That he would no way injure, fight with, or attack the Person he should find in the Island, who was so kind to send for them in order to their Deliverance; but that they would stand by and defend him against all such Attempts, and where-ever they went, would be entirely under and subjected to his Commands; and that this should be put in Writing, and signed with their Hands: How we were to have this done, when I knew they had neither Pen or Ink; that indeed was a question which we never asked.

Under these Instructions, the *Spaniard*, and the old *Savage* the Father of *Friday*, went away in one of the Canoes, which they might be said to come in, or rather were brought in, when they came as Prisoners to be devour'd by the *Savages*.

I gave each of them a Musket with a Firelock on it, and about eight Charges of Powder and Ball, charging them to be very good Husbands of both, and not to use either of them but upon urgent Occasion.

This was a chearful Work, being the first Measures used by me in View of my Deliverance for now 27 Years and some Days. I gave them Provisions of Bread, and of dry'd Grapes, sufficient for themselves for many Days, and sufficient for all their Country-men for about eight Days time; and wishing them a good Voyage, I see them go, agreeing with them about a Signal they should hang out at their Return, by which I should know them again, when they came back, at a Distance, before they came on Shore.

They went away with a fair Gale* on the Day that the Moon was at Full by my Account, in the Month of *October*: But as for an exact Reckoning of Days, after I had once lost it, I could never recover it again; nor had I kept even the Number of Years so punctually, as to be sure that I was right, tho' as it prov'd, when I afterwards examin'd my Account, I found I had kept a true Reckoning of Years.

It was no less than eight Days I had waited for them, when a strange and unforeseen Accident interven'd, of which the like has not perhaps been heard of in History: I was fast asleep in my Hutch one Morning, when my Man *Friday* came running in to me, and call'd aloud, Master, Master, they are come, they are come.

I jump'd up, and regardless of Danger, I went out, as soon as I could get my Cloaths on, thro' my little Grove, which by the Way was by this time grown to be a very thick Wood; I say, regardless of Danger, I went without my Arms, which was not my Custom to do: But I was surpriz'd, when turning my Eyes to the Sea, I presently saw a Boat at about a League and half's Distance, standing in for the Shore, with a *Shoulder of Mutton Sail*, as they call it; and the Wind blowing pretty fair to bring them in; also I observ'd presently, that they did not come from that Side which the Shore lay on, but from the Southermost End of the Island: Upon this I call'd *Friday* in, and bid him lie close, for these were not the People we look'd for, and that we might not know yet whether they were Friends or Enemies.

In the next Place, I went in to fetch my Perspective Glass, to see what I could make of them; and having taken the Ladder out, I climb'd up to the Top of the Hill, as I used to do when I was apprehensive of any thing, and to take my View the plainer without being discover'd.

I had scarce set my Foot on the Hill, when my Eye plainly discover'd a Ship lying at an Anchor, at about two Leagues and an half's Distance from me South-south-east, but not above a League and an half from the Shore. By my Observation it appear'd plainly to be an *English* Ship, and the Boat appear'd to be an *English* Long-Boat.

I cannot express the Confusion I was in, tho' the Joy of seeing a Ship, and one who I had Reason to believe was Mann'd by my own Country-men, and consequently Friends, was such as I cannot describe; but yet I had some secret Doubts hung about me, I cannot tell from whence they came, bidding me keep upon my Guard. In the first Place, it occurr'd to me to consider what Business an *English* Ship could have in that Part of the World, since it was not the Way to or from any Part of the World, where the *English* had any Traffick; and I knew there had been no Storms to drive them in there, as in Distress; and that if they were *English* really, it was most probable that they were here upon no good Design; and that I had better continue as I was, than fall into the Hands of Thieves and Murtherers.

Let no Man despise the secret Hints and Notices of Danger, which sometimes are given him, when he may think there is no Possibility of its being real. That such Hints and Notices are given us, I believe few that have made any Observations of things, can deny; that they are certain Discoveries of an invisible World, and a

Converse of Spirits,* we cannot doubt; and if the Tendency of them seems to be to warn us of Danger, why should we not suppose they are from some friendly Agent, whether supreme, or inferior, and subordinate, is not the Question; and that they are given for our Good?

The present Question abundantly confirms me in the Justice of this Reasoning; for had I not been made cautious by this secret Admonition, come it from whence it will, I had been undone inevitably, and in a far worse Condition than before, as you will see presently.

I had not kept my self long in this Posture, but I saw the Boat draw near the Shore, as if they look'd for a Creek to thrust in at for the Convenience of Landing; however, as they did not come quite far enough, they did not see the little Inlet where I formerly landed my Rafts; but run their Boat on Shore upon the Beach, at about half a Mile from me, which was very happy for me; for otherwise they would have landed just as I may say at my Door, and would soon have beaten me out of my Castle, and perhaps have plunder'd me of all I had.

When they were on Shore, I was fully satisfy'd that they were *English* Men; at least, most of them; one or two I thought were *Dutch*; but it did not prove so: There were in all eleven Men, whereof three of them I found were unarm'd, and as I thought, bound; and when the first four or five of them were jump'd on Shore, they took those three out of the Boat as Prisoners: One of the three I could perceive using the most passionate Gestures of Entreaty, Affliction and Despair, even to a kind of Extravagance; the other two I could perceive lifted up their Hands sometimes, and appear'd concern'd indeed, but not to such a Degree as the first.

I was perfectly confounded at the Sight, and knew not what the Meaning of it should be. *Friday* call'd out to me in *English*, as well as he could, *O* Master! *You see* English *Mans eat Prisoner as well as* Savage *Mans*. Why, says I, *Friday, Do you think they are a going to eat them then? Yes*, says Friday, *They will eat them: No, no*, says I, Friday, *I am afraid they will murther them indeed, but you may be sure they will not eat them*.

All this while I had no thought of what the Matter really was; but stood trembling with the Horror of the Sight, expecting every Moment when the three Prisoners should be kill'd; nay, once I saw

one of the Villains lift up his Arm with a great Cutlash, as the
Seamen call it, or Sword, to strike one of the poor Men; and I
expected to see him fall every Moment, at which all the Blood in my
Body seem'd to run chill in my Veins.

I wish'd heartily now for my *Spaniard*, and the *Savage* that was
gone with him; or that I had any way to have come undiscover'd
within shot of them, that I might have rescu'd the three Men; for I
saw no Fire Arms they had among them; but it fell out to my Mind
another way.

After I had observ'd the outragious Usage of the three Men, by
the insolent Seamen, I observ'd the Fellows run scattering about the
Land, as if they wanted to see the Country: I observ'd that the three
other Men had Liberty to go also where they pleas'd; but they sat
down all three upon the Ground, very pensive, and look'd like Men
in Despair.

This put me in Mind of the first Time when I came on Shore, and
began to look about me; How I gave my self over for lost: How wildly
I look'd round me: What dreadful Apprehensions I had: And how I
lodg'd in the Tree all Night for fear of being devour'd by wild Beasts.

As I knew nothing that Night of the Supply I was to receive by the
providential Driving of the Ship nearer the Land, by the Storms and
Tide, by which I have since been so long nourish'd and supported; so
these three poor desolate Men knew nothing how certain of Deliverance and Supply they were, how near it was to them, and how
effectually and really they were in a Condition of Safety, at the same
Time that they thought themselves lost, and their Case desperate.

So little do we see before us in the World, and so much reason
have we to depend chearfully upon the great Maker of the World,
that he does not leave his Creatures so absolutely destitute, but that
in the worst Circumstances they have always something to be thankful for, and sometimes are nearer their Deliverance than they
imagine; nay, are even brought to their Deliverance by the Means by
which they seem to be brought to their Destruction.*

It was just at the Top of High-Water when these People came
on Shore, and while partly they stood parlying with the Prisoners
they brought, and partly while they rambled about to see what kind
of a Place they were in; they had carelessly staid till the Tide was
spent, and the Water was ebb'd considerably away, leaving their
Boat a-ground.

They had left two Men in the Boat, who as I found afterwards, having drank a little too much Brandy, fell a-sleep; however, one of them waking sooner than the other, and finding the Boat too fast a-ground for him to stir it, hollow'd for the rest who were straggling about, upon which they all soon came to the Boat; but it was past all their Strength to launch her, the Boat being very heavy, and the Shore on that Side being a soft ousy Sand,* almost like a Quick-Sand.

In this Condition, like true Seamen who are perhaps the least of all Mankind given to fore-thought,* they gave it over, and away they stroll'd about the Country again; and I heard one of them say aloud to another, calling them off from the Boat, *Why let her alone*, Jack, *can't ye, she will float next Tide*; by which I was fully confirm'd in the main Enquiry, of what Countrymen they were.

All this while I kept my self very close, not once daring to stir out of my Castle, any farther than to my Place of Observation, near the Top of the Hill; and very glad I was, to think how well it was fortify'd: I knew it was no less than ten Hours before the Boat could be on float again,* and by that Time it would be dark, and I might be at more Liberty to see their Motions, and to hear their Discourse, if they had any.

In the mean Time, I fitted my self up for a Battle, as before; though with more Caution, knowing I had to do with another kind of Enemy than I had at first: I order'd *Friday* also, who I had made an excellent Marks-Man with his Gun, to load himself with Arms: I took my self two Fowling-Pieces, and I gave him three Muskets; my Figure indeed was very fierce; I had my formidable Goat-Skin Coat on, with the great Cap I have mention'd, a naked Sword by my Side, two Pistols in my Belt, and a Gun upon each Shoulder.

It was my Design, as I said above, not to have made any Attempt till it was Dark: But about Two a Clock, being the Heat of the Day, I found that in short they were all gone straggling into the Woods, and as I thought were laid down to Sleep. The three poor distressed Men, too Anxious for their Condition to get any Sleep, were however set down under the Shelter of a great Tree, at about a quarter of a Mile from me, and as I thought out of sight of any of the rest.

Upon this I resolv'd to discover my self to them, and learn something of their Condition: Immediately I march'd in the Figure as above, my Man *Friday* at a good Distance behind me, as formidable for his Arms as I, but not making quite so staring a *Spectre-like* Figure as I did.

I came as near them undiscover'd as I could, and then before any of them saw me, I call'd aloud to them in *Spanish, What are ye Gentlemen?*

They started up at the Noise, but were ten times more confounded when they saw me, and the uncouth Figure that I made. They made no Answer at all, but I thought I perceiv'd them just going to fly from me, when I spoke to them in *English*, Gentlemen, said I, do not be surpriz'd at me; perhaps you may have a Friend near you when you did not expect it. He must be sent directly from Heaven then, *said one of them very gravely to me, and pulling off his Hat at the same time to me*, for our Condition is past the Help of Man. All Help is from Heaven, *Sir, said I.* But can you put a Stranger in the way how to help you, for you seem to me to be in some great Distress? I saw you when you landed, and when you seem'd to make Applications to the Brutes that came with you, I saw one of them lift up his Sword to kill you.

The poor Man with Tears running down his Face, and trembling, looking like one astonish'd, return'd, *Am I talking to God, or Man! Is it a real Man, or an Angel!* Be in no fear about that, Sir, *said I*, if God had sent an Angel to relieve you, he would have come better Cloath'd, and Arm'd after another manner than you see me in; pray lay aside your Fears, I am a Man, an *English-man*, and dispos'd to assist you, you see; I have one Servant only; we have Arms and Ammunition; tell us freely, Can we serve you?—What is your Case?

Our Case, said he, Sir, is too long to tell you, while our Murtherers are so near; but in short, Sir, I was Commander of that Ship, my Men have Mutinied against me; they have been hardly prevail'd on not to Murther me, and at last have set me on Shore in this desolate Place, with these two Men with me; one my Mate, the other a Passenger, where we expected to Perish, believing the Place to be uninhabited, and know not yet what to think of it.

Where are those Brutes, your Enemies, said I, do you know where they are gone? *There they lye*, Sir, said he, pointing to a Thicket of Trees; *my Heart trembles, for fear they have seen us, and heard you speak, if they have, they will certainly Murther us all.*

Have they any Fire-Arms, *said I*, He answered they had only two Pieces, and one which they left in the Boat. Well then, said I, leave the rest to me; I see they are all asleep, it is an easie thing to kill them all; but shall we rather take them Prisoners? He told me there were two desperate Villains among them, that it was scarce safe to shew any Mercy to; but if they were secur'd, he believ'd all the rest would return to their Duty. I ask'd him, which they were? He told me he could not at that distance describe them; but he would obey my Orders in any thing I would direct. Well, says I, let us retreat out of their View or Hearing, least they awake, and we will resolve further; so they willingly went back with me, till the Woods cover'd us from them.

Look you, Sir, said I, if I venture upon your Deliverance, are you willing to make two Conditions with me? he anticipated my Proposals, by telling me, that both he and the Ship, if recover'd, should be wholly Directed and Commanded by me in every thing; and if the Ship was not recover'd, he would live and dye with me in what Part of the World soever I would send him; and the two other Men said the same.

Well, says I, *my Conditions are but two*. 1. That while you stay on this Island with me, you will not pretend to any Authority here; and if I put Arms into your Hands, you will upon all Occasions give them up to me, and do no Prejudice to me or mine, upon this Island, and in the mean time be govern'd by my Orders.

2. That if the Ship is, or may be recover'd, you will carry me and my Man to *England* Passage free.

He gave me all the Assurances that the Invention and Faith of Man could devise, that he would comply with these most reasonable Demands, and besides would owe his Life to me, and acknowledge it upon all Occasions as long as he liv'd.

Well then, *said I*, here are three Muskets for you, with Powder and Ball; tell me next what you think is proper to be done. He shew'd all the Testimony of his Gratitude that he was able; but offer'd to be wholly guided by me. I told him I thought it was hard venturing any thing; but the best Method I could think of was to fire upon them at once, as they lay; and if any was not kill'd at the first Volley, and offered to submit, we might save them, and so put it wholly upon God's Providence to direct the Shot.

He said very modestly, that he was loath to kill them, if he could help it, but that those two were incorrigible Villains, and had been the Authors of all the Mutiny in the Ship, and if they escaped, we should be undone still; for they would go on Board, and bring the whole Ship's Company, and destroy us all. *Well then*, says I, *Necessity* legitimates my Advice; for it is the only Way to save our Lives. However, seeing him still cautious of shedding Blood, I told him they should go themselves, and manage as they found convenient.

In the Middle of this Discourse, we heard some of them awake, and soon after, we saw two of them on their Feet, I ask'd him, if either of them were of the Men who he had said were the Heads of the Mutiny? He said, *No*: Well then, said I, you may let them escape, and Providence seems to have wakned them on Purpose to save themselves. Now, says I, if the rest escape you, *it is your Fault*.

Animated with this, he took the Musket, I had given him, in his Hand, and a Pistol in his Belt, and his two Comerades with him, with each Man a Piece in his Hand. The two Men who were with him, going first, made some Noise, at which one of the Seamen who was awake, turn'd about, and seeing them coming, cry'd out to the rest; but it was too late then; for the Moment he cry'd out, they fir'd; *I mean the two Men*, the Captain wisely reserving his own Piece: They had so well aim'd their Shot at the Men they knew, that one of them was kill'd on the Spot, and the other very much wounded; but not being dead, he started up upon his Feet, and call'd eagerly for help to the other; but the Captain stepping to him, told him, 'twas too late to cry for help, he should call upon God to forgive his Villany, and with that Word knock'd him down with the Stock of his Musket, so that he never spoke more: There were three more in the Company, and one of them was also slightly wounded: By this Time I was come, and when they saw their Danger, and that it was in vain to resist, they begg'd for Mercy: The Captain told them, he would spare their Lives, if they would give him any Assurance of their Abhorrence of the Treachery they had been guilty of, and would swear to be faithful to him in recovering the Ship, and afterwards in carrying her back to *Jamaica*, from whence they came: They gave him all the Protestations of their Sincerity that could be desir'd, and he was willing to believe them, and spare their Lives, which I was not against, only that I oblig'd him to keep them bound Hand and Foot while they were upon the Island.

While this was doing, I sent *Friday* with the Captain's Mate to the Boat, with Orders to secure her, and bring away the Oars, and Sail, which they did; and by and by, three straggling Men that were (happily for them) parted from the rest, came back upon hearing the Guns fir'd, and seeing their Captain, who before was their Prisoner, now their Conqueror, they submitted to be bound also; and so our Victory was compleat.

It now remain'd, that the Captain and I should enquire into one another's Circumstances: I began first, and told him my whole History, which he heard with an Attention even to Amazement; and particularly, at the wonderful Manner of my being furnish'd with Provisions and Ammunition; and indeed, as my Story is a whole Collection of Wonders, it affected him deeply; but when he reflected from thence upon himself, and how I seem'd to have been preserv'd there, on purpose to save his Life, the Tears ran down his Face, and he could not speak a Word more.

After this Communication was at an End, I carry'd him and his two Men into my Apartment, leading them in, just where I came out, *viz.* At the Top of the House, where I refresh'd them with such Provisions as I had, and shew'd them all the Contrivances I had made, during my long, long, inhabiting that Place.

All I shew'd them, all I said to them, was perfectly amazing; but above all, the Captain admir'd my Fortification, and how perfectly I had conceal'd my Retreat with a Grove of Trees, which having been now planted near twenty Years, and the Trees growing much faster than in *England*, was become a little Wood, and so thick, that it was unpassable in any Part of it, but at that one Side, where I had reserv'd my little winding Passage into it: I told him, this was my Castle, and my Residence; but that I had a Seat in the Country, as most Princes have, whither I could retreat upon Occasion, and I would shew him that too another Time; but at present, our Business was to consider how to recover the Ship: He agreed with me as to that; but told me, he was perfectly at a Loss what Measures to take; for that there were still six and twenty Hands on board, who having entred into a cursed Conspiracy, by which they had all forfeited their Lives to the Law, would be harden'd in it now by Desperation; and would carry it on, knowing that if they were reduc'd, they should be brought to the Gallows, as soon as they came to *England*, or to any of the *English* Colonies; and that therefore there would be no attacking them, with so small a Number as we were.

I mus'd for some Time upon what he had said; and found it was a very rational Conclusion; and that therefore something was to be resolv'd on very speedily, as well to draw the Men on board into some Snare for their Surprize, as to prevent their Landing upon us, and destroying us; upon this it presently occurr'd to me, that in a little while the Ship's Crew wondring what was become of their Comrades, and of the Boat, would certainly come on Shore in their other Boat, to see for them, and that then perhaps they might come arm'd, and be too strong for us; this he allow'd was rational.

Upon this, I told him the first Thing we had to do, was to stave the Boat, which lay upon the Beach, so that they might not carry her off; and taking every Thing out of her, leave her so far useless as not to be fit to swim; accordingly we went on board, took the Arms which were left on board, out of her, and whatever else we found there, which was a Bottle of Brandy, and another of Rum, a few Bisket Cakes, a Horn of Powder, and a great Lump of Sugar, in a Piece of Canvas; the Sugar was five or six Pounds; all which was very welcome to me, especially the Brandy, and Sugar, of which I had had none left for many Years.

When we had carry'd all these Things on Shore (the Oars, Mast, Sail, and Rudder of the Boat, were carry'd away before, as above) we knock'd a great Hole in her Bottom, that if they had come strong enough to master us, yet they could not carry off the Boat.

Indeed, it was not much in my Thoughts, that we could be able to recover the Ship; but my View was that if they went away without the Boat, I did not much question to make her fit again, to carry us away to the *Leeward* Islands, and call upon our Friends, the *Spaniards*, in my Way, for I had them still in my Thoughts.

While we were thus preparing our Designs, and had first, by main Strength heav'd the Boat up upon the Beach, so high that the Tide would not fleet her off at High-Water-Mark; and besides, had broke a Hole in her Bottom, too big to be quickly stopp'd, and were sat down musing what we should do; we heard the Ship fire a Gun, and saw her make a Waft with her Antient, as a Signal for the Boat to come on board; but no Boat stirr'd; and they fir'd several Times, making other Signals for the Boat.

At last, when all their Signals and Firings prov'd fruitless, and they found the Boat did not stir, we saw them by the Help of my Glasses, hoist another Boat out, and row towards the Shore; and we found as they approach'd, that there was no less than ten Men in her, and that they had Fire-Arms with them.

As the Ship lay almost two Leagues from the Shore, we had a full View of them as they came, and a plain Sight of the Men even of their Faces, because the Tide having set them a little to the *East* of the other Boat, they row'd up under Shore, to come to the same Place, where the other* had landed, and where the Boat lay.

By this Means, I say, we had a full View of them, and the Captain knew the Persons and Characters of all the Men in the Boat, of whom he said, that there were three very honest Fellows, who he was sure were led into this Conspiracy by the rest, being over-power'd and frighted.

But that as for the Boatswain, who it seems was the chief Officer among them, and all the rest, they were as outragious as any of the Ship's Crew, and were no doubt made desperate in their new Enter-prize, and terribly apprehensive he was, that they would be too powerful for us.

I smil'd at him, and told him, that Men in our Circumstances were past the Operation of Fear: That seeing almost every Condition that could be, was better than that which we were suppos'd to be in, we ought to expect that the Consequence, whether Death or Life, would be sure to be a Deliverance: I ask'd him, What he thought of the Circumstances of my Life? And, Whether a Deliverance were not worth venturing for? And where, Sir, said I, is your Belief of my being preserv'd here on purpose to save your Life, which elevated you a little while ago? For my Part, said I, there seems to be but one Thing amiss in all the Prospect of it; *What's that?* Says he; why, said I, 'Tis, that as you say, there are three or four honest Fellows among them, which should be spar'd; had they been all of the wicked Part of the Crew, I should have thought God's Providence had singled them out to deliver them into your Hands; for depend upon it, every Man of them that comes a-shore are our own, and shall die, or live, as they behave to us.

As I spoke this with a rais'd Voice and chearful Countenance, I found it greatly encourag'd him; so we set vigorously to our Busi-ness: We had upon the first Appearance of the Boat's coming from the Ship, consider'd of separating our Prisoners, and had indeed secur'd them effectually.

Two of them, of whom the Captain was less assur'd than ordinary, I sent with *Friday*, and one of the three (deliver'd Men) to my Cave, where they were remote enough, and out of Danger of being heard or discover'd, or of finding their way Out of the Woods, if they could have deliver'd themselves: Here they left them bound, but gave them Provisions, and promis'd them if they continu'd there quietly, to give them their Liberty in a Day or two; but that if they attempted their Escape, they should be put to Death without Mercy: They promis'd faithfully to bear their Confinement with Patience, and were very thankful that they had such good Usage, as to have Provisions, and a Light left them; for *Friday* gave them Candles (such as we made our selves) for their Comfort; and they did not know but that he stood Sentinel over them at the Entrance.

The other Prisoners had better Usage; two of them were kept pinion'd indeed, because the Captain was not free to trust them; but the other two were taken into my Service upon their Captain's Recommendation, and upon their solemnly engaging to live and die with us; so with them and the three honest Men, we were seven Men, well arm'd; and I made no doubt we shou'd be able to deal well enough with the Ten that were a coming, considering that the Captain had said, there were three or four honest Men among them also.

As soon as they got to the Place where their other Boat lay, they run their Boat in to the Beach, and came all on Shore, haling the Boat up after them, which I was glad to see; for I was afraid they would rather have left the Boat at an Anchor, some Distance from the Shore, with some Hands in her, to guard her; and so we should not be able to seize the Boat.

Being on Shore, the first Thing they did, they ran all to their other Boat, and it was easy to see that they were under a great Surprize, to find her stripp'd as above, of all that was in her, and a great hole in her Bottom.

After they had mus'd a while upon this, they set up two or three great Shouts, hollowing with all their might, to try if they could make their Companions hear; but all was to no purpose: Then they came all close in a Ring, and fir'd a Volley of their small Arms, which indeed we heard, and the Ecchos made the Woods ring; but it was all one, those in the Cave we were sure could not hear, and those in our keeping, though they heard it well enough, yet durst give no Answer to them.

They were so astonish'd at the Surprize of this, that as they told us afterwards, they resolv'd to go all on board again to their Ship, and let them know, that the Men were all murther'd, and the Long-

Boat stav'd; accordingly they immediately launch'd their Boat again, and gat all of them on board.

The Captain was terribly amaz'd, and even confounded at this, believing they would go on board the Ship again, and set Sail, giving their Comrades for lost, and so he should still lose the Ship, which he was in Hopes we should have recover'd; but he was quickly as much frighted the other way.

They had not been long put off with the Boat, but we perceiv'd them all coming on Shore again; but with this new Measure in their Conduct, which it seems they consulted together upon, *viz*. To leave three Men in the Boat, and the rest to go on Shore, and go up into the Country to look for their Fellows.

This was a great Disappointment to us; for now we were at a Loss what to do; for our seizing those seven Men on Shore would be no Advantage to us, if we let the Boat escape; because they would then row away to the Ship, and then the rest of them would be sure to weigh and set Sail, and so our recovering the Ship would be lost.

However, we had no Remedy, but to wait and see what the Issue of Things might present; the seven Men came on Shore, and the three who remain'd in the Boat, put her off to a good Distance from the Shore, and came to an Anchor to wait for them; so that it was impossible for us to come at them in the Boat.

Those that came on Shore, kept close together, marching towards the Top of the little Hill, under which my Habitation lay; and we could see them plainly, though they could not perceive us: We could have been very glad they would have come nearer to us, so that we might have fir'd at them, or that they would have gone farther off, that we might have come abroad.

But when they were come to the Brow of the Hill, where they could see a great way into the Valleys and Woods, which lay towards the *North-East* Part, and where the Island lay lowest, they shouted, and hollow'd, till they were weary; and not caring it seems to venture far from the Shore, nor far from one another, they sat down together under a Tree, to consider of it: Had they thought fit to have gone to sleep there, as the other Party of them had done, they had done the Jobb for us; but they were too full of Apprehensions of Danger, to venture to go to sleep, though they could not tell what the Danger was they had to fear neither.

The Captain made a very just Proposal to me, upon this Consultation of theirs, *viz.* That perhaps they would all fire a Volley again, to endeavour to make their Fellows hear, and that we should all Sally upon them, just at the Juncture when their Pieces were all discharg'd, and they would certainly yield, and we should have them without Blood-shed: I lik'd the Proposal, provided it was done while we were near enough to come up to them, before they could load their Pieces again.

But this Event did not happen, and we lay still a long Time, very irresolute what Course to take; at length I told them, there would be nothing to be done in my Opinion till Night, and then if they did not return to the Boat, perhaps we might find a way to get between them, and the Shore, and so might use some Stratagem with them in the Boat, to get them on Shore.

We waited a great while, though very impatient for their removing; and were very uneasy, when after long Consultations, we saw them start all up, and march down toward the Sea: It seems they had such dreadful Apprehensions upon them, of the Danger of the Place, that they resolv'd to go on board the Ship again, give their Companions over for lost, and so go on with their intended Voyage with the Ship.

As soon as I perceiv'd them go towards the Shore, I imagin'd it to be as it really was, That they had given over their Search, and were for going back again; and the Captain, as soon as I told him my Thoughts, was ready to sink at the Apprehensions of it; but I presently thought of a Stratagem to fetch them back again, and which answer'd my End to a Tittle.

I order'd *Friday*, and the Captain's Mate, to go over the little Creek *Westward*, towards the Place where the *Savages* came to Shore, when *Friday* was rescu'd; and as soon as they came to a little rising Ground, at about half a Mile Distance, I bad them hollow, as loud as they could, and wait till they found the Seamen heard them; that as soon as ever they heard the Seamen answer them, they should return it again, and then keeping out of Sight, take a round,* always answering when the other hollow'd, to draw them as far into the Island, and among the Woods, as possible, and then wheel about again to me, by such ways as I directed them.

They were just going into the Boat, when *Friday* and the Mate hollow'd, and they presently heard them, and answering, run along the Shore *Westward*, towards the Voice they heard, when they were presently stopp'd by the Creek, where the Water being up, they could not get over, and call'd for the Boat to come up, and set them over, as indeed I expected.

When they had set themselves over, I observ'd, that the Boat being gone up a good way into the Creek, and as it were, in a Harbour within the Land, they took one of the three Men out of her to go along with them, and left only two in the Boat, having fastned her to the Stump of a little Tree on the Shore.

This was what I wish'd for, and immediately leaving *Friday* and the Captain's Mate to their Business, I took the rest with me, and crossing the Creek out of their Sight, we surpriz'd the two Men before they were aware; one of them lying on Shore, and the other being in the Boat; the Fellow on Shore, was between sleeping and waking, and going to start up, the Captain who was foremost, ran in upon him, and knock'd him down, and then call'd out to him in the Boat, to yield, or he was a dead Man.

There needed very few Arguments to perswade a single Man to yield, when he saw five Men upon him, and his Comrade knock'd down; besides, this was it seems one of the three who were not so hearty in the Mutiny as the rest of the Crew, and therefore was easily perswaded, not only to yield, but afterwards to joyn very sincere with us.

In the mean time, *Friday* and the Captain's Mate so well manag'd their Business with the rest, that they drew them by hollowing and answering, from one Hill to another, and from one Wood to another, till they not only heartily tyr'd them, but left them, where they were very sure they could not reach back to the Boat, before it was dark; and indeed they were heartily tyr'd themselves also by the Time they came back to us.

We had nothing now to do, but to watch for them, in the Dark, and to fall upon them, so as to make sure work with them.

It was several Hours after *Friday* came back to me, before they came back to their Boat; and we could hear the foremost of them long before they came quite up, calling to those behind to come along, and could also hear them answer and complain, how lame and tyr'd they were, and not able to come any faster, which was very welcome News to us.

At length they came up to the Boat; but 'tis impossible to express their Confusion, when they found the Boat fast a-Ground in the

Creek, the Tide ebb'd out, and their two Men gone: We could hear them call to one another in a most lamentable Manner, telling one another, they were gotten into an inchanted Island; that either there were Inhabitants in it, and they should all be murther'd, or else there were Devils and Spirits in it, and they should be all carry'd away, and devour'd.

They hallow'd again, and call'd their two Comerades by their Names, a great many times, but no Answer. After some time, we could see them, by the little Light there was, run about wringing their Hands like Men in Despair; and that sometimes they would go and sit down in the Boat to rest themselves, then come ashore again, and walk about again, and so over the same thing again.

My Men would fain have me given them Leave to fall upon them at once in the Dark; but I was willing to take them at some Advantage, so to spare them, and kill as few of them as I could; and especially I was unwilling to hazard the killing any of our own Men, knowing the other were very well armed. I resolved to wait to see if they did not separate; and therefore to make sure of them, I drew my Ambuscade nearer, and order'd *Friday* and the Captain, to creep upon their Hands and Feet as close to the Ground as they could, that they might not be discover'd, and get as near them as they could possibly, before they offered to fire.

They had not been long in that Posture, but that the Boatswain, who was the principal Ringleader of the Mutiny, and had now shewn himself the most dejected and dispirited of all the rest, came walking towards them with two more of their Crew; the Captain was so eager, as having this principal Rogue so much in his Power, that he could hardly have Patience to let him come so near, as to be sure of him; for they only heard his Tongue before: But when they came nearer, the Captain and *Friday* starting up on their Feet, let fly at them.

The Boatswain was kill'd upon the Spot, the next Man was shot into the Body, and fell just by him, tho' he did not die 'till an Hour or two after; and the third run for it.

At the Noise of the Fire, I immediately advanc'd with my whole Army, which was now 8 Men, *viz.* my self *Generalissimo*, *Friday* my Lieutenant-General, the Captain and his two Men, and the three Prisoners of War, who we had trusted with Arms.

We came upon them indeed in the Dark, so that they could not see our Number; and I made the Man we had left in the Boat, who was now one of us, call to them by Name, to try if I could bring them to a Parley, and so might perhaps reduce them to Terms, which fell out just as we desir'd: for indeed it was easy to think, as their Condition then was, they would be very willing to capitulate; so he calls out as loud as he could, to one of them, *Tom Smith, Tom Smith; Tom Smith* answered immediately, *Who's that*, Robinson? for it seems he knew his Voice: T'other answered, *Ay, ay; for God's Sake*, Tom Smith, *throw down your Arms, and yield*, or, *you are all dead Men this Moment.*

Who must we yield to? where are they? (says *Smith* again;) *Here they are*, says he, here's our Captain, and fifty Men with him, have been hunting you this two Hours; the Boatswain is kill'd, *Will Frye* is wounded, and I am a Prisoner; and if you do not yield, you are all lost.

Will they give us Quarter then, (says *Tom Smith*) and we will yield?* *I'll go and ask, if you promise to yield*, says *Robinson*; so he ask'd the Captain, and the Captain then calls himself out, You *Smith*, you know my Voice, if you lay down your Arms immediately, and submit, you shall have your Lives all but *Will. Atkins.*

Upon this, *Will Atkins* cry'd out, *For God's Sake, Captain, give me Quarter, what have I done? They have been all as bad as I*, which by the Way was not true neither; for it seems this *Will. Atkins* was the first Man that laid hold of the Captain, when they first mutiny'd, and used him barbarously, in tying his Hands, and giving him injurious Language. However, the Captain told him he must lay down his Arms at Discretion, and trust to the Governour's Mercy, by which he meant me; for they all call'd me Governour.

In a Word, they all laid down their Arms, and begg'd their Lives; and I sent the Man that had parley'd with them, and two more, who bound them all; and then my great Army of 50 Men, which particularly with* those three, were all but eight, came up and seiz'd upon them all, and upon their Boat, only that I kept my self and one more out of Sight, for Reasons of State.*

Our next Work was to repair the Boat, and think of seizing the Ship; and as for the Captain, now he had Leisure to parley with them: He expostulated with them upon the Villany of their Practices with him, and at length upon the farther Wickedness of their Design, and how certainly it must bring them to Misery and Distress in the End, and perhaps to the Gallows.

They all appear'd very penitent, and begg'd hard for their Lives;

as for that, he told them, they were none of his Prisoners, but the Commander of the Island; that they thought they had set him on Shore in a barren uninhabited Island, but it had pleased God so to direct them, that the Island was inhabited, and that the Governour was an *English* Man; that he might hang them all there, if he pleased;* but as he had given them all Quarter, he supposed he would send them to *England* to be dealt with there, as Justice requir'd, except *Atkins*, who he was commanded by the Governour to advise to prepare for Death; for that he would be hang'd in the Morning.

Though this was all a Fiction of his own, yet it had its desired Effect; *Atkins* fell upon his Knees to beg the Captain to interceed with the Governour for his Life; and all the rest beg'd of him for God's Sake, that they might not be sent to *England*.

It now occurr'd to me, that the time of our Deliverance was come, and that it would be a most easy thing to bring these Fellows in, to be hearty in getting Possession of the Ship; so I retir'd in the Dark from them, that they might not see what Kind of a Governour they had, and call'd the Captain to me; when I call'd, as at a good Distance, one of the Men was order'd to speak again, and say to the Captain, *Captain, the Commander calls for you*; and presently the Captain reply'd, *Tell his Excellency, I am just a coming*: This more perfectly amused them;* and they all believed that the Commander was just by with his fifty Men.

Upon the Captain's coming to me, I told him my Project for seizing the Ship, which he lik'd of wonderfully well, and resolv'd to put it in Execution the next Morning.

But in Order to execute it with more Art, and secure of Success, I told him, we must divide the Prisoners, and that he should go and take *Atkins* and two more of the worst of them, and send them pinion'd to the Cave where the others lay: This was committed to *Friday* and the two Men who came on Shore with the Captain.

They convey'd them to the Cave, as to a Prison; and it was indeed a dismal Place, especially to Men in their Condition.

The other I order'd to my *Bower*, as I call'd it, of which I have given a full Description; and as it was fenc'd in, and they pinion'd, the Place was secure enough, considering they were upon their Behaviour.

To these in the Morning I sent the Captain, who was to enter into a Parley with them, in a Word to try them,* and tell me, whether he thought they might be trusted or no, to go on Board and surprize the Ship. He talk'd to them of the Injury done him, of the Condition they were brought to; and that though the Governour had given them Quarter for their Lives, as to the present Action, yet that if they were sent to *England*, they would all be hang'd in Chains,* to be sure; but that if they would join in so just an Attempt, as to recover the Ship, he would have the Governour's Engagement for their Pardon.

Any one may guess how readily such a Proposal would be accepted by Men in their Condition; they fell down on their Knees to the Captain, and promised with the deepest Imprecations, that they would be faithful to him to the last Drop,* and that they should owe their Lives to him, and would go with him all over the World, that they would own him for a Father to them as long as they liv'd.

Well, says the Captain, I must go and tell the Governour what you say, and see what I can do to bring him to Consent to it: So he brought me an Account of the Temper he found them in; and that he verily believ'd they would be faithful.

However, that we might be very secure, I told him he should go back again, and choose out five of them, and tell them, they might see that he did not want Men, that he would take out those five to be his Assistants, and that the Governour would keep the other two, and the three that were sent Prisoners to the Castle, (*my Cave*) as Hostages, for the Fidelity of those five; and that if they prov'd unfaithful in the Execution, the five Hostages should be hang'd in Chains alive upon the Shore.

This look'd severe, and convinc'd them that the Governour was in Earnest; however they had no Way left them, but to accept it; and it was now the Business of the Prisoners, as much as of the Captain, to perswade the other five to do their Duty.

Our Strength was now thus ordered for the Expedition: 1. The Captain, his Mate, and Passenger. 2. Then the two Prisoners of the first Gang, to whom having their Characters from the Captain, I had given their Liberty, and trusted them with Arms. 3. The other two who I had kept till now, in my Bower, pinion'd; but upon the Captain's Motion, had now releas'd. 4. These five releas'd at last: So that they were twelve in all, besides five we kept Prisoners in the Cave, for Hostages.

I ask'd the Captain, if he was willing to venture with these Hands on Board the Ship; for as for me and my Man *Friday*, I did not think it was proper for us to stir, having seven Men left behind; and it was Employment enough for us to keep them assunder, and supply them with Victuals.

As to the five in the Cave, I resolv'd to keep them fast, but *Friday* went in twice a Day to them, to supply them with Necessaries; and I made the other two carry Provisions to a certain Distance, where *Friday* was to take it.

When I shew'd my self to the two Hostages, it was with the Captain, who told them, I was the Person the Governour had order'd to look after them, and that it was the Governour's Pleasure they should not stir any where, but by my Direction; that if they did, they should be fetch'd into the Castle, and be lay'd in Irons; so that as we never suffered them to see me as Governour, so I now appear'd as another Person, and spoke of the Governour, the Garrison, the Castle, and the like, upon all Occasions.

The Captain now had no Difficulty before him, but to furnish his two Boats, stop the Breach of one, and Man them. He made his Passenger Captain of one, with four other Men; and himself, and his Mate, and five more, went in the other: And they contriv'd their Business very well; for they came up to the Ship about Midnight: As soon as they came within Call of the Ship, he made *Robinson* hale them, and tell them they had brought off the Men and the Boat, but that it was a long time before they had found them, and the like; holding them in a Chat 'till they came to the Ship's Side; when the Captain and the Mate entring first with their Arms, immediately knock'd down the second Mate and Carpenter, with the But-end of their Muskets, being very faithfully seconded by their Men, they secur'd all the rest that were upon the Main and Quarter Decks, and began to fasten the Hatches to keep them down who were below, when the other Boat and their Men entring at the fore Chains, secur'd the Fore-Castle of the Ship, and the Scuttle which went down into the Cook Room, making three Men they found there, Prisoners.

When this was done, and all safe upon Deck, the Captain order'd the Mate with three Men to break into the Round-House where the new Rebel Captain lay, and having taken the Alarm, was gotten up, and with two Men and a Boy had gotten Fire Arms in their Hands, and when the Mate with a Crow split open the Door, the new Captain and his Men fir'd boldly among them, and wounded the Mate with a Musket Ball, which broke his Arm, and wounded two more of the Men but kill'd no Body.

The Mate calling for Help, rush'd however into the Round-House, wounded as he was, and with his Pistol shot the new Captain thro' the Head, the Bullet entring at his Mouth, and came out again behind one of his Ears; so that he never spoke a Word; upon which the rest yielded, and the Ship was taken effectually, without any more Lives lost.

As soon as the Ship was thus secur'd, the Captain order'd seven Guns to be fir'd, which was the Signal agreed upon with me, to give me Notice of his Success, which you may be sure I was very glad to hear, having sat watching upon the Shore for it till near two of the Clock in the Morning.

Having thus heard the Signal plainly, I laid me down; and it having been a Day of great Fatigue to me, I slept very sound, 'till I was something surpriz'd with the Noise of a Gun; and presently starting up, I heard a Man call me by the Name of Governour, Governour, and presently I knew the Captain's Voice, when climbing up to the Top of the Hill, there he stood, and pointing to the Ship, he embrac'd me in his Arms, *My dear Friend and Deliverer*, says he, *there's your Ship, for she is all yours, and so are we and all that belong to her.* I cast my Eyes to the Ship, and there she rode within little more than half a Mile of the Shore; for they had weighed her Anchor as soon as they were Masters of her; and the Weather being fair, had brought her to an Anchor just against the Mouth of the little Creek; and the Tide being up, the Captain had brought the Pinnace in near the Place where I at first landed my Rafts, and so landed just at my Door.

I was at first ready to sink down with the Surprize. For I saw my Deliverance indeed visibly put into my Hands, all things easy, and a large Ship just ready to carry me away whither I pleased to go. At first, for some time, I was not able to answer him one Word; but as he had taken me in his Arms, I held fast by him, or I should have fallen to the Ground.

He perceived the Surprize, and immediately pulls a Bottle out of his Pocket, and gave me a Dram of Cordial, which he had brought on Purpose for me; after I had drank it, I sat down upon the Ground;

and though it brought me to my self, yet it was a good while before I could speak a Word to him.

All this while the poor Man was in as great an Extasy as I, only not under any Surprize, as I was; and he said a thousand kind tender things to me, to compose me and bring me to my self; but such was the Flood of Joy in my Breast, that it put all my Spirits into Confusion, at last it broke out into Tears, and in a little while after, I recovered my Speech.

Then I took my Turn, and embrac'd him as my Deliverer; and we rejoyc'd together. I told him, I look upon him as a Man sent from Heaven to deliver me, and that the whole Transaction seemed to be a Chain of Wonders; that such things as these were the Testimonies we had of a secret Hand of Providence governing the World, and an Evidence, that the Eyes of an infinite Power could search into the remotest Corner of the World, and send Help to the Miserable whenever he pleased.

I forgot not to lift up my Heart in Thankfulness to Heaven, and what Heart could forbear to bless him, who had not only in a miraculous Manner provided for one in such a Wilderness,* and in such a desolate Condition, but from whom every Deliverance must always be acknowledged to proceed.

When we had talk'd a while, the Captain told me, he had brought me some little Refreshment, such as the Ship afforded, and such as the Wretches that had been so long his Master had not plunder'd him of: Upon this he call'd aloud to the Boat, and bid his Men bring the things ashore that were for the Governour; and indeed it was a Present, as if I had been one not that was to be carry'd away along with them, but as if I had been to dwell upon the Island still, and they were to go without me.

First he had brought me a Case of Bottles full of excellent Cordial Waters, six large Bottles of *Madera* Wine; the Bottles held two Quarts a-piece; two Pound of excellent good Tobacco, twelve good Pieces of the Ship's Beef, and six Pieces of Pork, with a Bag of Pease, and about a hundred Weight of Bisket.

He brought me also a Box of Sugar, a Box of Flower, a Bag full of Lemons, and two Bottles of Lime-Juice, and Abundance of other things: But besides these, and what was a thousand times more useful to me, he brought me six clean new Shirts, six very good Neckcloaths, two Pair of Gloves, one Pair of Shoes, a Hat, and one Pair of

Stockings, and a very good Suit of Cloaths of his own, which had been worn but very little: In a Word, he cloathed me from Head to Foot.

It was a very kind and agreeable Present, as any one may imagine to one in my Circumstances: But never was any thing in the World of that Kind so unpleasant, awkard, and uneasy, as it was to me to wear such Cloaths at their first putting on.

After these Ceremonies past, and after all his good things were brought into my little Apartment, we began to consult what was to be done with the Prisoners we had; for it was worth considering, whether we might venture to take them away with us or no, especially two of them, who we knew to be incorrigible and refractory to the last Degree; and the Captain said, he knew they were such Rogues, that there was no obliging them, and if he did carry them away, it must be in Irons, as Malefactors to be delivered over to Justice at the first *English* Colony he could come at; and I found that the Captain himself was very anxious about it.

Upon this, I told him, that if he desir'd it, I durst undertake to bring the two Men he spoke of, to make it their own Request that he should leave them upon the Island: *I should be very glad of that*, says the Captain, *with all my Heart*.

Well, says I, I will send for them up, and talk with them for you; so I caused *Friday* and the two Hostages, for they were now discharg'd, their Comrades having perform'd their Promise; I say, I caused them to go to the Cave, and bring up the five Men pinion'd, as they were, to the Bower, and keep them there 'till I came.

After some time, I came thither dress'd in my new Habit, and now I was call'd Governour again; being all met, and the Captain with me, I caused the Men to be brought before me, and I told them, I had had a full Account of their villanous Behaviour to the Captain, and how they had run away with the Ship, and were preparing to commit farther Robberies, but that Providence had ensnar'd them in their own Ways, and that they were fallen into the Pit which they had digged for others.

I let them know, that by my Direction the Ship had been seiz'd, that she lay now in the Road; and they might see by and by, that their new Captain had receiv'd the Reward of his Villany; for that they might see him hanging at the Yard-Arm.

That as to them, I wanted to know what they had to say, why I should not execute them as Pirates taken in the Fact, as by my Commission they could not doubt I had Authority to do.

One of them answer'd in the Name of the rest, That they had nothing to say but this, That when they were taken, the Captain promis'd them their Lives, and they humbly implor'd my Mercy; But I told them, I knew not what Mercy to shew them; for as for my self, I had resolv'd to quit the Island with all my Men, and had taken Passage with the Captain to go for *England*: And as for the Captain, he could not carry them to *England*, other than as Prisoners in Irons to be try'd for Mutiny, and running away with the Ship; the Consequence of which, they must needs know, would be the Gallows; so that I could not tell which was best for them, unless they had a Mind to take their Fate in the Island; if they desir'd, that I did not care, as I had Liberty to leave it, I had some Inclination to give them their Lives, if they thought they could shift on Shore.

They seem'd very thankful for it, said they would much rather venture to stay there, than to be carry'd to *England* to be hang'd; so I left it on that Issue.

However, the Captain seem'd to make some Difficulty of it, as if he durst not leave them there: Upon this I seem'd a little angry with the Captain, and told him, That they were my Prisoners, not his; and that seeing I had offered them so much Favour, I would be as good as my Word; and that if he did not think fit to consent to it, I would set them at Liberty, as I found them; and if he did not like it, he might take them again if he could catch them.

Upon this they appear'd very thankful, and I accordingly set them at Liberty, and bad them retire into the Woods to the Place whence they came, and I would leave them some Fire Arms, some Ammunition, and some Directions how they should live very well, if they thought fit.

Upon this I prepar'd to go on Board the Ship, but told the Captain, that I would stay that Night to prepare my things,* and desir'd him to go on Board in the mean time, and keep all right in the Ship, and send the Boat on Shore the next Day for me; ordering him in the mean time to cause the new Captain who was kill'd, to be hang'd at the Yard-Arm that these Men might see him.

When the Captain was gone, I sent for the Men up to me to my Apartment, and entred seriously into Discourse with them of their Circumstances, I told them, I thought they had made a right Choice;

that if the Captain carry'd them away, they would certainly be hang'd. I shewed them the new Captain, hanging at the Yard-Arm of the Ship, and told them they had nothing less to expect.

When they had all declar'd their Willingness to stay, I then told them, I would let them into the Story of my living there, and put them into the Way of making it easy to them: Accordingly I gave them the whole History of the Place, and of my coming to it; shew'd them my Fortifications, the Way I made my Bread, planted my Corn, cured my Grapes; and in a Word, all that was necessary to make them easy: I told them the Story also of the sixteen *Spaniards* that were to be expected; for whom I left a Letter, and made them promise to treat them in common with themselves.

I left them my Fire Arms, *viz.* Five Muskets, three Fowling Pieces, and three Swords. I had above a Barrel and half of Powder left; for after the first Year or two, I used but little, and wasted none. I gave them a Description of the Way I manag'd the Goats, and Directions to milk and fatten them, and to make both Butter and Cheese.

In a Word, I gave them every Part of my own Story; and I told them, I would prevail with the Captain to leave them two Barrels of Gun-Powder more, and some Garden-Seeds, which I told them I would have been very glad of; also I gave them the Bag of Pease which the Captain had brought me to eat, and bad them be sure to sow and encrease them.

Having done all this, I left them the next Day, and went on Board the Ship: We prepared immediately to sail, but did not weigh* that Night: The next Morning early, two of the five Men came swimming to the Ship's Side, and making a most lamentable Complaint of the other three, begged to be taken into the Ship, for God's Sake, for they should be murthered, and begg'd the Captain to take them on Board, tho' he hang'd them immediately.

Upon this the Captain pretended to have no Power without me; But after some Difficulty, and after their solemn Promises of Amendment, they were taken on Board, and were some time after soundly whipp'd and pickl'd;* after which, they prov'd very honest and quiet Fellows.

Some time after this, the Boat was order'd on Shore, the Tide being up, with the things promised to the Men, to which the Captain at my Intercession caused their Chests and Cloaths to be added, which they took, and were very thankful for; I also encourag'd them, by telling them, that if it lay in my Way to send any Vessel to take them in, I would not forget them.

When I took leave of this Island, I carry'd on board for Reliques, the great Goat's-Skin-Cap I had made, my Umbrella, and my Parrot; also I forgot not to take the Money I formerly mention'd, which had lain by me so long useless, that it was grown rusty, or tarnish'd, and could hardly pass for Silver, till it had been a little rubb'd, and handled; as also the Money I found in the Wreck of the *Spanish* Ship.

And thus I left the Island, the Nineteenth of *December*, as I found by the Ship's Account, in the Year 1686, after I had been upon it eight and twenty Years,* two Months, and 19 Days; being deliver'd from this second Captivity, the same Day of the Month, that I first made my Escape in the *Barco-Longo*, from among the *Moors* of *Sallee*.

In this Vessel, after a long Voyage, I arriv'd in *England*, the Eleventh of *June*, in the Year 1687,* having been thirty and five Years absent.

When I came to *England*, I was as perfect a Stranger to all the World, as if I had never been known there. My Benefactor and faithful Steward, who I had left in Trust with my Money, was alive; but had had great Misfortunes in the World; was become a Widow the second Time, and very low in the World: I made her easy as to what she ow'd me, assuring her, I would give her no Trouble; but on the contrary, in Gratitude to her former Care and Faithfulness to me, I reliev'd her as my little Stock would afford, which at that Time would indeed allow me to do but little for her; but I assur'd her, I would never forget her former Kindness to me; nor did I forget her, when I had sufficient to help her, as shall be observ'd in its Place.

I went down afterwards into *Yorkshire*; but my Father was dead, and my Mother, and all the Family extinct, except that I found two Sisters, and two of the Children of one of my Brothers; and as I had been long ago given over for dead, there had been no Provision made for me; so that in a Word, I found nothing to relieve, or assist me; and that little Money I had, would not do much for me, as to settling in the World.

I met with one Piece of Gratitude indeed, which I did not expect; and this was, That the Master of the Ship, who I had so happily deliver'd, and by the same Means sav'd the Ship and Cargo, having given a very handsome Account to the Owners, of the Manner how I had sav'd the Lives of the Men, and the Ship, they invited me to meet them, and some other Merchants concern'd, and altogether made me a very handsome Compliment upon the Subject, and a Present of almost two hundred Pounds Sterling.

But after making several Reflections upon the Circumstances of my Life, and how little way this would go towards settling me in the World, I resolv'd to go to *Lisbon*, and see if I might not come by some Information of the State of my Plantation in the *Brasils*, and of what was become of my Partner, who I had reason to suppose had some Years now given me over for dead.

With this View I took Shipping for *Lisbon*, where I arriv'd in *April* following; my Man *Friday* accompanying me very honestly in all these Ramblings, and proving a most faithful Servant upon all Occasions.

When I came to *Lisbon*, I found out by Enquiry, and to my particular Satisfaction, my old Friend the Captain of the Ship, who first took me up at Sea, off of the Shore of *Africk*: He was now grown old, and had left off the Sea, having put his Son, who was far from a young Man, into his Ship; and who still used the *Brasil* Trade. The old Man did not know me, and indeed, I hardly knew him; but I soon brought him to my Remembrance, and as soon brought my self to his Remembrance, when I told him who I was.

After some passionate Expressions of the old Acquaintance, I enquir'd, you may be sure, after my Plantation and my Partner: The old Man told me he had not been in the *Brasils* for about nine Years; but that he could assure me, that when he came away, my Partner was living, but the Trustees, who I had join'd with him to take Cognizance of my Part, were both dead; that however, he believ'd that I would have a very good Account of the Improvement of the Plantation; for that upon the general Belief of my being cast away, and drown'd, my Trustees had given in the Account of the Produce of my Part of the Plantation, to the Procurator Fiscal, who had appropriated it, in Case I never came to claim it; one Third to the King, and two Thirds to the Monastery of St. *Augustine*, to be expended for the Benefit of the Poor, and for the Conversion of the *Indians* to the Catholick Faith; but that if I appear'd, or any one for me, to claim the Inheritance, it should be restor'd; only that the Improvement, or Annual Production, being distributed to charitable Uses, could not be restor'd; but he assur'd me, that the Steward of the King's Revenue (from Lands) and the Proviedore, or Steward of the Monastery, had taken great Care all along, that the Incumbent, that is to say my Partner, gave every Year a faithful Account of the Produce, of which they receiv'd duly my Moiety.

I ask'd him if he knew to what height of Improvement he had brought the Plantation? And, Whether he thought it might be worth looking after? Or, Whether on my going thither, I should meet with no Obstruction to my Possessing my just Right in the Moiety?

He told me, he could not tell exactly, to what Degree the Plantation was improv'd; but this he knew, that my Partner was grown exceeding Rich upon the enjoying but one half of it; and that to the best of his Remembrance, he had heard, that the King's Third of my Part, which was it seems granted away to some other Monastery, or Religious House, amounted to above two hundred Moidores a Year; that as to my being restor'd to a quiet Possession of it, there was no question to be made of that, my Partner being alive to witness my Title, and my Name being also enrolled in the Register of the Country; also he told me, That the Survivors of my two Trustees, were very fair honest People, and very Wealthy; and he believ'd I would not only have their Assistance for putting me in Possession, but would find a very considerable Sum of Money in their Hands, for my Account; being the Produce of the Farm while their Fathers held the Trust, and before it was given up as above, which as he remember'd, was for about twelve Years.

I shew'd my self a little concern'd, and uneasy at this Account, and enquir'd of the old Captain, How it came to pass, that the Trustees should thus dispose my Effects, when he knew that I had made my Will, and had made him, the *Portuguese* Captain, my universal Heir, &c.

He told me, that was true; but that as there was no Proof of my being dead, he could not act as Executor, until some certain Account should come of my Death, and that besides, he was not willing to intermeddle with a thing so remote; that it was true he had registred my Will, and put in his Claim; and could he have given any Account of my being dead or alive, he would have acted by Procuration, and taken Possession of the *Ingenio*, so they call'd the Sugar-House, and had given his Son,* who was now at the *Brasils*, Order to do it.

But, says the old Man, I have one Piece of News to tell you, which perhaps may not be so acceptable to you as the rest, and that is, That believing you were lost, and all the World believing so also, your

Partner and Trustees did offer to accompt to me in your Name, for six or eight of the first Years of Profits, which I receiv'd; but there being at that time, says he, great Disbursements for encreasing the Works, building an *Ingenio*, and buying Slaves, it did not amount to near so much as afterwards it produced: However, says the old Man, I shall give you a true Account of what I have received in all, and how I have disposed of it.

After a few Days farther Conference with this ancient Friend, he brought me an Account of the six first Years Income of my Plantation, sign'd by my Partner and the Merchants Trustees, being always deliver'd in Goods, *viz.* Tobacco in Roll, and Sugar in Chests, besides Rum, Molossus, &c. which is the Consequence of a Sugar Work;* and I found by this Account, that every Year the Income considerably encreased; but as above, the Disbursement being large, the Sum at first was small: However, the old Man let me see, that he was Debtor to me 470 Moidores of Gold, besides 60 Chests of Sugar, and 15 double Rolls of Tobacco which were lost in his Ship; he having been Ship-wreck'd coming Home to *Lisbon* about 11 Years after my leaving the Place.

The good Man then began to complain of his Misfortunes, and how he had been obliged to make Use of my Money to recover his Losses, and buy him a Share in a new Ship: However, my old Friend, says he, you shall not want a Supply in your Necessity; and as soon as my Son returns, you shall be fully satisfy'd.

Upon this, he pulls out an old Pouch, and gives me 160 *Portugal* Moidores in Gold; and giving me the Writing of his Title to the Ship, which his Son was gone to the *Brasils* in, of which he was a Quarter Part Owner, and his Son another, he puts them both into my Hands for Security of the rest.

I was too much mov'd with the Honesty and Kindness of the poor Man, to be able to bear this; and remembring what he had done for me, how he had taken me up at Sea, and how generously he had used me on all Occasions, and particularly, how sincere a Friend he was now to me, I could hardly refrain Weeping at what he said to me: Therefore, first I asked him, if his Circumstances admitted him to spare so much Money at that time, and if it would not straiten him? He told me, he could not say but it might straiten him a little; but however it was my Money, and I might want it more than he.

Every thing the good Man said was full of Affection, and I could hardly refrain from Tears while he spoke: In short, I took 100 of the Moidores, and call'd for a Pen and Ink to give him a Receipt for them; then I returned him the rest, and told him, If ever I had Possession of the Plantation, I would return the other to him also, as indeed I afterwards did; and that as to the Bill of Sale of his Part in his Son's Ship, I would not take it by any Means; but that if I wanted the Money, I found he was honest enough to pay me; and if I did not, but came to receive what he gave me reason to expect, I would never have a Penny more from him.

When this was pass'd, the old Man began to ask me, If he should put me into a Method to make my Claim to my Plantation? I told him, I thought to go over to it my self: He said, I might do so if I pleas'd; but that if I did not, there were Ways enough to secure my Right, and immediately to appropriate the Profits to my Use; and as there were Ships in the River of *Lisbon*,* just ready to go away to *Brasil*, he made me enter my Name in a Publick Register, with his Affidavit, affirming upon Oath that I was alive, and that I was the same Person who took up the Land for the Planting the said Plantation at first.

This being regularly attested by a Notary, and a Procuration affix'd, he directed me to send it with a Letter of his Writing, to a Merchant of his Acquaintance at the Place, and then propos'd my staying with him till an Account came of the Return.

Never any Thing was more honourable, than the Proceedings upon this Procuration; for in less than seven Months, I receiv'd a large Packet from the Survivors of my Trustees the Merchants, for whose Account I went to Sea, in which were the following particular Letters and Papers enclos'd.

First, There was the Account Current of the Produce of my Farm, or Plantation, from the Year when their Fathers had ballanc'd with my old *Portugal* Captain, being for six Years; the Ballance appear'd to be 1174 Moidores in my Favour.

Secondly, There was the Account of four Years more while they kept the Effects in their Hands, before the Government claim'd the Administration, as being the Effects of a Person not to be found, which they call'd *Civil Death*; and the Ballance of this, the Value of the Plantation encreasing, amounted to [38,892] Cruisadoes,* which made 3241 Moidores.

Thirdly, There was the Prior of the *Augustin's* Account, who had receiv'd the Profits for above fourteen Years; but not being to account for what was dispos'd to the Hospital, very honestly declar'd he had 872 Moidores not distributed, which he acknowledged to my Account; as to the King's Part, that refunded nothing.

There was a Letter of my Partner's, congratulating me very affectionately upon my being alive, giving me an Account how the Estate was improv'd, and what it produced a Year, with a Particular of the Number of Squares or Acres that it contained; how planted, how many Slaves there were upon it, and making two and twenty Crosses for Blessings, told me he had said so many *Ave Marias* to thank the Blessed Virgin that I was alive; inviting me very passionately to come over and take Possession of my own; and in the mean time to give him Orders to whom he should deliver my Effects, if I did not come my self; concluding with a hearty Tender of his Friendship, and that of his Family, and sent me, as a Present, seven fine Leopard's Skins, which he had it seems received from *Africa*, by some other Ship which he had sent thither, and who it seems had made a better Voyage than I: He sent me also five Chests of excellent Sweet-meats, and an hundred Pieces of Gold uncoin'd, not quite so large as Moidores.

By the same Fleet, my two Merchant Trustees shipp'd me 1200 Chests of Sugar, 800 Rolls of Tobacco, and the rest of the whole Accompt in Gold.

I might well say, now indeed, That the latter End of *Job* was better than the Beginning.* It is impossible to express here the Flutterings of my very Heart, when I look'd over these Letters, and especially when I found all my Wealth about me; for as the *Brasil* Ships come all in Fleets, the same Ships which brought my Letters, brought my Goods; and the Effects were safe in the River before the Letters came to my Hand. In a Word, I turned pale, and grew sick; and had not the old Man run and fetch'd me a Cordial, I believe the sudden Surprize of Joy had overset Nature, and I had dy'd upon the Spot.

Nay after that, I continu'd very ill, and was so some Hours, 'till a Physician being sent for, and something of the real Cause of my Illness being known, he order'd me to be let Blood;* after which, I had Relief, and grew well: But I verily believe, if it had not been eas'd by a Vent given in that Manner, to the Spirits, I should have dy'd.

I was now Master, all on a Sudden, of above 5000 *l. Sterling* in Money, and had an Estate, as I might well call it, in the *Brasils*, of above a thousand Pounds a Year, as sure as an Estate of Lands in *England*:* And in a Word, I was in a Condition which I scarce knew how to understand, or how to compose my self, for the Enjoyment of it.

The first thing I did, was to recompense my original Benefactor, my good old Captain, who had been first charitable to me in my Distress, kind to me in my Beginning, and honest to me at the End: I shew'd him all that was sent me, I told him, that next to the Providence of Heaven, which disposes all things, it was owing to him; and that it now lay on me to reward him, which I would do a hundred fold: So I first return'd to him the hundred Moidores I had receiv'd of him, then I sent for a Notary, and caused him to draw up a general Release or Discharge for the 470 Moidores, which he had acknowledg'd he ow'd me in the fullest and firmest Manner possible; after which, I caused a Procuration to be drawn, impowering him to be my Receiver of the annual Profits of my Plantation, and appointing my Partner to accompt to him, and make the Returns by the usual Fleets to him in my Name; and a Clause in the End, being a Grant of 100 Moidores a Year to him, during his Life, out of the Effects, and 50 Moidores a Year to his Son after him, for his Life: And thus I requited my old Man.

I was now to consider which Way to steer my Course next, and what to do with the Estate that Providence had thus put into my Hands; and indeed I had more Care upon my Head now, than I had in my silent State of Life in the Island, where I wanted nothing but what I had, and had nothing but what I wanted:* Whereas I had now a great Charge upon me, and my Business was how to secure it. I had ne'er a Cave now to hide my Money in, or a Place where it might lye without Lock or Key, 'till it grew mouldy and tarnish'd before any Body would meddle with it: On the contrary, I knew not where to put it, or who to trust with it. My old Patron, the Captain, indeed was honest, and that was the only Refuge I had.

In the next Place, my Interest in the *Brasils* seem'd to summon me thither, but now I could not tell, how to think of going thither, 'till I had settled my Affairs, and left my Effects in some safe Hands behind me. At first I thought of my old Friend the Widow, who I knew was honest, and would be just to me; but then she was in Years, and but poor, and for ought I knew, might be in Debt; so that in a Word, I had no Way but to go back to *England* my self, and take my Effects with me.

It was some Months however before I resolved upon this; and therefore, as I had rewarded the old Captain fully, and to his Satisfaction, who had been my former Benefactor, so I began to think of my poor Widow, whose Husband had been my first Benefactor, and she, while it was in her Power, my faithful Steward and Instructor. So the first thing I did, I got a Merchant in *Lisbon* to write to his Correspondent in *London*, not only to pay a Bill, but to go find her out, and carry her in Money, an hundred Pounds from me, and to talk with her, and comfort her in her Poverty, by telling her she should, if I liv'd, have a further Supply: At the same time I sent my two Sisters in the Country, each of them an Hundred Pounds, they being, though not in Want, yet not in very good Circumstances; one having been marry'd, and left a Widow; and the other having a Husband not so kind to her as he should be.

But among all my Relations, or Acquaintances, I could not yet pitch upon one, to whom I durst commit the Gross of my Stock, that I might go away to the *Brasils*, and leave things safe behind me; and this greatly perplex'd me.

I had once a Mind to have gone to the *Brasils*, and have settled my self there; for I was, as it were, naturaliz'd to the Place; but I had some little Scruple in my Mind about Religion, which insensibly drew me back, of which I shall say more presently. However, it was not Religion that kept me from going there for the present; and as I had made no Scruple of being openly of the Religion of the Country, all the while I was among them, so neither did I yet; only that now and then having of late thought more of it, (than formerly) when I began to think of living and dying among them, I began to regret my having profess'd my self a Papist, and thought it might not be the best Religion to die with.*

But, as I have said, this was not the main thing that kept me from going to the *Brasils*, but that really I did not know with whom to leave my Effects behind me; so I resolv'd at last to go to *England* with it, where, if I arrived, I concluded I should make some Acquaintance, or find some Relations that would be faithful to me; and according I prepar'd to go for *England* with all my Wealth.

In order to prepare things for my going Home, I first, the *Brasil*

Fleet being just going away, resolved to give Answers suitable to the just and faithful Account of things I had from thence; and first to the Prior of St. *Augustine* I wrote a Letter full of Thanks for their just Dealings, and the Offer of the 872 Moidores, which was indisposed of, which I desir'd might be given 500 to the Monastery, and 372 to the Poor, as the Prior should direct, desiring the good *Padres** Prayers for me, and the like.

I wrote next a Letter of Thanks to my two Trustees, with all the Acknowledgment that so much Justice and Honesty call'd for; as for sending them any Present, they were far above having any Occasion of it.

Lastly, I wrote to my Partner, acknowledging his Industry in the Improving the Plantation, and his Integrity in encreasing the Stock of the Works, giving him Instructions for his future Government of my Part, according to the Powers I had left with my old Patron, to whom I desir'd him to send whatever became due to me, 'till he should hear from me more particularly; assuring him that it was my Intention, not only to come to him, but to settle my self there for the Remainder of my Life: To this I added a very handsom Present of some *Italian* Silks* for his Wife, and two Daughters, for such the Captain's Son inform'd me he had; with two Pieces of fine *English* broad Cloath,* the best I could get in *Lisbon*, five Pieces of black Bays,* and some *Flanders* Lace* of a good Value.

Having thus settled my Affairs, sold my Cargoe, and turn'd all my Effects into good Bills of Exchange,* my next Difficulty was, which Way to go to *England*: I had been accustom'd enough to the Sea, and yet I had a strange Aversion to going to *England* by Sea at that time; and though I could give no Reason for it, yet the Difficulty encreas'd upon me so much, that though I had once shipp'd my Baggage, in order to go, yet I alter'd my Mind, and that not once, but two or three times.

It is true, I had been very unfortunate by Sea, and this might be some of the Reason: But let no Man slight the strong Impulses of his own Thoughts in Cases of such Moment: Two of the Ships which I had singl'd out to go in, I mean, more particularly singl'd out than any other, that is to say, so as in one of them to put my things on Board, and in the other to have agreed with the Captain; I say, two of these Ships miscarry'd, *viz.* One was taken by the *Algerines*, and the other was cast away on the *Start** near *Torbay*, and all the People drown'd except three; so that in either of those Vessels I had been made miserable; and in which most, it was hard to say.

Having been thus harass'd in my Thoughts, my old Pilot, to whom I communicated every thing, press'd me earnestly not to go by Sea, but either to go by Land to the *Groyne*,* and cross over the Bay of *Biscay* to *Rochell*,* from whence it was but an easy and safe Journey by Land to *Paris*, and so to *Calais* and *Dover*; or to go up to *Madrid*, and so all the Way by Land thro' *France*.

In a Word, I was so prepossess'd against my going by Sea at all, except from *Calais* to *Dover*,* that I resolv'd to travel all the Way by Land; which as I was not in Haste, and did not value the Charge, was by much the pleasanter Way; and to make it more so, my old Captain brought an *English* Gentleman, the Son of a Merchant in *Lisbon*, who was willing to travel with me: After which, we pick'd up two more *English* Merchants also, and two young *Portuguese* Gentlemen, the last going to *Paris* only; so that we were in all six of us, and five Servants; the two Merchants and the two *Portuguese*, contenting themselves with one Servant, between two, to save the Charge; and as for me, I got an *English* Sailor to travel with me as a Servant, besides my Man *Friday*, who was too much a Stranger to be capable of supplying the Place of a Servant on the Road.

In this Manner I set out from *Lisbon*; and our Company being all very well mounted and armed, we made a little Troop, whereof they did me the Honour to call me Captain, as well because I was the oldest Man, as because I had two Servants, and indeed was the Original of the whole Journey.

As I have troubled you with none of my Sea-Journals, so I shall trouble you now with none of my Land-Journal: But some Adventures that happen'd to us in this tedious and difficult Journey, I must not omit.

When we came to *Madrid*, we being all of us Strangers to *Spain*, were willing to stay some time to see the Court of *Spain*, and to see what was worth observing; but it being the latter Part of the Summer, we hasten'd away, and set out from *Madrid* about the Middle of *October*: But when we came to the Edge of *Navarre*,* we were alarm'd at several Towns on the Way, with an Account, that so much Snow was fallen on the *French* Side of the Mountains, that several Travellers were obliged to come back to *Pampeluna*,* after having attempted, at an extream Hazard, to pass on.

When we came to *Pampeluna* it self, we found it so indeed; and to me that had been always used to a hot Climate, and indeed to Countries where we could scarce bear any Cloaths on, the Cold was insufferable; nor indeed was it more painful than it was surprising, to come but ten Days before out of the old Castile* where the Weather was not only warm but very hot, and immediately to feel a Wind from the *Pyrenean* Mountains, so very keen, so severely cold, as to be intollerable, and to endanger benumbing and perishing of our Fingers and Toes.

Poor *Friday* was really frighted when he saw the Mountains all cover'd with Snow, and felt cold Weather, which he had never seen or felt before in his Life.

To mend the Matter, when we came to *Pampeluna*, it continued snowing with so much Violence, and so long, that the People said, Winter was come before its time, and the Roads which were difficult before, were now quite impassable: For in a Word, the Snow lay in some Places too thick for us to travel; and being not hard frozen, as is the Case in Northern Countries: There was no going without being in Danger of being bury'd alive every Step. We stay'd no less than twenty Days at *Pampeluna*; when seeing the Winter coming on, and no Likelihood of its being better; for it was the severest Winter all over *Europe* that had been known in the Memory of Man.* I propos'd that we should all go away to *Fonterabia*,* and there take Shipping for *Bourdeaux*, which was a very little Voyage.

But while we were considering this, there came in four *French* Gentlemen, who having been stopp'd on the *French* Side of the Passes, as we were on the *Spanish*, had found out a Guide, who traversing the Country near the Head of *Languedoc*,* had brought them over the Mountains by such Ways, that they were not much incommoded with the Snow; and where they met with Snow in any quantity, they said it was frozen hard enough to bear them and their Horses.

We sent for this Guide, who told us, he would undertake to carry us the same Way with no Hazard from the Snow, provided we were armed sufficiently to protect our selves from wild Beasts; for he said, upon these great Snows, it was frequent for some Wolves to show themselves at the Foot of the Mountains, being made ravenous for Want of Food, the Ground being covered with Snow: We told him, we were well enough prepar'd for such Creatures as they were, if he would ensure us from a Kind of two-legged Wolves, which we were told, we were in most Danger from, especially on the *French* Side of the Mountains.*

He satisfy'd us there was no Danger of that kind in the Way that we were to go; so we readily agreed to follow him, as did also twelve other Gentlemen, with their Servants, some *French*, some *Spanish*; who, as I said, had attempted to go, and were oblig'd to come back again.

Accordingly, we all set out from *Pampeluna*, with our Guide, on the fifteenth of *November*; and indeed, I was surpriz'd, when instead of going forward, he came directly back with us, on the same Road that we came from *Madrid*, above twenty Miles; when being pass'd two Rivers, and come into the plain Country, we found our selves in a warm Climate again, where the Country was pleasant, and no Snow to be seen; but on a sudden, turning to his left, he approach'd the Mountains another Way; and though it is true, the Hills and Precipices look'd dreadful, yet he made so many Tours, such Meanders, and led us by such winding Ways, that we were insensibly pass'd the Height of the Mountains, without being much incumbred with the Snow; and all on a sudden, he shew'd us the pleasant fruitful Provinces of *Languedoc* and *Gascoign*,* all green and flourishing; tho' indeed it was at a great Distance, and we had some rough Way to pass yet.

We were a little uneasy however, when we found it snow'd one whole Day, and a Night, so fast, that we could not travel; but he bid us be easy, we should soon be past it all: We found indeed, that we began to descend every Day, and to come more *North* than before; and so depending upon our Guide we went on.

It was about two Hours before Night, when our Guide being something before us, and not just in Sight, out rushed three monstrous Wolves, and after them a Bear,* out of a hollow Way, adjoyning to a thick Wood; two of the Wolves flew upon the Guide, and had he been half a Mile before us, he had been devour'd indeed, before we could have help'd him: One of them fastned upon his Horse, and the other attack'd the Man with that Violence, that he had not Time, or not Presence of Mind enough to draw his Pistol, but hollow'd and cry'd out to us most lustily; my Man *Friday* being next me, I bid him ride up, and see what was the Matter; as soon as *Friday* came in Sight of the Man, he hollow'd as loud as t'other, *O Master! O*

Master! But like a bold Fellow, rode directly up to the poor Man, and with his Pistol shot the Wolf that attack'd him into the Head.

It was happy for the poor Man, that it was my Man *Friday*; for he having been us'd to that kind of Creature in his Country,* had no Fear upon him; but went close up to him, and shot him as above; whereas any of us, would have fir'd at a farther Distance, and have perhaps either miss'd the Wolf, or endanger'd shooting the Man.

But it was enough to have terrify'd a bolder Man than I, and indeed it alarm'd all our Company, when with the Noise of *Friday's* Pistol, we heard on both Sides the dismallest Howling of Wolves, and the Noise redoubled by the Eccho of the Mountains, that it was to us as if there had been a prodigious Multitude of them; and perhaps indeed there was not such a Few, as that we had no cause of Apprehensions.

However, as *Friday* had kill'd this Wolf, the other that had fastned upon the Horse, left him immediately, and fled; having happily fastned upon his Head, where the Bosses of the Bridle had stuck in his Teeth; so that he had not done him much Hurt: The Man indeed was most Hurt; for the raging Creature had bit him twice, once on the Arm, and the other Time a little above his Knee; and he was just as it were tumbling down by the Disorder of his Horse, when *Friday* came up and shot the Wolf.

It is easy to suppose, that at the Noise of *Friday's* Pistol, we all mended our Pace, and rid up as fast as the Way (which was very difficult) would give us leave, to see what was the Matter; as soon as we came clear of the Trees, which blinded us before, we saw clearly what had been the Case, and how *Friday* had disengag'd the poor Guide; though we did not presently discern what kind of Creature it was he had kill'd.

But never was a Fight manag'd so hardily, and in such a surprizing Manner, as that which follow'd between *Friday* and the Bear, which gave us all (though at first we were surpriz'd and afraid for him) the greatest Diversion imaginable: As the Bear is a heavy, clumsey Creature, and does not gallop as the Wolf does, who is swift, and light; so he has two particular qualities, which generally are the Rule of his Actions; First, As to Men, who are not his proper Prey; I say, not his proper Prey; because tho' I cannot say what excessive Hunger might do, which was now their Case, the Ground being all cover'd with Snow; but as to Men, he does not usually attempt them, unless they first attack him: On the contrary, if you meet him in the Woods, if you don't meddle with him, he won't meddle with you; but then you must take Care to be very Civil to him, and give him the Road;* for he is a very nice Gentleman, he won't go a Step out of his Way for a Prince; nay, if you are really afraid, your best way is to look another Way, and keep going on; for sometimes if you stop, and stand still, and look steadily at him, he takes it for an Affront; but if you throw or toss any Thing at him, and it hits him, though it were but a bit of a Stick, as big as your Finger, he takes it for an Affront, and sets all his other Business aside to pursue his Revenge; for he will have Satisfaction in Point of Honour; that is his first Quality: The next is, That if he be once affronted, he will never leave you, Night or Day, till he has his Revenge; but follows at a good round rate, till he overtakes you.

My Man *Friday* had deliver'd our Guide, and when we came up to him, he was helping him off from his Horse; for the Man was both hurt and frighted, and indeed, the last more than the first; when on the sudden, we spy'd the Bear come out of the Wood, and a vast monstrous One it was, the biggest by far that ever I saw: We were all a little surpriz'd, when we saw him; but when *Friday* saw him, it was easy to see Joy and Courage in the Fellow's Countenance; *O! O! O!* says *Friday*, three Times, pointing to him; *O* Master! *You give me te Leave! Me shakee te Hand with him: Me make you good laugh.*

I was surpriz'd to see the Fellow so pleas'd; *You Fool you*, says I, *he will eat you up: Eatee me up! Eatee me up!* Says *Friday*, twice over again; *Me eatee him up: Me make you good laugh: You all stay here, me show you good laugh*; so down he sits, and gets his Boots off in a Moment, and put on a Pair of Pumps (as we call the flat Shoes they wear) and which he had in his Pocket, gives my other Servant his Horse, and with his Gun away he flew swift like the Wind.

The Bear was walking softly on, and offer'd to meddle with no Body, till *Friday* coming pretty near, calls to him, as if the Bear could understand him; *Hark ye, hark ye*, says *Friday*, *me speakee wit you:* We follow'd at a Distance; for now being come down on the *Gascoign* side of the Mountains, we were entred a vast great Forest, where the Country was plain, and pretty open, though many Trees in it scatter'd here and there.

Friday, who had as we say, the Heels of the Bear,* came up with him quickly, and takes up a great Stone, and throws at him, and hit him just on the Head; but did him no more harm, than if he had thrown it against a Wall; but it answer'd *Friday's* End;* for the Rogue was so void of Fear, that he did it purely to make the Bear follow him, and show us some Laugh as he call'd it.

As soon as the Bear felt the Stone, and saw him, he turns about, and comes after him, taking Devilish long Strides, and shuffling along at a strange Rate, so as would have put a Horse to a midling Gallop; away runs *Friday*, and takes his Course, as if he run towards us for Help; so we all resolv'd to fire at once upon the Bear, and deliver my Man; though I was angry at him heartily, for bringing the Bear back upon us, when he was going about his own Business another Way; and especially I was angry that he had turn'd the Bear upon us, and then run away; and I call'd out, *You Dog*, said I, *is this your making us laugh? Come away, and take your Horse, that we may shoot the Creature*; he hears me, and crys out, *No shoot, no shoot, stand still, you get much Laugh.* And as the nimble Creature run two Foot for the Beast's one, he turn'd on a sudden, on one side of us, and seeing a great Oak-Tree,* fit for his Purpose, he beckon'd to us to follow, and doubling his Pace, he gets nimbly up the Tree, laying his Gun down upon the Ground, at about five or six Yards from the Bottom of the Tree.

The Bear soon came to the Tree, and we follow'd at a Distance; the first Thing he did, he stopp'd at the Gun, smelt to it, but let it lye, and up he scrambles into the Tree, climbing like a Cat, though so monstrously heavy: I was amaz'd at the Folly, as I thought it, of my Man, and could not for my Life see any Thing to laugh at yet, till seeing the Bear get up the Tree, we all rod nearer to him.

When we came to the Tree, there was *Friday* got out to the small End of a large Limb of the Tree, and the Bear got about half way to him; as soon as the Bear got out to that part where the Limb of the Tree was weaker, *Ha*, says he to us, *now you see me teachee the Bear dance*; so he falls a jumping and shaking the Bough, at which the Bear began to totter, but stood still, and begun to look behind him, to see how he should get back; then indeed we did laugh heartily: But *Friday* had not done with him by a great deal; when he sees him stand still, he calls out to him again, as if he had suppos'd the Bear could speak *English*; *What you no come farther, pray you come farther*; so he left jumping and shaking the Tree; and the Bear, just as if he had understood what he said, did come a little further, then he fell a jumping again, and the Bear stopp'd again.

We thought now was a good time to knock him on the Head, and I call'd to *Friday* to stand still, and we would shoot the Bear; but he cry'd out earnestly, *O pray! O pray! No shoot, me shoot, by and then*; he would have said, *By and by*: However, to shorten the Story, *Friday* danc'd so much, and the Bear stood so ticklish, that we had laughing enough indeed, but still could not imagine what the Fellow would do; for first we thought he depended upon shaking the Bear off; and we found the Bear was too cunning for that too; for he would not go out far enough to be thrown down, but clings fast with his great broad Claws and Feet, so that we could not imagine what would be the End of it, and where the Jest would be at last.

But *Friday* put us out of doubt quickly; for seeing the Bear cling fast to the Bough, and that he would not be perswaded to come any farther; *Well, well*, says *Friday*, *you no come farther, me go, me go; you no come to me, me go come to you*; and upon this, he goes out to the smallest End of the Bough, where it would bend with his Weight, and gently lets himself down by it, sliding down the Bough, till he came near enough to jump down on his Feet, and away he run to his Gun, takes it up, and stands still.

Well, said I to him *Friday*, What will you do now? Why don't you shoot him? *No shoot*, says *Friday*, *no yet, me shoot now, me no kill; me stay, give you one more laugh*; and indeed so he did, as you will see presently; for when the Bear see his Enemy gone, he comes back from the Bough where he stood; but did it mighty leisurely, looking behind him every Step, and coming backward till he got into the Body of the Tree; then with the same hinder End foremost, he came down the Tree, grasping it with his Claws, and moving one Foot at a Time, very leisurely; at this Juncture, and just before he could set his hind Feet upon the Ground, *Friday* stept up close to him, clapt the Muzzle of his Piece into his Ear, and shot him dead as a Stone.

Then the Rogue turn'd about, to see if we did not laugh, and when he saw we were pleas'd by our Looks, he falls a laughing himself very loud; *so we kill Bear in my Country*, says *Friday*; so you kill them, says I, Why you have no Guns: *No*, says he, *no Gun, but shoot, great much long Arrow.*

This was indeed a good Diversion to us; but we were still in a wild

Place, and our Guide very much hurt, and what to do we hardly knew; the Howling of Wolves run much in my Head; and indeed, except the Noise I once heard on the Shore of *Africa*, of which I have said something already, I never heard any thing that filled me with so much Horrour.

These things, and the Approach of Night, called us off, or else, as *Friday* would have had us, we should certainly have taken the Skin of this monstrous Creature off, which was worth saving; but we had three Leagues to go, and our Guide hasten'd us, so we left him, and went forward on our Journey.

The Ground was still cover'd with Snow, tho' not so deep and dangerous as on the Mountains, and the ravenous Creatures, as we heard afterwards, were come down into the Forest and plain Country, press'd by Hunger to seek for Food; and had done a great deal of Mischief in the Villages, where they surpriz'd the Country People, kill'd a great many of their Sheep and Horses, and some People too.

We had one dangerous Place to pass, which our Guide told us, if there were any more Wolves in the Country, we should find them there; and this was in a small Plain, surrounded with Woods on every Side, and a long narrow Defile or Lane, which we were to pass to get through the Wood, and then we should come to the Village where we were to lodge.

It was within half an Hour of Sun-set when we entred the first Wood; and a little after Sun-set, when we came into the Plain. We met with nothing in the first Wood, except, that in a little Plain within the Wood, which was not above two Furlongs over, we saw five great Wolves cross the Road, full Speed one after another, as if they had been in Chase of some Prey, and had it in View; they took no Notice of us, and were gone, and out of our Sight in a few Moments.

Upon this our Guide, who by the Way was a wretched faint-hearted Fellow, bid us keep in a ready Posture; for he believed there were more Wolves a coming.

We kept our Arms ready, and our Eyes about us, but we saw no more Wolves, 'till we came thro' that Wood, which was near half a League, and entred the Plain; as soon as we came into the Plain, we had Occasion enough to look about us: The first Object we met with, was a dead Horse; that is to say, a poor Horse which the Wolves had kill'd, and at least a Dozen of them at Work; we could not say eating of him, but picking of his Bones rather; for they had eaten up all the Flesh before.

We did not think fit to disturb them at their Feast, neither did they take much Notice of us: *Friday* would have let fly at them, but I would not suffer him by any Means; for I found we were like to have more Business upon our Hands than we were aware of. We were not gone half over the Plain, but we began to hear the Wolves howl in the Wood on our Left, in a frightful Manner, and presently after we saw about a hundred coming on directly towards us, all in a Body, and most of them in a Line, as regularly as an Army drawn up by experienc'd Officers. I scarce knew in what Manner to receive them; but found to draw our selves in a close Line was the only Way:* so we form'd in a Moment: But that we might not have too much Interval, I order'd, that only every other Man should fire, and that the others who had not fir'd should stand ready to give them a second Volley immediately, if they continued to advance upon us, and that then those who had fir'd at first, should not pretend to load their Fusees again, but stand ready with every one a Pistol; for we were all arm'd with a Fusee, and a Pair of Pistols each Man; so we were by this Method able to fire six Volleys, half of us at a Time; however, at present we had no Necessity; for upon firing the first Volley, the Enemy made a full Stop, being terrify'd as well with the Noise, as with the Fire; four of them being shot into the Head, dropp'd, several others were wounded, and went bleeding off, as we could see by the Snow: I found they stopp'd, but did not immediately retreat; whereupon remembring that I had been told, that the fiercest Creatures were terrify'd at the Voice of a Man, I caus'd all our Company to hollow as loud as we could; and I found the Notion not altogether mistaken; for upon our Shout, they began to retire, and turn about; then I order'd a second Volley to be fir'd, in their Rear, which put them to the Gallop, and away they went to the Woods.

This gave us leisure to charge our Pieces again, and that we might loose no Time, we kept going; but we had but little more than loaded our Fusees, and put our selves into a Readiness, when we heard a terrible Noise in the same Wood, on our Left, only that it was farther onward the same Way we were to go.

The Night was coming on, and the Light began to be dusky, which made it worse on our Side; but the Noise encreasing, we could easily perceive that it was the Howling and Yelling of those hellish Creatures; and on a sudden, we perceiv'd 2 or 3 Troops of Wolves, one on our Left, one behind us, and one on our Front; so that we seem'd to be surrounded with 'em; however, as they did not fall upon us, we kept our Way forward, as fast as we could make our Horses go, which the Way being very rough, was only a good large Trot; and in this Manner we came in View of the Entrance of a Wood, through which we were to pass, at the farther Side of the Plain; but we were greatly surpriz'd, when coming nearer the Lane, or Pass, we saw a confus'd Number of Wolves standing just at the Entrance.

On a sudden, at another opening of the Wood, we heard the Noise of a Gun; and looking that Way, out rush'd a Horse, with a Saddle, and a Bridle on him, flying like the Wind, and sixteen or seventeen Wolves after him, full Speed; indeed, the Horse had the Heels of them; but as we suppos'd that he could not hold it at that rate, we doubted not but they would get up with him at last, and no question but they did.

But here we had a most horrible Sight; for riding up to the Entrance where the Horse came out, we found the Carcass of another Horse, and of two Men, devour'd by the ravenous Creatures, and one of the Men was no doubt the same who we heard fir'd the Gun; for there lay a Gun just by him, fir'd off; but as to the Man, his Head, and the upper Part of his Body was eaten up.

This fill'd us with Horror, and we knew not what Course to take, but the Creatures resolv'd us* soon; for they gather'd about us presently, in hopes of Prey; and I verily believe there were three hundred of them: It happen'd very much to our Advantage, that at the Entrance into the Wood, but a little Way from it, there lay some large Timber Trees, which had been cut down the Summer before, and I suppose lay there for Carriage;* I drew my little Troop in among those Trees, and placing our selves in a Line, behind one long Tree, I advis'd them all to light, and keeping that Tree before us, for a Breast Work, to stand in a Triangle, or three Fronts, enclosing our Horses in the Center.

We did so, and it was well we did; for never was a more furious Charge than the Creatures made upon us in the Place; they came on us with a growling kind of a Noise (and mounted the Piece of Timber, which as I said, was our Breast Work) as if they were only

rushing upon their Prey; and this Fury of theirs, it seems, was principally occasion'd by their seeing our Horses behind us, which was
the Prey they aim'd at: I order'd our Men to fire as before, every
other Man; and they took their Aim so sure, that indeed they kill'd
several of the Wolves at the first Volley; but there was a Necessity to
keep a continual Firing; for they came on like Devils, those behind
pushing on those before.

When we had fir'd our second Volley of our Fusees, we thought
they stopp'd a little, and I hop'd they would have gone off; but it was
but a Moment; for others came forward again; so we fir'd two Volleys
of our Pistols, and I believe in these four Firings, we had kill'd
seventeen or eighteen of them, and lam'd twice as many; yet they
came on again.

I was loath to spend our last Shot too hastily; so I call'd my
Servant, not my Man *Friday*, for he was better employ'd; for with
the greatest Dexterity imaginable, he had charg'd my Fusee, and his
own, while we were engag'd; but as I said, I call'd my other Man, and
giving him a Horn of Powder, I bad him lay a Train, all along the
Piece of Timber, and let it be a large Train; he did so, and had but
just Time to get away, when the Wolves came up to it, and some were
got up upon it; when I snapping an uncharg'd Pistol, close to the
Powder, set it on fire;* those that were upon the Timber were scorcht
with it, and six or seven of them fell, or rather jump'd in among us,
with the Force and Fright of the Fire; we dispatch'd these in an
Instant, and the rest were so frighted with the Light, which the
Night, for it was now very near Dark, made more terrible, that they
drew back a little.

Upon which I order'd our last Pistol to be fir'd off in one Volley,
and after that we gave a Shout; upon this, the Wolves turn'd Tail,
and we sally'd immediately upon near twenty lame Ones, who we
found struggling on the Ground, and fell a cutting them with our
Swords, which answer'd our Expectation; for the Crying and Howling they made, was better understood by their Fellows, so that they
all fled and left us.

We had, first and last, kill'd about three Score of them; and had it
been Day-Light, we had kill'd many more: The Field of Battle being
thus clear'd, we made forward again; for we had still near a League
to go. We heard the ravenous Creatures houl and yell in the Woods as
we went, several Times; and sometimes we fancy'd we saw some of

them, but the Snow dazling our Eyes, we were not certain; so in about an Hour more, we came to the Town, where we were to lodge, which we found in a terrible Fright, and all in Arms; for it seems, that the Night before, the Wolves and some Bears had broke into the Village in the Night, and put them in a terrible Fright, and they were oblig'd to keep Guard Night and Day, but especially in the Night, to preserve their Cattle, and indeed their People.

The next Morning our Guide was so ill, and his Limbs swell'd with the rankling of his two Wounds, that he could go no farther; so we were oblig'd to take a new Guide there, and go to *Tholouse*,* where we found a warm Climate, a fruitful pleasant Country, and no Snow, no Wolves, or any Thing like them; but when we told our Story at *Tholouse*, they told us it was nothing but what was ordinary in the great Forest at the Foot of the Mountains, especially when the Snow lay on the Ground: But they enquir'd much what kind of a Guide we had gotten, that would venture to bring us that Way in such a severe Season; and told us, it was very much* we were not all devour'd. When we told them how we plac'd our selves, and the Horses in the Middle, they blam'd us exceedingly, and told us it was fifty to one but we had been all destroy'd; for it was the Sight of the Horses which made the Wolves so furious, seeing their Prey; and that at other Times they are really afraid of a Gun; but the being excessive Hungry, and raging on that Account, the Eagerness to come at the Horses had made them sensless of Danger; and that if we had not by the continu'd Fire, and at last by the Stratagem of the Train of Powder, master'd them, it had been great Odds but that we had been torn to Pieces; whereas had we been content to have sat still on Horseback, and fir'd as Horsemen, they would not have taken the Horses for so much their own, when Men were on their Backs, as otherwise; and withal they told us, that at last, if we had stood altogether, and left our Horses, they would have been so eager to have devour'd them, that we might have come off safe, especially having our Fire Arms in our Hands, and being so many in Number.

For my Part, I was never so sensible of Danger in my Life; for seeing above three hundred Devils come roaring and open mouth'd to devour us, and having nothing to shelter us, or retreat to, I gave my self over for lost; and as it was, I believe, I shall never care to cross those Mountains again; I think I would much rather go a thousand

Leagues by Sea, though I were sure to meet with a Storm once a Week.

I have nothing uncommon to take Notice of, in my Passage through *France*; nothing but what other Travellers have given an Account of, with much more Advantage than I can. I travell'd from *Tholouse* to *Paris*, and without any considerable Stay, came to *Callais*, and landed safe at *Dover*, the fourteenth of *January*, after having had a severely cold Season to travel in.

I was now come to the Center of my Travels, and had in a little Time all my new discover'd Estate safe about me, the Bills of Exchange which I brought with me having been very currently paid.

My principal Guide, and Privy Councellor, was my good antient Widow, who in Gratitude for the Money I had sent her, thought no Pains too much, or Care too great, to employ for me; and I trusted her so entirely with every Thing, that I was perfectly easy as to the Security of my Effects; and indeed, I was very happy from my Beginning, and now to the End, in the unspotted Integrity of this good Gentlewoman.

And now I began to think of leaving my Effects with this Woman, and setting out for *Lisbon*, and so to the *Brasils*; but now another Scruple came in my Way, and that was Religion; for as I had entertain'd some Doubts about the *Roman* Religion, even while I was abroad, especially in my State of Solitude; so I knew there was no going to the *Brasils* for me, much less going to settle there, unless I resolv'd to embrace the *Roman* Catholick Religion, without any Reserve; unless on the other hand, I resolv'd to be a Sacrifice to my Principles, be a Martyr for Religion, and die in the Inquisition;* so I resolv'd to stay at Home, and if I could find Means for it, to dispose of my Plantation.

To this Purpose I wrote to my old Friend at *Lisbon*, who in Return gave me Notice, that he could easily dispose of it there: But that if I thought fit to give him Leave to offer it in my Name to the two Merchants, the Survivors of my Trustees, who liv'd in the *Brasils*, who must fully understand the Value of it, who liv'd just upon the Spot, and who I knew were very rich; so that he believ'd they would be fond of buying it; he did not doubt, but I should make 4 or 5000 Pieces of Eight, the more of it.

Accordingly I agreed, gave him Order to offer it to them, and he did so; and in about 8 Months more, the Ship being then return'd, he sent me Account, that they had accepted the Offer, and had remitted 33000 Pieces of Eight, to a Correspondent of theirs at *Lisbon*, to pay for it.

In Return, I sign'd the Instrument of Sale in the Form which they sent from *Lisbon*, and sent it to my old Man, who sent me Bills of Exchange for 32800 Pieces of Eight to me, for the Estate; reserving the Payment of 100 Moidores a Year to him, the old Man, during his Life, and 50 Moidores afterwards to his Son for his Life, which I had promised them, which the Plantation was to make good as a Rent-Charge. And thus I have given the first Part of a Life of Fortune and Adventure, a Life of Providence's Checquer-Work, and of a Variety which the World will seldom be able to show the like of: Beginning foolishly, but closing much more happily than any Part of it ever gave me Leave so much as to hope for.

Any one would think, that in this State of complicated good Fortune, I was past running any more Hazards; and so indeed I had been, if other Circumstances had concurr'd, but I was inur'd to a wandring Life, had no Family, not many Relations, nor however rich had I contracted much Acquaintance; and though I had sold my Estate in the *Brasils*, yet I could not keep the Country out of my Head, and had a great Mind to be upon the Wing again, especially I could not resist the strong Inclination I had to see my Island, and to know if the poor *Spaniards* were in Being there, and how the Rogues I left there had used them.

My true Friend, the Widow, earnestly diswaded me from it, and so far prevail'd with me, that for almost seven Years she prevented my running Abroad; during which time, I took my two Nephews, the Children of one of my Brothers into my Care: The eldest having something of his own, I bred up as a Gentleman, and gave him a Settlement of some Addition to his Estate, after my Decease; the other I put out to a Captain of a Ship; and after five Years, finding him a sensible bold enterprising young Fellow, I put him into a good Ship, and sent him to Sea: And this young Fellow afterwards drew me in, as old as I was, to farther Adventures my self.

In the mean time, I in Part settled my self here; for first of all I marry'd, and that not either to my Disadvantage or Dissatisfaction, and had three Children, two Sons and one Daughter: But my Wife dying, and my Nephew coming Home with good Success from a Voyage to *Spain*, my Inclination to go Abroad, and his Importunity prevailed and engag'd me to go in his Ship, as a private Trader to the *East Indies*: This was in the Year 1694.

In this Voyage I visited my new Collony in the Island, saw my Successors the *Spaniards*, had the whole Story of their Lives, and of the Villains I left there; how at first they insulted the poor *Spaniards*, how they afterwards agreed, disagreed, united, separated, and how at last the *Spaniards* were oblig'd to use Violence with them, how they were subjected to the *Spaniards*, how honestly the *Spaniards* used them; a History, if it were entred into, as full of Variety and wonderful Accidents, as my own Part, particularly also as to their Battles with the *Carribeans*, who landed several times upon the Island, and as to the Improvement they made upon the Island it self, and how five of them made an Attempt upon the main Land, and brought away eleven Men and five Women Prisoners, by which, at my coming, I found about twenty young Children on the Island.

Here I stay'd about 20 Days, left them Supplies of all necessary things, and particularly of Arms, Powder, Shot, Cloaths, Tools, and two Workmen, which I brought from *England* with me, *viz.* a Carpenter and a Smith.

Besides this, I shar'd the Island into Parts with 'em, reserv'd to my self the Property of the whole, but gave them such Parts respectively as they agreed on; and having settled all things with them, and engaged them not to leave the Place, I left them there.

From thence I touch'd at the *Brasils*, from whence I sent a Bark, which I bought there, with more People to the Island, and in it, besides other Supplies, I sent seven Women, being such as I found proper for Service, or for Wives to such as would take them: As to the *English* Men, I promis'd them to send them some Women from *England*, with a good Cargoe of Necessaries, if they would apply themselves to Planting, which I afterwards perform'd. And the Fellows prov'd very honest and diligent after they were master'd, and had their Properties set apart for them. I sent them also from the *Brasils* five Cows, three of them being big with Calf, some Sheep, and some Hogs, which, when I came again, were considerably encreas'd.

But all these things, with an Account how 300 *Caribbees* came and invaded them, and ruin'd their Plantations, and how they fought with that whole Number twice, and were at first defeated, and three of them kill'd; but at last a Storm destroying their Enemies Cannoes, they famish'd or destroy'd almost all the rest, and renew'd and recover'd the Possession of their Plantation, and still liv'd upon the Island.

All these things, with some very surprizing Incidents in some new Adventures of my own, for ten Years more, I may perhaps give a farther Account of hereafter.*

FINIS.

APPENDIX 1

Frontispiece and Preface to
Serious Reflections During the Life and Surprising Adventures of Robinson Crusoe (1720)

Serious Reflections, the second of Defoe's two sequels to *Robinson Crusoe*, was published on 6 August 1720. Whereas *The Farther Adventures of Robinson Crusoe*, published a year beforehand, is a straightforward continuation narrating Crusoe's return to the island and his later travels, *Serious Reflections* is a collection of essays on issues arising from the island experience, written in an unstable combination of the Crusoe persona and Defoe's own voice. In 'Robinson Crusoe's Preface', reprinted below, Defoe teasingly embraces and develops Charles Gildon's allegation, in *The Life and Strange Surprizing Adventures of Mr. D—— De F—, of London, Hosier* (1719), that Crusoe was 'the true Allegorick Image' of the author himself (p. ix). Also reproduced in this Appendix is the frontispiece to the volume, a folding engraved map of the island by the engravers John Clark and John Pine, illustrated with scenes from the original novel. At the centre of the map, Poll is shown crying 'poor Robin Cruso'.

Serious Reflections
DURING THE
LIFE
And Surprising
ADVENTURES
OF
ROBINSON CRUSOE:
WITH HIS
VISION
OF THE
Angelick WORLD.

Written by Himself.

LONDON: Printed for W. Taylor, at the *Ship* and *Black-Swan* in *Pater-noster-Row.* 1720.

Clark & Pine Sc. 1719.

PREFACE

As the Design of every Thing is said to be first in the Intention, and last in the Execution; so I come now to acknowledge to my Reader, That the present Work is not merely the Product of the two first Volumes, but the two first Volumes may rather be called the Product of this: The Fable is always made for the Moral, not the Moral for the Fable.

I have heard, that the envious and ill-disposed Part of the World have rais'd some Objections against the two first Volumes, on Pretence, *for want of a better Reason*; That (*as they say*) the Story is feign'd, that the Names are borrow'd, and that it is all a Romance; that there never were any such Man or Place, or Circumstances in any Mans Life; that it is all form'd and embellish'd by Invention to impose upon the World.

I *Robinson Crusoe* being at this Time in perfect and sound Mind and Memory, Thanks be to God therefore; do hereby declare, their Objection is an Invention scandalous in Design, and false in Fact; and do affirm, that the Story, though Allegorical, is also Historical; and that it is the beautiful Representation of a Life of unexampled Misfortunes, and of a Variety not to be met with in the World, sincerely adapted to, and intended for the common Good of Mankind, and designed at first, *as it is now farther apply'd*, to the most serious Uses possible.

Farther, that there is a Man alive, and well known too, the Actions of whose Life are the just Subject of these Volumes, and to whom all or most Part of the Story most directly alludes, this may be depended upon for Truth, and to this I set my Name.

The famous History of *Don Quixot*, a Work which thousands read with Pleasure, to one that knows the Meaning of it, was an emblematic History of, and a just Satyr upon the Duke *de Medina Sidonia*;* a Person very remarkable at that Time in *Spain*: To those who knew the Original, the Figures were lively and easily discovered themselves, as they are also here, and the Images were just; and therefore, when a malicious, but foolish Writer, in the abundance of his Gall, spoke of *the Quixotism* of *R. Crusoe*,* as he called it, he shewed evidently, that he knew nothing of what he said; and perhaps will be a little startled, when I shall tell him, that what he meant for a Satyr, was the greatest of Panegyricks.

Without letting the Reader into a nearer Explication of the Matter, I proceed to let him know, that the happy Deductions I have employ'd myself to make from all the Circumstances of my Story, will abundantly make him amends for his not having the Emblem explained by the Original; and that when in my Observations and Reflexions of any Kind in this Volume, I mention my Solitudes and Retirements, and allude to the Circumstances of the former Story, all those Parts of the Story are real Facts in my History, whatever borrow'd Lights they may be represented by: Thus the Fright and Fancies which succeeded the Story of the Print of a Man's Foot, and Surprise of the old Goat, and the Thing rolling on my Bed, and my jumping out in a Fright, are all Histories and real Stories; as are likewise the Dream of being taken by Messengers, being arrested by Officers, the Manner of being driven on Shore by the Surge of the Sea, the Ship on Fire, the Description of starving; the Story of my Man *Friday*, and many more most material Passages observ'd here, and on which any religious Reflections are made, are all historical and true in Fact: It is most real, that I had a Parrot, and taught it to call me by my Name, such a Servant a Savage, and afterwards a Christian, and that his Name was called *Friday*, and that he was ravish'd from me by Force, and died in the Hands that took him, which I represent by being killed; this is all litterally true, and should I enter into Discoveries, many alive can testify them: His other Conduct and Assistance to me also have just References in all their Parts to the Helps I had from that faithful Savage, in my real Solitudes and Disasters.

The Story of the Bear in the Tree, and the Fight with the Wolves in the Snow, is likewise Matter of real History; and in a Word, the Adventures of *Robinson Crusoe*, are one whole Scheme of a real Life of eight and twenty Years, spent in the most wandring desolate and afflicting Circumstances that ever Man went through, and in which I have liv'd so long in a Life of Wonders in continu'd Storms, fought with the worst kind of Savages and Man-eaters, by unaccountable surprising Incidents; fed by Miracles greater than that of Ravens, suffered all Manner of Violences and Oppressions, injurious Reproaches, contempt of Men, Attacks of Devils, Corrections from Heaven, and Oppositions on Earth; have had innumerable Ups and Downs in Matters of Fortune, been in Slavery worse than *Turkish*, escaped by an exquisite Management, as that in the Story of *Xury*, and the Boat at *Sallee*, been taken up at Sea in Distress, rais'd again and depress'd again, and that oftner perhaps in one Man's Life than ever was known before; Shipwreck'd often, tho' more by Land than by Sea: In a Word, there's not a Circumstance in the imaginary Story, but has its just Allusion to a real Story, and chimes Part for Part, and Step for Step with the inimitable Life of *Robinson Crusoe*.

In like Manner, when in these Reflections, I speak of the Times and Circumstances of particular Actions done, or Incidents which happened in my Solitude and Island-Life, an impartial Reader will be so just to take it as it is; *viz.* that it is spoken or intended of that Part of the real Story, which the Island-Life is a just Allusion to; and in this the Story is not only illustrated, but the real Part I think most justly approv'd: *For Example*, in the latter Part of this Work called the Vision,* I begin thus, *When I was in my Island Kingdom, I had abundance of strange Notions of my seeing Apparitions*, &c. all these Reflections are just History of a State of forc'd Confinement, which in my real History is represented by a confin'd Retreat in an Island; and 'tis as reasonable to represent one kind of Imprisonment by another, as it is to represent any Thing that really exists, by that which exists not. The Story of my Fright with something on my Bed, was Word for Word a History of what happened, and indeed all those Things received very little Alteration, except what necessarily attends removing the Scene from one Place to another.

My Observations upon Solitude* are the same, and I think I need say no more, than that the same Remark is to be made upon all the References made here, to the Transactions of the former Volumes, and the Reader is desired to allow for it as he goes on.

Besides all this, here is the just and only good End of all Parable or Allegorick History brought to pass, *viz.* for moral and religious Improvement. Here is invincible Patience recommended under the worst of Misery; indefatigable Application and undaunted Resolution under the greatest and most discouraging Circumstances; I say, these are recommended, as the only Way to work through those Miseries, and their Success appears sufficient to support the most dead-hearted Creature in the World.

Had the common Way of Writing a Mans private History been taken, and I had given you the Conduct or Life of a Man you knew, and whose Misfortunes and Infirmities, perhaps you had sometimes unjustly triumph'd over; all I could have said would have yielded no Diversion, and perhaps scarce have obtained a Reading, or at best no Attention; the Teacher, *like a greater*, having no Honour in his own Country.* Facts that are form'd to touch the Mind, must be done a great Way off, and by somebody never heard of: Even the Miracles of the Blessed Saviour of the World suffered Scorn and Contempt, when it was reflected, that they were done by the Carpenter's Son; one whose Family and Original they had a mean Opinion of, and whose Brothers and Sisters were ordinary People like themselves.

There even yet remains a Question, whether the Instruction of these Things will take place, when you are supposing the Scene, which is placed so far off, had its Original so near Home.

But I am far from being anxious about that, seeing I am well assur'd, that if the Obstinacy of our Age should shut their Ears against the just Reflections made in this Volume, upon the Transactions taken Notice of in the former, there will come an Age, when the Minds of Men shall be more flexible, when the Prejudices of their Fathers shall have no Place, and when the Rules of Vertue and Religion justly recommended, shall be more gratefully accepted than they may be now, that our Children may rise up in Judgment against their fathers, and one Generation be edified by the same Teaching, which another Generation had despised.

ROB. CRUSOE.

APPENDIX 2

A Chronology of *Robinson Crusoe*

THE plotting of *Robinson Crusoe* is meticulous, and Defoe robustly contested the efforts of early detractors to search the text for 'Inconsistency in the Relation, and Contradictions in the Fact' (*Farther Adventures*, Preface). Nevertheless, several anomalies complicate the time scheme of the novel, arising not only from Crusoe's own acknowledged uncertainties about his calendar of events but also from probable slips by Defoe and/or the compositors who worked from his manuscript. The following chronology should be read alongside, but at some points diverges from, the detailed analysis of Dewey Ganzel, 'Chronology in *Robinson Crusoe*', *Philological Quarterly*, 40 (1961), 495–512.

1632	30 September: Crusoe born in York.
1651	1 September: Crusoe runs away to sea and is promptly shipwrecked (19 September).
1652	1 September: Crusoe captured by Turkish pirates and enslaved for two years at Salé, on the Barbary Coast.
1654	19 September: Crusoe and Xury escape from Salé. Late November: Crusoe reaches Salvador da Bahia, in northern Brazil.
1655	Crusoe acquires and begins to cultivate his Brazilian plantation.
1658	14 June: one of Crusoe's brothers killed fighting the Spanish at the Battle of the Dunes, near Dunkirk.
1659	1 September: Crusoe leaves Brazil on his disastrous slaving voyage. 30 September: his shipwreck. 1–24 October: he salvages items from the wreck. 26 October–1 November: he establishes a semi-permanent habitation and, from 4 November, a daily routine. *c.*12 November: he begins his journal, making entries retrospectively from the date of his shipwreck.
1660	3 January–14 April: Crusoe builds breastworks around his habitation. 17 April: earthquake on the island. 1 May: wreck shifts. 5 May–15 June: salvage from the wreck continues. 18–29 June: Crusoe suffers a fever, culminating in his apocalyptic

vision. 21 June: Crusoe's first prayer for nearly eight years. 4 July: he begins to read the Bible in earnest. 15–17 July: he conducts a survey and discovers the other side of the island. By 31 July: he constructs a bower on the other side of the island. Early October: his ink begins to run short, and he gives up writing a daily journal. November–December: he unsuccessfully sows barley and rice.

1661   February–April: Crusoe successfully sows and cultivates barley and rice. *c.* July–August: he undertakes a month-long tour of the island on foot, and acquires his parrot, Poll.

1662   Crusoe learns to make earthenware, barley loaves, and rice cakes.

1663   Crusoe's estate in Brazil placed in the hands of receivers. July–December: he builds his first canoe but is unable to launch it.

1668   Crusoe finishes building a smaller canoe and undertakes (6 November) his near-fatal circumnavigation of the island.

1669–70   Crusoe snares and tames goats, for which he builds enclosures.

1674   Crusoe observes a single footprint in the sand late this year or early the next, and lives in great uneasiness for the next two years.

1675   Crusoe's dog dies.

1677   *c.* July–August. Crusoe finds the remains of a cannibal feast on the other side of the island. He continues pensive and sad for two further years, living largely within the confines of his habitations.

1679–80   Crusoe contemplates possible methods, and the rights and wrongs, of killing the cannibals en masse. He discovers his cave or grotto, which serves him as a magazine.

1681   Seventeen European sailors rescued from drowning by Friday's people at about this time. The sailors live among the friendly cannibals. December: Crusoe sees savages on his side of the island.

1683   March: Crusoe dreams that he rescues a savage from the cannibals. 16 May: a Spanish vessel founders in a great storm. Some days later, the corpse of a drowned boy is washed ashore. Crusoe rummages the wreck.

1684   November: Crusoe sees five canoes ashore on his side of the island. He rescues Friday.

1685   Crusoe commences his happiest year on the island. He and Friday construct a sailing vessel. November or December:

twenty-one cannibals land on the island with three captives. Crusoe ambushes them, killing at least seventeen, and frees Friday's father and a Spaniard (one of the sailors rescued by Friday's people some four years earlier).

1686   Crusoe increases the scale of his husbandry. Early October: Crusoe arms the Spaniard and Friday's father, who set out for the mainland. Eight days later an English vessel anchors close inshore. Eight mutineers land three prisoners, including the captain, in a long boat. Crusoe and Friday overthrow the mutineers and restore the captain to his command. 19 December: Crusoe leaves the island.

1687   11 June: Crusoe arrives in England.

1688   April: Crusoe arrives in Lisbon by sea. November: he receives news from trustees in Brazil concerning his plantation. In the following months, he settles his affairs from Lisbon before starting his overland journey to Calais.

1689   Mid-October: Crusoe sets out from Madrid. 15 November: Crusoe sets out from Pampeluna.

1690   14 January: Crusoe lands at Dover. In the following months, he sells his estate in Brazil and completes the settlement of his affairs. He buys a farm in Bedfordshire, marries, and takes two nephews into his care.

1694   With one of the nephews, Crusoe embarks on the voyage recorded in *The Farther Adventures of Robinson Crusoe*.

TEXTUAL NOTES

MORE than 14,000 changes were made in the text of *Robinson Crusoe* in the first eight authorized editions. The overwhelming majority of these variant readings involve matters of spelling, capitalization, internal punctuation, and italics, which, although of negligible individual significance, have a large cumulative effect on the total prose style. Almost 1,500 variants represent substantive word changes. Many of these are substitutions of one word for another; others are additions or deletions of phrases and clauses as well as single words such as articles, verbs, adverbs, adjectives, prepositions, and conjunctions. Few clear patterns of revision emerge in any single edition. The fact that about half of the substantive changes first occur in the seventh and eighth editions, which were printed for a new publisher, is but one of the many indications that even these alterations are the work of printers and reflect the imposition of a new printing house style on Defoe's original text. They are nevertheless interesting as editorial attempts, however misguided, to deal with the difficulties that Defoe's writing presents.

The following list is a limited selection of typical, and the most significant, revisions. References are to page and line; the first reading is that of the first edition, the reading after the bracket that of the edition in which the change first occurred.

6. 1 Fortunes] Fortune *2*. 7. 14 discharg'd] discharging *5*. 7. 29 did not know] did know *4*. 7. 36 and] but *7*. 8. 19 such a Discourse as I] the Discourse I *7*. 8. 30 miserablest] most miserablest *2*; most miserable *7*. 8. 33 continued] contained *4*. 9. 10 Winds] Sea *4*. 9. 27 thought,] thought it did, *7*. 9. 36 and I] and in short I *7*. 10. 22 made drunk] made half drunk *7*. 11. 6 to an Anchor] to Anchor *3*. 12. 10 protesting] protested *4*; protecting *5*. 12. 24 known] seen *8*. 14. 3 the Shore] the Stand *4*; the Strand *5*. 14. 24 rush] push *2*. 15. 10 Ship?] Ship; *2*; Ship! *5*. 16. 27 and who] this Captain *8*. 16. 28 not at all disagreeable] not disagreeable *8*. 17. 31 *Turkish*] *Moorish 7*. 17. 36 Ship] Ships *7*. 18. 21 it] I *3*. 19. 14 a stark calm] a calm *7*. 19. 19 Shoar] Land *7*. 19. 39 happen'd that] happen'd one day, that *7*. 20. 2 Distinction in that Place,] Distinction, *7*. 22. 33 Nations] Nation *2*. 22. 39 me not to] me to *5*. 23. 15 more] worse *7*. 23. 15 one of these mighty] one of the mighty *5*; one mighty *7*. 23. 20 says] said *4*. 23. 26 is impossible] was impossible *5*; was not impossible *7*. 23. 34 Hands] Paws *8*. 24. 34 hope was] Hopes were *4*. 25. 17 I was] we were *7*. 27. 33 upon any of the] upon the *7*. 28. 7 even ready] ready even *5*. 28. 17 on Shore] to the Shore *7*. 30. 37 now] how *5*. 31. 31 Canes] Canoes *7*. 33. 10 represented] presented *7*. 33. 30 might] my *2*; may *3*. 33. 33 bought] brought *7*. 35. 7 Company with] Company one Day with *7*. 35. 16 could not be carried on, because they could not publickly] could not publickly *7*. 35. 27 thus entered and established] thus establish'd *7*. 36. 17 furnished] finish'd *8*. 36. 18–19 the th of   ] 1st of *Sept*. 1659 *4*. 37. 3 whither ever] wherever *7*. 37. 13 *Guinea*] *Guiana 4*.

38. 2 immediately] even *7*. 38. 37 live] escape *8*. 39. 20 as] and *5*. 41. 32 with] like *7*. 42. 23 her up upon] her upon *7*. 43. 15 lose;] lose? *2*; lose. *5*. 43. 29 was not able] was able *4*. 44. 13 nor no] nor any *7*. 45. 7 Creek or River] Creek of the River *7*. 46. 26 I saw] I immediately saw *7*. 46. 29 great] large *7*. 48. 2 Creature] Creator *4*. 48. 38 to be Sails] to me for Sails *7*. 49. 10 also.] also, tho' at several times. *7*. 49. 19 Cove] Cave *2*. 50. 9 making] masting *5*. 50. 17 Sands] Sand *8*. 50. 34 against either] either against *4*. 51. 14 Front] Form *7*. 51. 14 was steep] was as steep *7*. 52. 17 uppermost with] uppermost part of it with *7*. 52. 17 large] larger *4*. 53. 14 in not] into no *8*. 54. 32 were expostulated] were expostulating *3*; were expostulate *4*; were, put in, expostulating *7*. 55. 3 Place where she first] Place she was first *4*; Place where first she *7*. 55. 6 Necessaries] any means *8*. 56. 4 out of] off *6*. 56. 16 may] must *7*. 56. 27 devise] get *7*. 58. 23 over looking out to] over the looking to *4*. 59. 6 me a Door] me Door *7*; my Door *8*. 60. 21 Ship, and got] Ship, I got *5*; Ship, and had got *7*. 60. 28 settled] settlest *5*. 62. 6 Cables] Cable *2*. 62. 15 driven] driving *3*. 63. 5 Sunday) I] Sunday, according to my Reckoning) I *4*. 63. 22 Two] Three *2*. 64. 18 fit] for *3*. 66. 38 joint] join *5*. 67. 13 with] by *8*. 67. 22 out of] upon *7*. 68. 28 could] should *7*; would *8*. 69. 13 crumbling] tumbling *7*. 69. 39 go] get *3*. 70. 8 Hurricane;] Hurricane of Wind: *8*. 73. 24 Plank] Timber *5*. 74. 22 horrid] horrible *5*. 74. 31 Storm off of] Storm of *4*. 77. 8 are] have *5*. 78. 3 for] from *8*.

79. 23 strangely] strongly *8*. 79. 34 had] has *3*; hath *4*. 80. 6 Man] Men *6*. 80. 36 Heat as almost for Suffocation] Heat as the Virtue of it, and I held it almost to Suffocation *7*. 81. 31 But certainly I lost a Day in my Accompt, and never] but in my Account, it was lost, and I never *7*. 85. 18 might] could *4*. 85. 18 be to be had] be had *4*. 87. 7 same] small *7*. 88. 9 differing] different *7*. 88. 32 expos'd, and open for any Thing to come in upon me; and yet] expos'd, and yet *5*. 99. 8 requir'd Speed. However] requir'd a great Deal of Speed; the Creatures daily spoiling my corn. However *7*. 104. 11 neither would] would neither *3*. 106. 35 have foreseen] have easily foreseen *5*. 106. 37 Levers] Leaves *7*. 107. 16 Tree.] Tree? *4*. 107. 22 it, when it was made, into the Water, a] it into the Water, when it was made; a *7*. 107. 25 much] great *5*. 108. 39 this was work'd] this work'd *4*. 110. 35 more upon] up more on *4*. 111. 27 *mine!*] *mine?* *5*. 111. 28 and their] and what their *7*. 112. 36 unhabitable] uninhabited *8*. 113. 1 venemous Creatures or poisonous] venemous or poisonous Creatures *4*. 114. 11 could not abide] could abide *5*; could I abide *7*. 114. 36 shoor] Shoot *6*. 115. 17 but if it] but it *5*. 115. 30 God himself] my Maker *7*. 115. 31 Ejaculations, was] Ejaculation and Petitions, was *7*. 116. 22 that little Journey] that Journey *7*. 117. 13 that, a Shoal] this Shoal *7*; this a Shoal *8*. 119. 30 Current which] Current lay, which *7*. 119. 38 a League] two leagues *7*. 119. 39 wake] West *8*. 122. 14 make] made *2*; have made *3*. 122. 32 yet they were such as were very handy and convenient] yet convenient *7*. 122. 39 Baskets.] Baskets instead of a Granary. *7*. 123. 30 Kids] Kid *4*. 123. 36 I learn'd] I recollected *4*; I had learned *5*. 125. 16 wanted,] wanted them, *7*. 127. 5 some-things] something *4*. 127. 21 nine or ten] nineteen *4*. 127. 39 is] I *5*. 128. 9 nearer] near *2*. 128. 10 from the Shore] from Shore *4*. 131. 4 remember; no, nor could I remember the next Morning,

for never] remember; for never 7. 132. 6 Imagination] Imaginations 7. 132. 33 call'd] call 3. 133. 35 me. In Answer,] me, and in return, 7. 136. 30 continual] continually 5. 136. 34 like my] as 4.

137. 24 Occasion, and began] Occasion, began 4. 138. 12 ten young She-Goats] ten She-Goats 5. 139. 14 more out without] more without 7. 142. 8 Thoughts too much upon] Thoughts upon 7. 142. 19 Things, notwithstanding, I verily believe, had not these Things interven'd] Things interven'd 7. 143. 11 was] were 5. 144. 29 Executioner] Executioners 5. 144. 38 it be] it to be 2. 146. 26 him] God 8. 147. 31 peeping] peering 4. 148. 3 should] would 4. 149. 35 this is by] this by 3. 151. 14 in Rock] in the Rock 2. 153. 1 who] which 2. 153. 5 know] knew 4. 153. 30 stepp'd] stopt 7. 153. 38 me, and made] me, having made 7. 156. 1 I provided for a] I had provided for a 7; I had provided a 8. 157. 28 their] the 4. 158. 2 stave] starve 4; stay 7. 159. 8 Fingers] Finger 4. 160. 29 little rising bit of Ground] little bit of rising Ground 7; little bit of rising Ground 8. 163. 5 Bars] Bags 4. 163. 10 of fine glaz'd] of glaz'd 7. 164. 17 has] hath 2. 164. 33 those whose] whose whole 4. 170. 33 saw plainly] knew 7. 170. 38 Persons] Pursuers 7. 171. 7 irresistibly] irresistible 4. 171. 10 fetches] fetch'd 3. 171. 24 pursu'd with him] pursu'd him 2. 172. 14 Twenty Five] five and twenty 7. 173. 21 strong] long 5. 176. 14 smaller] small 7. 178. 15 pointed] pointing 2. 180. 6 his] this 4. 181. 11 same] said 2. 181. 27 Mouth, or the Gulph of which] Mouth, of which 7. 182. 29 *do say*] *said* 2. 185. 9 good] great 8. 186. 18 in] to 2. 186. 20 Questionings] Questions 2. 187. 21 Country] Countries 7. 188. 25 upon] on 2. 191. 5 hastily, comes and gives] hastily, and gives 2. 192. 27 had to] us'd in 7. 193. 19 of the] of my 7. 194. 13 back] out 4. 194. 19 it was] there were 7. 197. 18 Feet, but did not immediately know] Feet, immediately, but did not know 7.

198. 7 see] saw 5. 198. 32 other two fell] other fell 4. 202. 24 strong] young 7. 203. 27 for] from 4. 203. 29 kill'd, when] kill'd: Then 7. 204. 32 Savages never] Savages of that Part never 7. 204. 39 me] we 4. 207. 1 we] he 5. 208. 8 Thought] Thoughts 4. 208. 17 above] about 5. 209. 9 Commands] Command 5. 209. 25 see] let 8. 212. 25 really] ready 3. 213. 27 fierce; I] fierce; and I 4. 213. 28 Sword by my Side,] Sword, 8. 214. 17 Applications] Application 3. 216. 35 only that I] only I 2. 220. 20 haling] hailing 3; halling 4; hauling 5. 220. 39 know,] know there, 2. 222. 38 hollow'd] follow'd 5. 223. 36 not able] not being able 7. 224. 5 and] or 5. 224. 13 given] give 2. 226. 8 who he was] who was 5; whom he was 7. 226. 27 secure] security 3. 227. 6 so just] such 5. 227. 23 and] but 7. 230. 24 Master] Masters 2. 231. 22 says] said 8. 233. 36 this, the Boat was order'd on] this, I went with the Boat on 8. 234. 4 and my Parrot] and one of my Parrots 5. 234. 17 was as perfect a Stranger] was a perfect Stranger 8. 235. 1 altogether] all together 2. 235. 20 but I soon brought him to my Remembrance, and as soon brought my] but I soon brought my 7. 236. 13 amounted] amounting 4. 240. 1 5000 *l.*] 50,000 *l.* 8. 242. 21 me he had] me had 4. 242. 38 *Algerine*] *Algerines* 2. 243. 15 two more *English* Merchants] two who were *English* and Merchants 7. 244. 9 Toes.] Toes, was very strange. 7. 244. 17 is] in 5. 244. 22 in the Memory of Man.] in many Years). 7. 245. 15 his] the 2. 246. 26 clearly] plainly 7. 247. 7 steadily] stedfastly 5. 247. 9 of a Stick]

or the Stick *5*; of Stick *7*. 248. 8 would have put] would put *5*. 248. 39 Tree] Bough *4*. 249. 16 says] said *5*.

249. 17 *me go come*] *me come 4*. 252. 19 But] For *5*. 254. 5 Village, in the Night, and] Village, and *4*. 255. 8 severely] severe *2*. 255. 24 unless] except *7*. 256. 6 328000] 32800 *7*. 257. 31 afterwards perform'd. And the] afterwards could not perform: The *7*. 257. 39 three] one *7*.

EXPLANATORY NOTES

THESE Explanatory Notes should be read in conjunction with the Textual Notes, which illustrate variant readings in early editions of *Robinson Crusoe*, and the Glossary, which defines nautical terms and other obsolete or unusual words and phrases used in the text. Variants and definitions are dealt with in the notes below only where confusion might otherwise arise or where supplementary explanation is needed.

3 *The Wonders of this Man's Life . . . extant*: heralding an insistent theme in *Robinson Crusoe* and its two sequels. Cf. the 'Croud of Wonders' to which Crusoe attributes his sustenance (112. 32–3); 'my Story is a whole Collection of Wonders' (217. 9–10); the 'Chain of Wonders' leading to his rescue (230. 12). Defoe habitually describes his own life in similar terms, as in the *Review* for 1711: 'I have gone through a Life of Wonders, and am the Subject of a vast Variety of Providences' (Vol. 8, Preface).

just History of Fact: a claim teasingly modified in Defoe's *Serious Reflections During the Life and Surprising Adventures of Robinson Crusoe* (1720), with its invitation to read the history as allegory: 'there's not a Circumstance in the imaginary Story, but has its just Allusion to a real Story, and chimes Part for Part, and Step for Step with the inimitable Life of *Robinson Crusoe*' (Preface; see also n. to 83. 12–13).

dispatch'd: altered to 'disputed' in the third and later editions, but the original reading makes sense. The editor suggests that since stories like Crusoe's are rapidly dispatched in the sense of being consumed and disposed of, the test of factual authenticity need not be strictly applied.

5 *City of York*: in electing to retire here, Crusoe's father may have been attracted by the antiquity and gentility of York, qualities stressed by Defoe when describing the city in *A Tour thro' the Whole Island of Great Britain* (1724–6). See the edition by G. D. H. Cole, 2 vols. (London: Peter Davies, 1927), ii. 636–42.

Foreigner of Bremen: this detail seems to identify Crusoe's father as a Protestant refugee from Catholic aggression during the Thirty Years War (1618–48). The word 'Foreigner' resonates with the loaded language of Defoe's *The True-Born Englishman* (1701), a poem that contests John Tutchin's *The Foreigners* (1700), a xenophobic attack on William III, by satirically debunking the idea of English racial purity. Bremen was an independent city-state and member of the Hanseatic League, strategically situated at the mouth of the River Elbe, the corridor for trade between Germany, England, and Holland. Defoe stresses the importance of Bremen and the need for its protection in the *Review* for 24 September 1709 (Vol. 6, No. 74, 296).

Hull: Defoe elsewhere describes the seaport of Hull, on the Humber estuary, as a place notable for 'Trade to all Parts of the known World' (*Tour*, ii. 652).

Kreutznaer . . . Crusoe: the German name indicates both religious and roving aspects of Crusoe's nature: either 'nearer the cross' or 'to cruise, to journey' (Robert Ayers, '*Robinson Crusoe*: Allusive Allegorick History', *PMLA* 82 (1967), 399–407). Elsewhere, Defoe plays on the etymological connection with '*Cruisado*' (*Serious Reflections*, 267), meaning 'crusade'. In its anglicized form, the name also recalls Defoe's schoolfellow at Charles Morton's Dissenting Academy at Newington Green, Timothy Cruso (1657–97), a Presbyterian minister and author of religious conduct literature.

Coll. Lockhart . . . Spaniards: Sir William Lockhart (1621–75), Scots soldier and diplomat, served in the Royalist army before switching allegiance to Cromwell in 1652. He was ambassador in Paris between 1656 and 1658, charged to promote England's alliance with France against Spain, and was in command of allied troops besieging Dunkirk when the Spanish defenders capitulated on 15 June 1658. Crusoe's brother is presumably a casualty of the pitched battle preceding this surrender, known as the Battle of the Dunes. Dunkirk was sold to France by Charles II on 17 October 1662.

6 *the wise Man . . . Poverty or Riches*: a favourite text with Defoe (cf. *Moll Flanders*, ed. G. A. Starr (Oxford: Oxford World's Classics, 1981), 191 and n.), the wise man being Solomon. 'Remove far from me vanity and lies: give me neither poverty nor riches; feed me with food convenient for me: | Lest I be full, and deny thee, and say, Who is the Lord? or lest I be poor, and steal, and take the name of my God in vain' (Proverbs 30: 8–9).

7 *my elder Brother . . . was kill'd*: subsequent indications place this conversation in 1650, eighteen years after Crusoe's birth in 1632 and a year before his departure in 1651; the bereavement mentioned at this point does not occur, however, until 1658 (see above, 5. 10–13 and n.). Either Crusoe's memory deceives him, or Defoe's own grasp of the time scheme is insecure. For other (sometimes self-conscious) slippages in the novel's chronology, see 81. 25–31, 113. 30–1, 156. 11, and 209. 30–4. An embittered rival, Charles Gildon, was quick to point out such inconsistencies in *The Life and Strange Surprizing Adventures of Mr. D—— De F—, of London, Hosier* (1719).

otherwise?: the edition of *Robinson Crusoe* on which the present text is based (ed. J. Donald Crowley (London: Oxford University Press, 1972)) follows the second and subsequent editions by emending the first-edition reading, 'otherwise;'. Similar emendations elsewhere are based by Crowley 'on the probability that the printers mistook Defoe's manuscript question marks and semicolons for each other' (Crowley, 310). Cf. 79. 2, originally 'in Reach of my Bed?'; see also, on the haphazard nature of press correction in the first edition, Henry Hutchins, *Robinson Crusoe and Its Printing, 1719–1731* (New York: Columbia University Press, 1925), 51.

9 *first of September 1651*: corrected from 1661 on the first edition errata page and in the second and subsequent editions. For the anniversary of this date and its significance, see below, 36. 18–20.

   the Wind began to blow, and the Waves to rise: originally 'and the Winds to rise'; altered to 'and the Sea to rise' in the fourth and later editions. Crowley retains 'Winds' as a possible unconscious repetition in Defoe's manuscript (which does not survive) rather than a compositor's error. But the likelihood is that Defoe wrote 'Waves', paraphrasing Psalms 107: 25 (see note below) and mirroring similar alliterative sequences in his writing elsewhere. Cf. 'the fierceness of the Wind, the dreadful height of the Waves' (*Roxana*, ed. John Mullan (Oxford: Oxford World's Classics, 1996), 123); 'many Lives were lost by the common accidents of Wind and Waves' (*A General History of Discoveries and Improvements* (1725–6), 56).

   All this while . . . many Vows and Resolutions: Crusoe's experience evolves, directly or indirectly, from Psalms 107: 23–8, a text regularly cited in the period on the emblematic spiritual status of the mariner before God: 'They that go down to the sea in ships, that do business in great waters: | These see the works of the Lord, and his wonders in the deep. | For he commandeth, and raiseth the stormy wind, which lifteth up the waves thereof. | They mount up to the heaven, they go down again to the depths, their soul is melted because of trouble. | They reel to and fro, and stagger like a drunken man, and are at their wit's end. | Then they cry unto the Lord in their trouble, and he bringeth them out of their distresses.' At this point, a somewhat ironic relationship to this text is implied by the inconstant and self-serving nature of Crusoe's vows.

   repenting Prodigal: alluding to the parable of the Prodigal Son (Luke 15: 11–32).

10 *Providence*: divine superintendence on earth. Crusoe later describes how Providence may be intuited (148. 10–149. 3); elsewhere he defines it as 'that Operation of the Power, Wisdom, Justice, and Goodness of God, by which he influences, governs, and directs, not only the Means, but the Events of all things, which concern us in this World' (*Serious Reflections*, 208).

11 *By Noon the Sea . . . to the better End*: mounting seas have caused the tension exerted by the anchor cable to pull the ship's head beneath the waves, resulting in her taking on board water. Afraid that the ship is dragging her anchor, the master orders the sheet anchor (the largest on board, used only in emergencies) to be let go. The vessel now rides with two anchors ahead, their cables paid out to their utmost length to reduce the risk of dragging.

12 *cut their Masts by the Board*: cut down their masts to reduce the ship's

surface area above the waterline, thereby lessening the effects of the wind.

13 *some light Colliers . . . were oblig'd to slip*: in their haste to put to sea, the colliers (coal barges) are forced to abandon their anchors by fully letting the cables go. If time permitted, buoys would be attached to the cables to facilitate later recovery.

Winterton Ness: sandy headland near the village of Winterton, about 10 miles (16 km) north from Great Yarmouth on the Norfolk coast. The effects on this area of the great hurricane that struck England on 26 and 27 November 1703 are recorded in Defoe's compilation of 1704, *The Storm* (ed. Richard Hamblyn (London: Penguin, 2005), 176–9); see also the *Tour*, which describes this stretch of coastline as 'particularly Famous for being one of the most dangerous and most fatal to the Sailors in all *England*, I may say in all *Britain*' (*Tour*, i. 69).

14 *the Land broke off . . . the Violence of the Wind*: the shoreline acts as a baffle to reduce the effects of the wind; cf. 39. 12 and n.

our Blessed Saviour's Parable: Luke 15: 11–32.

15 *Jonah in the Ship of Tarshish*: 'But Jonah rose up to flee unto Tarshish from the presence of the Lord, and went down to Joppa; and he found a ship going to Tarshish . . .' (Jonah 1: 3). As a rebel against God who experiences both punishment and deliverance at sea, Jonah is a prominent exemplar in devotional writing of the period aimed at mariners, and an implicit point of reference throughout the novel.

16 *Voyage to Guinea*: euphemism for a slaving voyage.

17 *competent Knowledge of . . . the Rules of Navigation*: Crusoe would have learned to calculate latitude (progress north–south) by measuring the angle of the sun above the horizon at noon (the sun's meridian altitude). He would then have used mathematical tables giving the sun's daily changing angle relative to the Equator (its declination) throughout the year. No generally reliable method of determining longitude (progress east–west) at sea existed until the later eighteenth century, and Crusoe would have learned the process known as 'dead reckoning'. After departure from a fixed point, the vessel's course and speed, weather conditions, sea state, currents, and factors impinging upon sailing performance would be reconciled to estimate progress daily. Crusoe glances at this process when describing his intended crossing to Africa (see 36. 31–8 and n.).

take an Observation: obtain a measurement of the sun's meridian altitude in order to calculate latitude. The instrument used would probably have been a quadrant or a cross-staff: cf. 24. 29–31, 36. 36–7, 37. 10–12, 55. 29.

L. 5. 9 Ounces: five pounds and nine ounces (approximately 2.5 kg).

the Line: the Equator, a notional line drawn on the earth's surface separating the northern and southern hemispheres.

17 *Turkish Rover of Sallee*: Turkish vessel from the port of Salé, near Rabat, on Morocco's Atlantic coast. The interception of Crusoe's vessel is a manifestation of the *corso*, a system of slave-raiding operating out of the North African Regencies or Barbary States, nominal dependencies of the Ottoman Empire, which yielded handsome profits from subsequent ransoms and sales. In 1632 (the year of Crusoe's birth) Charles I's navy attacked the port of Salé, effecting the release of many European hostages, but the threat still persisted a century later, when Defoe included in *A Plan of the English Commerce* (1728) 'a *Proposal* for rooting out those Nests of Pyrates and Rovers, the Turks or Moors of *Tunis*, *Tripoli*, *Algier*, and *Sallee*, who have for so many Ages infested the *Mediterranean* Seas, and the Coasts of *Spain* and *Portugal*, to the infinite Loss and Discouragement of all the trading Nations of *Europe*' (312). See G. A. Starr, 'Escape from Barbary: A Seventeenth Century Genre', *Huntington Library Quarterly*, 29 (1965), 35–52; Joe Snader, *Caught between Worlds: British Captivity Narratives in Fact and Fiction* (Lexington: University Press of Kentucky, 2000), 62–93; Linda Colley, *Captives: Britain, Empire, and the World, 1600–1850* (London: Pimlico, 2003), 23–134.

    bringing to . . . just athwart our Quarter: the pirate ship comes up into wind either too early or too late, losing way and exposing herself to guns positioned in the stern of Crusoe's ship.

18 *laying us on Board*: drawing alongside our ship.

19 *Maresco*: probably a misprint for 'Moresco', meaning a Moor from Spain; not corrected in any of the first eight authorized editions of *Robinson Crusoe*.

    hale home the Main-sheet: secure the mainsail.

    Room for him to lye, with a Slave or two: one of several sexual innuendoes (cf. 18. 16–17) that helps to explain Crusoe's determination to abscond. Allegations of homosexual rape were routinely made by returning Barbary captives, and were echoed in fiction: Colley (*Captives*, 129) compares Crusoe's hint with a more explicit passage in William Chetwood's *The Voyages and Adventures of Captain Robert Boyle* (1726), 34. For other examples, see Chetwood's *The Voyages, Travels and Adventures of William Owen Gwin Vaughan*, 2 vols. (1736), where an enslaved sailor, propositioned by his Tunisian master, 'would rather suffer Death, than comply with his infamous Desires' (ii. 129); also Penelope Aubin's *The Noble Slaves* (1722), where the hero's captor in Tunis 'had an ill Design upon me, and liked me for a use the *Mahometans* often keep young Men for' (139–40).

20 *for that*: because.

21 *he rise*: altered to 'rose' in the sixth edition, but a legitimate past tense in eighteenth-century usage; cf. 80. 10.

22 *the Straits-mouth*: the Strait of Gibraltar, the narrow passage connecting the Mediterranean Sea with the Atlantic Ocean and separating Spain from North Africa.

the truly Barbarian Coast: standard wordplay in the period, normally used to conflate the geographical term 'Barbary' (from 'Berbers' or indigenous North Africans) with 'barbarian' in the basic sense of uncivilized or brutish; Crusoe reworks it here to distinguish between the northern and tropical coasts of Africa.

devour'd by . . . Savages of humane kind: 'humane', the standard spelling throughout the first edition, is altered to 'human' in the second and subsequent editions. This is the first instance of Crusoe's paranoia concerning cannibals, foreshadowing a major theme of the novel: cf. 138. 17–28, 140. 33–141. 9. For context see Dianne Armstrong, 'The Myth of Cronus: Cannibal and Sign in *Robinson Crusoe*', *Eighteenth-Century Fiction*, 4.3 (1992), 207–20; Claude Rawson, *God, Gulliver, and Genocide: Barbarism and the European Imagination, 1492–1945* (Oxford: Oxford University Press, 2001), 17–91.

25 *Pico of Teneriffe*: Pico de Teide, the highest peak on the Spanish-ruled islands, 12,260 ft (3,715 m) (28° 3′ N 16° 6′ W).

almost Musquet-bore: the calibre of a musket in the period was between 10 and 20 bore, i.e. of a diameter to accommodate round lead balls weighing between one-tenth and one-twentieth of a pound. The range of a musket was about 240 yards (220 m).

26 *coming close to the Creature . . . dispatch'd him quite*: cf. 249. 31–3, where Friday exactly repeats Xury's action, reinforcing an implied connection between the two subaltern figures.

27 *lay by*: bows pointing into the wind, stationary except for movement caused by current.

bad Xury load both the other: asked Xury to load both the other guns.

29 *kept a large offing*: stayed well to seaward, away from the shore.

Cape de Verd . . . Cape de Verd Islands: the features Crusoe claims to see are in fact not intervisible, the distance between the cape and the islands (a Portuguese colony from the fifteenth century) being approximately 360 miles (600 km).

crowded to the utmost: set as much sail as possible to increase speed.

shortned Sail: reduced sail to decrease speed.

made a Waft of it: a waft was a signal, usually displayed astern, made by hoisting the ensign furled up in a long roll. It was commonly used to summon boats from the shore to return to their ship, or as a signal for a pilot to come aboard.

30 *ask'd me what I would have for it?*: 'The early editions very often print a question mark after an indirect question, and such pointing has been allowed to stand. It reflects Defoe's management of the narrative point of view, which continually shifts back and forth between direct and indirect statement and seems often to be a combination of both modes' (Crowley, 311).

30 *Pieces of Eight*: the Spanish silver dollar (*peso, piastre*, or *pieza de ocho reales*), first minted in 1497 and worth eight *reales*. Pieces of eight weighed between 27 and 30 grams, with an equivalent value in England of about 4*s*. 2*d*. Their silver content and intrinsic value remained remarkably unchanged in 400 years of issue. The coins were produced in large quantities in Spanish America at a time when English colonists were forbidden to mint their own coinage; thus the 'silver dollar' became the most common trade coin throughout the Americas.

very loath to sell the poor Boy's Liberty: Crusoe's bad conscience reflects the ambivalence about slavery of Defoe himself, who tends to deplore the practice in his religious writings and defend it when writing on trade. See Patrick J. Keane, 'Slavery and the Slave Trade: Crusoe as Defoe's Representative', in Roger D. Lund (ed.), *Critical Essays on Daniel Defoe* (New York: G. K. Hall, 1997), 97–120.

Todos los Santos, or All-Saints Bay: an Atlantic inlet (24 × 18 miles/ 40 × 30 km) in Northern Brazil. The Portuguese captain's destination is Salvador da Bahia (13° S 38° W), which lies at the entrance to the bay. Over half the Africans brought to the New World were landed in Brazil, many of them at Salvador.

32 *Sterl.*: sterling, originally the name given to a medieval English silver penny; a pound weight of sterlings became a unit of currency worth 240 pence. Historical monetary values are notoriously difficult to convert, but a stock of £200 is not insignificant. Elsewhere Defoe recommends 'a hundred pounds in goods' as the appropriate stock in trade of an ambitious young shopkeeper, adding that a tradesman clearing £500 a year is 'in a flourishing trade' and 'would certainly be a rich man, and get a good estate'. £200 a year would place its owner within the income range of 'the lower gentry' (*The Complete English Tradesman*, 2 vols. (1725–7), i. 318; i. 358; i. 375).

34 *100 Wt*: hundredweight, a standard English mercantile weight equal to four quarters, eight stone, or 112 pounds (50.5 kg).

St. Salvadore: Salvador da Bahia, the colonial capital of Brazil until 1762, was the centre of a sugar-producing area and a major slave port.

Guinea Grains: the seed capsules of *Aframomum melegueta*, a herbaceous perennial of the ginger family (*Zingiberaceae*), a variety of cardamom. Also known as 'Grains of Paradise', the seeds have medicinal properties and are used as spice.

35 *Assiento's*: since Spain had no foothold on the slave coasts, contracts were issued to foreign nations, companies, and individuals to furnish her dominions in the New World with African slaves. After the Portuguese *asiento de negros* ended in 1640, the slave trade to Spanish America became almost wholly contraband until 1702, when a monopoly was issued to the French Guinea Company. Crusoe is wrong to suggest that a contract was in force in 1659, though a formal *asiento* was briefly held by Genoese merchants from 1662. After the Treaty of Utrecht (1713), the

asiento was transferred to the South Sea Company (of Britain), but was relinquished in 1750 after several wartime suspensions, the first in 1718.

engross'd in the Publick . . . excessive dear: since the authorities controlled the monopoly on slaves, they were able to inflate prices accordingly.

36 *an evil Hour, the 1st of Sept. 1659*: blank spaces appear at this point ('the   th of   ') in the first three editions of *Robinson Crusoe*; the day, month, and year were first specified in the fourth edition, using the form reproduced here and matching the date of Crusoe's departure from Hull (see above, 9. 6–7). Crusoe puts to sea in the middle of the hurricane season, which lasts from August to October. The wording associates his embarkation, on the anniversary of his first disobedience towards his father, with the 'evil hour' of the original human sin against God in Milton's *Paradise Lost* (ix. 780; ix. 1067). For comparable 'evil hours' in Defoe's fiction, see *Captain Singleton*, ed. Shiv K. Kumar, introd. Penelope Wilson (Oxford: Oxford World's Classics, 1990), 138; also *Roxana*, 234.

120 Tun Burthen: tunnage or tonnage is the traditional measure of the carrying capacity or volume of a vessel, representing the number of tuns (casks of wine or beer holding approximately 200 gallons / 880 litres) capable of being stowed in her hold. The only system of ships' tonnage expressing the weight of the vessel is displacement, whereby the weight of water displaced by the underwater body of the ship equals the weight of the ship herself; this measurement was not widely used until the nineteenth century.

standing away to the Northward . . . till we came the Height of Cape St. Augustino: Crusoe indicates that his vessel follows the usual transatlantic route, which entails altering course somewhere between ten and twelve degrees of southern latitude. However, the height or latitude of Cape St Augustino, shown on many contemporary maps, including the world map in the fourth edition of *Robinson Crusoe*, as the easternmost tip of mainland Brazil, is eight degrees south (08° 20′ S 34° 55′ W). This detail indicates the caution of Crusoe's captain. He delays his wheel-over in order to fix his position precisely, availing himself of the last possible opportunity to do so before commencing his blue water passage. This prudence is consistent with the captain's reaction to the storm that follows, when he proposes 'going directly back to the Coast of *Brasil*' (37. 17).

Fernand de Noronha: Fernando de Noronha (04° S 32° W), a tropical archipelago first described by Amerigo Vespucci, lies about 220 miles (350 km) off the Brazilian coast, midway between South America and Africa. The Dutch possessed it (and Brazil) between 1635 and 1654, although both were under Portuguese control by the time Crusoe sets up as a planter.

37 *made an Observation as well as he could*: the heaving deck would make it difficult to hold the horizon still and thus measure the angle of the sun with accuracy.

37 *22 Degrees of Longitude difference West from Cape St. Augustino . . . upon the Coast of Guiana*: corrected in the fourth and subsequent editions from '. . . upon the Coast of Guinea', which would have placed the ship in the vicinity of 11° 00′ N 56° 55′ W, approximately 300 miles (480 km) east of Trinidad. Cf. 181. 36–7, which in all editions correctly reads 'from the Mouth of the River *Oroonooko* to *Guiana*'.

12 Deg. 18 Min: this places Crusoe some distance east of Grenada.

39 *Breach of the Sea*: breaking waves, crashing surf.

under the Lee of the Land: an area of water close to shore, offering shelter from the prevailing wind.

41 *turn'd off*: turned off the ladder, i.e. hanged. The figure of the malefactor reprieved at the last minute, used to highlight an incident where Crusoe brushes with death, returns at 119. 21–2.

For sudden Joys, like Griefs, confound at first: the line is from a controversial broadside of 1672 in which Robert Wild (1615/16–1679), nonconformist minister and satirical poet, congratulates Charles II on the extension of religious liberties to Dissenters proposed in the Declaration of Indulgence, but also provocatively denigrates the Anglican clergy. For full discussion of this poem (which Crusoe, strictly speaking, could not have seen), see Geoffrey Sill, 'The Source of Robinson Crusoe's "Sudden Joys" ', *Notes and Queries*, 45.1 (1998), 67–8. Originally entitled *Dr. Wild's Humble Thanks for His Majesties Gracious Declaration for Liberty of Conscience*, it was reprinted in *A Letter from Dr. Robert Wild . . . Together with His Poetica Licentia* (1709): 'Suspect us not (*Great Sir*) nor think the worst; | For sudden *Joys*, like *Griefs*, confound at first' (13). Defoe quotes the same memorable line (as 'that Saying of the Ancients') in *A Continuation of Letters Written by a Turkish Spy at Paris* (1718), 95, and again in *A New Family Instructor* (1727), 236. Cf. also 239. 32 below (Crusoe's 'sudden Surprize of Joy'), the verse introduction to *Jure Divino* (1706), p. v ('*Joy* strikes him dumb, and then *his Grief* confounds'), and the quaker's 'sudden Joy' in *Roxana*, 253.

43 *pull'd off my Clothes . . . fill'd my Pockets with Bisket*: 'I shall not take Notice of his striping himself to swim on Board, and then filling his Pockets with Bisket, because that is already taken Notice of in Publick' (Gildon, *Life and Strange Surprizing Adventures of Mr. D—— De F—*, 15). Even in the first edition, however, Defoe fixes this celebrated blunder by going on to specify that Crusoe has not pulled off *all* his clothes (44. 16–18).

46 *my Raft drew about a Foot of Water*: i.e. a foot is the minimum depth required to float the raft.

47 *hoise*: nautical term (as in 'to hoise sail') meaning to raise aloft by means of ropes or pulley and tackle; altered to 'hoist' in the fourth and later editions.

48 *an End*: on end.

49 *fain to dip for it*: obliged to dive under water to retrieve it.

thirteen Days on Shore . . . eleven Times on Board the Ship: in other words, a total of twenty-four days, thirteen spent entirely on land plus eleven of salvaging work. As Crusoe's journal specifies (61. 33–4), the wreck breaks up on 25 October following the original shipwreck of 30 September.

50 *Money, O Drug! . . . no Manner of use for thee*: Crusoe's musings may reflect contemporary debate about the intrinsic value of gold and silver and the practicality of substituting paper money for bullion, but are specific to his situation on the island. Elsewhere in Defoe, 'the drug money' (a phrase perhaps deriving from Ben Jonson, *The Alchemist* (1610), IV. i. 53) activates the circulating lifeblood of trade. As he writes in *The Complete English Tradesman*, 'The Country sends up their Corn, their Malt, their Cattle, their Fowls, their Coals, their Fish all to *London*; and *London* sends back Spice, Sugar, Wine, Druggs, Cotton, Linen, Tobacco, and all foreign necessaries to the Country; and above all the rest that useful drug call'd *Money*' (II. ii. 141).

52 *like a Spurr to a Post*: Crusoe lays the shorter stakes diagonally behind the uprights to brace them.

that so: so that.

53 *had the Powder took fire, I had never known who had hurt me*: had the gunpowder exploded, Crusoe would have been killed instantly.

Goats in the Island: European sailors sometimes left goats and pigs on remote islands to breed as a source of food on future visits. An example cited by William Dampier and others is Juan Fernández, the Spanish mariner who in 1563 discovered the archipelago that bears his name (30–4° S 80° W; see Dampier, *A New Voyage round the World*, 5th edn. (1703), 88). Goats imported by Fernández supported the Scottish sailor Alexander Selkirk throughout his years of isolation on Más a Tierra, part of the archipelago, in 1704–9.

55 *30th. of Sept. . . . 9 Degrees 22 Minutes North of the Line*: Crusoe confirms the date of his shipwreck and the latitudinal position of the island, which lies approximately 50 miles south-east of Trinidad. The ecliptic of the sun (its arc through the sky) intersects with a projection of the Equator (the celestial equator) on two occasions annually: the Vernal (Spring) Equinox and the Autumnal Equinox. Crusoe refers to the latter, which in the Julian calendar would have occurred on or about 11 September 1659, after which the sun passes from its northern into its southern declination. (The Gregorian calendar, in which the equinoxes fall on or about 20 March and 22 September, did not take effect in Britain until 1752.) Crusoe's remark that the sun 'was almost just over my Head' seems to confirm his latitudinal position (09° 22′ N), and we infer that it is early autumn on the island. For Crusoe's observations elsewhere in relation to the equinoxes, cf. 91. 1–4, 96. 4, 115. 9–10, 127. 19–22.

56 *not all*: not at all.

60 *my Journal . . . (tho' in it will be told all these Particulars over again)*:
    outweighing the disadvantage of factual repetition (and occasional incon-
    sistency) is the significance of the journal as a personal and exemplary
    spiritual exercise. John Ryther (1631/5?–81), a Dissenting minister born
    in York and known to his London congregation as the 'seaman's
    preacher', is typical in urging sailors to husband their immortal souls by
    keeping 'an exact Journal': 'by this God may have glory; you may have
    past experiences to feed your faith, and hope upon the future' (Ryther, *A
    Plat for Mariners; or, the Seaman's Preacher* (1675), sig. a3, quoted by
    J. Paul Hunter, *The Reluctant Pilgrim: Defoe's Emblematic Method and
    the Quest for Form in Robinson Crusoe* (Baltimore: Johns Hopkins Press,
    1966), 83–4).

62 *two or three Seals*: the Caribbean Monk Seal (*Monachus tropicalis*), once
    native to the waters around Crusoe's island, was last sighted in 1952.
    Descriptions of seals are ubiquitous in contemporary voyage narratives,
    which probably accounts for their inclusion here.

63 *Iron Tree: Caesalpinia ferrea*, a Brazilian hardwood tree.

66 *as may be observ'd hereafter upon a very remarkable Occasion*: for the
    episode foreshadowed here, see 213. 15–18 and ff.

67 *or had*: nor had I.

68 *I lost all that I sow'd . . . Of which in its Place*: 90. 1–12.

69 *thought nothing*: had no idea.

    Earthquake . . . at about eight Minutes Distance: Crusoe's specificity
    reflects the efforts made to document unusual natural phenomena in
    many contemporary voyage narratives, a practice encouraged by Royal
    Society scientists since the 1660s. On the relationship between Defoe's
    fiction and the 'Directions to Sea-men' prepared for Restoration voyagers
    by the Royal Society, see Ilse Vickers, *Defoe and the New Sciences*
    (Cambridge: Cambridge University Press, 1996), 99–138.

74 *Tortoise or Turtle*: Defoe uses these terms interchangeably (cf. 93. 37 and
    194. 11). Seven species of sea turtle are found near the specified location
    of Crusoe's island, four of which (Loggerhead, Green, Hawksbill,
    Leatherback) nest in the region from April to October. His claim to have
    found sixty eggs is plausible. Cf. the report of Henry Pitman, stranded
    on the island of Tortuga off the Venezuelan coast in 1687: 'each of these
    Tortoises lay about 140 Eggs at one time in almost an hours space, which
    are full as large as Hens Eggs' (*A Relation of the Great Sufferings and
    Strange Adventures of Henry Pitman* (1689), 23).

76 *Conscience of Evil*: inward knowledge or consciousness of evil.

    on the desperate Expedition . . . I was meerly thoughtless of a God: the
    passage in question, from Crusoe's escape from Salé (22. 8) to his rescue
    by the Portuguese captain (29. 39), matches this admission by entirely
    avoiding religious language and themes. Cf. 112. 8–16.

78 *That if I did take this foolish Step . . . my Recovery*: cf. 7. 24–7.

80 *What Use to make of the Tobacco*: Crusoe takes his tobacco cure by means of several preparations, a remedy that may derive from an abstract of a medical text edited by Jean Cornand de la Crose in *The History of Learning: or, An Abstract of Several Books* (1691). La Crose focuses on the traditional Galenic theories of Baron Theodore Turquet du Mayerne (1573–1655), which emphasize the importance of balancing the humours by evacuation (as seems to happen in Crusoe's case) but were discredited by the time of *Robinson Crusoe*. See Geoffrey M. Sill, 'A Source for Crusoe's Tobacco Cure', *English Language Notes*, 32.4 (1995), 46–8.

81 *Call on me . . . glorify me*: 'And call upon me in the day of trouble: I will deliver thee, and thou shalt glorify me' (Psalms 50: 15; invoked again below, 133. 27–8). Here Defoe supplies both natural and supernatural explanations for Crusoe's deliverance, which is not definitively attributed to either the tobacco or the Bible.

Can God Spread a Table in the Wilderness?: 'Can God furnish a table in the wilderness?' (Psalms 78: 19).

crossing and re-crossing the Line: referring to the 'circumnavigator's paradox', by which voyagers lose or gain a calendar day on crossing the meridian line in the Pacific that was later to be regularized as the International Date Line (180° W & E). The effect is noted by voyage writers such as Dampier, who observes during his circumnavigation that 'in the *East Indies*, we found them reckoning a Day before us, both Natives and *Europeans*' (*New Voyage round the World*, 375–6). Crusoe is nowhere near the date line, however, and he (or more likely Defoe) confuses it with the Equator, which entails no time difference when crossed.

brand Goose: Brent goose (*Branta bernicla*), the smallest species of wild goose, which visits the British Isles in winter. The southernmost extent of its range is in the southern United States, well to the north of Crusoe's island.

82 *in Barr of*: so as to prevent.

but: that, before.

He is exalted . . . to give Remission: 'Him hath God exalted with his right hand to be a Prince and a Saviour, for to give repentance to Israel, and forgiveness of sins' (Acts 5: 31).

83 *the Island was certainly a Prison to me*: cf. 96. 31–2, 'I was a Prisoner lock'd up with the Eternal Bars and Bolts of the Ocean.' Both passages look forward to the teasing preface to Defoe's *Serious Reflections*, which suggests an allegorical dimension to the text: 'all these Reflections are just History of a State of forc'd Confinement, which in my real History is represented by a confin'd Retreat in an Island; and 'tis as reasonable to represent one kind of Imprisonment by another, as it is to represent any Thing that really exists, by that which exists not.'

84 *Rain which came in the dry Season ... September and October*: 'We feel
    nothing here of the Hurricanes of *Barbadoes*', Defoe acknowledges else-
    where (*The Storm*, 39), and he underestimates them here. Climatically,
    the seasonal occurrence of hurricanes in September and October, near
    the end of the rainy season, makes these the most dangerous months.

    no humane Shape had ever set Foot upon that Place: a questionable assump-
    tion, in view of the presence of goats on the island (see above, n. to p. 53);
    this wording also foreshadows Crusoe's later discovery of a single foot-
    print on the shore (130. 20–39).

    Cassava Root: a plant also known by its Brazilian name, *Manioc*. Of
    the two species of Cassava native to tropical America, Sweet Cassava
    (*Manihot aipi*) is prized for its fleshy tuberous roots, which are prepared
    and eaten as a vegetable. Starch obtained by pressing the roots may be
    grated for use as bread-making flour.

    Plants of Alloes: aloes, various species of *Liliaceae*, plants whose leaves
    yield a bitter juice used as a purgative.

85 *indefeasibly*: in a way impossible to annul or make void. Here, as at later
    points, Defoe has Crusoe burlesque the discourse of Jacobite absolutism,
    in which the 'indefeasible' right to rule of the Stuart dynasty was a
    central claim. Cf. Defoe's ironic mimicry of the claim that 'Hereditary
    Right is Indefeasible' in his pamphlets *And What If the Pretender Should
    Come* (1713), 5–6, and *Reasons against the Succession of the House of
    Hanover* (1713), 43; see also, on this pattern in the novel as a whole,
    Manuel Schonhorn, *Defoe's Politics: Parliament, Power, Kingship, and
    Robinson Crusoe* (Cambridge: Cambridge University Press, 1991), 141–64.

90 *Rainy Seasons ... which were generally thus*: Crusoe's table of seasons is
    fanciful. Caribbean islands in the approximate latitude of Crusoe's, such
    as Trinidad and Tobago, experience a rainy season between June and
    October and a dry season from November to April.

92 *Tobacco-Pipe ... Contrivance for that too at last*: see 122. 19–28.

93 *Leaden-hall Market*: Leadenhall Market, so called because of the com-
    position of its roof, was situated in the City of London. Established by
    the thirteenth century, it became the major meat and game market in
    London. Defoe recalls elsewhere that 'a certain *Spanish* Ambassador said,
    There was as much Meat sold in it in one Month, as would suffice all
    Spain for a year' (*Tour*, i. 346).

94 *Penguins*: all seventeen species of *Spheniscidae*, flightless marine birds,
    inhabit islands or remote regions in the southern hemisphere. One
    Pacific species is found as far north as the Equator, but their range in the
    Atlantic is more limited, and no penguins are recorded in the specified
    vicinity of Crusoe's island.

    the next Journey ... Of which in its Place: Crusoe resumes this theme at
    120. 33.

95 *meer Domestick*: completely tame.

96 *my Affections chang'd their Gusts*: my inclinations shifted.

Eternal Bars and Bolts of the Ocean: Defoe may be recalling Milton's *Paradise Lost*, ii. 877–92, in which 'every bolt and bar' of hell opens to reveal 'a dark | Illimitable ocean without bound'. Cf. also Jonah's description of incarceration and isolation from God: 'The waters compassed me about, even to the soul: the depth closed me round about . . . | I went down to the bottoms of the mountains; the earth with her bars was about me for ever' (Jonah 2: 5–6).

97 *I will never . . . forsake thee*: 'I will be with thee: I will not fail thee, nor forsake thee' (Joshua 1: 5).

99 *every Grain . . . a Peck-loaf to me in the Consequence*: an extravagant hyperbole on Crusoe's part, a peck-loaf (of bread) being made from a measure of flour equivalent to two gallons in capacity.

100 *Hang'd them in Chains*: see below, 227. 5 and n.

104 *with the Help of Fire . . . make their Canoes*: a technique favoured later in the novel by Friday (191. 34–5). Dampier refers to its use among Amerindian peoples otherwise restricted to stone tools: 'their Digging or Hatchet-work they help out by Fire; whether for the felling of the Trees, or for the making the inside of their Canoa hollow' (*New Voyage round the World*, 85). Cf. Defoe's account elsewhere of the 'Natives of *America*, who, before the *Europeans* came among them, had their *Canoes*, and *Periaguaes*, made of the Trunk of a Tree, hollow'd in the middle by the help of Fire, and so form'd without so much as any Iron Tool to work with' (*General History of Discoveries and Improvements*, 22).

how I did afterwards . . . shew in its Place: one of several forecasts left unfulfilled in the text.

108 *Cedar Tree . . . Temple at Jerusalem*: referring to the cedars of Lebanon, proverbial for their might, that Solomon procures from King Hiram of Tyre to build the temple of Jerusalem (1 Kings 5: 5–1 Kings 6: 36). Cf. Defoe's discussion of this text elsewhere as evidence of ancient architectural skill: ' 'tis not to be suppos'd that their skill lay only in felling the Trees, very little Art being wanted for that kind of Work' (*General History of Discoveries and Improvements*, 89).

109 *Between me and thee is a great Gulph fix'd*: adapting Abraham's speech to the rich man in hell at the end of the parable of Lazarus: 'between us and you there is a great gulf fixed' (Luke 16: 26).

Lust of the Flesh . . . Pride of Life: 'For all that is in the world, the lust of the flesh, and the lust of the eyes, and the pride of life, is not of the Father, but is of the world' (1 John 2: 16).

112 *feeding Elijah by Ravens*: having prophesied a two-year drought to the idolatrous King Ahab, ruler over Israel in Samaria, Elijah is forced into hiding: 'And the ravens brought him bread and flesh in the morning, and bread and flesh in the evening; and he drank of the brook' (1 Kings 17: 6). This biblical episode resonated personally with Defoe when

contemplating his own fortunes and misfortunes: 'I have been fed more by Miracle than *Elija*, when the Ravens were his Purveyours' (*Review*, 8 (1711), preface).

113 *Concurrence of Days . . . great deal of Curiosity*: Defoe resumes this point in *Serious Reflections*, explaining the recurrence of key dates in private life and public history as providentially contrived 'for our Observation, and in some Things for our Instruction'. In particular, 'Providence causes the Revolutions of Days, to form a Concurrence between the Actions of Men . . . and the Reward of these Actions in this World'. The three examples he gives are all political, illustrating divine retribution for Stuart misrule in the 1640s and again in the 1680s: 'The same Day that King *James* the 2d came to the Crown against the Design of the Bill of Exclusion, the same Day he was voted Abdicated by Parliament, and the Throne fill'd with the Prince of *Orange*' (*Serious Reflections*, 219–20).

30th of September . . . 26 Year after: Crusoe's shipwreck on 30 September 1659 falls on his twenty-seventh birthday. This key date, mentioned no fewer than seven times in the text, may encode personal, political, and religious meanings commemorating Whig and Protestant resistance to James II. Two of Defoe's schoolfellows from Morton's Academy, Benjamin Hewling and William Jenkyn, were hanged on 30 September 1685 for their role in the failed rebellion of the Duke of Monmouth, in which Defoe himself took part. Three years later, on 30 September 1688, William of Orange (the future William III) issued his Declaration inaugurating a second, successful attempt to overthrow James. In a letter written on the day of his death and widely reprinted after William's intervention, Hewling predicted the support of Providence for this second attempt, 'and foretold our late Deliverance, more positively then any of the rest' (John Dunton, *The Merciful Assizes* (1701), 158). As Tom Paulin proposes, Crusoe's emphasis on this providential date suggests 'a commemoration of Benjamin Hewling's death day, possibly of Defoe's birthday and of his miraculous survival of . . . the notorious Bloody Assizes'; the novel as a whole is 'a parabolic vision of English history under the Stuarts from a Dissenter's point of view' ('Fugitive Crusoe', *London Review of Books*, 23. 14 (19 July 2001), 15–20).

115 *made very good shift with*: was able to cope well with.

Umbrella . . . as well for the Rains as the Heats: the first description in English of the use of umbrellas as a guard against the sun appears in *Coryats Crudities* by Thomas Coryate (1611), 111–12, with reference to practice in the Italian city of Cremona. Defoe's idea of equipping Crusoe with an umbrella against rain comes about three decades before the merchant and philanthropist Jonas Hanway introduced umbrellas into Britain for this purpose.

117 *the sixth of November, in the sixth Year of my Reign*: uncorrected in later editions, but 'sixth Year' is probably a compositorial error for 'tenth Year', influenced by the occurrence of 'sixth' earlier in the line. Five

years have now elapsed since the completion of Crusoe's first canoe after the start of his fifth year on the island (109. 16, 115. 33); a year later he is in his eleventh year (122.7, 123. 10).

for the Breach: because of the surf.

118 *warning Piece*: a signal gun discharged to give warning of some danger.

121 *poor Robin Crusoe? . . . Where have you been?*: consciously or otherwise, Defoe echoes his self-dramatizing lament on being imprisoned for seditious libel in 1703: 'Alas, *Poor De Foe!* What hast thou been doing, and for what hast thou suffer'd?' (*A New Test of the Church of England's Honesty* (1704), in *A Second Volume of the Writings of the Author of The True-Born Englishman* (1705), 313).

125 *us'd*: accustomed.

What a Table was here spread . . . perish for Hunger: see above, 81. 8–9 and n. Also in the background at this point is the complaint of the Israelites during the flight from Egypt ('for ye have brought us forth into this wilderness, to kill this whole assembly with hunger') and God's fulfilment of his promise to feed them (Exodus 16: 3 ff.).

It would have made a Stoick smile: alluding to the reputation of the Stoics (school founded by the Greek philosopher Zeno *c.*300 BC) for cultivating *apatheia* (freedom from the emotions, indifference to pleasure or pain) as a means of achieving psychological invulnerability. Proverbially, a Stoic neither laughs nor weeps. Cf. E. W., *Poems Written upon Several Occasions* (1711), 91: 'Humph, says old Greybeard with a Cough, | Which would have made a Stoick laugh'; also John Sheffield, Duke of Buckingham, 'Prologue to the Alteration of *Julius Caesar*', line 2: ' 'Tis such a Jest, would make a Stoick smile' (*Works*, 2 vols. (1723), ii. 211).

127 *within nine or ten Degrees of the Equinox*: the first three editions read 'within nineteen degrees', probably a compositor's error, corrected in the fourth edition.

128 *some great River on the Shore*: the Orinoco, as indicated by the latitudinal position of Crusoe's island (09° 22′ N) and the original title-page of the novel ('an un-inhabited Island . . . near the Mouth of the Great River of OROONOQUE'); see also 181. 26–8 and n. The mouth of the Orinoco had been proposed as the site of a new colony in a scheme promoted in *Mist's Weekly Journal* for 7 February 1719, for which Defoe was writing at the time, just weeks before the publication of *Robinson Crusoe*: see Maximillian E. Novak, *Daniel Defoe: Master of Fictions* (Oxford: Oxford University Press, 2001), 546.

132 *Chequer Work*: literally, ornamental work in chessboard pattern (cf. Crusoe's 'Chequer'd Shirt', 47. 20); hence anything diversified with contrasting shades. Defoe repeats this formulation in the opening words of *Colonel Jack*—'Seeing my Life has been such a Checquer Work of Nature . . .' (ed. Samuel Holt Monk, introd. David Roberts (Oxford: Oxford World's Classics, 1989), 3)—and applies it elsewhere to his own

tribulations: 'The Same Checquer-Work of Fortunes attends me still . . .' (*Review*, 8 (1711), preface).

133   *Call upon me . . . glorify me*: see above, 81 and n.

  Wait . . . on the Lord: 'Wait on the Lord: be of good courage, and he shall strengthen thine heart: wait, I say, on the Lord' (Psalms 27: 14). Defoe's biblical citations tend to be casual and from memory, but he seems to specify here that Crusoe's Bible (salvaged in 1659 from the shipwreck) is the Authorized or King James version. In the Geneva Bible, favoured by Puritans during the Commonwealth and beforehand, the text is as follows: 'Hope in the Lord: be strong, and he shall comfort thine heart, and trust in the Lord.'

135   *Saul, who complain'd . . . that God had forsaken him*: recalling the words of Saul, King of Israel, to the ghost of the prophet Samuel. 'I am sore distressed; for the Philistines make war against me, and God is departed from me, and answereth me no more, neither by prophets, nor by dreams' (1 Samuel 28: 15).

141   *it was . . . a very good Providence to me*: it served or provided me well.

143   *abated my Malice*: abetted my malice.

145   *if they attempted me*: if they sought to attack me.

  Conduct of the Spaniards . . . unjustifiable either to God or Man: a favourite theme in Defoe, though variably handled. In the *Review* for 28 June 1711, he treats as unavoidable *realpolitik* 'the Cruelty and Barbarity with which the *Spaniards* Treated the poor Natives of [Mexico], *and which all Writers, nay, even some of their own, exclaim against*'; he also represents the perfidy of Cortes as little worse than the conduct of the English in Virginia (Vol. 8, No. 41, 166). Elsewhere he straightforwardly reflects the 'black legend' of Spanish atrocity as promoted by rival colonial powers, drawing on the classic denunciation of conquistador genocide by Bartolomé de Las Casas, *A Short Account of the Destruction of the Indies* (1552), a well-known source in Britain since its first English translation of 1583. Las Casas is the authority cited when Defoe puts a figure of forty million on the number killed during 'the great Ravages which the *Spaniards* made in *America*, at their first landing among those innocent People' (*General History of Discoveries and Improvements*, 282).

  Bowels of Pity: in contemporary physiology, the bowels were the seat of gentle emotions such as pity, compassion, and tenderness.

148   *that I shall not discuss*: the syntax comes under strain towards the end of this serpentine sentence. There are two possible solutions: to read 'that' as a relative pronoun like 'which' or as a demonstrative pronoun inaugurating a new sentence; in either case, Crusoe is refusing to elaborate on the precise source of the 'secret Intimations of Providence'.

150   *He-goat . . . dying indeed of meer old Age*: a similar incident is recounted in J. Eden, 'Account of a Journey from the Port of Oratava in the Island of Tenerife to the Top of the Pike in that Island', *Philosophical Transactions*,

29 (1715), 317–25; see James Means, 'Crusoe's Dying Goat: A Possible
Source?', *Scriblerian*, 16.2 (1984), 184. The episode looks forward to
Defoe's ridicule elsewhere of traditional representations of Satan in the
form of a goat (*A Political History of the Devil* (1726), 265–81); see Aaron
Santesso, 'A Note on Goats: Defoe on Crusoe's "Devil" ', *Scriblerian*,
30.2 (1998), 48–9.

151 *Tinder-box . . . Pan*: a lock, which Crusoe here detaches from its musket
and uses as an improvised container for fire-lighting, is the device that
ignites a powder charge in the barrel of a muzzle-loaded weapon, thereby
causing a ball or shot to be discharged. It incorporates two jaws gripping
a flint, a steel frizzen or striking post, and a pan or depression designed to
hold a small quantity of gunpowder. When flint and steel are struck
together, a shower of sparks ignites the powder in the pan. Wildfire is
dampened gunpowder, to ignite tinder.

152 *taught my Poll, as I noted before . . . may be alive there still*: see above, 93.
25–9, where Crusoe teaches the parrot his name; also 234. 3–5, where, in
contradiction, he takes the parrot with him on leaving the island. The
present passage indicates not only that Crusoe will eventually escape, but
also (since he and Poll spend twenty-six years together) that he will not
do so for three more years.

153 *Southern Solstice*: the winter solstice, one of two points in the year (*circa*
10 June and 10 December in the Julian calendar), midway between the
two equinoxes, when the sun is at its furthest from the Equator.

stepp'd short: possibly a misprint for 'stopp'd short', but not corrected in
any of the six authorized editions of 1719. In military usage, '*to step short*
. . . is to diminish or slacken your pace' (*OED2*, quoting Charles James,
A New and Enlarged Military Dictionary (1802)).

158 *Breaking of the Sea . . . obliges Men to stave*: in severe weather the rapid
drainage of large volumes of seawater from the upper deck of a ship
is essential. Any impediment to this process is potentially fatal. In
exceptionally heavy conditions, crew members might be forced to stave
(break up) fixed objects on deck and throw them overboard.

Energy of Words: from *energeia*, a term in Aristotelian rhetoric denoting
the ability to create a semblance of actuality through mental picturing.
Cf. Defoe's preface to *A Continuation of Letters Written by a Turkish Spy
at Paris* (1718), which laments that the English language cannot 'express
the Story with the same Vivacity, the same Spirit, the same Energy of
Words as the old exquisitely qualified *Arabian* delivered it'.

159 *secret moving Springs . . . Motion carries out the Soul*: cf. above, 132. 25–6;
also Defoe's *The Mock Mourners: A Satyr* (1702), 10: 'By all endearing
stratagems he strove, | To draw us by the secret springs of Love.' Crusoe
flirts here with the controversial discourse of mechanism (from Descartes,
Hobbes, and others), which seeks to explain mental and emotional phenomena solely in terms of matter and motion, often by analogy with
clockwork ('secret moving springs . . . set a going'). This approach to the

inner life was widely feared to constitute a denial of the immaterial soul, but Crusoe embeds it securely in a Christian framework. For the philosophical context, see John S. Yolton, *Thinking Matter: Materialism in Eighteenth-Century Britain* (Minneapolis: University of Minnesota Press, 1983); for fiction after Defoe, see Thomas Keymer, 'Materialism, Mechanism, and the Novel', in David Womersley and Richard McCabe (eds.), *Text and Context: Essays in Literary History Presented to Howard Erskine-Hill* (Newark: University of Delaware Press, 2007), ch. 16.

159 *Naturalists*: empirical scientists, natural philosophers devoted to the explanation of sensible reality and the material world through observation, experiment, and discovery. The term is loosely applicable to the men of science who constituted the Royal Society from the 1660s. Defoe was schooled in the full flow of new scientific ideas at Morton's Academy (see Vickers, *Defoe and the New Sciences*, 32–51), and the goals and principles of natural philosophy are central to works in his canon such as *The Storm*. Cf. *The Storm*, 18: 'I wish our Naturalists would explain that Wind to us, and tell us which way it blew, or how it is possible that any direct Wind could cause the Waters to ebb . . .'

161 *jaum'd*: dialect spelling of 'jammed', this being the earliest occurrence recorded in *OED2*. Cf. *Captain Singleton*, 40: 'Her Stern seem'd to be jaum'd in between two Ridges of the Rock, and so remained fast, all the Fore-part of the Ship having been beaten to Pieces.'

Cookroom, or Forecastle of the Ship: in wooden vessels the cookroom, or galley, was the only space where naked lights were permitted below deck. It was often located forward, towards the fo'c'sle, so that in the event of fire the ship could be turned downwind to contain the blaze.

162 *room to suppose . . . perhaps to Spain*: Crusoe's assumption is later confirmed when a second Spanish vessel, steering the same course, is hijacked and puts in at the island. With light touches, Defoe begins to outline a trade route plied by richly laden but poorly defended Spanish vessels. See also 205. 13–17 and n.

several Muskets . . . no occasion for them: muskets were muzzle-loaded, shoulder-borne firearms, usually matchlock, and the primary weapons used by the Spanish in the conquest of the Americas. Matchlock incorporated a slow-match to ignite the powder, but the match could be difficult to light and easily extinguished in wet weather. Matchlock was finally superseded by the general introduction of flintlock in the early 1700s. Crusoe already possesses flintlocks ('Two Fowling-Pieces', 151. 27), which probably accounts for his decision to forgo these weapons.

164 *my ORIGINAL SIN*: literally, a state of corruption and sinfulness innate to all humans as a consequence of the Fall, but a term frequently applied by Defoe to specific individual character faults. Cf. 'Thirst of Gold was his *Original Sin*' (*Jure Divino* (1706), 228, on William Rufus); 'Satan's original Sin *Ambition*' (*Political History of the Devil*, 146). Crusoe refers here to filial disobedience, but commentators have found a rich variety of

further implications in the term. For the standard explanations, see Pat Rogers, *Robinson Crusoe* (London: Allen and Unwin, 1979), 61–6.

166 *Curlieu*: curlew, *Numenius arquata*, Britain's largest wader, grey-brown in colour with a slender curved bill.

171 *to be kill'd*: about to be killed.

172 *as cleaverly*: so cleverly (variant spelling, with a pun on 'cleaver').

    no Executioner in Germany: shorthand for the preferred method of decapitation on the Continent, by wielding a sword with a horizontal stroke. This was relatively clean and efficient compared with the axe, which continued to be used in England until 1747 for beheading traitors of noble birth. Defoe may be recalling the execution of James Scott, Duke of Monmouth, on Tower Hill on 15 July 1685, when the executioner is said to have struck eight blows before resorting to his knife.

173 *a comely handsome Fellow . . . white as Ivory*: detailed physical description of native peoples was a standard feature of contemporary travel writing, driven in part by the expectations of the Royal Society. Dampier's crude ethnographic description of a New Holland aborigine in *A New Voyage round the World* is one example: 'They are tall, strait bodied, and thin, with small long Limbs. They have great Heads, round Foreheads, and great Brows . . . They have great Bottle Noses, pretty full Lips, and wide Mouths . . . They are long visaged, and of a very unpleasing Aspect, having no one graceful Feature in their Faces. Their Hair is black, short and curl'd, like that of the Negroes; and not long and lank like the common *Indians*. The colour of their Skins, both of their Faces and the rest of their Body, is coal black, like that of the Negroes of *Guinea*' (464). Defoe's description of Friday seems pointedly antithetical to this norm, and more akin to Aphra Behn's idealizing portrait of Oroonoko in her novel of 1688 (*Oroonoko*, ed. Paul Salzman (Oxford: Oxford World's Classics, 1994), 11–12).

174 *I was very well pleas'd with him . . . his Name should be Friday*: Crusoe echoes the words of God at the baptism of Christ ('This is my beloved Son, in whom I am well pleased' (Matthew 3: 17)). The name he bestows has related connotations, Friday being the weekly commemoration of Christ's crucifixion and salvation of humankind. The irony is that Crusoe has previously lost 'a Day out of my Reckoning of the Days in the Week', as he notes above (81. 27–31); his new companion is really Man Saturday.

177 *a Law to themselves*: 'For when the Gentiles, which have not the law, do by nature the things contained in the law, these, having not the law, are a law unto themselves' (Romans 2: 14).

    Clay in the Hand of the Potter . . . form'd me thus?: the biblical sources for Crusoe's rumination are various: 'Surely your turning of things upside down shall be esteemed as the potter's clay: for shall the work say of him that made it, He made me not?' (Isaiah 29: 16); 'Woe unto him that striveth with his Maker! Let the potsherd strive with the potsherds of the

earth. Shall the clay say to him that fashioneth it, What makest thou?'
(Isaiah 45: 9); 'Nay but, O man, who art thou that repliest against God?
Shall the thing formed say to him that formed it, Why hast thou made
me thus?' (Romans 9: 20). Defoe left a 195-page signed notebook, dated
1681, including the author's holograph transcript of sermons and several
verse 'Meditãcions', one of which resonates with Crusoe's theme: 'shall
The Clay Say Unto the Potter? &ca' (*The Meditations of Daniel Defoe*,
ed. G. H. Healey (Cummington, Mass.: Cummington Press, 1946),
17–18).

177   *aptest Schollar*: most fit and ready pupil.

179   *not a great while*: not until after a great while.

181   *Oroonooko*: the Orinoco, discovered by Columbus, the third largest river
system in the world, draining an area comprising most of modern
Venezuela and the northern regions of Brazil. The river flows into the
Caribbean through a delta stretching over 11,600 square miles (30,000
square km), just south of Trinidad and Tobago.

   Caribs ... Caribbees: the Caribs are a people native to islands in the
southern Caribbean (the Caribbees), commonly associated with cannibalism in the period.

   St. Martha: Santa Marta, coastal town situated in modern Colombia,
founded by Roderigo de Bastidas in 1525, and prey to pirates in the
sixteenth and seventeenth centuries.

182   *Friday's Discourse began to relish with me very well*: Friday's information
began to give me much pleasure.

183   *Priestcraft ... among all Religions in the World*: cf. Defoe's *Political
History of the Devil*, in which Jesuits in China 'joining the priestcraft of
both religions together, they brought *Jesus Christ* and *Confucius* to be so
reconcilable, that the *Chinese* and the *Roman* idolatry appeared capable of
a confederacy' (8). Crusoe's brief and apparently conciliatory aside about
the universality of priestcraft notwithstanding, his primary target here is
Roman Catholicism.

   great first Cause: philosophical term for God as originator and creator.
Crusoe's efforts to catechize Friday look forward to the religious dia-
logues of Defoe's *A New Family Instructor* (1727): 'It follows naturally, if
there is an infinite eternal Being, a great first Cause of all Things, He
must be infinitely Wise, God, Righteous, Holy and Just' (256).

184   *dreadful Nature to Sin*: profound aversion to sin.

   consuming Fire: 'For the Lord thy God is a consuming fire, even a jealous
God' (Deuteronomy 4: 24); the passage that follows is a tissue of biblical
quotations and allusions.

   Workers of Iniquity: sinners. 'Is not destruction to the wicked? and a
strange punishment to the workers of iniquity?' (Job 31: 3); 'The foolish
shall not stand in thy sight: thou hatest all workers of iniquity' (Psalms 5:
5); 'Depart from me, all ye workers of iniquity; for the Lord hath heard

the voice of my weeping' (Psalms 6: 8); 'But he shall say, I tell you, I know you not whence ye are; depart from me, all *ye* workers of iniquity' (Luke 13: 27).

tread him down: 'And I will put enmity between thee and the woman, and between thy seed and her seed; it shall bruise thy head, and thou shalt bruise his heel' (Genesis 3: 15); 'And the God of peace shall bruise Satan under your feet shortly' (Romans 16: 20).

enable us to . . . quench his fiery Darts: 'Above all, taking the shield of faith, wherewith ye shall be able to quench all the fiery darts of the wicked' (Ephesians 6: 16).

Doctor . . . or a Solver of Difficulties: one qualified and proficient in casuistry, a theological technique for resolving cases of conscience or conflicts of duty generated by special circumstance. Cf. *Roxana*, 68 ('I had no Casuists to resolve this Doubt'). On the significance of casuistry for Defoe's fiction overall, see G. A. Starr, *Defoe and Casuistry* (Princeton: Princeton University Press, 1971); Crusoe applies the term here to problems of divinity in general.

cast into the Bottomless-Pit . . . everlasting Fire: 'God spared not the angels that sinned, but cast them down to hell, and delivered them into chains of darkness, to be reserved unto judgement' (2 Peter 2: 4); 'Then shall he say also unto them on the left hand, Depart from me, ye cursed, into everlasting fire, prepared for the devil and his angels' (Matthew 25: 41); 'And I saw an angel come down from heaven, having the key of the bottomless pit and a great chain in his hand' (Revelation 20: 1).

Jesus Christ . . . Mediator of the new Covenant: Crusoe endeavours to explain to Friday the relationship between God and his people. The Old Covenant or pledge between God and the Israelites inscribed in the Ten Commandments (Exodus 34: 27–8) expires with the birth of Jesus (Galatians 4: 4–7). The New Covenant (Hebrews 8: 6) is mediated by Jesus, who gives new laws to the Church (Galatians 3: 24–5; Hebrews 7: 11–12), and symbolized by Christ's crucifixion: 'God so loved the world, that he gave his only begotten Son, that whosoever believeth in him should not perish, but have everlasting life' (John 3: 16).

185 *Intercessor, at the Foot-stool of God's Throne*: a recollection from the Sermon on the Mount: 'Swear not at all; neither by heaven; for it is God's throne: | Nor by the earth; for it is his footstool' (Matthew 5: 34–5).

our Blessed Redeemer . . . Seed of Abraham: Jesus takes on human form, and is born a Jew, 'For verily he took not on him the nature of angels; but he took on him the seed of Abraham' (Hebrews 2: 16).

only to the lost Sheep of the House of Israel: the twelve disciples are appointed by Jesus to minister to the Jews, and to no other nation. 'These twelve Jesus sent forth, and commanded them, saying, Go not into the way of the Gentiles, and into any city of the Samaritans enter ye not: | But go rather to the lost sheep of the house of Israel' (Matthew 10: 5–6).

186　*no farther off from his Spirit to instruct*: no more distanced from his enlightening spirit.

187　*leading us into all Truth*: Crusoe recalls Jesus's words of comfort to his disciples against tribulation by the promise of the Holy Ghost: 'when he, the Spirit of truth, is come, he will guide you into all truth' (John 16: 13).

188　*They no eat Mans but when make the War fight*: Friday's assertion recalls Montaigne's account of the Brazilian Tupinamba, who roast and eat enemy warriors 'not . . . for Nourishment . . . but as a Representation of an extream Revenge' (*Essays*, trans. Charles Cotton, 4th edn., 3 vols. (1711), i. 294). This passage also looks forward to modern anthropological theories concerning 'ritual exocannibalism' among the Caribs; the act was largely symbolic, expressing revenge and allowing the spiritual essence of captured enemies to be incorporated by the victors. Crusoe encounters the custom again in the sequel: 'they never eat Men or Women, except only such as they took in the Wars, and then they own'd that they made a great Feast' (*The Farther Adventures of Robinson Crusoe* (1719), 83).

191　*Fustic*: a tropical hardwood tree, *Chlorophora tinctoria*, native to Central and South America and the West Indies, the wood of which yields a yellow dye. The term also refers to various European trees and shrubs that yield a similar dye, especially *Rhus cotinus*.

　　　Nicaragua Wood: any of several species of *Caesalpinia*, tropical hardwood trees native to Central and South America that yield a red dye.

195　*fetch'd a Compass*: made a sweeping circle.

　　　shoot: range; distance or reach of a shot; shooting distance. The usage here is the last example of this obsolete sense noted in *OED2*.

196　*which*: whom.

　　　within half Shot of them: well within shot, well within range.

197　*loose*: altered to 'lose' in the third edition, but a variant spelling current in the period and used elsewhere in the text (99. 26; 251. 34).

　　　see me cock, and present: saw me cock my weapon and take aim. The same colloquial past tense (or historic present) recurs elsewhere: cf. 198. 7, 209. 25, and 249. 25.

198　*answer'd in Latin*: European cultures in the early modern period preserved the Latin language as a shared inheritance; educated Europeans would routinely use it to communicate in the absence of a shared modern language.

199　*tho' undermost, wisely quitting the Sword, drew the Pistol*: having been wrestled to the ground, the Spaniard is unable to wield his sword effectively, so he relinquishes it and draws his pistol.

200　*filial Affection . . . Sight of his Father*: the natural scenes of love between Friday and his parent stand in contrast not only to Crusoe's relations with his father, but also to a public scandal flirted with by Defoe in his monthly journal, *Mercurius Politicus*. In the January 1718 number, Defoe guardedly alludes to a recent breakdown in relations between George I and the Prince of Wales that had led the latter to remove his household from the court; he returns to it indirectly in the ensuing months. On the implications for *Robinson Crusoe*, see Novak, *Daniel Defoe: Master of Fictions*, 543–4.

203 *my own meer Property*: my exclusive property. As elsewhere, Crusoe poses whimsically as a divine-right monarch, making the claims to absolute authority and dominion that Defoe satirizes in *Jure Divino* and elsewhere.

Liberty of Conscience throughout my Dominions: Crusoe continues to mimic the language of Stuart autocracy, alluding now to one of the most vexed political issues of the period and a central theme of Defoe's writing elsewhere, that of religious toleration. His words recall the Declarations of Indulgence issued by Charles II (1672) and James II (1687, 1688), especially the latter, which courted Dissenters while serving the ulterior purpose of admitting Catholics to civil and military office. James's first 'declaration to all his loving subjects for liberty of conscience' announces that among 'all the people of our dominions . . . conscience ought not to be constrained'; see also above, 41. 8 and n.

205 *Spanish Ship bound . . . to the Havana*: Defoe sketches more definitely the navigational track taken by the first Spanish trader (162. 8 ff.). He scopes the ship's lading, strengthening the evidence that places Crusoe's island somewhere adjacent to an important Spanish trade route. The implication is that Spain's decline will be hastened by trade with, or plunder of, her assets in the Americas. Elsewhere Defoe argues explicitly that strategically sited English colonies might sever Spain's silver lifeline close to its source, divert its output into English coffers, and shift the balance of power in Europe: see *Review*, Vol. 4, No. 110, 438 (25 October 1707); Vol. 8, No. 181, 727 (20 May 1712); Vol. 9, No. 87, 73–4 (23 April 1713).

Gratitude . . . in the Nature of Man: Defoe is preoccupied here and elsewhere with the theme of gratitude, typically presenting ingratitude as the quintessential English vice. See Maximillian E. Novak's chapter on 'The Worst of Crimes and the Meaning of Gratitude' in *Defoe and the Nature of Man* (Oxford: Clarendon Press, 1963), 113–28.

206 *the Inquisition*: a formal papal policy, instituted by Pope Gregory IX in the 1230s to obliterate heresy, later a crucial factor in sustaining the Counter-Reformation. Inquisitors were originally licensed to convict and burn suspected heretics without appeal, thus incorporating a legal mechanism for mass intimidation and even extermination. Thereafter the Inquisition developed into a smooth administrative machine for the investigation, indictment, trial, torture, and execution of its victims, beginning to abate in the eighteenth century, but still the subject of British captivity narratives such as *The Trial and Sufferings of Mr. Isaac Martin, Who Was Put into the Inquisition in Spain, For the Sake of the*

Protestant Religion (1723). See Michael Baigent and Richard Leigh, *The Inquisition* (London: Penguin, 1999); also, on inquisition narratives, Snader, *Caught between Worlds*, 70–7. Crusoe resumes this theme in *Serious Reflections*, recalling a victim who 'had much rather die, than be carry'd back to the Prison of the Inquisition, where their Cruelties were worse than Death' (148).

206 *Holy Sacraments*: there is an irony in the Spaniard's suggestion that his countrymen should swear loyalty to Crusoe based on the mysterious ceremonies of the Christian church. As Catholics, the Spaniards observe seven sacraments, whereas Defoe's Protestant readers would recognize only two, Baptism and the Eucharist.

207 *fourteen*: the number sixteen is mentioned later (208. 30).

Children of Israel . . . Bread in the Wilderness: 'And the children of Israel said unto [Moses and Aaron], Would to God we had died by the hand of the Lord in the land of Egypt, when we sat by the flesh pots, and when we did eat bread to the full; for ye have brought us forth into this wilderness, to kill this whole assembly with hunger' (Exodus 16: 3). The same text is in play above, 125. 32–4.

Land cur'd and trim'd up: land prepared for seeding.

208 *Alicant*: coastal city in south-east Spain, famous for its wine. Crusoe suggests that if only he had had access to a sufficient store of barrels, such as existed at Alicante, he might have been able to fill a great number.

209 *strict Charge in Writing*: a strange oversight, in view of the way this paragraph concludes. Crusoe has already stressed the inconvenience caused by his shortage of ink (56. 23–6), his inability to produce a substitute (56. 26–7), and the consequence of his supply running out (60. 29–32; 113. 12–14). 'He had done well if he had inform'd us, how he could give them Instructions in Writing, when his *Ink* was gone so many Years before' (Gildon, *Life and Strange Surprizing Adventures of Mr. D—— De F—*, 27).

fair Gale: stiff breeze.

211 *invisible World, and a Converse of Spirits*: a theme resumed at length in the final section of *Serious Reflections*, headed 'A Vision of the Anglick World'. Here Crusoe writes of 'Intimations given us, by which a prudent Man may sometimes foresee Evil, and hide himself'. He adds that 'Providence at the Head of the invisible World . . . may, and I believe does, direct from thence silent Messengers on many Occasions, whether sleeping or waking, whether directly or indirectly, whether by Hints, Impulses, Allegories, Mysteries, or otherwise, we know not' (212).

212 *So little do we see . . . Destruction*: a conspicuous instance of the moralizing that fulfils Defoe's prefatory account of *Robinson Crusoe* as 'told . . . with Seriousness, and with a religious Application of Events to the Uses to which wise Men always apply them' (3). Early critics rejoined that the

work was 'clog'd with Moral Reflections, as you are pleas'd to call them, every where insipid and aukward, and . . . put in by you to swell the Bulk of your Treatise up to a five Shilling Book' (Gildon, *Life and Strange Surprizing Adventures of Mr. D—— De F—*, 30–1).

213 *ousy Sand*: oozy, loose, and yielding sand, similar in effect to the sand described by Defoe near the mouth of the Thames. 'Several Ships drove on shoar below *Tilbury* Fort . . . but as the shoar is ouzy and soft, the Vessels sat upright and easy, and here the high Tides which follow'd, and which were the ruin of so many in other places, were the deliverance of all these Ships whose lading and value was very great, for the Tide rising to an unusual height, floated them all off' (*The Storm*, 138).

true Seamen . . . least of all Mankind given to fore-thought: a sentiment reflecting the main thrust of Crusoe's characterization as a mariner. For Defoe's low opinion of seafarers elsewhere, see the *Review* for 31 March 1705 (Vol. 2, No. 12, 47), with a conclusion that casts interesting light on the objections of Crusoe's father to his son's intended career: 'They Sware Violently, Whore Violently, drink Punch Violently, Spend their Money when they have it Violently, and when they han't it, run in Debt Violently; at Sea they'll be Violent Sick, when they come to Short-Allowance they'll Fast Violently; in a Storm they'll Pray Violently . . . In short, they are Violent Fellows, and ought to be Encourag'd to go to Sea.'

no less than ten Hours before the Boat could be on float again: with two tides in any given twenty-four hour period, high tide occurs every twelve hours. The mutineers will have to wait for the water to rise sufficiently with the next flood tide before the boat can be refloated.

219 *the other*: the other men (one of Defoe's habitual uninflected plurals, as above, 27. 38 and n.).

222 *take a round*: circle round.

225 *give us Quarter . . . and we will yield?*: spare our lives . . . if we surrender?

particularly with: even including.

Reasons of State: another political buzzword of the age, typically used to denote a pragmatic suspension of principle or legality on the part of a ruler. In *The Original Power of the Collective Body of the People of England, Examined and Asserted* (1701), Defoe lists this expression under 'the different Terms which Statesmen turn so often into fine Words to serve their Ends' (8). But he elsewhere condones *realpolitik* in cases of need: 'Reasons of State are principally the Great Doctrine of Self-preservation, which branches it self in such Methods as these: Keeping Danger at a distance. Keeping a good Barrier between Our selves and powerful Neighbours, that you may not be forced to a Defensive War. Preventing the Union of Neighbours of different Interests from Our selves' (*The Danger of the Protestant Religion Consider'd* (1701), 30).

226 *Governour . . . might hang them all there, if he pleased*: before 1700, all

pirates apprehended by colonial authorities were required to be returned to England for trial. After 1700, governors were commissioned to set up courts of Vice Admiralty in their jurisdiction for the trial and punishment of pirates. Cf. also 232. 1–2.

226 *more perfectly amused them*: deceived them even more.

try them: examine them (to test their loyalty).

227 *hang'd in Chains*: throughout the later seventeenth and eighteenth centuries, the bodies of notorious felons, notably pirates, were often hanged in chains after execution. Daubed with pitch or tar and held fast in a full-length brace of iron hoops and chains suspended from a gibbet, the decomposing corpse would retain human semblance and serve as a grisly deterrent. A relevant case is that of Captain William Kidd, hanged for piracy at Wapping on 23 May 1701, whose body was hanged in chains on the lower reaches of the Thames at Tilbury Point (where Defoe had his brick and tile works at the time) as an example to passing mariners. The practice of hanging in chains was not abolished until 1834.

faithful to him to the last Drop: a grim double entendre, signifying not only the last drop of lifeblood but also the fatal drop from the gallows.

230 *miraculous Manner . . . Wilderness*: another allusion to the feeding of the Israelites in the wilderness (cf. 125. 32–4, 207. 23–6), with a pun on 'manna' (as in Exodus 16: 15: 'It is manna . . . the bread which the Lord hath given you to eat').

232 *stay that Night to prepare my things*: one of several passages connecting Crusoe with Shakespeare's Prospero, who similarly decides to remain on his island one final night (*The Tempest*, v. i. 301–12).

233 *weigh*: weigh anchor.

whipp'd and pickl'd: wounds caused by flogging were commonly dressed with salt water to stave off infection and accelerate the healing process. The aim was to render the seaman fit for duty in the shortest time.

234 *eight and twenty Years*: another of Crusoe's miscalculations. He arrives on the island on 30 September 1659 and departs on 19 December 1686, making the tally twenty-seven years.

Eleventh of June, in the Year 1687: another date implying thematic correspondence between Crusoe's island exile of 1659–86 and the alienation of English Dissenters under the restored Stuart monarchy of 1660–88 (see above, n. to p. 113). 'Not only is this date [11 June 1687] of historical importance to Defoe for personal reasons as the second anniversary of Monmouth's rebellion against James II, in which Defoe himself took part, but it was precisely at this time in England that leading national figures officially invited the Protestant Dutch prince, William, to mount an invasion and wrest the monarchy from Stuart possession. In a sense, Crusoe's salvation and rearrival home allegorize the English salvation to follow' (Michael Seidel, 'Crusoe in Exile', *PMLA* 96 (1981), 374; see also Paulin, 'Fugitive Crusoe').

236 *had given his Son*: would have given his son.

237 *Consequence of a Sugar Work*: by-product of refining sugar in a factory.

238 *River of Lisbon*: the Tagus, longest river of the Iberian Peninsula, rises in eastern central Spain and flows 626 miles (1,004 km), passing through Lisbon into the Atlantic.

[38,892] *Cruisadoes*: editions published in Defoe's lifetime leave this number blank. The usual figure of 38,892 was first calculated by W. P. Trent; an alternative estimate of '19,446 crusadoes' appears in a London edition published by J. Walter in 1790 (340). Cruisadoes were Portuguese silver coins marked with a cross, estimated in 1695 to be worth 3 shillings and sixpence apiece. This was also Defoe's habitual spelling for 'crusades': 'all the Cruisadoes and Expeditions to the *Holy-Land*, which cost *Europe* a Million of Lives, and an immense Treasure, during one Hundred and twenty Years, to no Purpose' (*A Plan of the English Commerce*, 321).

239 *latter End of Job . . . the Beginning*: 'So the Lord blessed the latter end of Job more than his beginning: for he had fourteen thousand sheep, and six thousand camels, and a thousand yoke of oxen, and a thousand she asses. | He had also seven sons and three daughters' (Job 42: 12–13). Like several of the Psalms recollected by Crusoe, the Old Testament Book of Job confronts the problem of unjust suffering and interrogates the connection between righteousness and reward. Both sources amplify Crusoe's experience as a character led by affliction and endurance into new awareness of God.

order'd me to be let Blood: phlebotomy was commonplace in Defoe's day, when good health was widely held to depend on a balance between the four bodily humours of blood, phlegm, black bile, and yellow bile. As the most prolific humour, blood was subject to the most governance, and would usually be drawn from incisions to surface veins in the forearm. Crusoe's pallor and subsequent nausea are perceived to be symptomatic of 'plethora', an excess of blood in the body; hence the prescription of bleeding.

240 *now Master . . . Lands in England*: Crusoe now enjoys material wealth equivalent to that of the middling or even higher landed gentry. He resembles in this the entrepreneurs of trade, commerce, and navigation celebrated in Defoe's economic writings: 'How ordinary is it to see a tradesman . . . with, from ten to forty thousand pounds estate, to divide among his family? when, on the contrary, take the gentry in *England* from one end to the other . . . we find few families of the lower gentry, that is to say, from six or seven hundred a year downwards, but they are in debt and in necessitous circumstances, and a great many of greater estates also' (*Complete English Tradesman*, i. 373).

more Care . . . nothing but what I wanted: Crusoe's observation concerning his finances resembles Alexander Selkirk's reported attitude after his return from four years and four months of isolation on Juan Fernández:

'*I am now worth 800 Pounds, but shall never be so happy, as when I was not worth a Farthing*' (Richard Steele, *The Englishman*, No. 26 (3 December 1713)).

241 *no Scruple . . . best Religion to die with*: Crusoe has presented himself as a Catholic when living in Brazil, and would do so again, but now begins to worry about dying in the wrong religion (a position that hardens below, 255. 19–29). Similar anxieties are in play in Defoe's *Religious Courtship* (1722), which warns against the spiritual dangers of conversion to Catholicism in cases of interdenominational marriage.

242 *Padres*: Padre's. Deriving from the Latin *pater* (father), the term was in general use throughout Italy, Spain, Portugal, and Spanish and Portuguese America to denote any regular clergy, especially Catholic priests; cf. the 'kind *Padre*' in *Colonel Jack*, 231.

      Italian Silks: fabric made from the fibres of the silkworm's cocoon, prized for its texture and lustre, and chiefly used in the manufacture of garments, upholstery, and ecclesiastical vestments. Finished Italian silk was considered the most exquisite variety available, and a byword for luxury. Defoe comments elsewhere on the superiority of 'fine *Italian* and *Piedmont* thrown Silks' (*Plan of the English Commerce*, 277), and notes the restriction forbidding its importation through any port other than London (*Complete English Tradesman*, II. ii. 130).

      English broad Cloath: plain-wove, double-width black cloth, of high quality, chiefly used in making men's garments.

      black Bays: baize, coarse woollen stuff having a long nap, formerly used for making garments. During his years as a hose factor, Defoe would have dealt in broadcloth and baize.

      Flanders Lace: Flanders (modern Belgium) produced extremely high-quality fine linen thread, which made the best lace in Europe, used in making clothing, coverings, and furnishings. The success of the Flemish lace industry owed much to the business acumen of its traders, who adapted lace production to suit the latest tastes in European court circles, and led to repeated bans on importation into Britain. This commodity is a favourite target of Defoe's Moll Flanders, who notes that 'Flanders-Lace, being then Prohibited . . . was a good Booty to any Custom-House Officer that could come at it' (*Moll Flanders*, 210).

      turn'd all my Effects into good Bills of Exchange: Crusoe has exchanged his personal possessions for promissory notes, comparable to modern cheques, from reliable sources. These guarantee him a specified sum either on demand or on a certain date.

      the Start: Start Point (50° 13′ 30″ N 03° 38′ 47″ W), south of Dartmouth, Devon, one of the most exposed peninsulas on the English coast, running sharply into the sea for almost a mile.

243 *the Groyne*: La Coruña or Corunna, a port town situated in an inlet on the extreme north-west coast of Spain, important since Roman times.

Rochell: La Rochelle, the most important port on France's Atlantic seaboard, founded in the tenth century. The city was a Protestant enclave from 1598 until 1628, when its resistance to Richelieu's scheme to unify France collapsed under siege. In *Lex Talionis; or, An Enquiry into the most Proper Ways to Prevent the Persecution of the Protestants in France* (1698), Defoe bitterly recalls 'the Taking of *Rochelle*; the Protestants being miserably deserted by the *English*, and Thirteen Thousand People starv'd to death in the Town' (17); cf. also *Review*, Vol. 8, No. 111 (8 December 1711), 446).

Calais to Dover: Crusoe's determination to minimize time spent at sea in returning home leads him to cross the English Channel at its narrowest point (14 miles/22 km).

Navarre: when Crusoe visits Navarre in 1688, it is a separate kingdom under the crown of France, ruled by Louis XIV. Modern Navarre is an autonomous community in Spain, its territory limited to the west by the Basque Country, to the south-west by La Rioja, to the south-east and east by Aragon, and to the north by France.

Pampeluna: Pamplona, capital of Navarre, a city of pre-Roman origins situated 1,460 ft (444 m) above sea level on the southern edge of the Pyrenees.

244 *old Castile*: the central region of northern Spain, situated mostly on a vast arid plain, the Meseta Norte (Northern Plateau), bounded to the north by mountains and sea and to the south by the Sierra de Guadarrama, which separates it from New Castile.

severest Winter . . . in the Memory of Man: an assertion impossible to verify, though in England the winter of 1688–9 is recorded as unusually severe, and the Thames froze over.

Fonterabia: Fuenterrabia, a strategically important northern Spanish town situated on the French border near the Bay of Biscay. Milton erroneously connects Fuenterrabia with Charlemagne in *Paradise Lost*, i. 587. In June 1719, two months after first publication of *Robinson Crusoe*, the town was reduced by Catholic troops commanded by James Fitzjames, Duke of Berwick, the illegitimate son of James II.

Languedoc: region in south-eastern France, bordering on the Mediterranean, with a strong Protestant tradition. During the War of the Spanish Succession, Defoe called on the province to recover its lost independence: 'now is the Time for the Protestants in *Languedoc* to put their Hands to the Work, and wake out of the Sleep of despairing Circumstances; they seem to be summoned by Heaven to the Agency of their own Deliverance' (*Review*, Vol. 4, No. 90 (9 September 1707), 360). Crusoe passes through Languedoc in 1688, when Protestants were being vigorously persecuted as part of a drive by Catholics to reassert authority in the region; his itinerary may be designed to register the plight of beleaguered Protestants across Europe.

245 *two-legged Wolves . . . on the French Side of the Mountains*: Crusoe implies
the Catholic authorities, perhaps specifically the agents of the Inquisition. His image recalls the words of Jesus in the Sermon on the Mount,
echoed by St Paul: 'Beware of false prophets, which come to you in
sheep's clothing, but inwardly they are ravening wolves' (Matthew 7: 15);
'after my departing shall grievous wolves enter in among you, not sparing
the flock' (Acts 20: 29). There may also be a memory here of Milton's
'grim wolf with privy paw' (*Lycidas*, line 128), 'hireling wolves' ('To
the Lord General Cromwell', line 14), and 'grievous wolves' (*Paradise
Lost*, xii. 508), all representing the corrupted and acquisitive church
hierarchy.

Gascoign: Gascogne, region in France on the northern edge of the
Pyrenees, held by the kings of England in the twelfth century, and
annexed by France in 1453. Elsewhere Defoe laments that 'we have lost
all the dominions which our antient Kings for some hundreds of years
held in *France*; such as the rich and powerful provinces of *Normandy,
Poictou, Gascogne . . .*' (*Complete English Tradesman*, i. 382).

three monstrous Wolves . . . a Bear: on 4 January 1718 *Mist's Weekly
Journal* carried an article reporting heavy snow in the Pyrenees and an
attack on villagers near Languedoc by a troop of wolves and six bears;
Defoe was contributing to the paper at this date, and may have written
this piece. There may also be an allegorical element, with the wolves and
bear alluding respectively to the Catholic powers and the belligerent
Russian Czar, Peter the Great, as the chief dangers to the Protestant
interest in Europe. Cf. the *Review* for 2 April 1713, in which Defoe
represents Peter, then thought to be on the brink of invading Sweden,
as '*a Siberian BEAR*', and urges the British government to 'do justice
upon him, and all the Humane Bears of his Country' (*Review*, Vol. 9,
No. 79, 156).

246 *Friday . . . us'd to that kind of Creature in his Country*: wolves in America
are to be found as far south as Mexico, though not in Friday's homeland.
Crusoe's account bears interesting resemblance to a contemporary
description of wolves at the extremity of their range: 'in this place are a
multitude of *Wolves*, which are the boldest that I ever met with; for they
would come so near, as to be almost ready to pull the Flesh out of our
Hands: Yet we durst not shoot them for fear the noise of our Guns should
call more to their assistance' (Lionel Wafer, *A New Voyage and Description
of the Isthmus of America* (1699), 191).

247 *give him the Road*: make way for him, get out of his way.

Friday, who had . . . the Heels of the Bear: Friday is capable of outstrip-
ping, outrunning, outdistancing the bear.

248 *answer'd Friday's End*: served Friday's purpose.

great Oak-Tree: Defoe may be poking fun at Stuart iconography by
staging this spectacle in an oak, the tree in which Charles II is said to
have hidden from Cromwell's soldiers after his defeat at the battle of

Worcester (1651). Elsewhere Defoe comments sardonically on the damage done by souvenir hunters to 'the Royal Oak, the famous Retreat of King *Charles* II' (ii. 477), and satirizes Stuart loyalists who 'drink the King's Health, with the Healths of all the Royal-Family, and of General *Monk*, and of the Royal-Oak, and of every simple mad thing they cou'd think of' (*The Great Law of Subordination Consider'd* (1724), 60).

251 *all in a Body . . . close Line was the only Way*: representing the encounter in technical military vocabulary of a kind that Defoe makes sustained use of elsewhere, notably *Memoirs of a Cavalier* (1720) and *Colonel Jack*. Cf. *Farther Adventures of Robinson Crusoe*, 130: 'they made their Way with their Halbards and Pieces, standing close together in a Line, thro' a Body of above a thousand Savages'; see also, on this technique in general, Maximillian E. Novak, 'Defoe and the Art of War', *Philological Quarterly*, 75.2 (1996), 197–214.

252 *the Creatures resolv'd us*: the wolves made our minds up for us.

    lay there for Carriage: lay awaiting disposal.

253 *snapping an uncharg'd Pistol . . . set it on fire*: Crusoe pulls the trigger of an unloaded flintlock pistol, generating sparks which ignite the gunpowder.

254 *Tholouse*: Toulouse in southern central France was the first city in which the Inquisition was instituted (in 1234), and espoused the Catholic interest during the French Wars of Religion in the sixteenth century. More than 4,000 Huguenots (Protestants of Calvinistic temper) were massacred in the city in 1564.

    very much: very fortunate.

255 *Sacrifice to my Principles . . . die in the Inquisition*: underlying Crusoe's fear is the suspicion that one of his surviving trustees might denounce him as a heretic for personal gain. The apparatus of the Inquisition was often misused to settle old scores or eliminate rivals in wills, business, and commerce.

258 *All these things . . . farther Account of hereafter*: as Crusoe duly does in *The Farther Adventures of Robinson Crusoe*, published four months after the original novel. The detailed narrative foreshadowing in these closing paragraphs suggests that Defoe may already have been at work on the sequel advertised here. On the conventions governing sequels in the period, see J. Paul Hunter, 'Serious Reflections on Farther Adventures: Resistances to Closure in Eighteenth-Century English Novels', in Albert J. Rivero (ed.), *Augustan Subjects: Essays in Honor of Martin C. Battestin* (Newark: University of Delaware Press, 1997), 276–94.

265 *famous History of Don Quixot . . . Duke de Medina Sidonia*: referring to Alonso Pérez de Guzmán, 7th Duke of Medina Sidonia (1550–1619), best known to English readers as the ineffectual commander in chief of the Spanish Armada of 1588. Cervantes lampooned him in a sonnet ('Vimos en julio') on his failure to protect Cadiz from English retaliation in 1596, but there is little evidence to connect him with *Don Quixote* (1605–15).

265 *malicious, but foolish Writer . . . Quixotism of R. Crusoe*: apparently a reference to Charles Gildon's attack on *Robinson Crusoe* in *The Life and
Strange Surprizing Adventures of Mr. D—— De F—, of London, Hosier*
(1719), though the exact phrase does not appear in surviving editions of
this work. In general, Gildon was fond of ridiculing his enemies for '*Don
Quixotism*, encountering Windmills, or making a monstrous Bustle to
no manner of Purpose' (*The Post-Man Robb'd of His Mail* (1719), 35,
his target on this occasion being the Society for the Reformation of
Manners), and he may have applied the term to Defoe elsewhere.

267 *latter Part of this Work called the Vision*: the lengthy closing chapter of
Serious Reflections, entitled 'A Vision of the Angelick World'.

Observations upon Solitude: the opening chapter of *Serious Reflections*,
which presents Crusoe's island confinement as merely the intensification
of a shared human condition: 'Life in general is, or ought to be, but one
universal Act of Solitude' (2).

268 *the Teacher . . . in his own Country*: 'For Jesus himself testified, that a
prophet hath no honour in his own country' (John 4: 44).

GLOSSARY

The following Glossary defines nautical terms and other unfamiliar words and phrases in *Robinson Crusoe*; definitions are also supplied for obsolete senses (but not the only senses) in which familiar words are sometimes used.

abroad without confinement, widely, at large, in another country

accompt account, reckon

acre 4,840 square yards/4,046 square metres (originally a measure of land that could be ploughed in a day by a yoke of oxen)

acted activated

ad infinitum without limit, endlessly, forever

admiration surprise, wonder, amazement

admir'd wondered at

adze axe-like tool for cutting or slicing away the surface of wood

affection, affections devotion, passions, zeal, states of mind

Africk Africa

ague acute fever, especially malarial, with intermittent cold and hot fits

Algerines pirate vessels operating in the Mediterranean Sea and beyond from bases on the Barbary coast

amusement distraction, perplexity, bewilderment

animal spirits the principle of energy, feeling, and movement, transported through the nervous system

antick bizarre, grotesque, fantastic

antient ensign, banner, standard, flag

application remedy

arms firearms

attempt try to capture or kill

auning awning, a canvas cover suspended over the deck of a vessel as protection from the elements

awkard awkward

bad him invited or enjoined him

Barbary coastal region roughly corresponding to Morocco, Algeria, and Tunisia. The three North African Regencies of Algiers, Tunis, and Tripoli, known in Europe as the 'Barbary States', were ostensibly dependencies of the Ottoman Empire but in practice semi-independent states with politics largely driven by private interests

Barco-Longo longboat (a corruption of the Portuguese *barca longa*)

barricado'd hastily fortified, barricaded

bays baize, coarse woollen stuff with a heavy nap

beachy shingly

bethought called to mind

Bills of Exchange promissory notes, cheques

bisket ship's biscuit or hard tack, made from stoneground flour, water, and salt, mixed into a stiff dough, and left after baking to harden and dry. Ship's biscuit was an important dietary item at sea, designed to withstand storage on long voyages

boat-swain boatswain, a ship's officer responsible for boats, sails, rigging, ground tackle (anchors and their cables), and colours (flags, especially the national ensign)

boltsprit bowsprit, a boom or spar projecting forward of the ship's head, to which the foremast stays are fastened, and below which a spritsail may be suspended

boom light running spar (pole), particularly one used to spread the foot (bottom) of a sail

bosses conjunctions, studs, protrusions

bow the rounded forward parts of a vessel, commencing where the sides arch inwards on either side and terminating at the stem or prow

brace pair

bread breed

breast work makeshift or temporary defensive fortifications

broil'd grilled

bulg'd staved, holed

bushel measure of capacity for dry goods. The Winchester bushel was the standard dry measure, equivalent to 4 pecks or 8 gallons (36.5 litres), but there were many local variations

by and by in time, in due course, eventually

cable large, strong, hemp rope or hawser of considerable length, usually made up of three strands, used to retain a ship at anchor. The standard length of an anchor cable was 120 fathoms or 240 yards (220 m). Ships properly carried three cables, a sheet-cable and two bower-cables

calenture tropical disease, associated with seafarers, symptomatized by fever and delirium

case bottle shaped bottle, most often square, designed to fit with others of the same shape into a case

charg'd loaded

charge load a weapon / weapons (to be *discharged* on firing)

chests secure wooden boxes used by sailors to stow personal possessions

chickens meat chicken feed

chimera idle conceit, whim, fancy

chop'd upon chanced, happened, upon

clapp'd interposed suddenly and unexpectedly

clifts cliffs

coast along perform coastal navigation; shape a course determined by the topography of the shoreline, remaining within sight of land

cognizance acknowledgement, recognition, conviction

compleat without defects, perfect, full

conceits fanciful notions

confound perplex, put out of countenance

consequence production, output, effect

converse communication

cordial waters liqueurs thought to have a tonic or stimulating quality due to the medicinal properties of their flavourings

coup de grace 'stroke of grace', a blow by which a condemned or mortally wounded victim is quickly dispatched; a stroke that puts an end to something

crow stave or metal bar used as a lever

cur'd preserved, cleared, prepared

cutlash Cutlass, a short, slightly curved, flat-bladed, single-edged sword used for cutting and hacking rather than thrusting

defaced removed, erased, obliterated

depending impending

design intention, purpose, scheme

dextrous handy, skilful, expert

dials sun-dials, portable instruments each incorporating a gnomon, or pointer, which casts a shadow on a graduated surface indicating the hour of the day

discourse (n.) speech, an act of comprehension processed verbally, reasoned argument; (v.) talk, consult, reason

discover'd disclosed, expressed, exhibited

discoveries intimations, disclosures, revelations

discover the country to search out, reveal, ascertain the lie of the land

discretion whim, will, disposal

dispatch'd killed

distemper bodily disorder, sickness, disease

diswaded dissuaded

diversion amusement

divert amuse

doubloons Spanish gold coins, double the value of *pistoles*, worth approximately 30–5 English shillings each

draft outflow, flood, effluence, efflux

dram small draught, or quantity, of spirits, usually consumed at once

dram of cordial tonic or pick-me-up used to restore vigour

drawers undergarment drawn on over the legs and reaching to the waist; long johns

dress prepare (of food)

drills rills, small streams, springs

drive run before the wind, with minimal control, to drift

ducats gold coins of varying values in use in many European countries

durst dared

ebb'd out drained

ejaculations short prayers darted out spontaneously

elephants teeth tusks, ivory

engagement word, promise, commitment, obligation

entertain'd preoccupied, abstracted, diverted

essays attempts, trials

expect our crop wait for our crop

fain glad, glad under the circumstances, necessitated, obliged

fancy imagination

fancy'd imagined

fathom 6 feet (2 m)

firelock flintlock, a gunlock incorporating a flint screwed to the cock which, when it strikes the hammer, produces sparks to ignite the priming in the flash-pan

flaggs, flags the blades or slender leaves of plants belonging to the Iris family; more generally, rushes, reeds, coarse grass used for binding persons or things

flea flay, skin, pare

fleet float

flower flour

fluxes severe diarrhoea, dysentery

forecastle fo'c'sle, a short deck situated in the forepart of the ship, sometimes above the main deck, the site of any foremast, and the area where anchor work takes place

fore-chains iron plates or links bolted to the sides of the ship to secure the standing rigging which braces the masts

foremast mast situated in the forward part of a vessel, its exact position determined by that of the mainmast

foresail sail positioned towards the bows of a vessel, forward of any other canvas

founder fill with water and sink

fowl birds, especially game birds and wildfowl (ducks, geese)

fowling-piece light gun used for shooting fowl

frigate term originally denoting a lightly armed, manoeuvrable craft powered by oars and sails, operating in the Mediterranean; swift craft

frog loop fitted to a belt in order to secure a sword or dagger

furlong an eighth part of a mile, 220 yards (198 m)

fuzees, fusees light muskets

gat thither arrived there

Generalissimo Italian superlative of *Generale*, thus Captain General

genius nature, natural inclination toward particular employment

gib'd, gyb'd a sail gybes when a vessel turns downwind and her bows pass through the line of the wind so that contact between the wind and one surface of a boom-sail shifts to the opposite side. In light winds, or if the vessel is cumbersome, gybing is often easier than tacking (turning the vessel's bows through the wind)

glass spy glass, telescope, any hand-held optic used for magnification

graplin small anchor fitted with four or five flukes, or claws, commonly used to ride a small boat

great cabin quarters allotted to the captain or master of a vessel

gridiron iron cooking utensil in the form of a frame, equipped with legs, housing parallel bars for cooking flesh or fish over a fire

gross twelve dozen

grutches begrudges

gudgeons sockets or housings to support both ends of an axle

guinea trader euphemism for a slave trader

half-pikes short-hafted lances, for use in close-quarter battle

haling, hall'd, hale, hal'd, hawl variants of the verb *to haul*, meaning to pull directly on a rope without the assistance of blocks

halter rope used to lead malefactors by the neck

hand-barrow stretcher

hanger short broad sword originally hung from a belt

hardily confidently, robustly, audaciously

hatches square or oblong openings in decks and bulkheads, allowing the movement of men and material throughout a ship, secured by means of lockable covers

hawser large, strong, hemp rope, a size smaller than cable, used for warping and mooring a vessel

head ornamental figure erected on the stem of a ship, usually bearing some relation with war, navigation, or some virtue. More generally, the

Glossary

    forward parts of a vessel including the bows (which part the column of
    water through which the vessel passes)

historical part of things chronological relation of events and facts

hogshead large cask used for liquid and dry storage, liquid volumes
    ranged between about 50 and 140 gallons (230 and 640 litres)

hold the lowest internal space in a vessel, between the keel and the lower
    deck, running along the length of the ship, containing ballast, stores,
    and provisions

hollow, hollowing a cry or cries uttered in exhortation or exultation

houl howl

humane human

hundred weight 112 pounds weight, equivalent to 46.267 kg

hurdles sticks bound together with horizontal strengtheners to form a
    frame, placed over the pit-fall trap

husband person concerned with tillage, cultivation, the improvement of
    land and, more generally, the management of resources

hutch pen or small compartment accommodating animals or human
    beings

ingenio *ingenio de azucar*, a Spanish term denoting the machinery used
    to mill sugar cane in a refinery or factory

ingenuity freedom, high-mindedness, nobility

insensibly unwittingly, unconsciously

instrument of sale conveyance, transfer deed

intermeddle interpose

interval time between shots

iron crows crowbars, iron bars with flattened bent ends, sometimes
    forked, used to lever or prise objects

jealous suspicious, apprehensive, fearful, vigilant

jealousy suspicion

jerkin waistcoat, jacket, short coat

kalander calendar

laths pieces of wood fashioned into pliable strips used in building to
    support roof tiles and plasterwork

latitude the angular distance of any designated point on the earth's sur-
    face north or south of the Equator, expressed in degrees, minutes, and
    seconds. The Equator is a notional line drawn on the earth's surface sep-
    arating the northern and southern hemispheres, represents zero degrees
    latitude; the two poles represent 90 degrees north and south respectively

league unit of distance measuring 3 miles (5 km). The nautical mile is properly one minute of arc of latitude or 6,080 feet (1,842 m), although most contemporary navigators equated the mile with an average minute of longitude, 5,000 feet (1,515 m)

leave liberty, allowance, permission, licence

long-boat the largest and stoutest boat belonging to a ship, used to carry heavy weights such as anchors, cable, ordnance, and ballast

longitude the angular distance of any designated point on the earth's surface east or west of the Prime Meridian, expressed in degrees, minutes, and seconds. Meridians are continuous notional lines drawn on the earth's surface, extending from pole to pole. The Prime Meridian passes through Greenwich and intersects with the Equator at a point representing zero degrees longitude. The Equator (a circle) is divisible into 360 degrees, so the longitudinal position of any point on earth depends upon the position of its meridian relative to the Prime Meridian, i.e. up to 180 degrees east or west of it

lustily with great gusto, urgently

madera wine naturally light, acidic, white wine produced on Madeira, an island situated about 400 miles (640 km) off the north-west coast of Africa. Madeira, which was often fortified with brandy for use at sea, improved greatly on long sea voyages, particularly when the ship entered the tropics and the heated wine was allowed to cool slowly afterwards

magazine, maggazin, magazin warehouse, store of munitions and general provisions, a repository in a ship or on shore

main mainland

main and quarter decks the main-deck is usually the principal upper-most horizontal surface area of a vessel. The quarterdeck is an elevation above the main-deck extending from the stern towards the mainmast, the area from which command is usually exercised

mainmast mast situated towards the middle part of a vessel, ideally positioned at the axis where water exerts maximum resistance against the hull

mark aim

mate the officer who commands in the absence of the master of a small merchant vessel, and who shares the duty with him at sea

mechanick pitiful, mean, servile

medium compromise

meer downright, simple, unmixed

melancholly pensive, gloomy, dejected, depressed in spirit. The physiological cause of melancholy was supposed to be an excess of black bile in the body, or the presence of heavy blood

mend improve
mended our pace altered pace
miscarry'd met with disaster, shipwrecked
missen-yard yard affixed to the aftermost mast of the ship, the mizzen mast
moiety half, one of two equal parts
moletta mulatto, a person of mixed descent or race, European and African
molossus molasses, uncrystallized syrup drained from raw sugar, also the syrup obtained from the process of refining sugar
momento memento, a salutary reminder, warning, hint
Moors Muslim peoples inhabiting north-west Africa, of mixed Berber and Arab descent
motion the effect of the moving parts of a mechanical device such as the 'movement' of a clock or watch
move recommend
moydors, moidores Portuguese gold coins each worth about 27 shillings
murthering humour murderous temper, disposition, state of mind
muschatoes moustache

naked defenceless, unprepared
New Spain Spanish colonies and the territory and waters claimed in America by Spain
nice, nicest most exacting, scrupulous, painstaking, punctilious
Notary clerk whose function it is to prepare formal documents, contracts, and financial undertakings
nourish comfort

oakum the hemp strands of old rope picked apart and untwisted, then mixed with tar to form a fibrous, watertight, material for use in caulking (filling) seams in the sides and decks of ships
obligation written undertaking
offensive displeasing, disgusting, repulsive to any of the senses
opticks eyes
original origin, history, rise, originator
osiers species of willow (genus *Salix*)
over-against situated opposite

pale defensive enclosure bounded by a fence of stakes
papist Catholic
parley discussion, negotiation, agreement, oral treaty
parley'd with them treated with them

past pastry

patroon patron, a master of slaves or captives in Barbary

pease peas

peck measure of capacity for dry goods equivalent to 2 gallons (9 litres) or a quarter of a bushel

pendants pennants

penthouse shelter over a door or window

periagua large canoe common in the Caribbean basin and coastal South America

perspective, perspective glass spy glass or telescope; any hand-held optic used for magnification

physical restorative, curative, medicinal

piece pistol, musket, or other firearm

pilot person embarked in a vessel whose local knowledge enables him to advise the captain concerning safe conduct and navigation in unfamiliar waters

pinnace small vessel carried on board a ship, generally having two masts and capable of being rowed, whose shallow draft and manoeuvrability suit inshore work

pipkins small earthenware vessels

pitch upon settle on, fix upon, select

powder gunpowder, an explosive mixture of about thirty parts saltpetre, three parts sulphur, and three parts charcoal

powder-chests wooden, triangular chests filled with gunpowder, stones, and other projectiles, designed to explode towards boarders

powder-horns portable containers for gunpowder

primitive condition primary state, early childlike disposition unaffected by reason

prevailed influenced, persuaded, overruled

procuration delegation of authority, power of attorney, written authorization empowering one party to act on another's behalf

proper convenient, serviceable, suitable, fitting

prudential wisdom, discretion

pumps thin soled shoes without heels

punch liquor made by mixing brandy, water, lemon juice, and sugar

quarter the upper part of a ship's side between the main chains and the stern

rack arrack, name applied to any liquor of native manufacture, especially that distilled from the sap of coco-palm, or from rice and sugar mixed with coconut water

rankling festering

ready posture alert or vigilant state

reflux reflow, ebb, refluence

retire withdraw, retreat

roads, road sheltered waters, usually inshore, offering safe anchorage

rod rode

round-house cabin or set of apartments built in the after part of the quarter-deck (sometimes occupied by sailmakers and carpenters, sometimes used as a place of detention), the roof of which forms the poop deck

rude bandage rough, coarse, crude, makeshift fetters

rumag'd rummaged, searched thoroughly (especially the hold of a ship)

runlets casks for holding spirits; liquid volumes ranged between about 3 and 20 gallons (90 litres)

ryals reals, small Spanish silver coins, notionally worth one-eighth of a piece of eight (Spanish silver dollar) or about sixpence in English money

sallows species of willow, of low-growing or shrubby habit

sally upon them burst forth upon them, descend upon them, attack them

salvages archaic form of 'savages'

sand sandbank

score twenty

scuttle opening in a deck or in the sides of a vessel to permit light and ventilation, secured by means of a lockable cover

sea-fowls seabirds

search strainer or searce

seasonable opportune, timely

seiling ceiling

sensible sensitive towards, perceptive, cognizant

sensibly surpriz'd astonished, shocked, traumatized

set sit

shift improvise, make do, manage, survive

shift me change into

ship's pinnace tender to a larger vessel, usually equipped with oars and sails, and of shallow draft to facilitate inshore work

shod iron plate fastened under leather heels, wooden handles, etc., to protect from wear

shoor off repel

shoulder of mutton sail lateen or tri-cornered sail suspended from a lateen yard, typical of vessels navigated in the Mediterranean sea and still in use on the Nile

signals signs

skipper (slang) captain or master of a vessel

skirt of the wood edge, extremity, of the wood

skirts parts of a garment below the waist

skrew-jack lifting-jack or jack-screw, a portable device for lifting heavy objects

simple naive, silly, foolish

slugs cylindrical or oval pieces of lead or other metal shot from a gun; roughly cast bullets

small-shot small calibre pellets or bullets discharged from muskets

softly quietly, placidly, yieldingly, meekly

spatter-dashes leggings, gaiters

sprit small boom, or pole, attached to the mast by a collar (snotter) and extending to the upper hindmost corner of a sail to elevate and extend its surface area

sprit-sail small quadrilateral sail suspended at the peak from a sprit, or boom, positioned beneath the bowsprit itself. A forerunner of the jib, the spritsail was designed to prevent the ship's head from turning into wind. In heavy seas the belly of the sail sometimes collected seawater, which was drained away through holes in the lower corners

sprye spray

stay strong rope extending from an elevated position on a mast to the fore part of a ship and used in conjunction with shrouds (similar lines extending to the sides and aft) to brace the mast itself; standing rigging

steerage apartment in the after part of the ship normally adjacent to the great cabin from which it is separated by a thin partition. In merchant ships, it was generally the junior officers' berth or accommodation for crew members

step block of wood fixed onto the deck or keel of a vessel, shaped to receive the heel of a mast

stern after end of a ship

strait narrow entrance, passage, or channel

string ties forming a secure brace around a piece of meat, allowing it to be suspended under a cross-piece and roasted over a fire

strook struck

sublunary beneath the moon, earthly

subtile crafty, cunning

succades sweetmeats, confectionery

suffer indulge, permit, enable

super-cargo, supra-cargo supercargo, an officer in a merchant vessel charged by the freighters to manage, protect, and account for their commercial interests

swan-shot large shot, fifteen pellets weighing an ounce

sweetmeats delicacies made of fruits, vegetables, or nuts, candied or preserved in syrup

swim remain afloat

tarpaulin piece of canvas coated with tar to render it waterproof

tell, told count, counted

terra firma the mainland

terras bank of earth

ticklish unsteady, precarious, insecure

till small draw or box containing money

tinder-box waterproof container containing implements for lighting fire including flint and steel (for striking a spark) and tinder

top of high-water peak of high tide

toys playthings, trifles, baubles

traffick intercourse, dealings, trade

train trail of gunpowder

transports of soul raptures, exaltations, exhilarations

treat bargain, negotiate, deal with, handle

twist fork or junction of the thighs

unaccountable extraordinary, strange, puzzling

understand recognize

unhabitable uninhabited

vapours exhalations developed by bodily organs and ascending to the brain, supposed to cause anguish, depression, hypochondria, hysteria, and other mental or nervous disorders

ventrous adventurous, venturesome

vesting investing

victual our vessel store our vessel (in preparation for sea)

victuals, vittle foodstuffs, rations, provisions, prepared to last some period of time

viz. *videlicet*, that is to say

waft wave, signal

wanting lacking, deficient, remiss

wasted much used up

whelming down covering or turning the open side of a vessel downwards

whether whither
without doors outside, in the open

yard(s) wooden spar attached by its centre to a mast to sit horizontally, serving to support and extend a sail bent to it
yard-arm tapered extremity of a yard

Anthony Trollope

The American Senator

An Autobiography

Barchester Towers

Can You Forgive Her?

The Claverings

Cousin Henry

The Duke's Children

The Eustace Diamonds

Framley Parsonage

He Knew He Was Right

Lady Anna

Orley Farm

Phineas Finn

Phineas Redux

The Prime Minister

Rachel Ray

The Small House at Allington

The Warden

The Way We Live Now

The Oxford World's Classics Website

www.oup.com/uk/worldsclassics

- Information about new titles
- Explore the full range of Oxford World's Classics
- Links to other literary sites and the main OUP webpage
- Imaginative competitions, with bookish prizes
- Articles by editors
- Extracts from Introductions
- Special information for teachers and lecturers

www.oup.com/uk/worldsclassics

American Literature

Authors in Context

British and Irish Literature

Children's Literature

Classics and Ancient Literature

Colonial Literature

Eastern Literature

European Literature

History

Medieval Literature

Oxford English Drama

Poetry

Philosophy

Politics

Religion

The Oxford Shakespeare

A complete list of Oxford World's Classics, including Authors in Context, Oxford English Drama, and the Oxford Shakespeare, is available in the UK from the Marketing Services Department, Oxford University Press, Great Clarendon Street, Oxford OX2 6DP, or visit the website at www.oup.com/uk/worldsclassics.

In the USA, visit www.oup.com/us/owc for a complete title list.

Oxford World's Classics are available from all good bookshops. In case of difficulty, customers in the UK should contact Oxford University Press Bookshop, 116 High Street, Oxford OX1 4BR.